THE BEST OF
GEORGE
ADE

THE BEST OF
GEORGE ADE

─────────────

With Illustrations by
John T. McCutcheon

─────────────

SELECTED AND EDITED
BY A. L. LAZARUS

INDIANA UNIVERSITY PRESS

Bloomington

First Midland Book Edition 1985

Illustrations reprinted by
permission of John T. McCutcheon, Jr.

Introductory material and notes copyright © 1985 by A. L. Lazarus

Manufactured in the United States of America

Library of Congress Cataloging in Publication Data

Ade, George, 1866–1944.
  The best of George Ade.

  I. Lazarus, Arnold Leslie.   II. Title.
PS1006.A6A6   1985   818'.409   84-43170
ISBN 0-253-10609-5

1 2 3 4 5   89 88 87 86 85

Contents

III. *Plays*

IV. *Essays*

V. *Verses and Songs*

VI. *Selected Letters*

PREFACE

The BEST of George Ade! "Best," here, must not be dismissed as an honorific. Inasmuch as Ade's total output* varies in quality from the banal (as in certain early fables) to the sublime (as in certain later stories), the editor of this anthology has measured each candidate-for-inclusion against criteria of literary excellence, universality of appeal, and promise of permanence. It was no doubt those qualities of Ade's best work which elicited praise from such luminaries as Mark Twain, W. D. Howells, and H. L. Mencken.

Mark Twain said (particularly about *Pink Marsh*): "I have been reading him again, and my admiration overflows all limits. . . . How effortless the limning! It is as if the work did itself, without help of the master's hand."—From a letter to Howells, tipped between pages 8 and 9 in Ade's *One Afternoon with Mark Twain* (Chicago: Mark Twain Society, 1939).

W. D. Howells said (refuting the claim that Ade was a mere regionalist): "In Mr. George Ade the American spirit arrives . . . that whole vast droll American world, alike in Maine and Oregon and all the hustling regions between."—From "The Chicago School of Fiction," *North American Review* (May, 1904), 739ff.

H. L. Mencken said, "Ade is one of the few genuinely original literary craftsmen now in practice among us. . . . The whole body of his work is thoroughly American in cut and color, tang and savor, structure and point of view . . . in vivid and accurate evocation of the American scene, the whole American *Kultur.* . . . No other writer of our generation is more inescapably national."—From "George Ade," Chapter IX, *Prejudices, First Series* (New York: Alfred Knopf, 1919), pages 118–119.

At the turn of the century Ade's fans also included thousands of readers of his (and illustrator John T. McCutcheon's) *Chicago Record* column "Stories of the Streets and of the Town," albeit printed without by-line. When some of those pieces appeared in book form Ade enjoyed even more immense popularity, to say nothing of the accolades he received when three of his plays ran simultaneously, in 1904, on Broadway and in road shows across the country.

And yet today, alas, he remains all but forgotten. It is hoped that *The Best of George Ade* will afford not only entertainment (some of the selections do induce belly-shaking hilarity) but also recognition, at last, for George Ade as a humorist of world class.

A. L. Lazarus

---

*His substantial output is chronicled in Dorothy Russo's book-length *A George Ade Bibliography* (Indianapolis: Indiana Historical Society, 1947). I am grateful to all the copyright holders for permission to reprint pieces not yet in the public domain. Specific credit lines are printed in the NOTES.

A Note on the Illustrations

Both at Purdue University and for many years in Chicago, George Ade fraternized with John T. McCutcheon. McCutcheon, who helped Ade get his reporting job on the *Chicago Record*, illustrated several of Ade's fables when they first appeared in that newspaper in 1894. McCutcheon also illustrated most of Ade's books—among them *Stories of the Streets and of the Town*, first and second series (1894), third and fourth series (1895); *Bird Center* (1896); *Artie* (1896); *Pink Marsh* (1897); *Doc' Horne* (1899); *Fables in Slang* (1899); *More Fables in Slang* (1900); *Forty Modern Fables* (1901); parts of *The Girl Proposition* (1902); and, in *Verses and Jingles* (1911), "Il Janitoro."

For permission to reprint cartoons and sketches from these works, warm thanks are extended to John T. McCutcheon, Jr., formerly Editorial Director of the *Chicago Tribune*.

INTRODUCTION

One year after the end of the War Between the States, on February 6, 1866, George Ade was born in Kentland, Indiana. His father, John Hazleton Ade, had migrated from Lewes (near Brighton), England to Cheviot (near Cincinnati), Ohio. Adaline Bush, a native of Cheviot, became John's wife in 1851, when she was eighteen and he was twenty-three.

In 1866 the population of Kentland was about 600. Because it had more saloons than churches (an anomaly in Indiana) it seemed to be singled out by temperance crusaders, who swept through the town quite frequently. As a boy George abhorred demon rum, but in his maturity he opposed the Volstead Act; indeed, during his impoverished first months in Chicago he relied heavily on the saloons that offered free lunches and nickel beers, as he later revealed in *The Old-Time Saloon* (1931). As for church-going, he accompanied his mother to her Methodist meetings more often than he accompanied his father to the Campbellite services, but this can hardly explain why George ultimately gravitated to agnosticism.

He enjoyed a happy childhood. The youngest of three sons—in fact, the youngest survivor of seven children—he was very much catered to. The summers afforded swimming in nearby ponds and berry-picking in the fields adjacent to town. The winters provided snow-balling, sledding, and on the frozen ponds all manner of fancy skating. One evening in October, at the age of five, George joined his sisters and brothers in marveling at the blazing skies to the north, the first night of Chicago's great fire of 1871.

For several hours a week George's father "cashiered" at the Kentland Discount and Deposit Bank. For most of the other hours of the week he farmed the open field behind their frame house, the front of which faced the town's courthouse square and wooden sidewalks. Much of the corn that John grew was used, during the harsh winters, to fuel their pot-bellied stove. George helped only reluctantly with the weeding, and he sometimes used schoolwork, at which he excelled, as an excuse for getting out of chores. "From the time I could read," he writes in his *Autobiography*, "I had my nose in a book, and I lacked enthusiasm for manual labor."

George attended the local schools and was regarded as something of a prodigy. In 1881, when he was fifteen, one of his teachers persuaded the local newspaper to print George's bumptious essay "A Basket of Potatoes" ("Life is but a basket of potatoes. . . . Keep away from the rotten potatoes and you will get to the top.") The "Keep away" caveat foreshadowed some of the "morals" that would tag the ends of his "fables in slang."

In the fall of 1883 John Ade did not have to be coaxed to send George, then seventeen, away to college. They settled on Purdue, which had opened in 1874, in Lafayette, about fifty miles south of Kentland. Purdue appealed to John Ade for its excellent reputation in agricultural and mechanical arts. Early on, these were Purdue's emphases, along with mathematics and science. But its *Annual Register* of 1882 reveals that "students in any of the programs . . . are required to spend five terms in the study of French and seven terms in the study of German Language and Literature. . . . The time given by the student to English, French, and German affords a general knowledge which must prove of practical advantage in any pursuit."

George won his father's reluctant consent to take the scientific curriculum "because I had no ambition to become an engineer or an agriculturist." Although he was, as he said, "a total loss in mathematics," he excelled in literature and composition, especially under the tutelage of Professor Annie Peck. George did not take the agricultural chemistry course, which was directed by Professor Harvey Wiley, M.D., who would become nationally visible as the author of the nation's first Food and Drug Act (1906). But George did play on the varsity baseball team coached by Dr. Wiley and must have relished Wiley's irreverent epithets, especially toward manufacturers who were adulterating Purdue's "naturally pure" corn products. No doubt some of Wiley's irreverence rubbed off on George Ade. At Purdue George also developed a crush on a coed by the name of Lillian Howard, who did not reciprocate, and who instead married a minister from Minnesota. Ade later rationalized her marriage as a good reason for remaining a bachelor.

George was elected president of the Irving Literary Society (rival of the Carlyle Society) and of his fraternity, Sigma Chi. At Sigma Chi he met Purduvian John T. McCutcheon, who would soon become his best friend and life-long illustrator. Although John's older brother, George Barr McCutcheon, was not a member of Sigma Chi, "G B Mc," too, became one of Ade's close friends, especially during Ade's apprenticeship as a reporter for the *Lafayette News*, the *Morning Call*, and the *Evening Call*. For after graduation from Purdue (1887) and after abortive ventures in studying law and writing advertisements for Cascarets, a patent laxative ("It works overnight"), Ade devoted two years (1888–1890) to reporting as a friendly rival of G B Mc, who was working for the *Lafayette Journal* and who would become City Editor of the *Lafayette Courier*.

With John T. and G B Mc and another Purduvian, Booth Tarkington, before Tark transferred to Princeton, Ade enjoyed triple dates—picnics on the banks of the Wabash, Indianapolis cotillions on North Meridian Street, theatre parties at English's Opera House— with debutantes Tark had "fixed up" for Ade and the McCutcheon brothers. In *Drawn from Memory* (Indianapolis: Bobbs-Merrill, 1950), p. 53, John T. recalls Ade's persiflage and practical jokes on these dates, in which the tall gaunt Ade capitalized on his deadpan face and vaudeville timing. "One of his stunts that brought down the house," writes John T., "was the one in which I'd start a serious [recitation] with my hands clasped behind my back, while Ade, stooping behind me with his arms through mine, made gestures such as pulling out my watch, blowing my nose, and picking my teeth."

Ade, along with G B Mc, frequently attended the Lafayette Opera House, where the offerings ranged from Shakespearean plays (starring such artists as Edwin Booth, Helena Modjeska, and Otis Skinner) to Gilbert and Sullivan operettas (starring, among others, Minnie Maddern Fiske) and above all to the most popular of the shows—melodramas. Some of the more absurd scenes of these melodramas ("full of foolish solemnities and unintended humor"), to which the two Georges could not accord willing suspension of disbelief, elicited their uncontrolled hooting, which in turn elicited cutting stares from the innocent devotees in the audience.

In 1890, on an invitation from John T., who was "making it" in Chicago as a cartoonist on the *Chicago News* (later called the *News-Record* and still later the *Record*), Ade moved to Chicago, in fact moved in with John McCutcheon. On the latter's recommendation Ade got a job as a reporter on the *News*, albeit at a next-to-starvation salary. But the turning point in his Chicago career, thanks to the Columbian Exposition of 1893, came with Ade's column "All Roads Lead to the Fair," illustrated by John T. So successful was this column (next to Eugene Field's column "Sharps and Flats") that at the close of the Exposition Ade persuaded City Editor Charles Dennis to print a successor column, "Stories of the Streets and of the Town" (inaugurated November 20, 1893).

By now Ade's reporting had exposed him to Chicago's melting pot of Scandinavians, Germans, Poles, Greeks, and Bohemians; to politicians, ward-heelers, policemen, prostitutes, stenographers, shop-

John T. labeled this sketch, which dates from their days at
Purdue, "GEORGE ADE has apparently just heard the
dinner bell at the boarding hall"

girls, peddlers, bootblacks, and other people from almost every other walk of life. Although the new column was printed without a by-line, it became a hit from its very inception. For the next three years its popularity generated not only substantial pay raises but also an invitation from Chicago publisher Herbert Stone to publish book-length collections of the column's fables and stories.

In prolific succession there appeared Ade's story collection *Artie* (1896), about the exploits of the brash and opportunistic office boy Artie Blanchard; *Pink Marsh* (1897), about the natively shrewd bootblack who gleaned a practical education from his affluent customers; *Doc' Horne* (1899), about a resident retiree at the Alfalfa European Hotel who excelled as a raconteur; *Fables in Slang* (1899); *More Fables in Slang* (1900); *Forty Modern Fables* (1901); *The Girl Proposition: A Book of He and She Fables* (1902); *Breaking into Society* (1902); and *People You Know* (1903).

In Ade's fables one notices on the surface certain trademark features: an Aesopian moral-at-end drawn from the protagonist's foibles, often ironic (e.g., in the "Fable of Sister Mae," in which the skinflint Mae "rewards" her poor sister Luella with a next-to-starvation wage, the end-moral reads "Industry and Perseverance bring a sure Reward"); and a heavy use of capitalization, in part a vestige of the noun-capitalizations in the German literature Ade had studied at Purdue, in part a substitute for italics, to slow down the readers, to make them take notice. Also in first evidence is of course Ade's use of slang expressions. But on deeper levels, Ade's originality emerges, especially his ear for the vernacular, for the very rhythms of speech and dialogue. Two prime examples: the dialogue of the two young men "In the Roof Garden" and of the parents in "When Father Meets Father."

Except briefly in "Dubley, '89," Ade used no ethnic dialects. He left Irish brogues, for example, to Finley Peter Dunne's Mr. Dooley even while sharing with Dunne the mill-grist of Chicago's typical persons and places. Ade's use of the vernacular did inspire at least in part Ring Lardner's *You Know Me Al* (1916), consisting of letters home by Jack Keefe, a half-educated bush-league baseball player.

In Babel (1903), which sold 70,000 copies within its first few months off the press, remains Ade's most distinguished collection of stories and essays. It competes with Theodore Dreiser in authentic portraits (e.g., Effie Whittlesy and Olof Lindstrom) and in verisimilitude of scenes (e.g., Lincoln Park and the Art Institute). No doubt Dreiser's *Sister Carrie* (1900) was not indebted to Ade's "The Two Mandolin Players" (see Part VI), nor was Dreiser's *The Titans* (1914) indebted to Ade's "Some Instances of Political Devotion."

Dreiser and Ade after all had access to the same raw materials. But how much lighter is Ade's treatment! Whereas Dreiser's Charles Drouet comes on to Carrie as an unvarnished masher, Ade's hilarious Cousin Gus in "The Two Mandolin Players" is a much subtler and more imaginative operator. Whereas in *The Titan* Dreiser's scenes of vote buying remain primarily reportage ("Say what you will, Mr. Hand, but it's the two-, and five-, and ten dollar bills paid out at the last moment over the saloon bars and polling places that do the work," p. 266), in "Some Instances of Political Devotion" *Stories of the Streets and of the Town, First Series* (1894) Ade not only reports; he injects ironic humor: "There can be no greater disgrace for a working politician than to lodge a man for two weeks before election and then lose his vote on election morning." One hastens to add that each in his own way Dreiser and Ade contributed significantly to realism in American literature—only Ade had more "heart" and a greater sense of humor.

What with royalties from book sales, to say nothing of royalties from his column, which by now was syndicated in newspapers across the country, Ade was able to leave the *Record* and devote himself to freelance writing and to travel. As a "mesmeree of single blessedness" he could afford to travel all over the world. And travel he did: to the Philippines, China, and Japan in 1900; to Egypt and the Middle East in 1905; and almost annually thereafter to England and the Continent. Recounting some of his experiences in Cairo, London, Paris, and Naples, his book *In Pastures New* (1906)—even more irreverent than Mark Twain's *Innocents Abroad* (1869)—mercilessly satirizes the idiotic behavior of certain American tourists.

For Ade perhaps the most intellectually exciting phase of his career (1902–1905) started when he collaborated with the composer Alfred Wathall on *The Sultan of Sulu* (Part III), a comic operetta in the tradition of Gilbert and Sullivan, satirizing American jingoism and gunboat diplomacy in the Philippines. After it underwent a few major revisions, including a tryout at the Lafayette (Indiana) Opera House, it became a "smash" in Chicago, in New York, and on the road. *The Sultan* remains a brilliant satire—timeless and universal in its appeal.

Encouraged by the success of *The Sultan*, Ade wrote several more comedies in rapid, no doubt too rapid, succession: *Peggy from Paris*, a potpourri and a failure; *The Night of the Fourth*, another failure; *The County Chairman*, a successful satire of American grassroots politics; *The College Widow* (published 1904), his most successful comedy, assigning to college football more glory than deprecation, with its

McCutcheon's tongue-in-cheek drawing of Hazelden
poked fun at the huge parties Ade liked to give

"Atwater" setting said to be a thinly disguised replica of Wabash College, Crawfordsville, Indiana; *The Sho-Gun*, a successful musical comedy set in the Korean kingdom of Ka-Choo and satirizing (as the program notes said) "Yankee commercial invasions"; and two failed comedies, *The Bad Samaritan* and *Just Out of College*. In the last play the "Pure Food Exhibit" represented Ade's homage to Purdue's Harvey Wiley. *Artie* (1907), a dramatization of the 1896 novel *Artie*, closed after only twenty-two performances. *The Fair Co-ed* (1909), written originally for Purdue's Harlequin Club, was a musical adaptation of *The College Widow*.

During 1904, when three of his most successful plays were running simultaneously, packing audiences into theatres on Broadway and on the road, his royalties exceeded $5,000 a week. With part of these proceeds he paid off the mortgage on Hazelden, his recently acquired country estate, complete with pool, tennis court, and golf course, in Brook, near Kentland, Indiana. Here he played host to rich and poor Republicans at lavish parties and picnics, barbecues, ice cream and lemonade socials. Visitors to Hazelden included such celebrities as Warren Harding, William Howard Taft, Charles

Dawes, Booth Tarkington, James Whitcomb Riley, Franklin P. Adams, John Studebaker, Jesse Lasky, and May Robson.

Through the years the only friend that declined invitations to Hazelden was George Barr McCutcheon, pleading his—or his wife Marie's—illness. But according to John Raleigh (Jessie McCutcheon Raleigh's son) a coolness between G B Mc and Ade developed soon after Ade wrote *The Slim Princess* (published in 1907), satirizing edelweiss romances like G B Mc's *Graustark* (1901) and its sequels. Actually *The Slim Princess* (in which a Morovenian count faces the dilemma that Kalora, the older of his two daughters, is too thin to win a husband before Jeneka, the younger and more appropriately plump daughter, does), was intended as a parody—one of the more sincere forms of flattery, or so Ade thought. But G B Mc did not see it as such. He felt wounded, especially since it was on Ade's advice that G B Mc had accepted the Stone Publishing Company's parsimonious contract in the first place. Perhaps in a penitential mood, Ade regaled several of the McCutcheon families (G B Mc's, John T's, Ben's, and Jessie's) with a farcical skit* based on *The Slim Princess* in a private performance during a darked-out night at the Studebaker Theatre in Chicago. G B Mc could have smiled all the way to the bank—his Graustarkian romances sold in the millions (about 5,000,000 each, according to *The Bookman*). Still the coolness persisted, gradually on Ade's part too, as reflected in at least two letters: one from G B Mc, New York, October 13, 1915, "Marie was just saying, 'Why don't we ever see George Ade when he comes to town?' And I had to reply, 'Damned if I know!'"; one from Ade to John T.: "Hazelden, October 29, 1928" [the day after G B Mc's death] "I was terrible [sic] shocked and grieved to learn of George's sudden death. . . . I tried to keep track of the funeral arrangements, but I am greatly worried now for fear that I should have shown up in Lafayette. . . . George and I were such good friends in the old days that I was in readiness to start down but I was really in doubt as to whether I should go or not."

When Ade was not writing, or presiding at Hazelden picnics, or wintering in Florida, or attending Republican meetings, or traveling around the world, he busied himself with a variety of charitable ac-

---

*The dramatized version of *The Slim Princess* remains as yet unlocated and for now must be listed, along with *The Night of the Fourth* and several one-act play manuscripts, as lost. For an important account of a document which by implication throws light on George Ade's attitude, in his prosperity, toward G B Mc in *his* prosperity, see James L. W. West, "George Barr McCutcheon's Literary Ledger," *Yale University Library Gazette* (April, 1985), 155–161.

tivities. He gave huge monetary gifts to Sigma Chi and to Purdue, for which he served as a trustee. He and his fellow alumnus Dave Ross gave Purdue the Ross-Ade Stadium.

With such absorbing and immensely satisfying activities Ade lived to the age of 78. On May 16, 1944, after a brief illness, he died at Brook, Indiana. Ade's reputation had declined sharply after World War I, perhaps (according to an entry in the *Dictionary of American Biography*) "because he had followed too closely the moral of one of his fables, 'Give the People what they Think they want.'" He no doubt believed that "People" prefer light verse to serious poetry. In diametric contrast to James Whitcomb Riley, Ade was a much less accomplished writer of verse than of prose. Yet even Ade's verse (light verse, one reiterates, not poetry) and especially his songs still entertain with a satiric sparkle.

What, finally, was Ade's vision of life? Was he truly the gentle, the "warm-hearted" satirist of the Kelly* biography? On the whole, perhaps yes. Implicit in much of his satire, both the benign and the acerbic, is the hope that humans can become more human that they sometimes seem to be. And aside from his sentimental verses ("When Maidens Wait," for example, and "The Games We Used to Play") some of his stories are charmingly romantic. Cases in point: "Our Private Romance," in which, quite publicly, some sympathetically portrayed eavesdroppers watch from their front steps the progress of an enchanting courtship across the street; "Sophie's Sunday Afternoon," in which is evoked a delicate Impressionist painting; the idyllic suburban family in "The Buell Cherry"; "When Father Meets Father," admiring infants on an El train.

At best supercilious and snobbish, however, is Ade's attitude toward some of the unfortunates, and the half-educated, and the untalented and manqué among his dramatis personae—among them, Sister Mae's sister Luella; Lutie, the would-be vocalist; the Dawsons and the Hanrahans in "The Intellectual Awakening in Burton's Row."

Far from being an unadulterated idealist, then, Ade must at least at times have believed in the reality of evil; indeed, not a few of his fables and stories chuckle with an almost Satanic cynicism. Against the benign Olof Lindstrom, who goes fishing from the shores of Lake Michigan, consider the malignancies (to say nothing of the male chauvinism) in "The Honest Money-Maker"—the skinflint

---

*Fred C. Kelly, *George Ade: Warm-Hearted Satirist* (Indianapolis: The Bobbs-Merrill Company, 1947).

farmer who literally works his wife to death—and in "Mr. Payson's Satirical Christmas"—the man whose Scroogelike behavior ("Some of [Payson's] friends used to say that Satan had got the upper hand with him") is only mitigated by the comeuppance he gets from the recipients of his "gifts." In "The Fable of How the Fool-Killer Backed Out of a Contract," although the Fool-Killer was and is a folk character in rural Indiana, for Ade he seems to evoke Satan himself. He is endowed with much more perspicacity and urbanity than is the oafish burly character of Indiana folklore. Ade's creature shudders at the behavior of the fools—people at a country fair—and decides that they are beneath his handling, contract or no contract. Such a sophisticated vision of evil evokes the Fellow-Traveler in Hawthorne's "Young Goodman Brown" and even Mark Twain's *Mysterious Stranger*, Ade's county fair conjuring up the gothic Eseldorf or "Jackassville."

Finally, in Perspective (to use Ade's style of emphasis), Ade has left us a Priceless Legacy: the Hilarity generated by such Triumphs as "Il Janitoro," "Dubley, '89," "The Fable of What Happened the Night the Men Came to the Women's Club," and—above all—*The Sultan of Sulu*.

THE BEST OF
GEORGE
ADE

I

Fables in Slang

THE FABLE OF
SISTER MAE, WHO DID
AS WELL AS
COULD BE EXPECTED[1]

Two Sisters lived in Chicago, the Home of Opportunity.

Luella was a Good Girl, who had taken Prizes at the Mission Sunday School, but she was Plain, much. Her Features did not seem to know the value of Team Work. Her Clothes fit her Intermittently, as it were. She was what could be called a Lumpy Dresser. But she had a good Heart.

Luella found Employment at a Hat Factory. All she had to do was to put Red Linings in Hats for the Country Trade; and every Saturday Evening, when Work was called on account of Darkness, the Boss met her as she went out and crowded three Dollars on her.

The other Sister was Different.

She began as Mary, then changed to Marie, and her Finish was Mae.

From earliest Youth she had lacked Industry and Application.

She was short on Intellect but long on Shape.

The Vain Pleasures of the World attracted her. By skipping the Long Words she could read how Rupert Banisford led Sibyl Gray into the Conservatory and made Love that scorched the Begonias. Sometimes she just Ached to light out with an Opera Company.

When she couldn't stand up Luella for any more Car Fare she went out looking for Work, and hoping she wouldn't find it. The sagacious Proprietor of a Lunch Room employed her as Cashier. In a little While she learned to count Money, and could hold down the Job.

Marie was a Strong Card. The Male Patrons of the Establishment hovered around the Desk long after paying their Checks. Within a Month the Receipts of the Place had doubled.

It was often remarked that Marie was a Pippin. Her Date Book had to be kept on the Double Entry System.

Although her Grammar was Sad, it made no Odds. Her Picture was on many a Button.

3

Sister Mae

A Credit Man from the Wholesale House across the Street told her that any time she wanted to see the Telegraph Poles rush past, she could tear Transportation out of his Book. But Marie turned him down for a Bucket Shop Man, who was not Handsome, but was awful Generous.

They were Married, and went to live in a Flat with a Quarter-Sawed Oak Chiffonier and Pink Rugs. She was Mae at this Stage of the Game.

Shortly after this, Wheat jumped twenty-two points, and the Husband didn't do a Thing.

Mae bought a Thumb Ring and a Pug Dog, and began to speak of the Swede Help as "The Maid."

Then she decided that she wanted to live in a House, because, in a Flat, One could never be sure of One's Neighbors. So they moved into a Sarcophagus on the Boulevard, right in between two Old Families, who had made their Money soon after the Fire, and Ice began to form on the hottest Days.

Mae bought an Automobile, and blew her Allowance against Beauty Doctors. The Smell of Cooking made her Faint, and she couldn't see where the Working Classes came in at all.

When she attended the theater a Box was none too good. Husband went along, in evening clothes and a Yachting Cap, and he had two large Diamonds in his Shirt Front.

Sometimes she went to a Vogner Concert, and sat through it, and she wouldn't Admit any more that the Russell Brothers, as the Irish Chambermaids, hit her just about Right.

She was determined to break into Society if she had to use an Ax.

At last she Got There; but it cost her many a Reed Bird and several Gross of Cold Quarts.

In the Hey-Day of Prosperity did Mae forget Luella? No, indeed.

She took Luella away from the Hat Factory, where the Pay was three Dollars a Week, and gave her a Position as Assistant Cook at five Dollars.

MORAL: *Industry and Perseverance bring a sure Reward.*

THE FABLE OF THE LAWYER WHO BROUGHT IN A MINORITY REPORT[2]

At a Bazaar, the purpose of which was to Hold Up the Public for the Benefit of a Worthy Cause, there were many Schemes to induce Visitors to let go of their Assets. One of the most likely Grafts perpetrated by the astute Management was a Voting Contest to Determine who was the Most Beautiful and Popular Young Lady in the City. It cost Ten Cents to cast one Vote. The Winner of the Contest was to receive a beautiful Vase, with Roses on it.

A prominent Young Lawyer, who was Eloquent, Good Looking, and a Leader in Society, had been selected to make the Presentation Speech after the Votes had been counted.

In a little while the Contest had narrowed down until it was Evident that either the Brewer's Daughter or the Contractor's Daughter was the most Beautiful and Popular Young Lady in the City. The Brewer and his Friends pushed Ten Dollar Bills into the Ballot Box, while the Contractor, just before the Polls closed, slipped in a Check for One Hundred Dollars.

When the Votes were counted, the Management of the Bazaar was pleased to learn that the Sixty-Cent Vase had Netted over Seven Hundred Dollars. It was Announced that the Contractor's Daughter was exactly Nine Dollars and Twenty Cents more Beautiful and Popular than the Brewer's Daughter.

Thereupon the Committee requested that the Eloquent Young Lawyer step to the Rostrum and make the Presentation Speech. There was no Response; the Young Lawyer had Disappeared.

The Church Bazaar

One of the Members of the Committee started on a Search for him, and found him in a dusky Corner of the Japanese Tea Garden, under the Paper Lanterns, making a Proposal of Marriage to a Poor Girl who had not received one Vote.

MORAL: *Never believe a Relative.*

WHAT THEY HAD LAID OUT FOR THEIR VACATION[3]

A man who had three weeks of Vacation coming to him began to get busy with an Atlas about April 1st. He and his Wife figured that by keeping on the Jump they could do Niagara, Thousand Islands, Atlantic City, The Mammoth Cave and cover the Great Lakes.

On April 10th they decided to charter a House-Boat and float down the Mississippi.

On April 20th he heard of a Cheap Excursion to California with a stop-over Privilege at every Station and they began to read up on Salt Lake and Yellowstone.

On May 1st she flashed a Prospectus of a Northern Lake Resort where Boats and Minnows were free and Nature was ever smiling.

By May 10th he had drawn a Blue Pencil all over a Folder of the Adirondack Region, and all the Hotel Rates were set down in his Pocket Memorandum Book.

Ten days later she vetoed the Mountain Trip because she had got next to a Nantucket Establishment where Family Board was $6 a Week, with the use of a Horse.

On June 1st a Friend showed him how, by making two Changes and hiring a Canoe, he could penetrate the Deep Woods, where the Foot of Man had never Trod and the Black Bass came to the Surface and begged to be taken out.

On June 15th he and Wifey packed up and did the annual Hike up to Uncle Foster's Place in Brown County, where they ate with the Hired Hand and had Greens three times a Day. There were no Screens on the Windows, but by climbing a Hill they could get a lovely View of the Pike that ran over to the County Seat.

MORAL: *If Summer came in the Spring there would be a lot of Travel.*

THE FABLE OF THE MAN
WHO WAS GOING TO RETIRE[4]

A Business Slave was pulling like a Turk so that his Wife could wear three Rings on every Finger. Also, he wanted to put aside something for a Rainy Day. He put it aside as if expecting another Deluge.

He always said that he was going to Retire when he had Enough. When he was 20 years old he hoped to amass $10,000. At 30 he saw that he would not be able to peg along on less than $100,000. When he was 40 he realized that a Man that didn't have a Million was little better than a Tramp. At 50 he wanted to make the Elkins-Widener Syndicate look like a band of Paupers.

At 60 he still promised himself that he would retire. Just as soon as he had cabbaged everything Getatable, then he was going to lie back in an Invalid Chair and read the 18,000 Books he had collected, but he had not found time to cut the Leaves.

In order to get ready for his Lay-Off he built a Home in the Country. He told the Architect to throw himself on something compared with which Windsor Castle would be a Woodman's Hut. He decided on a Deer Park, a Poultry Farm and Ancestral Oaks, so as to have something Ancestral.

He put up a Shack that reminded one of the State Capitol at Springfield. It was big enough for a Soldiers' Home. The Family consisted of himself and his Wife, and the architect allowed them 19 Bath-Rooms apiece.

The Rugs and Tapestries cost $1.75 a Thread. Every Painting was fresh from the Salon and had the Cost-Mark attached to show that it was Good Goods.

When the Place was completed he handed the Business over to the Junior Partners and went out to Rest. He turned on all the Fountains and ordered the Birds to strike up. The Dream of his Life had come True. He had no Cares, no Responsibilities. All he had to do was sit there and watch the Grass grow.

He enjoyed it for nearly 25 minutes and then he began to Fidget, so he went and sat in the Marie Antoinette Room for a while and counted the Stripes in the Fresco. Afterward he took a Turn about the Grounds and came back and wondered if everything was running along all right at the Office.

"Gee, but this is Tame!" said the Retired Hustler. "I think I'd better take a little Run into Town to be sure that the Under-Strappers are not making a Botch of it."

At 11 o'clock he was back at the Old Stand, hovering about like an Uneasy Spirit. He looked over the Correspondence and dictated a few Letters and got the Noise in his Ears and he began to feel Good again.

His Associates told him to clear out and play with the Deer and the Prize Chickens.

"I have been Associating with them all Morning," was the Reply. "They did not seem disposed to close any Contracts, so their Society palled on me. Besides, I have been looking around and see that you can't get along without me. Furthermore, it is all Tommy-Rot for a man of 68 and just entering the Prime of Life to talk of Retiring."

When the Reaper finally came the old Gentleman was found in the Tread-Mill but he was still counting on making use of the Country Place, next Year or possibly the Year after.

MORAL: *One cannot Rest except after steady Practice.*

THE FABLE OF HOW
THE FOOL-KILLER BACKED
OUT OF A CONTRACT[5]

The Fool-Killer came along the Pike Road one Day and stopped to look at a Strange Sight.

Inside of a Barricade were several Thousands of Men, Women and Children. They were moving restlessly among the trampled Weeds, which were clotted with Watermelon Rinds, Chicken Bones, Straw and torn Paper Bags.

It was a very hot Day. The People could not sit down. They shuffled Wearily and were pop-eyed with Lassitude and Discouragement.

A stifling Dust enveloped them. They Gasped and Sniffled. Some tried to alleviate their Sufferings by gulping down a Pink Beverage made of Drug-Store Acid, which fed the Fires of Thirst.

Thus they wove and interwove in the smoky Oven. The Whimper or the faltering Wail of Children, the quavering Sigh of overlaced Women, and the long-drawn Profanity of Men—these were what the Fool-Killer heard as he looked upon the Suffering Throng.

"Is this a new Wrinkle on Dante's Inferno?" he asked of the Man on the Gate, who wore a green Badge marked "Marshal," and was taking Tickets.

"No, sir; this is a County Fair," was the reply.

"Why do the People congregate in the Weeds and allow the Sun to warp them?"

"Because Everybody does it."

"Do they Pay to get in?"

"You know it."

"Can they Escape?"

"They can, but they prefer to Stick."

The Fool-Killer hefted his Club and then looked at the Crowd and shook his Head doubtfully.

"I can't tackle that Outfit today," he said. "It's too big a Job."

So he went on into Town, and singled out a Main Street Merchant who refused to Advertise.

MORAL: *People who expect to be Loony will find it safer to travel in a Bunch.*

THE FABLE OF THE TWO MANDOLIN PLAYERS AND THE WILLING PERFORMER[6]

A Very Attractive Debutante knew two Young Men who called on her every Thursday Evening, and brought their Mandolins along.

They were Conventional Young Men, of the Kind that you see wearing Spring Overcoats in the Clothing Advertisements. One was named Fred, and the other was Eustace.

The Mothers of the Neighborhood often remarked, "What Perfect Manners Fred and Eustace have!" Merely as an aside it may be added that Fred and Eustace were more Popular with the Mothers

than they were with the Younger Set, although no one could say a
Word against either of them. Only it was rumored in Keen Society
that they didn't Belong. The Fact that they went Calling in a Crowd,
and took their Mandolins along, may give the Acute Reader some
Idea of the Life that Fred and Eustace held out to the Young
Women of their Acquaintance.

The Debutante's name was Myrtle. Her Parents were very
Watchful, and did not encourage her to receive Callers, except such
as were known to be Exemplary Young Men. Fred and Eustace were
a few of those who escaped the Black List. Myrtle always appeared to
be glad to see them, and they regarded her as a Darned Swell Girl.

Fred's Cousin came from St. Paul on a Visit; and one Day, in the
Street, he saw Myrtle, and noticed that Fred tipped his Hat, and
gave her a Stage Smile.

"Oh, Queen of Sheba!" exclaimed the Cousin from St. Paul,
whose name was Gus, as he stood stock still, and watched Myrtle's
Reversible Plaid disappear around a Corner. "She's a Bird. Do you
know her well?"

"I know her Quite Well," replied Fred, coldly. "She is a Charming Girl."

"She is all of that. You're a great Describer. And now what Night
are you going to take me around to Call on her?"

Fred very naturally Hemmed and Hawed. It must be remembered that Myrtle was a member of an Excellent Family, and had
been schooled in the Proprieties, and it was not to be supposed that
she would crave the Society of slangy old Gus, who had an abound-
ing Nerve, and furthermore was as Fresh as the Mountain Air.

He was the Kind of Fellow who would see a Girl twice, and then,
upon meeting her the Third Time, he would go up and straighten
her Cravat for her, and call her by her First Name.

Put him into a Strange Company—en route to a Picnic—and by
the time the Baskets were unpacked he would have a Blonde all to
himself, and she would have traded her Fan for his College Pin.

If a Fair-Looker on the Street happened to glance at him Hard
he would run up and seize her by the Hand, and convince her that
they had Met. And he always Got Away with it, too.

In a Department Store, while waiting for the Cash Boy to come
back with the Change, he would find out the Girl's Name, her Favorite Flower, and where a Letter would reach her.

Upon entering a Parlor Car at St. Paul he would select a Chair
next to the Most Promising One in Sight, and ask her if she cared to
have the Shade lowered.

Before the Train cleared the Yards he would have the Porter bringing a Foot-Stool for the Lady.

At Hastings he would be asking her if she wanted Something to Read.

At Red Wing he would be telling her that she resembled Maxine Elliott, and showing her his Watch, left to him by his Grandfather, a Prominent Virginian.

At La Crosse he would be reading the Menu Card to her, and telling her how different it is when you have Some One to join you in a Bite.

At Milwaukee he would go out and buy a Bouquet for her, and when they rode into Chicago they would be looking out of the same Window, and he would be arranging for their Baggage with the Transfer Man. After that they would be Old Friends.

Now, Fred and Eustace had been at School with Gus, and they had seen his Work, and they were not disposed to Introduce him into One of the most Exclusive Homes in the City.

They had known Myrtle for many Years; but they did not dare to Address her by her First Name, and they were Positive that if Gus attempted any of his usual Tactics with her she would be Offended; and, naturally enough, they would be Blamed for bringing him to the House.

But Gus insisted. He said he had seen Myrtle, and she Suited him from the Ground up, and he proposed to have Friendly Doings with her. At last they told him they would take him if he promised to Behave. Fred Warned him that Myrtle would frown down any Attempt to be Familiar on Short Acquaintance, and Eustace said that as long as he had known Myrtle he had never Presumed to be Free and Forward with her. He had simply played the Mandolin. That was as Far Along as he had ever got.

Gus told them not to Worry about him. All he asked was a Start. He said he was a Willing Performer, but as yet he never had been Disqualified for Crowding. Fred and Eustace took this to mean that he would not Overplay his Attentions, so they escorted him to the House.

As soon as he had been Presented, Gus showed her where to sit on the Sofa, then he placed himself about Six Inches away and began to Buzz, looking her straight in the Eye. He said that when he first saw her he Mistook her for Miss Prentice, who was said to be the Most Beautiful Girl in St. Paul, only, when he came closer, he saw that it couldn't be Miss Prentice, because Miss Prentice didn't have such Lovely Hair. Then he asked her the Month of her Birth and

Gus and Myrtle

told her Fortune, thereby coming nearer to Holding her Hand within Eight Minutes than Eustace had come in a Lifetime.

"Play something, Boys," he Ordered, just as if he had paid them Money to come along and make Music for him.

They unlimbered their Mandolins and began to play a Sousa March. He asked Myrtle if she had seen the New Moon. She replied that she had not, so they went Outside.

When Fred and Eustace finished the first Piece, Gus appeared at the open Window, and asked them to play "The Georgia Camp-Meeting," which had always been one of his Favorites.

So they played that, and when they had Concluded there came a Voice from the Outer Darkness, and it was the Voice of Myrtle. She said: "I'll tell you what to Play; play the Intermezzo."

Fred and Eustace exchanged Glances. They began to Perceive

that they had been backed into a Siding. With a few Potted Palms in front of them, and two Cards from the Union, they would have been just the same as a Hired Orchestra.

But they played the Intermezzo and felt Peevish. Then they went to the Window and looked out. Gus and Myrtle were sitting in the Hammock, which had quite a Pitch toward the Center. Gus had braced himself by Holding to the back of the Hammock. He did not have his Arm around Myrtle, but he had it Extended in a Line parallel with her Back. What he had done wouldn't Justify a Girl in saying, "Sir!" but it started a Real Scandal with Fred and Eustace. They saw that the only Way to Get Even with her was to go Home without saying "Good Night." So they slipped out the Side Door, shivering with Indignation.

After that, for several Weeks, Gus kept Myrtle so Busy that she had no Time to think of considering other Candidates. He sent Books to her Mother, and allowed the Old Gentleman to take Chips away from him at Poker.

They were Married in the Autumn, and Father-in-Law took Gus into the Firm, saying that he had needed a good Pusher for a Long Time.

At the Wedding the two Mandolin Players were permitted to act as Ushers.

MORAL: *To get a fair Trial of Speed, use a Pace-Maker.*

THE FABLE OF THE GRASS WIDOW AND THE MESMEREE AND THE SIX DOLLARS[7]

One day a keen Business manager who thought nobody could Show him was sitting at his Desk. A Grass Widow floated in, and stood Smiling at him. She was a Blonde, and had a Gown that fit her as if she had been Packed into it by Hydraulic Pressure. She was just as Demure as Edna May ever tried to be, but the Business Manager was a Lightning Calculator, and he Surmised that the Bunk was about to be Handed to him. The Cold Chills went down his Spine when he caught a Flash of the Half-Morocco Prospectus.

If it had been a Man Agent he would have shouted "Sick 'em" and reached for a Paper-Weight. But when the Agent has the Venus de Milo beaten on Points and Style, and when the Way the Skirt sets isn't so Poor, and she is Coy and introduces the Startled Fawn way of backing up without getting any farther away, and when she comes on with short Steps, and he gets the remote Swish of the Real Silk, to say nothing of the Faint Aroma of New-Mown Hay, and her Hesitating Manner seems to ask, "Have I or have I not met a Friend?"—in a Case of that kind, the Victim is just the same as Strapped to the Operating-Table. He has about One Chance in a Million.

The timorous but trusting little Grass Widow sat beside the Business Manager and told him her Hard-Luck Story in low, bird-like Notes. She said she was the only Support of her Little Boy, who was attending a Military School at Syracuse, N.Y. She turned the Liquid Orbs on him and had him to the Bad. He thought he would tell her that already he had more Books at Home than he could get on the Shelves, but when he tried to Talk he only Yammered. She Kept on with her little Song, and Smiled all the Time, and sat a little Closer, and he got so Dizzy he had to lock his Legs under the Office Chair to keep from Sinking Away.

When she had him in the Hypnotic State she pushed the Silver Pencil into his Right Hand, and showed him where to sign his Name. He wrote it, while the dim Sub-Consciousness told him that probably he was the Softest Thing the Lady Robber had Stood Up that Season. Then she recovered the Pencil, which he was confusedly trying to put into his Vest Pocket, and missing it about Six Inches, and with a cheery Good Bye she was gone.

He shook himself and took a Long Breath, and asked where he was. Then it all came back to him and he felt Ornery, and called himself Names and roasted the Office Boy in the Next Room, and made a Rule that hereafter Nobody could get at him except by Card, and if any Blonde Sharks in Expensive Costumes asked for him, to call up the Chief and ask for a Squad.

He was so Wrothy at himself for being Held Up that he could not find any Consolation except in the Fact that he had seen on the List of Subscribers the name of nearly every well-known married Citizen above the Age of 35. He was not the Only One. She had Corralled the Street.

When the Man came around to deliver the seven-pound copy of "Happy Hours with the Poets," and he paid out his Six Silver Pieces for a queer Volume that he would not have Read for Six an Hour, he hated himself worse than ever. He thought some of giving the Book to the Office Boy, by way of Revenge, but he hit upon a Better Use for it. He put it back into the Box and carried it Home, and said to his Wife, "See what I have Bought for you."

It occurred to him that after getting a Present like that, she ought to let him stay out every Night for a Month. But she could not see it that Way. He had to tell her that Some Women never seem to Appreciate having Husbands to Grind and Toil all day, so as to be able to purchase Beautiful Gifts for them. Then she told him that all the Women of her Acquaintance had received these Books as Presents, and a crowd of Married Men must have been given a Club Rate. Then he Spunked up and said that if she was going to look a Gift Horse in the Mouth, they wouldn't Talk about it any more.

In the meantime the Grass Widow was living at the Waldorf-Astoria.

MORAL: *Those who are Entitled to it Get it sooner or later.*

THE FABLE OF WHAT HAPPENED THE NIGHT THE MEN CAME TO THE WOMEN'S CLUB[8]

In a Progressive Little City claiming about twice the Population that the Census Enumerators could uncover, there was a Literary Club. It was one of these Clubs guaranteed to fix you out with Culture while you wait. Two or three Matrons, who were too Heavy for Light Amusements, but not old enough to remain at Home and Knit, organized the Club. Nearly every Woman in town rushed to get in, for fear somebody would say she hadn't been Asked.

The Club used to Round Up once a week at the Homes of Members. There would be a Paper, followed by a Discussion, after which somebody would Pour.

The Organization seemed to be a Winner. One Thing the Lady Clubbers were Dead Set On. They were going to have Harmony with an Upper Case H. They were out to cut a seven-foot Swath through English Literature from Beowulf to Bangs, inclusive, and no petty Jealousies or Bickerings would stand in the Way.

So while they were at the Club they would pull Kittenish Smiles at each other, and Applaud so as not to split the Gloves. Some times they would Kiss, too, but they always kept their Fingers crossed.

Of course, when they got off in Twos and Threes they would pull the little Meat-Axes out of the Reticules and hack a few Monograms, but that was to have been expected.

Everything considered, the Club was a Tremendous Go. At each Session the Lady President would announce the Subject for the next Meeting. For instance, she would say that Next Week they would take up Wyclif. Then every one would romp home to look in the Encyclopedia of Authors and find out who in the world Wyclif was. On the following Thursday they would have Wyclif down Pat, and be primed for a Discussion. They would talk about Wyclif as if he had been down to the House for Tea every evening that Week.

After the Club had been running for Six Months it was beginning to be Strong on Quotations and Dates. The Members knew that Mrs. Browning was the wife of Mr. Browning, that Milton had Trouble with his Eyes, and that Lord Byron wasn't all that he should have been, to say the Least. They began to feel their Intellectual Oats. In the meantime the Jeweler's Wife had designed a Club Badge.

The Club was doing such Notable Work that some of the Members thought they ought to have a Special Meeting and invite the Men. They wanted to put the Cap-Sheaf on a Profitable Season, and at the same time hand the Merited Rebuke to some of the Husbands and Brothers who had been making Funny Cracks.

It was decided to give the Star Programme at the Beadle Home, and after the Papers had been read then all the Men and Five Women who did not hold office could file through the Front Room and shake Hands with the President, the Vice-President, the Recording Secretary, the Corresponding Secretary, the Treasurer, and the members of the various Committees, all of whom were to line up and Receive.

The reason the Club decided to have the Brain Barbecue at the

Beadle Home was that the Beadles had such beautiful big Rooms and Double Doors. There was more or less quiet Harpoon Work when the Announcement was made. Several of the Elderly Ones said that Josephine Beadle was not a Representative Member of the Club. She was Fair to look upon, but she was not pulling very hard for the Uplifting of the Sex. It was suspected that she came to the Meetings just to Kill Time and see what the Others were Wearing. She refused to buckle down to Literary Work, for she was a good deal more interested in the Bachelors who filled the Windows of the new Men's Club than she was in the Butler who wrote "Hudibras." So why should she have the Honor of entertaining the Club at the Annual Meeting? Unfortunately, the Members who had the most Doing under their Bonnets were not the ones who could come to the Front with large Rooms that could be Thrown together, so the Beadle Home got the Great Event. . . . The men managed to get Rear Seats or stand along the Wall so that they could execute the Quiet Sneak if Things got too Literary. The Women were too Flushed and Proud to Notice.

At 8:30 P. M. the Lady President stood out and began to read a few Pink Thoughts on "Woman's Destiny—Why Not?" Along toward 9:15, about the time the Lady President was beginning to show up Good and Earnest, Josephine Beadle, who was Circulating around on the Outskirts of the Throng to make sure that everybody was Happy, made a Discovery. She noticed that the Men standing along the Wall and in the Doorways were not more than sixty per cent En Rapport with the Long Piece about Woman's Destiny. Now Josephine was right there to see that Everybody had a Nice Time, and she did not like to see the Prominent Business Men of the Town dying of Thirst or Leg Cramp or anything like that, so she gave two or three of them the Quiet Wink, and they tiptoed after her out to the Dining Room, where she offered Refreshments, and said they could slip out on the Side Porch and Smoke if they wanted to.

Probably they preferred to go back in the Front Room and hear some more about Woman's Destiny not.

As soon as they could master their Emotions and get control of their Voices, they told Josephine what they thought of her. They said she made the Good Samaritan look like a Cheap Criminal, and if she would only say the Word they would begin to put Ground Glass into the Food at Home. Then Josephine called them "Boys," which probably does not make a Hit with one who is the sloping side of 48. More of the Men seemed to awake to the Fact that they were

Overlooking something, so they came on the Velvet Foot back to the Dining Room and declared themselves In, and flocked around Josephine and called her "Josie" and "Joe." They didn't care. They were having a Pleasant Visit.

Josephine gave them Allopathic Slugs of the Size that they feed you in the Navy and then lower you into the Dingy and send you Ashore. Then she let them go out on the Porch to smoke. By the time the Lady President came to the last Page there were only two Men left in the Front Room. One was Asleep and the other was Penned In.

The Women were Huffy. They went out to make the Men come in, and found them Bunched on the Porch listening to a Story that a Traveling Man had just brought to Town that Day.

Now the Plan was that during the Reception the Company would stand about in little Groups, and ask each other what Books they liked, and make it something on the order of a Salon. This Plan miscarried, because all the Men wanted to hear Rag Time played by Josephine, the Life-Saver. Josephine had to yield, and the Men all clustered around her to give their Moral Support. After one or two Selections, they felt sufficiently Keyed to begin to hit up those low-down Songs about Baby and Chickens and Razors. No one paid any Attention to the Lady President, who was off in a Corner holding an Indignation Meeting with the Secretary and the Vice-President.

When the Women began to sort out the Men and order them to start Home and all the Officers of the Club were giving Josephine the frosty Good Night, any one could see that there was Trouble ahead.

Next day the Club held a Special Session and expelled Josephine for Conduct Unbecoming a Member, and Josephine sent Word to them as follows: "Rats."

Then the Men quietly got together and bought Josephine about a Thousand Dollars' Worth of American Beauty Roses to show that they were With her, and then Homes began to break up, and somebody started the Report that anyway it was the Lady President's Fault for having such a long and pokey Essay that wasn't hers at all, but had been Copied out of a Club Paper published in Detroit.

Before the next Meeting there were two Factions. The Lady President had gone to a Rest Cure, and the Meeting resolved itself into a Good Cry and a general Smash-Up.

MORAL: *The only Literary Men are those who have to Work at it.*

THE FABLE OF LUTIE, THE FALSE ALARM, AND HOW SHE FINISHED ABOUT THE TIME THAT SHE STARTED[9]

Lutie was an Only Child. When Lutie was eighteen her Mother said they ought to do something with Lutie's Voice. The Neighbors thought so, too. Some recommended killing the Nerve, while others allowed that it ought to be Pulled.

But what Mamma meant was that Lutie ought to have it Cultivated by a Professor. She suspected that Lutie had a Career awaiting her, and would travel with an Elocutionist some day and have her Picture on the Programme.

Lutie's Father did not warm up to the Suggestion. He was rather Near when it came to frivoling away the National Bank Lithographs. But pshaw! The Astute Reader knows what happens in a Family when Mother and the Only Child put their Heads together to whipsaw the Producer. One Day they shouldered him into a Corner and extorted a Promise. Next Day Lutie started to Take.

She bought a red leather Cylinder marked "Music," so that people would not take it to be Lunch. Every Morning about 9 o'clock she would wave the Housework to one side and tear for a Trolley.

Her Lessons cost the Family about twenty cents a Minute. She took them in a large Building full of Vocal Studios. People who didn't know used to stop in front of the Place and listen, and think it was a Surgical Institute.

There were enough Soprani in this one Plant to keep Maurice Grau stocked up for a Hundred Years. Every one thought she was the Particular One who would sooner or later send Melba back to Australia and drive Sembrich into the Continuous. Lutie was just about as Nifty as the Next One.

When she was at Home she would suck Lemons and complain about Draughts and tell why she didn't like the Other Girls' Voices. She began to act like a Prima Donna, and her Mother was encouraged a lot. Lutie certainly had the Artistic Temperament bigger than a Church Debt.

Now before Lutie started in to do Things to her Voice she occasionally Held Hands with a Young Man in the Insurance Business, named Oliver. This Young Man thought that Lutie was all the Merchandise, and she regarded him as Permanent Car-Fare.

But when Lutie began to hang out at the Studios she took up with the Musical Set that couldn't talk about anything but Technique and Shading and the Motif and the Vibrato. She began to fill up the Parlor with her new Friends, and the first thing Oliver knew he was in the Side Pocket and out of the Game.

In his own Line this Oliver was as neat and easy-running as a Red Buggy, but when you started him on the topic of Music he was about as light and speedy as a Steam Roller. Ordinarily he knew how to behave himself in a Flat, and with a good Feeder to work back at him he could talk about Shows and Foot-Ball Games and Things to Eat, but when any one tried to draw him out on the Classics, he was unable to Qualify.

When Lutie and her Musical acquaintances told about Shopan and Batoven he would sit back so quiet that often he got numb below the Hips. He was afraid to move his Feet for fear some one would notice that he was still in the Parlor and ask him how he liked Fugue No. 11, by Bock. He had never heard of any of these People, because they did not carry Tontine Policies with his Company.

Oliver saw that he would have to Scratch the Musical Set or else begin to Read Up, so he changed his Route. He canceled all Time with Lutie, and made other Bookings.

Lutie then selected for her Steady a Young Man with Hair who played the 'Cello. He was so wrapped up in his Art that he acted Dopey most of the time, and often forgot to send out the Laundry so as to get it back the same Week. Furthermore, he didn't get to the Suds any too often. He never Saw more than $3 at one time; but when he snuggled up alongside of a 'Cello and began to tease the long, sad Notes out of it, you could tell that he had a Soul for Music. Lutie thought he was Great, but what Lutie's Father thought of him could never get past the Censor. Lutie's Father regarded the whole Musical Set as a Fuzzy Bunch. He began to think that in making any Outlay for Lutie's Vocal Training he had bought a Gold Brick. When he first consented to her taking Lessons his Belief was that after she had practiced for about one Term she would be able to sit up to the Instrument along in the Dusk before the Lamps were lit, and sing "When the Corn Is Waving, Annie Dear," "One Sweetly Solemn Thought," or else "Juanita." These were the Songs linked in

"... she would approach the Piano timidly and sort of
Trifle with it ..."

his Memory with some Purple Evenings of the Happy Long Ago. He
knew they were Chestnuts, and had been called in, but they suited
him, and he thought that inasmuch as he had put up the Wherewith
for Lutie's Lessons he ought to have some kind of a Small Run for
his Money.

Would Lutie sing such Trash? Not she. She was looking for
Difficult Arias from the Italian, and she found many a one that was
Difficult to sing, and probably a little more Difficult to Listen To.

The Voice began to be erratic, also. When Father wanted to sit by
the Student's Lamp and read his Scribner's, she would decide to
hammer the Piano and do the whole Repertoire.

But when Mother had Callers and wanted Lutie to Show Off, then she would hang back and have to be Coaxed. If she didn't have a Sore Throat, then the Piano was out of Tune, or else she had left all of her Good Music at the Studio, or maybe she just couldn't Sing without some one to Accompany her. But after they had Pleaded hard enough, and everybody was Embarrassed and sorry they had come, she would approach the Piano timidly and sort of Trifle with it for a while, and say they would have to make Allowances, and then she would Cut Loose and worry the whole Block. The Company would sit there, every one showing the Parlor Face and pretending to be entranced, and after she got through they would Come To and tell her how Good she was.

She made so many of these Parlor Triumphs that there was no Holding her. She had herself Billed as a Nightingale. Often she went to Soirées and Club Entertainments, volunteering her Services, and nowhere did she meet a Well-Wisher who took her aside and told her she was a Shine—in fact, the Champion Pest.

No, Lutie never got out of her Dream until she made a bold Sashay with a Concert Company. It was her Professional Debut.

Father fixed it. The Idea of any one paying Real Money to hear Lutie sing struck him as being almost Good enough to Print. But she wouldn't be Happy until she got it, and so she Got It right where the Newport Lady wears the Rope of Pearls.

On the First Night the mean old Critics, who didn't know her Father or Mother, and had never been entertained at the House, came and got in the Front Row, and defied Lutie to come on and Make Good. Next Morning they said that Lutie had Blow-Holes in her Voice; that she hit the Key only once during the Evening, and then fell off backward; that she was a Ham, and her Dress didn't fit her, and she lacked Stage Presence. They expressed Surprise that she should be attempting to Sing when any bright Girl could learn to pound a Type-Writer in Four Weeks. They wanted to know who was responsible for her Appearance, and said it was a Shame to String these Jay Amateurs. Lutie read the Criticisms, and went into Nervous Collapse. Her Mother was all Wrought Up, and said somebody ought to go and kill the Editors. Father bore up grimly.

Before Lutie was Convalescent he had the Difficult Italian Arias carted out of the house. The 'Cello Player came to call one Day, and he was given Minutes to get out of the Ward.

By the time Oliver looked in again Lutie was more than ready to pay some Attention to him. She is now doing a few quiet Vocaliza-

tions for her Friends. When some one who hasn't Heard tells her
that she is good enough for Opera, they have to open the Windows
and give her more Air.

MORAL: *When in Doubt, try it on the Box-Office.*

THE FABLE OF THE
HONEST MONEY-MAKER
AND THE PARTNER OF
HIS JOYS, SUCH
AS THEY WERE[10]

The Prosperous Farmer lived in an Agricultural Section of the
Middle West. He commanded the Respect of all his Neighbors. He
owned a Section, and had a Raft of big Horses and white-faced Cows
and Farm Machinery, and Money in the Bank besides. He still had
the first Dollar he ever made, and it could not have been taken away
from him with Pincers.

Henry was a ponderous, Clydesdale kind of Man, with Warts on
his Hands. He did not have to travel on Appearances, because the
whole County knew what he was Worth. Of course he was Married.
Years before he had selected a willing Country Girl with Pink
Cheeks, and put her into his Kitchen to serve the Remainder of her
Natural Life. He let her have as high as Two Dollars a Year to spend
for herself. Her Hours were from 6 A. M. to 6 A. M., and if she got
any Sleep she had to take it out of her Time. The Eight-Hour Day
was not recognized on Henry's Place.

After Ten Years of raising Children, Steaming over the Washtub,
Milking the Cows, Carrying in Wood, Cooking for the Hands, and
other Delsarte such as the Respected Farmer usually Frames Up for
his Wife, she was as thin as a Rail and humped over in the Shoulders. She was Thirty, and looked Sixty. Her Complexion was like
Parchment and her Voice had been worn to a Cackle. She was losing
her Teeth, too, but Henry could not afford to pay Dentist Bills because he needed all his Money to buy more Poland Chinas and build

other Cribs. If she wanted a Summer Kitchen or a new Wringer or a Sewing Machine, or Anything Else that would lighten her Labors, Henry would Moan and Grumble and say she was trying to land him in the Poorhouse.

They had a dandy big Barn, painted Red with White Trimmings, and a Patent Fork to lift the Hay into the Mow, and the Family lived in a Pine Box that had not been Painted in Years and had Dog-Fennel all around the Front of it.

The Wife of the Respected Farmer was the only Work Animal around the Place that was not kept Fat and Sleek. But, of course, Henry did not count on Selling her. Henry often would fix up his Blooded Stock for the County Fair and tie Blue Ribbons on the Percherons and Herefords, but it was never noticed that he tied any Blue Ribbons on the Wife.

And yet Henry was a Man to be Proud of. He never Drank and he was a Good Hand with Horses, and he used to go to Church on Sunday Morning and hold a Cud of Tobacco in his Face during Services and sing Hymns with Extreme Unction. He would sing that he was a Lamb and had put on the Snow-White Robes and that Peace attended him. People would see him there in his Store Suit, with the Emaciated Wife and the Scared Children sitting in the Shadow of his Greatness, and they said that she was Lucky to have a Man who was so Well Off and lived in the Fear of the Lord.

Henry was Patriotic as well as Pious. He had a Picture of Abraham Lincoln in the Front Room, which no one was permitted to Enter, and he was glad that Slavery had been abolished.

Henry robbed the Cradle in order to get Farm-Hands. As soon as the Children were able to Walk without holding on, he started them for the Corn-Field, and told them to Pay for the Board that they had been Sponging off of him up to that Time. He did not want them to get too much Schooling for fear that they would want to sit up at Night and Read instead of Turning In so as to get an Early Start along before Daylight next Morning. So they did not get any too much, rest easy. And he never Foundered them on Stick Candy or Raisins or any such Delicatessen for sale at a General Store. Henry was undoubtedly the Tightest Wad in the Township. Some of the Folks who had got into a Box through Poor Management, and had been Foreclosed out of House and Home by Henry and his Lawyer, used to say that Henry was a Skin, and was too Stingy to give his Family enough to Eat, but most People looked up to Henry, for there was no getting around it that he was Successful.

When the Respected Farmer had been Married for Twenty Years

and the Children had developed into long Gawks who did not know Anything except to get out and Toil all Day for Pa and not be paid anything for it, and after Henry had scraped together more Money than you could load on a Hay-Rack, an Unfortunate Thing happened. His Wife began to Fail. She was now Forty, but the Fair and Fat did not go with it. At that Age some Women are Buxom and just blossoming into the Full Charm of Matronly Womanhood. But Henry's Wife was Gaunt and Homely and all Run Down. She had been Poorly for Years, but she had to keep up and do the Chores as well as the House-Work, because Henry could not afford to hire a Girl. At last her Back gave out, so that she had to sit down and Rest every Once in a While. Henry would come in for his Meals and to let her know how Hearty all the Calves seemed to be, and he began to Notice that she was not very Chipper. It worried him more than a little, because he did not care to pay any Doctor Bills. He told her she had better go and get some Patent Medicine that he had seen advertised on the Fence coming out from Town. It was only Twenty-Five cents a Bottle, and was warranted to Cure Anything. So she tried it, but it did not seem to restore her Youth and she got Weaker, and at last Henry just had to have the Doctor, Expense or No Expense. The Doctor said that as nearly as he could Diagnose her Case, she seemed to be Worn Out. Henry was Surprised, and said she had not been Complaining any more than Usual.

Next Afternoon he was out Dickering for a Bull, and his Woman lying on the cheap Bedstead, up under the hot Roof, folded her lean Hands and slipped away to the only Rest she had known since she tied up with a Prosperous and Respected Farmer.

Henry was all Broken Up. He Wailed and Sobbed and made an Awful Fuss at the Church. The Preacher tried to Comfort him by saying that the ways of Providence were beyond all Finding Out. He said that probably there was some Reason why the Sister had been taken right in the Prime of her Usefulness, but it was not for Henry to know it. He said the only Consolation he could offer was the Hope that possibly she was Better Off. There did not seem to be much Doubt about that.

In about a Month the Respected Farmer was riding around the Country in his Buck-Board looking for Number Two. He had a business Head and he knew it was Cheaper to Marry than to Hire one. His Daughter was only Eleven and not quite Big Enough as yet to do all the Work for five Men.

Finally he found one who had the Reputation of being a Good

Worker. When he took her over to his House to Break Her In, the Paper at the County Seat referred to them as the Happy Couple.

MORAL: *Be Honest and Respected and it Goes.*

NOTES ON THE FABLES

1. From *Fables in Slang* (Chicago: Herbert Stone & Company, 1899). This version of Ade's first published fable in slang represents one of his revisions—deletion of a passage in which he originally had Mae sing a racist song. "Vogner" is of course Mae's rendition of Wagner. "Reed Bird" is probably pheasant, duck, or some other expensive game bird, and "Cold Quarts" probably refers to champagne.

2. From *Fables in Slang*.

3. From *People You Know* (New York: Harper & Brothers, 1902).

4. From *Fables in Slang*.

5. From *Fables in Slang*.

6. From *Fables in Slang*. This is the fable Ade said Dreiser "may have seen in the Chicago Record" and may or may not have had in mind when he was writing the first chapter of *Sister Carrie* (1900). See, in Part IV of this anthology, Ade's letter to the editor of the *New York Herald-Tribune* (September 8, 1926). Maxine Elliott was a cover-girl of the day.

7. From *More Fables in Slang* (Chicago: Herbert Stone & Company, 1900). 1900).

8. From *More Fables in Slang*. Although this fable reflects a condescending attitude toward women, it also depicts the men's behavior in an unflattering light. "English literature from Beowulf to Bangs": John Kendrick Bangs (1862–1922) was an American humorist, lecturer, and New York editor for the British magazine *Punch*.

9. From *More Fables in Slang*. The personages referred to in paragraph six are Maurice Grau (1857–1934), American theatrical talent representative; Nellie Melba (1861–1931), Australian coloratura soprano; and Marcella Sembrich (d. 1935), an Austrian opera star.

10. From *More Fables in Slang*.

II

Short Stories

ARTIE BLANCHARD[1]

Artie Blanchard went to the charity entertainment, and, as he said afterward, he had "no kick comin'," although it wasn't exactly his kind of a show. Artie had started in at the general offices as messenger boy and had earned promotion on his merits. What he lacked in schooling he made up in good sense, industry and a knowledge of human nature.

He had the reputation of being worldly, even "tough," but he didn't deserve it. He was simply overmasculine. If he used slang it was because slang helped him to express his feelings with greater force and directness.

He was always interested in prize-fighting because he admired gameness and muscular power and had both of them pretty well developed in his own well-knit figure.

If he showed a disposition to "kid" on all sorts of topics it was because he took a cheerful and good-natured view of life and also gave his hearers credit for having enough perception to understand that he didn't mean all that he said.

Artie was well dressed, although he was inclined to follow his own notions as to personal adornment. He was jaunty rather than "swell," and like all hard-headed men he hated any sort of an extreme, such as a very high collar or a very low-cut vest. He had no evening dress, or "first-party clothes" as he called them, because he had a jovial contempt for "society" as he had caught glimpses of it, although he was on cordial terms with many young men who devoted all of their leisure time to it.

On the other hand, he had the utmost respect for women. In fact, he held all good women in such deep and tender regard that he seldom attempted to express himself on the subject, holding that it was too sacred for the every-day fool intercourse of men in this world. Only to those who knew him well and had proved themselves worthy of such confidence did he reveal himself. Others, who were but partly acquainted with him, held him to be a person of rather low morals.

Not that he was a drunkard or a gambler or a rowdy, but he lacked reverence and repose. His language was that of the streets, and he was an anarchist regarding so-called "good form."

There is no excuse for telling so much about Artie except that

31

there are so many young men of his kind in Chicago who combine good conduct of life and strict attention to business with a playful pretense to heathen depravity. . . .

One day Mrs. Morton, wife of the city manager, came into the offices and "held up" the boys for 50 cents apiece, and then gave each of them a ticket to the charity entertainment to be given in the parlors of a certain south side church on the following Wednesday evening. Artie had to "cough up," and he did it with apparent willingness.

"I don't want you young men to think that I am robbing you of this money," said Mrs. Morton. "I want you to come to this entertainment. I know you'll enjoy it."

"Blanchard can go all right," suggested Miller, with a wink at the man next to him. "He lives only about three blocks from the church."

"Then he must come," said Mrs. Morton. "Won't you, Mr. Blanchard?"

"Sure," replied Artie, blushing deeply.

"Why, Mrs. Morton, he hasn't been in a church for three years," said Miller.

"I don't believe it," and she turned to Artie, who was making motions to "call off" Miller. "Now, Mr. Blanchard, I want you to promise me faithfully that you'll come."

"I'll be there all right," he replied, smiling feebly.

"Remember, you've promised," and as she went out she shook her finger at him as a final reminder.

"Well, are you going?" asked Miller.

"What's it to you?" asked Artie. "Didn't you hear what I said to her? Sure I'm goin'. I've got as much right to go out and do the heavy as any o' you pin-heads. If I like their show I'll help 'em out next time—get a couple o' handy boys from Harry Gilmore's and put on a six-round go for a finish. Them people never saw anything good."

"I'll bet the cigars you don't go," spoke up young Mr. Hall.

"You'd better make it chewin' gum," replied Artie. "Next thing you'll be bettin' real money. You guys must think I'm a quitter, to be scared out by any little old church show. I don't think it'll be any worse than a barn fight over in Indiana." . . .

Ellipsis points are the editor's. In keeping with Ade's characteristic concision, I have taken the liberty of making a few—very few—cuts. I have omitted passages that struck me as expendable because of their repetitiousness or uninteresting, probably unintended, prolixity.—A.L.L.

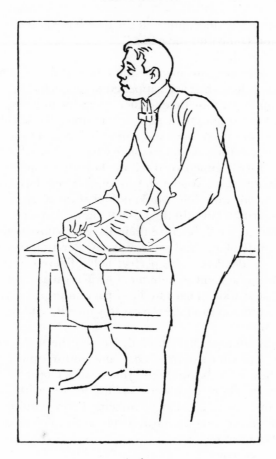

Artie

. . . . .

"Well, I goes," said Artie, the morning after the charity entertainment.

"Where?" asked Miller, who had forgotten.

"Where? Well, that's a good thing. To the church show—the charity graft. I didn't do a thing but push my face in there about 8 o'clock last night and I was it from the start. Say, I like that church, and if they'll put in a punchin' bag and a plunge they can have my game, I'll tell you that."

"Did you see Mrs. Morton?"

"How's that, boy? Did I see her? Say, she treated me out o' sight.

She meets me at the door, puts out the glad hand and says: 'Hang up your dicer and come into the game.'"

"That's what she said, eh?"

"Well, that's what she meant. She's all right, too, and the only wonder to me is how she ever happened to tie herself up to that slob. It's like hitchin' up a four-time winner alongside of a dog. He ain't in her class, not for a minute, a part of a minute. What kills me off is how all these dubs make their star winnin's. Why, out there last night I saw the measliest lot of jays, regular Charley-boys, floatin' around with queens. I wish somebody'd tell me how they cop 'em out. Don't it kill you dead to see a swell girl, you know, a regular peach, holdin' on to some freak with side whiskers and thinkin' she's got a good thing? That's right. She thinks he's all right. Anyway, she acts the part, but you can't tell, because them fly girls know how to make a good many bluff plays. And say, you know Percival, that works over in the bank—little Percy, the perfect lady. There's a guy that I've known for five years and so help me if he gets on a street car where I am I get off and walk. That's no lie. I pass him up. I say, 'You're all right, Percy, and you can take the car to yourself,' and then I duck."

"Was he there?"

"The whole thing! That's no kid. He was the real papa—the hit of the place. One on each arm, see?—and puttin' up the large, juicy con talk. They were beauts, too; you couldn't beat 'em, not in a thousand years. There they were, holdin' to this wart. Up goes my hands into the air and I says to myself: 'Percy, you're all right. I wouldn't live on the same street with you, but you're all right at that.' But he couldn't see me."

"Couldn't see you?"

"No, he lost his eyesight. He looked at me, but he was too busy to see me. No, he had on his saucy coat and that touch-me-not necktie, and oh, he was busy. He wasn't doin' a thing. I think I'll give the bank a line on Percy. Any man that wears that kind of a necktie hadn't ought to be allowed to handle money. But you ought to have seen the two he had. I'd like to know how he does it. I had a notion to go up to one of the girls and say: 'What's the matter? Haven't you ever seen any others?'". . .

"Did you like the show," asked Miller.

"It's this way. They liked it and so"—with a wave of the hand—"let 'em have it. If they put the same turns on at the Olymp the people'd tear down the buildin' tryin' to get their coin back. Mrs. Morton got me a good seat and then backcapped the show a little before it opened up, so I didn't expect to be pulled out of my chair—and I wasn't. If I'd been near the door I'd have sneaked early in the game, but, like a farmer, I let her put me way up in front. I saw I was up against it, so I lasted the best way I could. Two or three of the songs were purty fair, but the woman that trifled with the piano for about a half-hour was very much on the bummy bum. Then there was a guy called an entertainer that told some of the Billy Rice gags that I used to hear when my brother took me to the old Academy and held me on his lap. But he got 'em goin' just the same. Well, I says to myself, 'What'd Weber and Fields[2] do to this push?" On the dead, I don't believe any of them people out there ever saw a good, hot variety show. It just goes to show that there are a lot of people with stuff who think they know what's goin' on in town, but they don't. I've got no kick comin', only it was a yellow show, and I'm waitin' for 45 cents change."

"I should think you would have got the worth of your money simply by seeing so many good-looking girls," said Miller.

"The girls are all right, only I think they're losin' their eyesight. If I had time I'd go over to that church and make a lot o' them Reubs look like 30-cent pieces. Not that I'm strong on the con talk, but I know I'd be in it with them fellows. I think it must be a case of nerve. That's all there is to 'em—is nerve. But the girls—wow!"

"Fine creatures, eh?"

"Lallypaloozers!"

HOW "PINK"
WAS REFORMED[3]

It was very difficult to tell whether "Pink" had been drinking or not. The only signs were a slight reddening of the eyeballs and an increased violence of laughter.

There was no such thing as detecting an alcoholic flush in a face which had the dull brown-black color of chocolate. It was generally known around the building, however, that "Pink" was addicted to spiritous, vinous, malt and other intoxicating liquors, with a racial preference for gin. He had other worldly habits, which he gladly confessed. These were "craps" and "policy." Even to the customers

"Pink had aspirations to leave the lowly job of cleaning
shoes . . ."

who could have no possible interest in such lowly speculation he
confided stories about "passin' de bones," "Little Joe" and "gettin' ole
eight," whatever he may have meant. One day when he appeared
with a new suit of checked garments he announced that he had hit
the "Kentucky row" on a "gig," or something of that kind. This was
conclusive evidence that he gambled at times and was a person of
bad habits.

However, he was so obliging, so ready to laugh at jokes and so
conscientious in his work of polishing shoes that his faults were overlooked. His chair was in the main corridor of the building near the
elevator. Those who were well acquainted with him knew that his
name was William Pinckney Marvin, and that he had aspirations to
leave the lowly occupation of cleaning shoes and get a job at one of
the race-tracks. . . .

It has already been intimated that "Pink" sometimes drank, but
seldom to the neglect of business.

From the story afterward told by him it would appear that on the day of misfortunes "Wilse" Johnson, who worked in the hotel, approached the boot-blacking stand and asked: "Are you strong?"

"Pink" gave him the white of his eyes and said: "Man, I'm too strong for any hotel colo'ed person."

Wilse suggested that he had some "bones" in his pocket and "Pink" said: "I ain't got no strength to run; mus' stay here and get action."

They began rolling at 10 cents a crap, but too many people stopped to watch them, and "Pink," who had been "got into" for 30 cents, advised an adjournment to the alley, where he knew of a good place. They sought the quiet alley, "Pink" leaving his business interests to go to rack, and for the next hour there was a rattle of dry "bones," accompanied by a chanting duet of such expressions: "Come on, seven" and "I mus' have fo'." At the end of that time Mr. "Wilse" Johnson was bankrupted, for "Pink" had "faded" him to the extent of $3.50.

In the flush of success "Pink" offered to buy, and the two sought a neighboring saloon which fronted on the alley. "Pink" met some white men in there and called up the house. The white gentlemen waived all prejudice as to color and accepted his hospitality. After that there were other drinks, and he was introduced to a number of colored men, who were apparently friends of "Wilse" Johnson. . . .

"Pink" remembered distinctly next day that he made speeches on several topics, feeling that he had a right to do so, because he had done most of the buying. "Wilse" Johnson was gloomy and unsociable. It was during a discussion of the freedman's condition that they fell into an argument over the question: "Isn't a colored man as good as anybody else?" While "Pink" was addressing himself to the question "Wilse" Johnson made some disparaging remark, which the speaker properly resented. It was all a misty recollection, but "Pink" knew that some one pushed him from behind, while some one else struck him over the head with what felt to be a billiard cue. Something landed in his eye, and he felt himself lying on the floor being jumped on.

At about 6 o'clock that evening he reached his "stand" in the lobby, his legs describing strange curves, his garments torn and bloody and his face an awful picture of dark, rare meat.

A sympathetic man sent for the janitor and the latter dragged "Pink" into a wash-room and with the aid of cotton and arnica dressed his wounds. The injured and betrayed man could give no account of what had happened, although he constantly mumbled an intention to cut out several important parts from some one's anatomy. Shortly after 7 o'clock he was able to walk around and the janitor had him put on a State Street car, with instructions to the conductor to dump him off at the right corner. . . .

At the very hour when "Pink" Marvin and "Wilse" Johnson got into a dispute over the civil rights of the colored man, a murder was done in a "levee" saloon about ten blocks distant. Two colored men engaged in a fight. One stabbed the other and escaped through the back door. The wounded man died within an hour and that evening every policeman in uniform and every "fly" man was on the lookout for a murderer, a colored man of whom there was but a vague description. . . .

• • •

"Pink," slightly repaired, and with his head tied up, leaned heavily back in the corner and dozed as the car moved southward. He did not see the two officers in plain clothes studying him from the back platform, and was considerably surprised when awakened by a rough shake.

"We want you," said one of the men.

"Wha' fo'," asked "Pink."

"Aw, come on and don't talk. You're the guy that had the fight in that saloon."

"Yes, sah, but——"

"Aw, come on," and they had him between them running him toward a patrol box. There was the usual crowd and a great many people pushed around and wanted to know what he had done. "Pink" was too thoroughly sick and miserable to care what happened to him. He was thrown into the wagon, the bell went ding-ding-ding, and he rode to the station in a hurry. The moment they pushed him into a cell he collapsed and did not waken until broad daylight.

Then, with a racking headache, a burning throat and a dull ache wherever he had been struck or kicked, he tried to figure why he should be in the police station. It was the first time he had ever been arrested and he remembered that when taken into custody he was riding peaceably in a cable car. After breakfast a turnkey unlocked the cell door and said: "Come out here, Marvin, the captain wants to talk with you." So he had told his right name.

Sore and limping he followed upstairs and was pushed into a small room, bare of carpet and with no furniture save a small desk and several chairs. The captain was a large man with a small mustache and a uniform very new and bright. He spoke rather kindly to the prisoner.

"You were out drinking a little yesterday."

"Tha's right, boss; I don't deny it."

"Got purty full, eh?"

"I had too much, fo' a fac'."

"Got into a little fight?"

"They jumped on me, seh; I didn't do nothin'."

"How did you happen to go in there?"

"Well, seh, me and a frien' o' mine goes in to take a drink. We meets some mo' fellows."

"I see. What started the fight?"

"I don' 'zactly remembeh."

"What became of your knife?"

"I didn' have no knife at all."

"Is that so?" There was a sudden change in the tone. "Do you know that you got into a fight in there and killed a man?"

"Wha's dat—wha' you say!" He was staring at the captain and trembling like a leaf. Then, with a cry like that of a frightened child, he fell across the arm of his chair in a dead faint. The captain threw open the door and motioned to an officer, who roused "Pink" and half dragged him back to the cell.

"He's the man all right," said the captain.

"He just the same as admitted it last night," remarked the desk sergeant. . . .

"Pink" lay crouched in his cell for two hours, crying in terror, before he thought to send for his friend the janitor. He was a murderer and entitled to special privileges. The janitor was summoned. He stood at the bars and listened to "Pink's" choking narrative.

"That's funny," said he. "Larry was up this morning and said you broke a looking glass in his place, but he didn't say you stabbed any one. Did you have two fights?"

"Pink" gave it up. He was ready to give up everything. But the janitor sent for "Larry," who came and told a straight story and the captain, much puzzled, sent for the colored bartender, who had seen the stabbing. He took one look at "Pink" and that settled it. He said the guilty man was a light yellow. "Git out," said the captain, giving "Pink" a shove, and "Pink" ran.

Each Sunday morning at the African Methodist Episcopal Church the minister says: "The offering will now be taken" and Brother William Pinckney Marvin marches up in front and starts around with the basket. When the hymns are sung his voice rises loudly and joyously above all others. Since that morning when he rushed from the station he has shunned the "bones" and the "gigs" and if any one dares to suggest drinking he quotes scripture, his favorite passage being: "De way of de transgressor's hard, and no mistake."

THE ALFALFA
EUROPEAN HOTEL[4]

Chicago is a city made up of country people. It is a metropolis having a few saving virtues of a village.[5] It is spread over so many square miles of prairie and has so many farms alternating with scanty suburbs that no one has been able to draw the line between urban and suburban, or the line between suburban and rural. When one is in State Street he finds proof that Chicago is urban, suburban and rural.

In 1880 the population was 500,000 and a few over. In 1900 it is to be 2,000,000 census or no census. Ask any real estate man. Was not a club organized in 1896 to concede the 2,000,000 mark?[6]

Whence came the 1,500,000 increase? From Germany, Italy, Sweden, Norway, Ireland, Poland, Russia, China, Austria, Greece, and any other country you choose to name. Also from all those towns set in close columns in the United States Postal Guide.

Not long ago, before the Spanish-American war was fought and while women still wore puff sleeves, there stood in a street toward the smoky center of town a hotel, not of the first class. The building was thin, and might have appeared tall but for the fact that it was overtopped by two mountainous structures, shutting out the eastern sky. The street front was mostly buffet, but there was a hallway leading back to a dim apartment, called the office, and here there were chairs and a counter, and behind the counter a box of pigeon-holes for keys and letters. From the office a stairway and an elevator shaft led to the upper region of narrow hallways and cramped bedchambers.

It was the Alfalfa European Hotel. Alfalfa, because the name had a pleasing sound; European, because no meals were served in the house.

Of the men who lived at the Alfalfa Hotel, either as transient guests or on arrangement for a weekly rate, the one worth knowing was Calvin Horne, called Doc' Horne by his familiars. His age cannot be given. He never told it. He was bald on the top of his head. His face had the fullness of youth, but it was wrinkled. The chin beard was white. When it is said, further, that he wore clothes such as might be worn by any old gentleman who had ceased to be fastidious on the point of personal adornment, the reader knows as much as any one would know in taking a first glance at Doc' Horne as he sat in the office of the Alfalfa European Hotel with his satellites grouped about him. His daily employment at the time of the beginning of this story called him to the Federal offices, where he checked pension lists or classified vouchers or performed some other kind of labor quite unsuited to him. Doc' overshadowed his occupation, and it is doubtful if there will be another reference to it anywhere in this book.

In the succeeding pages, when it is related that Doc' and his companions moved in and about the hotel, it is not to be concluded that they had the hotel to themselves. Many strangers came to the desk and claimed their keys and rode upward in the tremulous elevator. Men whose names do not appear and whose comments will be suppressed stood at a respectful distance and heard what Doc' had to say of love and life. Mr. Ike Francis, proprietor, is somewhere in the office, smoking a pipe, and other persons are in the background, reading newspapers. These are mere details of the setting and will not be pointed out again.

To recur to the original proposition, that Chicago is a city made up of country people: one evening Doc' sat in the office and told a chapter to an actor from a farm in Ohio, a drinking man from a village in New York, a lightning dentist from an interior county of Indiana, and a race-track man from the bluegrass part of Kentucky.

They were talking of women, and the topic lasted well at the Alfalfa Hotel, as elsewhere. The actor had said that once upon a time he went up a ladder and into a burning house to save a young woman. That reminded Doc' Horne of Crosbyville.

"Let's see—I spent two or three years in Crosbyville, off and on," he began, "and this must have happened in the fall of '51 or the spring of '52. I remember that I left Crosbyville just about the time of the presidential campaign, and that was—well, it must have been about June, '52. No matter; the date doesn't make any difference.

"In order that you may understand this story better, I'll have to go back a little. The first time I ever visited in Crosbyville I was invited out to a shooting-match. We didn't shoot at glass balls or live pigeons in those days. We usually put a white square of paper up against a tree and blazed away at it with rifles, and, although our firearms were of defective bore, I can assure you that some of the best shooting I ever saw was at these old-time matches out in the woods. However, that has nothing to do with the story.

"One of my friends invited me to go to the shooting-match, and after I got out there I was asked to enter the contest. Well, I went in and I happened to get a rifle that sighted just right for me, and I won. A man who had been introduced to me as Capt. Jaynes made the next highest score. It seemed to me that the other contestants took their defeat good-naturedly, but on the way home my friend told me to look out for this Capt. Jaynes. He was a hot-headed Kentuckian, and it seems that this was the first time he had been defeated in years, and it worried him a good deal. My friend told me that he had taken a dislike to me and would probably try to pick a quarrel at the first opportunity.

"Well, that same afternoon I invited all the men who had been at the shooting-match to come over to the tavern. It was customary for the winner of the match to stand treat to the others. Capt. Jaynes came in rather late, while we were all sitting round and talking. I arose and asked him to join the party. He bowed very coldly and said that he was not in the habit of drinking with strangers. Now, I was rather touchy in my younger days. I said: 'Very well, captain; I withdraw the invitation. I made the mistake of supposing that you would feel at home in a company of gentlemen.' I knew what to expect when I said that. He started to draw a knife, but before he could lift it I had hold of him. They pulled us apart and tried to quiet him, but he went away raving mad. They all said he would kill me the first time we met, but he must have cooled down when he had time to think it over. I saw him often after that—passed him on the street. He never made a move, but I knew that he hated me and would be glad of a chance to do me an injury.

"The captain's house was right on the bank of the Green River, and stood near his mill. It was an old-fashioned two-story house, very broad and well built, and thickly surrounded by trees. It was considered the best house in Crosbyville. The captain was the wealthiest and one of the most prominent citizens of the town. He was a widower and had two children—a son of fourteen or so, and a daughter named Elizabeth. She was a very beautiful girl—very charming. I had met her several times, but, of course, I had never become well acquainted with her on account of my standing feud with her father.

"Well, to make a long story short, the whole town was aroused by an alarm of fire one night, and when we turned out the Jaynes' mill was one mass of flames. It was an old-style structure, with a framework of heavy logs, and it made a fearful blaze. The wind was blowing the flames toward the house. Every one saw that it was no use to try and save the mill, so we turned in to defend the house— got up on the roof and passed buckets and put out wet blankets to catch the sparks, but all in vain, gentlemen, all in vain. The men were driven off the roof, and the water dried as fast as it was thrown on. All at once one whole side of the house seemed to spring into a flame. There was a general shout, and everybody retreated to a safe distance. The members of the family and the neighbors had been removing the household goods. Just as the house caught fire, and all the men were getting out of it as fast as they could, I heard Elizabeth Jaynes cry out: 'The canary!' Then she ran back into the house, with every one calling to her to stop. I didn't hesitate a moment, I assure you. She went through that terrific heat and dense smoke right up the stairway, and I followed. I caught her by the arm at the top of the stairs and told her to come back. She was hysterical and excited—said she wouldn't leave until she got the bird. In spite of all I could do she pulled away from me and ran to the front room—her bedroom, I believe—and felt her way to where the bird-cage was hanging. Gentlemen, it was never any hotter in any bake-oven than it was in that room. As soon as she got the bird-cage I dragged her back through the hall. The smoke was not so thick now because the fire had got a free draught through the house and was making a fearful roar and spreading rapidly. When we reached the stairway the whole lower end of it was ablaze. I dragged the girl away to the front window, but by that time the whole veranda was on fire. The crowd outside saw us, and shouted something—I couldn't tell what. I saw there was no escape over that burning veranda. When the people shouted, the girl fainted dead away. I threw her across my shoulder and started for the rear of the house, because I knew that was my only salvation. The whole stairway was ablaze by that time, and flames were creeping up through the floor. I closed my lips tightly and in about four leaps I reached a back window. Outside there was a big tree, almost brushing the window. I kicked out the window sash and simply jumped into the tree. It was the only thing to be done. Luckily, I got my arm over a limb, which sagged with us and dropped us to the ground. I scrambled to my feet and ran, with the girl still hanging absolutely limp and helpless over my shoulder. I went straight for the river with the intention of jumping in. The heat was something awful. It had driven away the men who had been filling their buckets at the river.

"Just as I staggered down the river bank I saw a skiff. Some one had probably rowed across the river to the fire, for the boat was not fastened. I dropped the girl into the boat and gave it a strong push out into the current, and in a few seconds we were floating down stream and were safe."

"She had the canary, I suppose?" said the lightning dentist.

"Oh, yes. She was in a dead faint, but she hadn't let go of the cage. As soon as I recovered my breath and wet my clothes in two or three places where they were on fire, I splashed water in the girl's face and she recovered consciousness, but was still hysterical and did not seem to realize fully what had happened.

"We could look up the river and see the burning house. It made a huge blaze and threw a bright glare across the river. I remember the peculiar effect of this glare on the windows of the houses across the river. It caused them to glow as if the houses were filled with live flames. The girl was so frightened that she thought all the houses were afire.

"When I got ready to row back I discovered that I hadn't any oars. The current was swift and we were drifting rapidly, so I pulled out a seat-board and used it as a rudder, and in a few minutes I had made a landing near a house occupied by a Mr. Wesley. Miss Jaynes was so weak and nervous that she could hardly walk, but I assisted her to this house and aroused the family.

"The woman of the house was very kind. She cared for the young lady for about two hours and had one of the boys drive us back to Crosbyville. Now, in the general excitement we had forgotten that the people in Crosbyville had every reason to believe that we had perished in the flames. You couldn't blame them for thinking so. The window from which I had leaped was well hidden by trees, and there was no one at the river bank when we leaped into the boat. We learned afterward that the men had pulled down the burning veranda and had planted a ladder at the front window where we had been seen, but the blaze was so fierce that they had been driven back.

"As I say, every one supposed that we were lost; so you can imagine what happened when we drove up in front of the ruins about seven o'clock in the morning. They were already searching for our bodies. Yes, sir; they thought we were ghosts. As soon as I explained

Doc' and his companions

to them how we got away you never heard such cheering in your life. They lifted Miss Jaynes out of the wagon and took her over to a neighboring house, to which the captain had been taken. The man was almost wild with grief. Those who went over to the house say it was one of the most affecting meetings that could be imagined. First he wept like a baby and then he jumped up and laughed like a boy and said he didn't care for the loss of his buildings so long as his daughter was safe. I suppose his daughter must have given him a very favorable account of my efforts in her behalf, for presently he came out of the house and walked up to where I was standing and said: 'Mr. Horne, you have done me the greatest service that one man can do another. All that I have is at your command now and forever. I once did you an injustice. You have repaid me. Will you take the hand of a man who honestly admits himself beaten and humiliated?' I said to him: 'Captain, you are a brave and gallant man, but you were mistaken for once. Let us say no more about the misunderstandings of the past.' We shook hands, and from that day forward we were friends. He was a man of passions and prejudices, but if he came to know you and like you he was the truest friend a man ever had."

"There's only one thing needed to make that a good story," suggested the dentist. "You ought to say that you married the captain's daughter."

"I am not going to sacrifice truth in order to make a fancy romance," replied Doc'.

EFFIE WHITTLESY[7]

Mrs. Wallace was in a good humor.

She assisted her husband to remove his overcoat and put her warm palms against his red and windbeaten cheeks.

"I have good news," said she.

"Another bargain sale?"

"Pshaw, no. A new girl, and I really believe she's a jewel. She isn't young or good looking, and when I asked her if she wanted any nights off she said she wouldn't go out after dark for anything in the world. What do you think of that?"

"That's too good to be true."

"No, it isn't. Wait till you see her. She came here from the intelligence office about 2 o'clock and I put her to work at once. You wouldn't know that kitchen. She has it as clean as a pin."

"What nationality?"

"None—or I mean she's from the country. She's as green as she can be, but she's a good soul, and I know we can trust her."

"Well, I hope so. If she is all that you say, why, for goodness' sake give her any pay she wants—put lace curtains in her room and subscribe for all the story papers on the market."

"Bless you, I don't believe she'd read them. Every time I've looked into the kitchen she's been working like a Trojan and singing 'Beulah Land.'"

"Oh, she sings, does she? I knew there'd be something wrong with her."

"You won't mind that. We can keep the doors closed.". . .

The dinner table was set in tempting cleanliness. Bradley Wallace, aged 8, sat at the left of his father, and Mrs. Wallace, at the right, surveyed the arrangements of glass and silver and gave a nod of approval. Then she touched the bell and in a moment the new servant entered.

She was a tall woman who had said her last farewell to girlhood. She had a nose of honest largeness and an honest spread of freckles, and yet her face was not unattractive. It suggested good nature and homely candor. The cap and apron were of snowy white. She was modest, but not flurried.

Then a very strange thing happened.

Mr. Wallace turned to look at the new girl and his eyes enlarged. He gazed at her as if fascinated either by cap or freckles. An expression of wonderment came to his face and he said: "Well, by George!"

The girl had come very near the table when she took the first overt glance at him. Why did the tureen sway in her hands? She smiled in a frightened way and hurriedly set the tureen on the table.

Mr. Wallace was not long undecided, but during that moment of hesitancy he remembered many things. He had been reared in the democracy of a small community and the democratic spirit came uppermost.

"This isn't Effie Whittlesy?" said he.

"For the land's sake!" she exclaimed, backing away, and this was a virtual confession.

"You don't know me."

"Well, if it ain't Ed Wallace!"

Would that words were ample to tell how Mrs. Wallace settled back in her chair, gaping first at her husband and then at the new girl, stunned with surprise and vainly trying to understand what it all meant.

She saw Mr. Wallace reach awkwardly across the table and shake hands with the new girl and then she found voice to gasp: "Of all things!"

Mr. Wallace was painfully embarrassed. He was wavering between his formal duty as an employer and his natural regard for an old friend. Anyway, it occurred to him that an explanation would be timely.

"This is Effie Whittlesy from Brainerd," said he. "I used to go to school with her. She's been at our house often. I haven't seen her for—I didn't know you were in Chicago."

"Well, Ed Wallace, you could knock me down with a feather," said Effie, who still stood in a flustered attitude a few paces back from the table. "I had no more idee when I heard the name Wallace that'd it be you, though knowin', of course, you was up here. Wallace is such a common name I never give it a second thought. But the minute I saw you, law! I knew who it was well enough."

"I thought you were still at Brainerd," said Mr. Wallace, after a pause.

"I left there a year ago November, and came to visit Mort's people. Mort has a real nice place with the street-car company and is doin' well. I didn't want to be no burden on him, so I started out on my own hook, seein' that there was no use of going back to Brainerd to slave for $2 a week. I had a good place with Mr. Sanders, the railroad man on the north side, but I left because they wanted me to serve liquor. I'd about as soon handle a toad as a bottle of beer. Liquor was the ruination of Jesse. He's gone to the dogs, and been off with a circus somewhere for two years."

"The family's all broken up, eh?" asked Mr. Wallace.

"Gone to the four winds since mother died. Of course, you know that Lora married Huntford Thomas and is livin' on the old Murphy place. They're doin' so well."

"Yes? That's good," said Mr. Wallace.

Was this an old settlers' reunion or a quiet family dinner? The soup had been waiting.

Mrs. Wallace came into the breach.

"That will be all for the present, Effie," said she. Effie gave a startled "Oh!" and vanished into the kitchen.

"What does this mean?" asked Mrs. Wallace, turning to her husband. "Bradley, behave!" This last was addressed to the 8-year-old, who had followed the example of his father and was snickering violently.

"It means," said Mr. Wallace, "that we were children together, made mud pies in the same puddle and sat next to each other in the old schoolhouse at Brainerd. The Whittlesy family was as poor as a church mouse, but they were all sociable—and freckled. Effie's a good girl."

"Effie? Effie? And she called you Ed!"

"My dear, you don't understand. We lived together in a small town where people don't stand on their dignity. She never called me anything but Ed, and everybody called her Effie. I can't put on any airs with her, because, to tell the truth, she knows me too well. She's seen me licked in school and has been at our house, almost like one of the family, when mother was sick and we needed an extra girl. If my memory serves me right I took her to more than one school exhibition. I'm in no position to lord it over her and I wouldn't do it anyway. She's a good-hearted girl and I wouldn't want her to go back to Brainerd and say that she met me up here and I was too 'stuck up' to remember old times."

"You took her to school exhibitions?" asked Mrs. Wallace, with a gasp and an elevation of the eyebrows.

"Fifteen years ago, my dear—in Brainerd. I told you you wouldn't understand. You're not jealous, are you?" and he gave a side-wink at his son, who once more giggled.

"Jealous! I'm only thinking how pleasant it will be when we give a dinner party to have her come in and address you as 'Ed.'"

Mr. Wallace laughed as if he enjoyed the prospect, which led his wife to remark: "I really don't believe you'd care."

"Well, are we going to have any dinner?" he asked.

The soup had become cold and Effie brought in the next course.

"Do you get the Brainerd papers?" she asked, when encouraged by an amiable smile from Mr. Wallace.

"Every week. I'll give you some of the late ones," and he had to bite his lips to keep from laughing, seeing that his wife was really in a worried state of mind. . . .

"Something must be done."

Such was the edict issued by Mrs. Wallace. She said she had a sufficient regard for Effie, but she didn't propose to have every meal converted into a social session, with the servant girl playing the star part.

"Never worry, my dear," said Mr. Wallace, "I'll arrange that. Leave it to me."

• • • • •

Effie was "doing up" the dishes when Mr. Wallace lounged up to the kitchen doorway and began his diplomatic campaign.

His wife, seated in the front room, heard the prolonged purr of conversation. Ed and Effie were going over the family histories of Brainerd and recalling incidents that may have related to mud pies or school exhibitions. Somehow Mrs. Wallace did not feel entirely at ease, and yet she didn't want to go any nearer the conversation. It would have pleased her husband too well.

This is how Ed came to the point. Mrs. Wallace really should have heard this part of it.

"Effie, why don't you go down and visit Lora for a month? She'd be glad to see you."

"I know, Ed, but I can't hardly afford—"

"Pshaw! I can get you a ticket to Brainerd tomorrow, and it won't cost you anything down there."

"But what'll your wife do? I know she ain't got any other help to look to."

"To tell you the truth, Effie, you're an old friend of mine, and I don't like to see you here in my house except as a visitor. You know Chicago's different from Brainerd."

"Ed Wallace, don't be foolish. I'd as soon work for you as any one, and a good deal sooner."

"I know, but I wouldn't like to see my wife giving orders to an old friend, as you are. You understand, don't you?"

"I don't know. I'll quit if you say so."

"Tut! tut! I'll get you that ticket and you can start for Brainerd tomorrow. Promise me, now."

"I'll go, and tickled enough, if that's the way you look at it."

"And if you come back I can get you a dozen places to work."

·   ·   ·   ·   ·

Next evening Effie departed by carriage, although protesting against the luxury.

"Ed Wallace," said she, pausing in the hallway, "they never will believe me when I tell it in Brainerd."

"Give them my best regards, and tell them I am the same as ever."

"I'll do that. Good-bye. Good-bye."

Mrs. Wallace, watching from the window, saw Effie disappear into the carriage. "Thank goodness," said she.

"Yes," said Mr. Wallace, dryly, "I've invited her to call when she comes back."

"To call—here? What shall I do?"

"Don't you know what to do when she comes?"

"Oh, of course I do. I didn't mean what I said."

"That's right. I knew you'd take a sensible view of the thing— even if you never did live in Brainerd."

SOPHIE'S
SUNDAY AFTERNOON[8]

Sophie slipped out into the sunlight through the big oak side door of Mr. Hamilton Jefferson's residence and walked down the crooked path to the gateway, humming a little tune to herself.

Sophie was Mrs. Hamilton Jefferson's girl and Mrs. Hamilton Jefferson was proud of her. When there was a tea and Sophie in her puckered cap and dainty apron flitted about with the salvers Mrs. Hamilton Jefferson would lean forward and say to her guests behind her pudgy hand:

"She's a jewel of a girl and she sews beautifully. No, no, you can't have her at any price."

During all the week Sophie was just Sophie and she conversed with nodded "Yes m'm's" and "No m'm's," as any well-trained girl would do.

But on Sunday afternoon as soon as the dishes shone on the shelves of the china closet Sophie became Miss Sophie Johnson and she walked out of Mrs. Hamilton Jefferson's domain into a world of her own.

Sophie couldn't help humming. It was something to get out into the spring sunlight with a whole afternoon and the savings of a week to spend. And Sophie had a new hat—and wasn't that enough to make any girl hum? It was a mere bit of a thing—a knot of blue ribbons, a queer little twisted body and a red rose on a long stem nodding a perpetual "how-d'y-do" above it. The hat was perched on Sophie's yellow hair combed back straight and smooth and wound in a tight little knot at the back of her head.

Sophie wore a pink dress with ribbon bows playing hide and seek all over it, and a belt of leather with a shiny buckle, and her skirts kept up a bustling as she walked. Sophie's shoes were new and squeaky and they hurt her a little, too, but she wouldn't have admitted it for anything.

Sophie's face—a round, pink and white dumpling of a face— beamed out from under her parasol with a soap and water freshness and a consciousness of looking very well indeed.

When Sophie had walked several blocks she met a young man on the sidewalk.

He stopped and smiled.

Now Sophie looked very much surprised. She had never expected to see Mr. Carl Lindgren out there.

"Good day," he said.

"Good day," she answered.

Then they shook hands.

Sophie blushed a little. So did Mr. Carl Lindgren.

Presently he said something about Humboldt Park, and Sophie laughed and nodded her head. Then she put her hand with its silk mitt—a very neat silk mitt it was, too, only a little old-fashioned—on his arm and they walked down the street together under one parasol.

Mr. Carl Lindgren worked in a factory and he had bought ten shares of stock in a building and loan association in Chicago Avenue with his savings, for Carl belonged to a frugal, hard-working race, and he was thinking of getting married.

Carl's mustache—the color of raveled rope—bristled with much brushing and his brown derby tilted back on his yellow hair. He wore a shiny celluloid collar and a flat tie—one of the kind crocheted from silk twist and presented by way of the Christmas tree. His coat had been pressed until it shone and the corner of a red silk handkerchief looked out with artful carelessness from his breast pocket. A huge watch-chain with a heavy fob dangled from his vest and a dandelion was stuck in his buttonhole.

They walked to North Avenue and took the electric cars. The car bumped along past the rows of small stores and houses with the Sunday crowds strolling up and down the sidewalks in front. There were children everywhere, romping, shouting and playing, many of them bare-headed.

At last they reached the park. The trees were just leafing out, the grass was green and inviting, with little patches of dandelions yellowing it here and there. Crowds of people, men, women and children, streamed into the park past the saloons, peanut stands and photograph galleries which cluster around its entrance.

Sophie and Carl strolled along arm in arm. They didn't have much to say—not yet, at least.

Now they were walking hand in hand. Carl had picked up Sophie's handkerchief and in returning it had forgotten to let go of her fingers. And Sophie didn't say a word.

The path led to the pavilion, the broad verandas of which swirled with children and young girls chewing gum and young men joking with them. In the lagoon boats, unevenly rowed, dragged about, splashing the water.

They sat down at a table in the basement.

"What will you have?" said Carl.

"Chocolate," said Sophie.

"One chocolate an' one wanilla," ordered Carl.

Then the waiter rushed to the counter where a man with the perspiration rolling down his face was dishing ice cream, twirling cakes across the counter and drawing sizzling soda water with almost frantic rapidity.

Carl and Sophie didn't say much. Sophie fingered her little handkerchief and Carl watched her out of the tail of his eye. Once she caught him at it and they both laughed. Carl took some money out of his pocket and paid the waiter with a little flourish. Sophie looked at him admiringly.

Just as they were going out Carl spied a fortune-telling machine—a gypsy with pointing finger and a knowing look. Carl produced some pennies and Sophie thrust one of them into the slot. The gypsy girl whirled around dizzily and finally stopped with her finger pointing to the words:

> YOU ARE NEARER GREAT DANGER
> THAN YOU ARE AWARE.

Sophie looked serious.
"I wonder what it is," she said.
"That's a bad fortune," answered Carl. "Try again."
The next penny brought better luck.

> AN UNKNOWN LOVER ADORES YOU.

Carl laughed and Sophie blushed.
"It tells lies," said Sophie.
Then Carl tried. The gypsy bluntly pointed to the words:

> YOU ARE IN LOVE

"'At's the truth," said Carl, without looking at Sophie.

• • •

Then they went out and walked along the path until they came to a popcorn booth. Here Carl bought a big sticky ball for 5 cents, and he and Sophie went to a grassy spot on the bank of a lagoon and sat down to eat it. A boy not far away was dangling his bare legs in the water and some little girls were rolling about on the grass. Ducks and swans nodded as they swam in the lagoon. In the middle of a shawl sat a baby, with her father and mother paying court to her not far away.

Carl talked now pretty steadily, but in a low tone, so that no one but Sophie could hear him. Here are some of the things which Sophie answered him:

"So?"

"Et's too bad about you!"

"Now, behave."

"Don't you tease."

"Sure."

When the popcorn was all gone Carl wanted Sophie to go boat-riding. Sophie said she was afraid. So they walked through the greenhouse and Sophie told Carl something about the flowers.

Then they walked, hand in hand, swinging their arms just a little, down to North Avenue and went into one of the photographers' tents with the pictures hung in tempting array outside. Here a busy, nervous man seated Sophie in a chair, tipped her chin a little back and folded her hands. Sophie pulled off one mitt so that a ring would show. Then Carl stood up behind, put one of his big hands on Sophie's shoulder and the other behind him. Then he advanced one foot and looked up.

"Now look pleasant," said the busy, nervous man.

He clicked the plates into the camera, thrust his head under the curtain, jerked it out and pulled the slide.

"All right," he shouted, and then shot into his little darkroom.

Sophie drew a long sigh and Carl smiled reassuringly at her.

•   •   •

An hour later Carl and Sophie were hurrying from the park. A great black cloud reached out of the west and a stiff wind was blowing.

Sophie and Carl had been so much occupied that they had not noticed the coming rain. Just before they reached North Avenue a few big drops began to fall and they made a wild race for the car. But Sophie was laughing and holding fast to Carl's hand. By the time the car stopped at their street the shower was at its height.

Sophie and Carl crowded under the parasol and hurried down the dripping street. When they reached the residence of Mr. Hamilton Jefferson Sophie's skirts were soaking wet and her hair flew about her face. She had covered her new bonnet with her handkerchief so that is was fairly dry. The coloring from her parasol had dripped down Carl's neck and his coat was bedraggled and shapeless.

For a moment they paused in the entry where no one could see them. Then Carl came out with his face beaming and walked away regardless of the rain.

OLOF LINDSTROM
GOES FISHING[9]

Olof Lindstrom was going fishing. All winter long he had worked at his bench in the cabinet-shop. He made carved bureau tops from day's end to day's end. It was a hard, monotonous life—earn and spend, eat and sleep, week in and week out.

Olof was a little pale-faced man, with a straw-colored mustache. On weekdays he wore a faded brown derby, white with sawdust. On Sunday, when he and his family went to the Lutheran Church in the next street, he changed it for a neat black derby, his coat was as smooth as Mrs. Lindstrom's flatiron could make it and the corner of a silk handkerchief thrust itself into notice from his breast pocket.

The idea of going fishing had come to him suddenly, as it had done every spring for years. Perhaps it was the compelling sunshine that opened the doors of the wooden cottages and brought the children and the pet puppies swarming to the sidewalk, or, perhaps, it was merely the inherited instinct of a man whose fathers and grandfathers in Norway calked their fishing smacks each spring and mended their carp nets as soon as the sun had opened the rugged coves on the coast.

It was Saturday night. Olof had secured a fishing pole and bait. He was just setting out.

"Tomorrow is Sunday," said Mrs. Lindstrom, as if warning him to be back in time.

Olof did not answer. He was going fishing and the fish were hungriest an hour before sunrise.

Oak Street runs as far as the lake wall with all the paved and guttered respectability of a great city thoroughfare. But eastward from the Lake Shore Drive it pitches off into a waste of ash-piles and garbage heaps which have usurped a part of the domain of Lake Michigan. Here it meanders around in an aimless, lawless way with a self-made, independent air, as if in contempt of the general orderliness and conventionality of city life.

Just at dark Olof followed Oak Street out among the garbage piles. It was with a feeling of rebellious freedom that he left behind the carved bureau tops and Mrs. Lindstrom's strident voice. At the extreme point in the bumpy expanse of desert he found a newly dumped pile of paper, rags and broken boxes, and he set it afire. Then he built up a seat from some old bricks and a board and sat down with his face to the blaze, which he occasionally encouraged

"... every audible reminder of city life ... was drowned
out by the thumping and mumbling of the waves ..."

with a broken barrel hoop. There was not a human being within shouting distance, not even a policeman. Although the spot was hardly half
a mile from the Lake Shore Drive it was quite as lonely as an African
jungle.

Darkness settled down and every audible reminder of city life,
except the intermittent screeching of tugboats, was drowned out by
the thumping and mumbling of the waves among the ragged rows of
piling. The lighthouse reflector began to wink crimson and yellow
over the black stretch of water. A few dim squares and specks of
light with a smudge of black above them, crawling along apparently
through space, indicated the course of vessels outbound on their first
voyage of the season. The city was a wall of black from north to
south, with a few towers, spires and the huge bulk of a great building or two extending into the murky blue sky, where the moon
hung—Olof didn't often have an opportunity to see the moon. He
didn't care much about it either—it was only one of the things that
united to make up a stolid sense of freedom, which he could not
have explained. A long row of electric lights along the lake shore
appeared like holes in the dark wall—as if the city blazed beyond.

A stiff, chilly wind sprang up as night deepened, and Olof set up
a plank at his back and then sat quietly, unthinkingly watching the
burning bits of paper scurry over the garbage heaps whenever he
stirred the fire. Occasionally he nibbled a cracker from a bundle
which he had brought with him.

Toward morning he grew cold and had to run up and down a hardened ash pile to keep warm. The wind cut through his thin clothing and pinched his shop-faded face. He had not dreamed that it would blow so cold.

At last, when the moon had gone down behind the waterworks tower and a faint gray streak of light cut the lake horizon, Olof baited his hook with a minnow from the pail and crawled carefully to the outer row of piling. Here he mounted, shivering with cold, and cast his line. The waves still beat heavily and the spray dashed up and drenched him.

At the end of half an hour he had caught one little perch, and half of his bait was gone. But the keen delight of watching that fish squirm on the bank was worth a great deal of misery—it gave him more pleasure than a thousand carved bureau tops.

An hour later the sun came up over the rim of the lake and laid a ladder of gold across the water. But Olof didn't notice it—he felt a nibble at his line. He had never learned to revere sunrises—the nibble of a fish was ecstasy enough.

Later the church bells began to ring for early mass. For a moment they made Olof feel guilty and uncomfortable, but his joy was restored by catching a second fish, a shade larger than the first. He was still wet and chilly, and he knew that the twinges in his knees meant rheumatism.

At ten o'clock the sun blazed high and hot. The reflection in the water blinded the eyes of the solitary fisher and burned his face. At noon, after an endless series of nibbles, he caught one more fish and then his bait was gone. He felt hungry and tired, too—it had been a long night without a wink of sleep. His head ached.

Olof strung the three little fishes on a splinter and dragged himself back over the garbage heaps and ash-piles with his fish-pole on his shoulder. He met throngs of well-dressed people on their way home from church. He thought they looked at him chidingly for breaking the sabbath, and so he walked with his eyes cast down.

When Olof reached his home he found his wife in a temper. He laid the three little fish on the table as a peace-offering, but she only scolded him roundly. She said it was a shame, and that every one of the neighbors would be talking about him before the day was over.

"Can't a man have a little time to himself?" he said to her meekly in Norwegian. She did not deign to answer him.

The next day he went back to his bench and the carved bureau tops. He had a cold in the head and painful twinges of rheumatism in his knees. His face was red and sore with sunburn and his eyes saw green.

Yet he knew that if he was alive another spring he would go fishing again—even on Sunday if necessary.

It was in his blood.

THE BUELL CHERRY[10]

"This is the place," said Mr. Buell, as he stopped in front of a new cottage with a wrinkled lawn in front of it.

The breezes came freely from across the prairies. Over toward the trolley track the white and blue flowers of spring peeped timidly from the new grass. Mrs. Buell gave every symptom of delight. She knew that she would fall in love with the place. The children would have a play-ground at last. Mr. Buell predicted that the whole family would become brown and heavy from living in the suburbs.

> Domestic happiness, thou only bliss
> Of paradise that has survived the fall.[11]

It was spring-time when the Buells moved to Arcadian Heights, a mountainous suburb, rising at points to a height of fifteen feet above the level of the lake.

Arcadian Heights was then the skeleton framework of a town. It had a railway-station, a grass-plot with the name of the suburb tastefully set in whitewashed rocks, and the streets were already marked out and fringed with spidery shade-trees.

Cement sidewalks parted the bushy weeds. Rusted hydrants lifted themselves about the dandelions in evidence of the fact that the town had a water-supply, even if it had no one to use the water.

A dozen new houses were sprinkled on the checkerboard plain to the west of the station. It was to one of these houses that the Buells came with two cavernous wagons full of furniture. They had given up the close communion of life in a flat building and preferred an association with Nature.

> An elegant sufficiency, content,
> Retirement, rural quiet, friendships, books,
> Ease and alternate labour, useful life,
> Progressive virtue and approving heaven![12]

The Buell place was not large, as compared with the country seats of the 300-page novel, but it was all theirs.

Every spear of grass assumed a pleasant relation toward the new-comers.

Mr. and Mrs. Buell had something like a parental interest in the slender shade-trees at the front, the bushes behind the house, and the two cherry-trees which stood near the walk spurring out from the veranda.

Within a few days after the Buells first moved in, one of these trees unfolded a few milky blossoms.

> *For, lo! the winter is past, the rain is over and gone; the flowers appear on the earth; the time of the singing of birds is come, and the voice of the turtle is heard in the land.*[13]

The Buells did not hear the dove, but they were entertained nightly by the frogs, and sitting on the front veranda at dusk all four would sniff hard in an effort to corroborate Mrs. Buell's firm belief that she could detect the odour of cherry-blossoms.

> *Now came still evening on, and twilight grey*
> *Had in her sober livery all things clad;*
> *Silence accompany'd; for beast and bird,*
> *They to their grassy couch, these to their nests,*
> *Were slunk.*[14]

Mrs. Buell plucked a few of the blossoms and copied them imperfectly in water-colours. The other tree produced nothing but waxen leaves. Mr. Buell examined it studiously and conferred with a neighbour who had made a study of small fruits, and it was decided that it would produce, in time, the ox-heart cherry, which is a pleasant edible.

The first tree, blossoming so promptly, was a common specimen of the *prunus cerasus*, the fruit being known as the "cooking cherry."

> *Hope springs eternal in the human breast;*
> *Man never is, but always to be blest.*[15]

During the long winter the trees were banked about with earth and kept in swaddling clothes, and early in the second spring they fulfilled the promise of the season and put out an abundance of green leaves. A mother guiding the steps of her first-born could not have been more solicitous than were the Buells as they searched the long branches and found, here and there, the beginning of a white blossom.

"The ox-heart tree is going to blossom," said Mrs. Buell to the children one afternoon.

"The ox-heart tree is going to blossom!" shouted the children to Mr. Buell as he walked over from the station that afternoon.

"By George, the ox-heart tree *is* going to blossom," said Mr. Buell, as he pulled down the branches and examined them with a surgeonly tenderness.

> *It is the month of June,*
> *The month of leaves and roses,*
> *When pleasant sights salute the eyes*
> *And pleasant scents the noses.*[16]

Yet the month of June held one cruel disappointment for the Buell family.

The ox-heart tree which had blossomed so sturdily, showed not a cherry. The other tree bore thirteen. For a long time the count was twelve, but one day little Grace, who had sharper eyes than the others, discovered one cherry on a high branch, partly hidden by the leaves, and thirteen was thereafter taken as the official count.

The cherries ripened one at a time and were devoured. An equitable division was made, although thirteen cherries cannot be divided exactly by four.

It will be understood that in the spring of the third year there was a lack of confidence in the ox-heart tree. It had grown taller and extended its branches and the blossoms hung rich and heavy, but the Buells did not permit themselves to be lifted by vain hopes. They were waiting for it to perform actual service.

The common tree, producing the cooking cherries, blossomed more bounteously than ever before, and, it may be added, bore nearly four quarts of cherries, which were put into pies.

But what of the other?

The white petals fell and there was a period of uncertainty. One day Mr. Buell (credit where credit is due!) discovered on the eastward branch which extended toward the walk, one small, hard cherry. It seemed normal and without defect.

After three years of care and nursing the ox-heart tree was about to yield the first evidence of gratitude.

From one stand-point the Buell cherry was a small and insignificant part of the vegetable growth of North America. From the other stand-point it was the symbol of all the beauty in Nature's excellent laws. It was the essential poetry in the quatrain of seasons.

> *Warmed by the sun*
> *And wet by the dew,*

It grew, it grew—
Listen to my tale of woe.[17]

All values are comparative.

The Buells had been fruit-growers for three years, and at last they had produced one edible cherry.

According to market quotations the value of this cherry was the decimal part of one cent. The Buells justly regarded it as a priceless treasure. The children stood guard over it, to keep the robins away, and there was never a day that the family did not gather at the tree and remark the growing blush.

What was to be done with the cherry? It was too valuable and epoch-marking to be gulped down in the ordinary off-hand manner. Rabelais spoke of a man who would take three bites at a cherry, but Mr. Buell could not see a fair plan of division among four.

Like a gallant man and a good husband, he decreed that Mrs. Buell should eat the cherry.

The ceremony of the eating was to be as follows: Mrs. Buell's sister and the sister's husband were to come out from town for Sunday dinner. At the serving of dessert the girl was to bring in the cherry on the genuine Delft plate which Mrs. Buell's brother had brought from Holland. Mr. Buell would make a few remarks, touching on the sweetness of life in the suburbs and the felicities of horticulture. Mrs. Buell would then bite the cherry to the accompaniment of applause.

It was eventide. Mr. and Mrs. Buell sat on the cool veranda, arranging for the celebration. Suddenly they were interrupted.

"Mr. Buell, that was a mighty fine cherry."

There stood the man who delivered the papers. He was smacking his lips.

Mr. Buell looked to where the branch of the tree was outlined against the darkening, turquoise sky. The cherry was gone! A low moan escaped him.

He turned to where his wife sat. She was mute and staring. Then she saw his white face and burst into convulsive sobbing.

This, this is misery—the last, the worst
That man can feel.[18]

"Walk down to the gate with me, Jefferson, and I'll pay you," said Mr. Buell, taking him by the arm.

"Why, what's the matter with Mrs. Buell?" asked Jefferson, looking back at her.

"She has bad news. One of her cousins is dead—out in Kansas."

OUR PRIVATE ROMANCE[19]

It is a boarding-house privilege to sit on the front stoop at dusk. The rooms are small and stuffy. Our landlady cannot afford to provide a roof-garden when rates are $5 per week per person, or $9 a week for a married couple, provided the husband will agree not to come home to luncheon.

On this evening in June we noticed the two across the way. These two sat on the stone steps in front of what had been an aristocratic residence five years after the fire. Lest it should degenerate into a ruin, it had become a boarding-house. We lived in a street of boarding-houses.

The house was of three stories and the architecture was gloomy and most respectable. The basement, which was really the ground floor, had been thrown into one long dining-room, and here, when the lights were on, we could see the boarders flocked at a series of rectangular tables sparsely set with glass and white ware. It was much like our own ground floor.

The three floors above this tunnel-like dining-room were filled with families and roomers. We had come to know two old men who went in and out at irregular intervals. Then there were at least three elderly women, and the tall one with the military bearing was generally supposed to be the mistress of the boarding department. In addition to these there was the usual straggle of men. The time to see them was near 7:45 each morning as they came slamming out of the house, one after another, and raced away to their eight o'clock jobs. Three children played in front of the house occasionally, or else looked out from the second-story window.

Then there was the girl. She was with a young man who did not belong to the establishment, as we suspected at the time and came to know later on. His summer suit was a real triumph of soft grey, and the straw hat was in the very moment of fashion, being woven of rough straw, the rim very narrow and the ribbon a dazzling tricolour. We could see that he was young and self-satisfied. We felt that perhaps he boarded at an $8 house.

The men on our stoop preferred to look at the young woman. She had spread a rug on the landing above the top step and sat in a kind of oriental sprawl, looking down at the young man, who was two steps below. Her shirt-waist was of some light material, and the skirt was of a darker stuff, and her brown hair was wavy and rebellious. Also, she was very pretty, with eyes and lips, etc. This is a man's description, of course. Our two young women criticized her apparel,

"It is a boarding-house privilege to sit on the front stoop at
dusk . . ."

but the men silently agreed with the law-student when he said, "She
suits *me*."

The majority of us were country-born and we had not overcome
that early habit, honestly inherited, of taking a lively interest in the
affairs of other people. So we watched the two across the way and
talked about them. The men were inwardly jealous of the attractive
youth in the grey suit, and the young women were outwardly displeased at his lack of taste.

The two sat on the front steps and looked at each other steadily,
talking but little. After a little while one of the roomers came out and
joined the two on the steps. He was a confident young man with a
toss of hair on his forehead and a grating haw-haw laugh, intended
to be a token of sociability.

For a few minutes he had the conversation all to himself. Then
the two came to an agreement, evidently through some code known
only to themselves, for they came down the steps and sauntered

away together, leaving the hairy young man to trim his nails and smoke his cigar in solitary self-satisfaction.

We saw them again, a night or two after that.

They sat together on the steps until one of the women came out to join them, and they wandered away into the twilight, their arms touching.

In a little while we had learned his average. It was three times a week. They seemed most happy when there was no third person near. A happy sign.

It is tantalising to assist in a love-affair and not know the names.

She did not hurry away in the morning with the other eight-o'clock sleepy-heads, but our landlady said that usually she went out at ten, returning not later than four. If she was not regularly employed, perhaps she was merely visiting the woman who took boarders. Probably this woman was her aunt. Mere speculation, all of it.

The young man usually approached from the south. Presumably he lived on the south side. A poor fragment of unsatisfactory evidence.

After two or three weeks, when any one of the boarders spoke of "he" it was known that he referred to the young man across the way. The girl was "she"—the couple "they."

The new bulletins came at breakfast and dinner. They were somewhat after the style of the following:

"*They* went out again last night."

"A messenger boy brought a note today. I suppose it was from *him*."

"*She* sat at the window for nearly an hour today and seemed, oh, so lonesome!"

"*They* were out walking all afternoon."

"A boy brought a box this afternoon. It looked like a box of flowers. I suppose they were for *her*."

As the colder weather came on and the days were shorter, the men had little opportunity to learn for themselves what was happening. The women made two important discoveries:

1. *She* was doing a great deal of department-store shopping, for the shiny wagons from State Street stopped in front of the place nearly every day.

2. *She* now had as a companion an older woman, who accompanied her as she went out each day.

Was this woman her mother? How could she afford to buy so many clothes? Was it possible that the young man was paying for her trousseau? What were in the boxes?

No one at our boarding-house could answer these questions, but the young women built a romance around the slender framework of circumstantial evidence. The young man was rich and the girl the daughter of an aristocratic widow who had lost her property, and the young man's parents opposed the match because the girl was poor and had to live in a boarding-house, but the young man, thank heaven, was true to the girl he loved, and so the mother had come from the old home and had made every sacrifice in order that her daughter might be married in proper style, and so they were to be united and fly away to a honeymoon in Florida, and then come back to live forever in a magnificent flat with rugs and things and their own servants.

We hoped that it might be true, and it came about sooner than we expected.

When we trooped home the other evening the landlady and her daughter were throbbing with information. It had happened!

The arrival of two carriages first caused comment. The landlady had said to her daughter, "I wonder who"—but there is no need of recounting all that.

Strange people came—strange people in their best clothes. This was near twelve o'clock. Then a preacher—walking. Any one could have told he was a preacher—sickly looking man in black. Then *he* came. Lovely! Black clothes—silk hat. Then other people—on foot. The landlady and her daughter straining their eyes to see what was happening inside the house.

About 1.30 the front door opened. Carriage in waiting. Bride looked sweet and wore a going-away gown of—but no! courage fails. Every one waved and said good-bye. The landlady (not ours) and the other woman (suspected to be the mother) stood on the steps and watched the carriage until it was out of sight. The other woman cried a little. She must have been the mother.

Alackaday! It is all over. The tingle of romance has gone out of our street.

THE MYSTERY OF THE
BACK-ROOMER[20]

There went the front doorbell again! Mrs. Morgane's hopes rose accordingly.

The bell gave forth a hollow gong-like sound. It was required to make a good deal of noise, as Mrs. Morgane's furnished apartments were on the second and third floors of the red-brick building, a tailoring and cleansing establishment having the first floor.

When the door-bell rang Mrs. Morgane at once said: "Some one for the top back room." She had been trying for over a month to rent it. All sorts and conditions of men had climbed the stairs and followed her into the room. She always pulled the curtain away up and began by telling that the last young man who occupied it—a very nice young man, by the way—had gone out on the road as a salesman and of course he couldn't keep a room in the city.

"It is small but comfortable," she would say. "We get steam heat from the building next to us. The bed has a lovely set of springs. The bath-room is on the floor below, but of course you have your pitcher here. I did get $3 for this room, but you may have it for $2.50."

They made all sorts of excuses to get out of the house. One would say the room was too small. Another insisted on running water. In some instances the room was too far up or too far back. An occasional caller would promise to "look around," and perhaps come back. Only a week before an elderly man with a shawl-strap full of books, after pointing out the danger of living on a third floor without a fire escape, had said in a roundabout way that he "guessed" he would move in. But he didn't come.

Now Mrs. Morgane, having primped a little before her glass, hurried down-stairs to welcome another. Much depended on renting the top back room. With the other rooms taken her profits were but slight. All revenues from the back room would be so much clear gain.

She found at the door a rather pale man, apparently between 30 and 35 years of age. He was smooth-shaven and had an aquiline nose and melancholy eyes. The closely buttoned Prince Albert told in his favor, although it did seem to go badly with the striped shirt. Mrs. Morgane had ceased to be a stickler as to attire. The only man who had ever defrauded her of a full month's rent dressed beautifully.

The stranger was quiet and attentive as she told him the old story of the peculiar advantages of the top back room. She was more than surprised when he thrust a cameoed finger into his vest pocket and produced a $5 bill in payment for two weeks' rent.

No questions were asked. . . .

Mrs. Morgane did not require the usual exchange of references. Like a court of exact justice, she regarded every person as respectable and trustworthy until he or she was shown to be something else and then she acted with great firmness. Her furnished apartments were for people more or less restricted as to finances and she didn't object if, instead of getting their refreshments outside, they sent out a pitcher and a dime. When she found a steady and reliable roomer she did all she could to keep him and for a year there had not been a change, except in the top back room. The furniture man had moved out a year before when an increase of salary changed his notions of life, and the first to succeed him was a very blonde young woman who asked a great many questions about the other people in the house and remarked that one couldn't be too particular. Her husband was out of town most of the time and during his absence she employed herself in reading woodcut weeklies and going to the theaters. The tickets came to her with some regularity and were always in plain envelopes. As for the husband, he proved to be a man of the most variable habits, calling sometimes twice a day and sometimes once in two weeks. Finally Mrs. Morgane grew weary at these eccentricities and so the blonde young woman was requested to go elsewhere.

The next one was a whistling young man, whose personal effects seemed to consist largely of photographs and Indian clubs. This young man, who professed an ardent admiration of pugilism and the dramatic art, was employed in the packing department of a wholesale hardware house. He had a disturbing habit of dropping his Indian clubs during practice, and one day while attempting an entirely new juggle he smashed two panes of glass from the window. There was a difference of opinion as to whether or not he should pay for the glass and it was compromised by his moving away.

What need to tell of the three who came after him?

The last was a heavily mustached person who sang when he felt like it, and felt like it when he came home along after midnight. Mrs. Morgane couldn't stand that.

She now felt overjoyed to have in the room a man who moved in so quietly that morning that he did not disturb her at her work in the front room. He remained in the room all day and that evening went out carrying what appeared to be a small tin cash-box. She learned that he had been in bed all day and she observed, with some apprehension, that he and his tin box returned at 7 o'clock the next morning. The second day he remained in his room and on the second evening he departed in the same mysterious manner. . . .

Mrs. Morgane was at the head of a strangely assorted community. Two steady men, given to early hours, had the large front rooms on the second floor. Behind them was the old book-keeper, who had been in that room ever since the furniture was carried in. At the rear was the woman who had separated from her husband. The exact trouble was not known to the other people in the house, but they agreed that the husband must be a brute. Mr. Morgane and the girl who helped her had the top front rooms. The young woman stenographer, who was distantly related to Mrs. Morgane, had the next room back and then came the department-store young man, who performed wonders in the way he managed to get along on a small salary. He had two good suits and was saving up to buy a wheel. Farther to the rear of his little pocket apartment was a young man who worked in a book-bindery and employed his evenings in writing long letters. Then came the unlucky room, which had been taken by the stranger with the tin box. Mrs. Morgane had not so much as asked his name, and he had such a retiring way of turning the key in the lock as he went in that no one ventured to break in upon him or to try to scrape an acquaintance. . . .

For a week he kept up his routine. In the afternoon or early evening, as the others would be going to their rooms or preparing for a cheerful reunion in Mrs. Morgane's parlor, they would see him stealthily going down-stairs. In the morning they would sometimes meet him coming back. It was no wonder that they began to peer around corners at him and that Mrs. Morgane tried to learn something from a study of his personal property.

There was but little to study. The wardrobe was limited, the trunk was always locked and the linen was marked "X9." No letters were left lying about and no mail came.

One morning when she met him on the stairway she said: "You're getting in late."

He smiled rather sadly and said: "A man in my profession can't sleep when other people do."

And before she could press further inquiries he paid another $5, which action she construed to mean that he did not choose to talk about himself. . . .

That evening she found a pretext, however, for when he was about to depart she pounced out upon him and said: "I started to make out your receipt, but do you know I haven't learned your name yet?"

Three persons were waiting behind doors and at key-holes to catch his answer, which was most disappointing. He gave a name which may be found duplicated twenty times in the city directory and then he slipped away.

That evening there was an animated discussion of the stranger by

"It was no wonder that they began to peer around
corners at him"

Mrs. Morgane, the stenographer, the department-store young man
and the woman who had experienced trouble with her husband.

"Now, what does he do?"

"Maybe he's a doctor."

"No; doctors have people send for them."

"But he said he was a professional man."

"He can't be a lawyer. They don't go around at night with tin
boxes."

"Oh, I'll tell you, he might be a burglar and have his tools in that
box."

"Get out! You can see that he is a gentleman. He doesn't look as
though he drank."

"How about a gambler?"

"No; gamblers don't carry boxes, either."

All agreed that he should be questioned. The good name of the
house demanded it.

The next Sunday afternoon the stenographer and the young
man were present in the parlor as witnesses, when Mrs. Morgane by
the most urgent methods lured him thither, and, after the com-
monplace remarks, asked: "By the way, what is your profession?"

He looked at her reproachfully as he answered: "I am a chiropodist in a Turkish bath."

"A what?"

"He removes corns," explained the department-store young man.

"And bunions," added the professional man.

They were interested and he told them of the work he did for the night customers. He was a professional man, after all. He became a favored member of the Morgane community and was afterward best man at the wedding of the stenographer and the department-store young man. It was in the morning, and he came around a trifle sleepy, for it had been a busy night.

MR. PAYSON'S SATIRICAL CHRISTMAS[21]

Mr. Sidney Payson was full of the bitterness of Christmas-tide. Mr. Payson was the kind of man who loved to tell invalids that they were not looking as well as usual, and who frightened young husbands by predicting that they would regret having married. He seldom put the seal of approval on any human undertaking. It was a matter of pride with him that he never failed to find the sinister motive for the act which other people applauded. Some of his pious friends used to say that Satan had got the upper hand with him, but there were others who indicated that it might be Bile.

Think of the seething wrath and the sense of humiliation with which Mr. Sidney Payson set about his Christmas-shopping! In the first place, to go shopping for Christmas-presents was the most conventional thing that any one could do, and Mr. Payson hated conventionalities. For another thing, the giving of Christmas-presents carried with it some testimony of affection, and Mr. Payson regarded any display of affection as one of the crude symptoms of barbarous taste.

If he could have assembled his relatives at a Christmas-gathering and opened a few old family wounds, reminding his brother and his two sisters of some of their youthful follies, thus shaming them before the children, Mr. Sidney Payson might have managed to make out a rather merry Christmas. Instead of that, he was condemned to go out and purchase gifts and be as cheaply idiotic as the other wretched mortals with whom he was being carried along. No wonder that he chafed and rebelled and vainly wished that he could hang crape on every Christmas-tree in the universe.

Mr. Sidney Payson hated his task and he was puzzled by it. After wandering through two stores and looking in at twenty windows he had been unable to make one selection. It seemed to him that all the articles offered for sale were singularly and uniformly inappropriate. The custom of giving was a farce in itself, and the store-keepers had done what they could to make it a sickening travesty.

"I'll go ahead and buy a lot of things at haphazard," he said to himself. "I don't care a hang whether they are appropriate or not."

At that moment he had an inspiration. It was an inspiration which could have come to no one except Mr. Sidney Payson. It promised a speedy end to shopping hardships. It guaranteed him a Christmas to his own liking.

He was bound by family custom to buy Christmas-presents for his relatives. He had promised his sister that he would remember every one in the list. But he was under no obligation to give presents that would be welcome. Why not give to each of his relatives some present which would be entirely useless, inappropriate, and superfluous? It would serve them right for involving him in the childish performances of the Christmas-season. It would be a burlesque on the whole nonsensicality of Christmas-giving. It would irritate and puzzle his relatives and probably deepen their hatred of him. At any rate, it would be a satire on a silly tradition, and, thank goodness, it wouldn't be conventional.

Mr. Sidney Payson went into the first department-store and found himself at the book-counter.

"Have you any work which would be suitable for an elderly gentleman of studious habits and deep religious convictions?" he asked.

"We have here the works of Flavius Josephus in two volumes," replied the young woman.

"All right; I'll take them," he said. "I want them for my nephew Fred. He likes Indian stories."

The salesgirl looked at him wonderingly.

"Now, then, I want a love-story," said Mr. Payson. "I have a maiden sister who is president of a Ruskin club and writes essays about Buddhism. I want to give her a book that tells about a girl named Mabel who is loved by Sir Hector Something-or-Other. Give me a book that is full of hugs and kisses and heaving bosoms and all that sort of rot. Get just as far away from Ibsen and Howells and Henry James as you can possibly get."

"Here is a book that all the girls in the store say is very good," replied the young woman. "It is called 'Virgie's Betrothal; or, the Stranger at Birchwood Manor.' It's by Imogene Sybil Beauclerc."

"If it's what it sounds to be, it's just what I want," said Payson, showing his teeth at the young woman with a devilish glee. "You say the girls here in the store like it?"

"Yes; Miss Simmons, in the handkerchief-box department, says it's just grand."

"Ha! All right! I'll take it."

He felt his happiness rising as he went out of the store. The joy shone in his face as he stood at the skate-counter.

"I have a brother who is forty-six years old and rather fat," he said to the salesman. "I don't suppose he's been on the ice in twenty-five years. He wears a No. 9 shoe. Give me a pair of skates for him."

A few minutes later he stood at the silk-counter.

"What are those things?" he asked, pointing to some gaily coloured silks folded in boxes.

"Those are scarfs."

"Well, if you've got one that has all the colors of the rainbow in it, I'll take it. I want one with lots of yellow and red and green in it. I want something that you can hear across the street. You see, I have a sister who prides herself on her quiet taste. Her costumes are marked by what you call 'unobtrusive elegance.' I think she'd rather die than wear one of those things, so I want the biggest and noisiest one in the whole lot."

The girl didn't know what to make of Mr. Payson's strange remarks, but she was too busy to be kept wondering.

Mr. Payson's sister's husband is the president of a church temperance society, so Mr. Payson bought him a buckhorn corkscrew.

There was one more present to buy.

"Let me see," said Mr. Payson. "What is there that could be of no earthly use to a girl six years old?"

Even as he spoke his eye fell on a sign: "Bargain sale of neckwear."

"I don't believe she would care for cravats," he said. "I think I'll buy some for her."

He saw a box of large cravats marked "25 cents each."

"Why are those so cheap?" he asked.

"Well, to tell the truth, they're out of style."

"That's good. I want eight of them—oh, any eight will do. I want them for a small niece of mine—a little girl about six years old."

Without indicating the least surprise, the salesman wrapped up the cravats.

———————

Letters received by Mr. Sidney Payson in acknowledgment of his Christmas-presents:

1.

"Dear Brother: Pardon me for not having acknowledged the receipt of your Christmas-present. The fact is that since the skates came I have been devoting so much of my time to the re-acquiring of one of my early accomplishments that I have not had much time for writing. I wish I could express to you the delight I felt when I opened the box and saw that you had sent me a pair of skates. It was just as if you had said to me: "Will, my boy, some people may think that you are getting on in years, but I know that you're not.' I suddenly remembered that the presents which I have been receiving for several Christmases were intended for an old man. I have received easy-chairs, slippers, mufflers, smoking-jackets, and the like. When I received the pair of skates from you I felt that twenty years had been lifted off my shoulders. How in the world did you ever happen to think of them? Did you really believe that my skating-days were not over? Well, they're *not.* I went to the pond in the park on Christmas-day and worked at it for two hours and I had a lot of fun. My ankles were rather weak and I fell down twice, fortunately without any serious damage to myself or the ice, but I managed to go through the motions, and before I left I skated with a smashing pretty girl. Well, Sid, I have you to thank. I never would have ventured on skates again if it had not been for you. I was a little stiff yesterday, but this morning I went out again and had a dandy time. I owe the renewal of my youth to you. Thank you many times, and believe me to be, as ever, your affectionate brother,

"WILLIAM."

2.

"Dear Brother: The secret is out! I suspected it all the time. It is needless for you to offer denial. Sometimes when you have acted the cynic I have almost believed that you were sincere, but each time I have been relieved to observe in you something which told me that underneath your assumed indifference there was a genial current of the romantic sentiment of the youth and the lover. How can I be in doubt after receiving a little book—a love-story?

"I knew, Sidney dear, that you would remember me at Christmas. You have always been the soul of thoughtfulness, especially to those of us who understood you. I must confess, however, that I expected you to do the deadly conventional thing and send me something heavy and serious. I knew it would be a book. All of my friends send me books. That comes of being president of a literary club. But you are the only one, Sidney, who had the rare and kindly judgment to appeal to the woman and not to the club president. Because I am interested in a serious literary movement it need not follow that I want my whole life to be overshadowed by the giants of the kingdom of letters. Although I would not dare confess it to Mrs. Peabody or Mrs. Hutchens, there are times when I like to spend an afternoon with an old-fashioned love-story.

"You are a bachelor, Sidney, and as for me, I have long since ceased to blush at the casual mention of 'old maid.' It was not for us to know the bitter-sweet experiences of courtship and marriage, and you will remember that we have sometimes pitied the headlong infatuation of sweethearts and have felt rather superior in our freedom. And yet, Sidney, if we chose to be perfectly candid with each other, I dare say that both of us would confess to having known something about that which men call *love*. We might confess that we had felt its subtle influence, at times and places, and with a stirring uneasiness, as one detects a draught. We might go so far as to admit that sometimes we pause in our lonely lives and wonder what might have been and whether it would not have been better, after all. I am afraid that I am writing like a sentimental school-girl, but you must know that I have been reading your charming little book, and it has come to me as a message from you. Is it not really a confession, Sidney?

"You have made me very happy, dear brother. I feel more closely drawn to you than at any time since we were all together at Christmas, at the old home. Come and see me. Your loving sister,

"GERTRUDE."

3.

"Dear Brother: Greetings to you from the happiest household in town, thanks to a generous Santa Claus in the guise of Uncle Sidney.

I must begin by thanking you on my own account. How in the world did you ever learn that Roman colors had come in again? I have always heard that men did not follow the styles and could not be trusted to select anything for a woman, but it is a libel, a base libel, for the scarf which you sent is quite the most *beautiful* thing I have received this Christmas. I have it draped over the large picture in the parlor, and it is the envy of every one who has been in today. A *thousand, thousand* thanks, dear Sidney. It was perfectly sweet of you to remember me, and I call it nothing less than a stroke of genius to think of anything so appropriate and yet so much out of the ordinary.

"John asks me to thank you—but I must tell you the story. One evening last week we had a little chafing-dish party after prayer-meeting, and I asked John to open a bottle of olives for me. Well, he broke the small blade of his knife trying to get the cork out. He said: 'If I live to get downtown again, I'm going to buy a corkscrew.' Fortunately he had neglected to buy one, and so your gift seemed to come straight from Providence. John is very much pleased. Already he has found use for it, as it happened that he wanted to open a bottle of household ammonia the very first thing this morning.

"As for Fred's lovely books, thank goodness you didn't send him any more story-books. John and I have been trying to induce him to take up a more serious line of reading. The Josephus ought to help him in the study of his Sunday-school lessons. We were pleased to observe that he read it for about an hour this morning.

"When you were out here last fall did Genevieve tell you that she was collecting silk for a doll quilt? She insists that she did not, but she must have done so, for how could you have guessed that she wants pieces of silk above anything else in the world? The perfectly lovely cravats which you sent will more than complete the quilt, and I think that mamma will get some of the extra pieces for herself. Fred and Genevieve send love and kisses. John insists that you come out to dinner some Sunday very soon—next Sunday if you can. After we received your presents we were quite ashamed of the box we had sent over to your hotel, but we will try to make up the difference in heart-felt gratitude. Don't forget—any Sunday. Your loving sister,

"KATHERINE."

It would be useless to tell what Mr. Sidney Payson thought of himself after he received these letters.

DUBLEY, '89 [22]

Mr. Dubley, '89, was flattered to receive an invitation to attend the annual dinner of the Beverly alumni and respond to the toast, "College Days." Mr. Dubley, class of '89, in his days pointed out as a real ornament to the campus, had allowed his interest in college matters to ooze away from him. He had been in Chicago three years and had not attended an annual dinner, but now, being invited to speak, he felt it his duty to step in and accept the honor.

See Mr. Dubley in his room at night—writing, writing. He was writing about "College Days"—but he erased much more than he wrote. When he had completed a sentence he would read it aloud to make sure that it had the swing and cadence so pleasing to the ear.

One week before the dinner and Mr. Dubley's speech regarding "College Days" was a finished thing. It had been typewritten, with broad spaces, and there were parenthetical reminders such as: (Pause), (full breath), (gesture with right hand), etc. Mr. Dubley had witnessed the pitiable flunks resulting from a state of unpreparedness, and he was not going to rely upon momentary inspiration. He was going to rehearse every part of his speech, and when he arose to respond to the toast "College Days" that speech would be a part of his mental fibre.

If Mr. Dubley talked mutteringly as he hid behind his newspaper on the elevated train or made strange gestures as he hurried along Dearborn Street, it was not to be inferred that Mr. Dubley had lost his mind. He was practising—that is all.

The speech:

"Mr. President and Gentlemen: The toastmaster has told you that I am to speak of 'College Days,' a subject that must arouse the tenderest and sweetest memories in the bosom of every one here. When I look about me and see all these faces beaming with good-fellowship and fraternal love, I realise that there are no ties as lasting as those that we form in the bright days of our youth, within the college halls. No matter what experiences may befall us after we have gone out into the world, we can always look back with pleasure on the days that we spent in college.

> *You may break, you may shatter, the vase if you will,*
> *But the scent of the roses will cling 'round it still.*[23]

"I sometimes think that in the rush and hurry of business life, here in this great metropolis, we make a serious mistake in neglecting to keep up the friendships formed in college. I tell you, fellow-alumni, we ought to extend a helping hand to every man who comes to this city from old Beverly. Let us keep alive the holy torch ignited at the altar of youthful loyalty.

"The enthusiasm manifested here this evening proves that you indorse what I have just said. I know that your hearts beat true to our dear alma mater; that other institutions, larger and more pretentious, perhaps, can never hold the same place in your affections.

"Oh, that we might again gather on the campus in the same company that was once so dear to us, there to sing the old college songs, to feel the hand-clasp of our college mates, and listen to the sweet chiming of the chapel bell. These are memories to be treasured. In the years to come we shall find that they are the brightest pages in life's history.

"Gentlemen, I have no wish to tire you. There are other speakers to follow me. In conclusion I merely wish to relate a little anecdote which is suggested to me by the opening remarks of our worthy toastmaster. It seems there was an Irishman who had been in this country but a few days, and he was looking for work, so he said to himself one morning: 'Begob, Oi think Oi'll go down be the dock to see if I can't be afther gettin' a job unloadin' a ship.' So he went down to the dock, but couldn't get any work. While he was standing there looking down into the water, a man in a diving-suit came up through the waves and climbed up on the dock. Pat looked at him in great surprise and said: 'Begob, if Oi'd known where to get a suit loike that, I'd have walked over mesilf.'"

During the gale of laughter which was to follow this story, Mr. Dubley would sit down.

Now, in order that he might not become confused as to the order of his paragraphs and to guard against the remote possibility of his forgetting some part of the address, Mr. Dubley had the opening words of each paragraph jotted down on a card, to which he might refer if necessary:

The president has told, etc.

I sometimes think, etc.

The enthusiasm manifested, etc.

Oh, that we might, etc.

Gentlemen, I have no wish, etc.

The annual dinner of the Beverly alumni was an unqualified success.

Three tables were filled. Two of these were long tables joining a short transverse table, at which sat the chairman and the speakers. Dubley, '89, was at this head table.

Dinner came on with a great clatter. The mandolin orchestra played . . . and the young men bellowed the choruses. An ex-star of the football team was carried thrice round the table on the billowing shoulders of his friends, who chanted and rahrahed and stepped high.

Mr. Dubley, '89, who was dieting and abstaining, in order that he might be in good voice and have possession of his faculties when the critical moment came, began to suspect that the assemblage was in no mood to give serious attention to the memories of college days. His fellow-alumni sat low in their chairs, with their white fronts very convex, and pounded the tables rhythmically, causing the small coffee-cups to jump and jingle.

Cigars succeeded cigarettes. A blue fog obscured the far end of the double perspective of long tables, and the hurrah was unabated.

The chairman pounded on the table.

"I am glad," he shouted, "to see such a large and disorderly mob here this evening. (*Cheers.*) I understand that Mr. Dubley of the class of '89 has something to say to you, and I will now call on him."

And Mr. Dubley arose. The clamorous applause helped to encourage him. He took a drink of water.

A voice: "What is the gentleman's name, please?"

The chairman: "Dubley—this is Mr. Dubley of the class of '89."

A voice: "Never heard of him before." (*Laughter*)

Dubley: "Mr. President and gentlemen."

A voice: "Mr. President *and* gentlemen'?"

Another voice: "Yes—why this distinction?"

Dubley (*Smiling feebly*): "Of course—you understand—when I say 'Mr. President and gentlemen' I don't mean to insinuate that the president is not a gentleman. I think he is a gentleman."

A voice: "You *think* he is?"

Dubley: "The toastmaster has told you that I am to speak of 'College Days.'"

A voice: "I didn't hear him."

Dubley: "Well, he—ah—should have announced that as the subject of my toast. (*Cries of "All right," "Go ahead," "Make good."*)—'College Days,' a subject that must arouse the tenderest and sweetest memories in the bosom of every one here." (*Applause.*)

A voice: "Say, this fellow's eloquent." (*Laughter.*)

Dubley: "Tenderest and sweetest memories in the bosom of every one here."

A voice: "No encores."

Another voice: "You said that once."

Dubley: "Pardon me; I—ah——"

A voice: "Go ahead! you're all right—maybe."

Dubley: "When I look around me and see all these faces beaming with good-fellowship and fraternal love I——"

Grand chorus: "Ah-h-h-h-h!"

Dubley: "I say, when I look around——"

A voice: "That's twice you've looked around."

Dubley: "I realise that there are no ties as lasting as those that we form in the bright days of our youth within the college halls. (*Cries of "Good boy" and "Right you are, old fox."*) No matter what experiences may befall us——"

Distant voice: "Mr. Toastmaster! Mr. Toastmaster!"

Chairman: "Well, what is it?"

Distant voice: "There are several of us down at this end of the table who did not catch the gentleman's name. He is making a good speech, and we want to know who he is—let go of my coat!"

The Chairman: "Gentlemen, I will announce for the third time that the speaker who now has the floor is Mr. Harold Dubley of the class of '89, sometimes known as the boy orator of Danville."

A voice: "Harold's such a sweet name."

The Chairman: "I may add that Mr. Dubley has prepared his speech with great care and I hope you'll give him your quiet attention." (*Cries of "All right!" and "Let 'er go!"*)

Dubley (*hesitatingly*):

> 'You may break, you may shatter, the vase if you will,
> But the scent of the roses will cling 'round it still.'

A voice: "Oh, Lizzie!" (*Prolonged howls.*)

Dubley: "I sometimes think——"

A voice: "You don't look it." (*Renewed laughter.*)

Dubley: "I say, I sometimes think——"

A voice: "Did anybody else ever say it?"

Dubley: "—that in the rush and hurry of business life here in the great metropolis we make a serious mistake in neglecting to keep up the friendships formed in college. (*Indian yell. Someone throws a stalk of celery at Dubley.*) Ah—let us keep alive the holy torch ignited at the altar of youthful loyalty."

A voice: "Mr. Toastmaster!"

The Chairman: "What is it?"

A voice: "I propose three cheers for the holy torch." (*Tremendous cheering and laughter.*)

Dubley: "The enthusiasm manifested here this evening proves that you indorse what I have just said."

A voice: "You haven't said anything yet." (*Cries of "Order!" and "Give him a chance."*)

Dubley: "I know that your hearts—I know that your hearts——"

One of the rioters (*arising*): "Mr. Toastmaster, I move you that Mr. Jubley or Gubley or whatever his name is, be directed to omit all anatomical references. He should remember that there are gentlemen present."

The Chairman: "I have every confidence in Mr. Dubley's sense of propriety and must ask him to continue."

Dubley (*hesitating and referring to his card*): "Oh—Oh that we might—might again gather on the campus——"

A voice: "Wouldn't that be nice?"

Dubley: "—in the same company that was once so dear to us, there to sing the old college songs, to ——"

A voice: "Mr. Toastmaster!"

The Chairman: "What is it?"

The voice: "I suggest that Mr. Bubley sing one of those college songs to which he refers with so much feeling."

The Chairman: "Again I will inform the company that the speaker's name is not Bubley, but Dubley."

A voice: "With the accent on the 'Dub'."

The Chairman: "Mr. Dubley has promised to sing a song if you will permit him to finish his speech." (*Cries of "All right!" "Go ahead."*)

Dubley (*Once more referring to his card*): "Gentlemen, I have no wish to tire you. (*Cries of "Hear! hear!"*) There are other speakers—"

A voice: "You *bet* there are!"

Dubley: "Er—in conclusion, I merely wish to relate a little anecdote (*Cries of "Ah-h-h-h!"*) which is suggested to me by the opening remarks of our worthy toastmaster. (*Laughter.*) It seems there was an Irishman (*Groans*) who had been in this country but a few days and he was looking for work." (*Loud laughter.*)

The Chairman: "I will have to ask the gentlemen to come to order. Mr. Dubley hasn't finished his story yet."

Dubley: "As I say, this Irishman was looking for work, so he said to himself one morning, 'Begob, Oi think Oi'll go down be the dock to see if I can't be after getting a job un——"

A voice: "'ster Toastmaster!"

The Chairman: "What is it?"

The voice: "A point of order."

The Chairman: "State your point."

The voice: "The gentleman is telling an Irish story with a Swedish dialect."

The Chairman: "The point is well taken. If Mr. Dubley wishes to go ahead with his anecdote, he will please use an Irish dialect."

Dubley (*On the verge of collapse*): "Well, Mr. Toastmaster, the story's nearly over. (*Cries of "Hooray!"*) All there was to it is that while the Irishman was at the dock he saw a diver in a divingsuit come up out of the water and he thought, of course—I should have told you that this Irishman had lately come over from the old country—then—well—he saw the diver and he thought the diver had walked over from Ireland, so he said——" (*General uproar, during which Dubley dodges a French roll. Some one pulls him into a chair.*)

Dubley: "But I hadn't finished my story."

The man next to him: "Yes, you had."

Although the toastmaster referred to Mr. Dubley's speech in very complimentary terms, Dubley will always have his doubts.

THE INTELLECTUAL AWAKENING IN BURTON'S ROW[24]

Burton's Row was, in some respects, a little world to itself. It was the nucleus of a new suburb, sprung up at the end of a narrow wooden sidewalk which spanned the prairie to the south. In winter the sidewalk was sometimes hopelessly lost in the snow. In the early spring sections of it were either submerged or else floated about as rafts for the Hanrahan boys.

The implement factory, where all but one of the men were employed, was half a mile distant, and the school was three-quarters of a mile in another direction. The man who didn't work at the implement factory was Mr. Dawson, who was a photographer with two small rooms near the factory. The neighborhood was not much addicted to the folly of posing before a camera, and Mr. Dawson depended largely on the tin-type habit among the younger people, with a sprinkling of babies and brides-to-be done in cabinet size.

Mr. Dawson could properly be called the prominent man of Burton's Row, not only because of his superior attainments, but also because of his wife. It was understood that she had been a school-teacher out in the country somewhere before she became Mrs. Dawson.

Mr. and Mrs. Dawson were responsible for the literary movement in Burton's Row.

The owner of the six houses was a hopeful speculator of the name of Burton. It was his policy to go out into the country and begin a town and then permit the city to "build out to it," buying the lots from him. In this instance the city had been backward in filling up the gap. By some calculation Burton had discovered that his six houses had numbers and were on an extension of some city street. The numbers were quite large and the figures many; so it was easier to speak of the six houses as Burton's Row and to number them from 1 to 6, beginning at the east.

The Swansons lived at No. 1. Mr. Swanson was a sober, industrious young man and the father of a flaxen-haired girl. Mr. and Mrs. Hanrahan and their two children were in the next house. The Williams couple, lately married, were in No. 3 with a lot of new furniture. The Dawsons were in No. 4. Old Mr. McClatchey, day watchman at the factory, was a widower. His youngest daughter, 15 years old, attended to the household affairs. They lived at No. 5. At No. 6 resided the Neinbergers, he and she and the three children. Therefore the little world had eighteen persons.

The row was built after a socialistic pattern. Each house was exactly like every other. They were all the same height and width. One fence reached the length of the row. The only differences were trivial. The Dawsons had a door-mat on the low front stoop. Mrs. Swanson always kept flowers in the window. In the McClatchey front yard was a stake, to which the goat was usually tied. Mrs. Neinberger's curtains had scenery painted on them. A drunken man would have had some trouble in picking out the right place, but Mr. Williams, who was the only one addicted to strong drink, never made a mistake. He would pick out the two middle houses and enter the one that had no door-mat in front.

The women, being left to themselves all day, soon became fast friends. They found material for gossip in the routine of their daily life, and when nothing else could be done they compared husbands.

It was during these talks with the other women that Mrs. Dawson became impressed with the idea that she should be an instrument for lifting Burton's Row to something above the dull consideration of eating, working and sleeping. In the outside world great things were transpiring. They, as wage-workers, were affected and they should know the truth and be guided by it. So she spoke to her husband.

"Let us organize a neighborhood club," said she. "We will meet once a week to discuss matters of current interest. The men will be encouraged to read the newspapers, and the exchange of opinions cannot help but broaden their views."

"I think it's a good plan, Luella. It'll give me a chance to buckle McClatchey and Hanrahan on this tariff business. They're free-traders, but they don't know why. I can show them why they've been working half-time all winter."

"Yes, but you must be careful and not antagonize them too much. We want to discuss everything fairly and without passion. Now, what shall we call it?"

He left it all to her, and she selected "The Circle of Inquiry."

The first meeting was called for the following Monday evening. The cards of invitation caused such a commotion as had not been known since the day the Hanrahan boy had been knocked senseless by the McClatchey goat. Mrs. Dawson followed up the cards with calls along the row, and she secured the cooperation of all the women, except the McClatchey girl, who, she said, was hardly old enough to grasp the subjects to be taken up. Having the women, she was sure of the men, although Mrs. Swanson experienced great difficulty in convincing her husband that he should attend.

This was to be the first formal gathering of the residents of Burton's Row. As announced by word of mouth, the program was to consist of a paper on "Immigration," read by Mrs. Dawson, after which the members of the circle would be expected to join in a general discussion.

The Dawson front room was dusted and tidied on Monday evening. In the dining-room a cocoanut cake, a bowl of apples and several pies were in readiness for the "lap supper," which was to be served as soon as the immigration problem had been solved.

Never before, it is safe to say, had there been so much scrubbing, button-hunting and shoe-polishing all at one time as on this Monday evening. Mrs. Dawson was amazed at the change in her neighbors as they arrived in twos, all except old Mr. McClatchey, who came alone with a clean shave, a long black coat and a huge black cravat. They

"Mrs. Dawson had taken her place at the center table"

sat timidly around the wall. Under the restraining influence of their best clothes and the impending solemnity they appeared to forget that they knew one another.

"Well, Mr. Hanrahan, it is quite a nice night outside," remarked Mr. Williams.

"It is that, the finest I ever see," said Mr. Hanrahan.

"I think we'll have some good weather now," joined in Mr. Swanson, shifting his feet uneasily.

Old Mr. McClatchey, who had been gazing thoughtfully at the floor, nodded his head in assent.

Just then there was a rustling of manuscript. Mrs. Dawson had taken her place at the center table and unrolled her "paper." A most profound silence was given her. She began to read.

It appeared that she regarded the United States as an asylum for the poor and downtrodden of the earth, but she was bitterly opposed to the importation of the criminal and pauper elements of Europe. She was also against anarchy, and believed that unless immigrants were willing to accept our institutions, abide by our laws and become good American citizens they should at once return to their native lands.

These highly original views were indorsed by Mr. McClatchey, who not only nodded his head, but said aloud several times "Y'r right."

Mrs. Dawson concluded with a brief extract from Emerson and then said: "We shall be glad to hear from any one on the subject."

After a few moments of awkward silence McClatchey began.

He said, in opening, that we are all foreigners. Because some one got here twenty years ahead of somebody else was no reason why the second man should be shut out of the game. He was in favor of letting in everybody except the Chinese. These, however, were not his exact words.

"I'll just tell you what's the trouble," broke in Mrs. Williams. "The foreigners come in here and take all the offices. I don't object to them coming here, but they ought to wait awhile before they run everything."

"Who runs everything?" asked Mr. Hanrahan, who was becoming agitated.

"The Irish!" she answered, sharply.

"Y'r right," he said, smiting the table. "And why?"

He told them. The Irishman got out and hustled. He always voted, he attended the primaries and he stood up for his rights. What did the American do? Stayed at home and kicked. He finished by telling Mrs. Williams that she talked like a "female depaty."

"Hold on, Terry," broke in Mr. Williams. "Don't talk like that. You know that I don't care a continental where a man was born, but I do say we don't want no cheap labor piled in on us."

Hanrahan arose. "I'm a mimber of the union. No man can iver saay I worked cheap. Can they, McClatchey?"

Mr. McClatchey shook his head.

Mr. Williams hastened to apologize. Mr. Hanrahan still had the floor. "I do move," said he, "that immigration is all right except for crooks."

The American-born vote was disconcerted and saw itself beaten. "All in favor," said Mr. Hanrahan. It was carried unanimously. He sat down.

Another painful pause and Mrs. Neinberger came in. She asked Mr. McClatchey about the goat. He chuckled at the suggestion and began to talk. When he concluded it was time for the lap supper.

On the following Monday evening the meeting was at the Hanrahan house, the host entertaining his guests by playing the flute.

Mr. Neinberger, when it came his time to receive on Monday evening, had a German supper. The men played seven-up in the front room and the women got together in the back room. Thus it was that the Circle of Inquiry became a popular institution in Burton's Row.

IL JANITORO[25]

Mr. Tyler paid $7 for two opera tickets.

Although he slept through one duet he felt fully repaid for going, because Mrs. Tyler raved over the opera and wasted all her superlatives on it. The music was "heavenly," the prima donna "superb" and the tenor "magnificent."

There is nothing so irritates a real enthusiast as the presence of calm scorn.

"Don't you like it?" asked Mrs. Tyler, as she settled back after the eighth recall of the motherly woman who had been singing the part of a 16-year-old maiden.

"Oh, yes; it's all right," replied Mr. Tyler, as if he were conceding something.

"All right! Oh, you iceberg! I don't believe you'd become enthusiastic over anything in the world."

"I like the music, my dear, but the grand opera drags so. Then the situations are so preposterous they always appeal to my sense of humor. I can't help it. When I see Romeo and Juliet die, both singing away as if they enjoyed it, I have to laugh."

"The idea!"

"You take it in this last act. Those two fellows came out with the soldiers and announced that they were conspiring and didn't want to be heard by the people in the house, and then they shouted in chorus until they could have been heard two miles away."

"Oh, you are prejudiced."

"Not at all. I'll tell you, a grand opera's the funniest kind of a show if you only take the right view of it."

Thus they argued, and even after they arrived home she taunted him and told him he could not appreciate the dignity of the situations.

It was this nagging which induced Mr. Tyler to write an act of grand opera. He chose for his subject an alarm of fire in an apartment house. He wanted something modern and up-to-date, but in his method of treatment he resolved to reverently follow all the traditions of grand opera. The act, hitherto unpublished, and written solely for the benefit of Mrs. Tyler, is here appended:

(*Mr. and Mrs. Taylor are seated in their apartment on the fifth floor of the Behemoth residential flat building. Mrs. Taylor arises, places her hand on her heart, and moves to the center of the room. Mr. Taylor follows her, with his right arm extended.*)

Mrs. Taylor:	I think I smell smoke.
Mr. Taylor:	She thinks she smells smoke.
Mrs. Taylor:	I think I smell smoke.
Mr. Taylor:	Oh. What is it? She says she thinks she smells smoke.
Mrs. Taylor:	What does it mean, what does it mean?
	This smell of smoke may indicate,
	That we'll be burned—oh-h-h, awful fate!
Mr. Taylor:	Behold the smell grows stronger yet,
	The house is burning, I'd regret
	To perish in the curling flames;
	Oh, horror! horror! horror!!!
Mr. and Mrs. Taylor:	
	Oh, sad is our lot, sad is our lot,
	To perish in the flames so hot,
	To curl and writhe and fry and sizz,
	Oh, what a dreadful thing it is
	To think of such a thing!
Mrs. Taylor:	We must escape!
Mr. Taylor:	Yes, yes, we must escape!
Mrs. Taylor:	We have no time to lose.
Mr. Taylor:	Ah, bitter truth, Ah, bitter truth,
	We have no time to lose.
Mr. and Mrs. Taylor:	
	Sad is our lot, sad is our lot,
	To perish in the flames so hot.
Mr. Taylor:	Hark, what is it?
Mrs. Taylor:	Hark, what is it?
Mr. Taylor:	It is the dread alarm of fire.
Mrs. Taylor:	Ah, yes, ah, yes, it is the dread alarm.
Mr. Taylor:	The dread alarm strikes on the ear
	And chills me with an awful fear.
	The house will burn, oh, can it be
	That I must die in misery,
	That I must die in misery,
	The house will burn, oh, can it be
	That I must die in misery?
Mrs. Taylor:	Come, let us fly!
Mr. Taylor:	'Tis well. 'Tis well. We'll fly at once.

(Enter all the other residents of the fifth floor.)

Mr. Taylor:	Kind friends, I have some news to tell.
	This house is burning; it were well

"Oh hasten, oh hasten, oh hasten away.
Our terror we should not conceal"

	That we should haste ourselves away
	And save our lives without delay.
Chorus:	What is this he tells us?
	It must be so;
	The building is on fire
	And we must go.
	Oh, hasten, oh, hasten, oh, hasten away.
	Our terror we should not conceal,
	And language fails to express the alarm
	That in our hearts we feel.
Mr. and Mrs. Taylor:	
	Oh, language fails to express the alarm
	That in their hearts they feel.

(Enter the Janitor)

Janitor:	Hold, I am here.
Mr. Taylor:	Ah, it is the Janitoro.
Mrs. Taylor:	Can I believe my senses,
	Or am I going mad?
	It is the Janitoro,
	It is indeed the Janitoro

Janitor:	Such news I have to tell.
Mr. Taylor:	Ah, I might have known
	He has such news to tell.
	Speak and break the awful suspense.
Mrs. Taylor:	Yes, speak.
Janitor:	I come to inform you
	That you must quickly fly
	The fearful blaze is spreading,
	To tarry is to die.
	The floors underneath you
	Are completely burned away.
	They cannot save the building,
	So now escape I pray.
Mrs. Taylor:	Oh, awful message
	How it chills my heart.
Janitor:	The flames are roaring loudly,
	Oh, what a fearful sound!
	You can hear the people shrieking
	As they jump and strike the ground.
	Oh, horror overtakes me,
	And I merely pause to say
	That the building's doomed for certain
	Oh, haste, oh, haste away.
Mrs. Taylor:	Oh, awful message.
	How it chills my heart.
	Yet we will sing a few more arias
	Before we start.
Mr. Taylor:	Yes, a few more arias and then away.
Chorus:	Oh, hasten, oh, hasten, oh hasten away.
Mrs. Taylor:	Now, e'er I retreat,
	Lest death o'ertakes me
	I'll speak of the fear
	That convulses and shakes me,
	I sicken to think what may befall,
	Oh, horror! horror!! horror!!!
Mr. Taylor:	The woman speaks the truth,
	And there can be no doubt
	That we will perish soon
	Unless we all clear out.
Chorus:	Oh, hasten, oh, hasten, oh, hasten away!

(But why go further? The supposition is that they continued the dilatory tactics of grand opera and perished in the flames.)

IN THE ROOF GARDEN[26]

Ollie and Fred were up at the roof garden one night this week and it was just like getting into the younger set to sit and listen to them.

Ollie wore one of his new summer suits, with the adhesive trousers, and his soft white hat had been folded in from the top until it was not much higher than the silvery hat-band. Fred was in blue and held his gloves all evening. They tilted forward as they walked along the aisle and both of them stared seriously into space.

"Say, old man, where shall we sit?" asked Ollie, halting suddenly.

"I don't mind, old chap."

"We might sit at this table."

"All right. Can we get a table to ourselves?"

"I don't know, old man. I think so."

"Well, let's sit here."

"All right."

"Well, you take this place."

"No, really, old chap, you know, I don't care so much for the show."

"I'd rather you would."

"No, really, I'd just as soon sit here."

"Would you, really, old man?"

"Yes, I would, really."

So they seated themselves and Fred picked up a program.

"What's on the bill, old man?" asked Ollie.

"I don't know who they are."

"I'll tell you who I'd like to see tonight."

"Who's that?"

"Vesta Tilly."

"That's right. I think she's great."

"She's dog-goned fine."

"I liked Yvette Guilbert, too."

"Yes, I think she's elegant."

"Did you think she was good-looking?"

"No, I didn't think she was, but Billy Pendleton says he thinks she's good-looking."

"The dickens he does! No, I don't think she is."

"Neither do I. She's good, though."

"Yes, I always thought she was elegant."

"You know when she sings those French songs, there's

something—I don't know, but she has that—well, by George, she's fine."

"Yes, I always thought she was great. I wish Anna Held was here tonight. Don't you like her?"

"Yes, I liked her pretty well."

"I think she's elegant. There's something, you know, when she comes out and starts in—well, you know—er—. It's something in the—you can't hardly say what it is, but I think it's fine, don't you?"

"Yes, she's elegant. Did you buy a picture of her?"

"Yes, I've got mine in that frame where I used to have Della Fox."

"Say, old man, is Della Fox married?"

"I'll be dog-goned if I know. Somebody told me she was, and then I heard somewhere else that she wasn't."

"Lean over here, your tie's coming up."

"The dickens it is! If anything make me mad it's to have my tie come up."

"I should say so. It's horrible."

"I used to have trouble all the time with my ties coming up, but, by George, you know, Crossley made me some new shirts that won't let your tie work up at all. They're great."

"I must get me some."

"That's what you want to do, old man. Tell Crossley I sent you."

"What did Crossley charge you for your last shirts?"

"I don't know. He sent the bill to the guv'nor. Say, tell that dog-goned waiter to come over here."

Ollie beckoned to a waiter, who came up briskly and asked: "Well, what will it be, gents?"

Ollie flinched as if cut by a whip, and then he gave the waiter a reproving look.

"What do you want, old man?" he asked.

"Oh, I'll be dog-goned if I care."

"Don't you want some beer?"

Fred glanced apprehensively to right and left and then said in a careless manner, brushing his trousers leg with the gloves, "I don't care, old chap. Go ahead and order."

"Waiter, have you good beer here?" asked Ollie.

"Sure," replied the waiter. "How many—two?"

"Yes—I think so," said Ollie. "Say, waiter, now don't be in a hurry. Have you got mugs here?"

"Two mugs you want?"

"What do you think about it, old man?"

"Yes, I'd just as soon have mine in a mug."

"All right, waiter, two mugs."

The waiter dashed away, and Ollie looked after him, moodily. "Dog-gone!" he exclaimed. "It makes me mad to have a waiter try to hurry me."

"That's right."

"Do you see anybody you know?"

"No; I guess it's all right."

"Hat Elliott saw me drinking beer here one night last summer and she raised the dickens with me."

"Oh, thunder! A man's got a right to drink a mug of beer if he wants it."

"Well, that's what I said."

"Will Martin says that in the east everybody drinks beer out of mugs."

"Look out, Ollie, there's Mr. Kirby coming."

The two sat very quiet as an elderly gentleman passed along the aisle. Just as he was passing the waiter brought the two mugs.

"Do you think he saw us?" asked Fred.

"What the dickens do I care?" said Ollie. He took a gulp of the fluid and made a sour face. "Got a cigarette, old man?" he asked, throwing himself back in the chair.

"Yes, I've got a new Turkish kind here. I think they're great."

"I had some up at Burchard's the other night that were elegant. George Burchard got them in New York."

"Is that so?"

"Yes," and he lighted the cigarette which he had chosen from Fred's leather case. He timidly inhaled a draw of smoke and then said, hoarsely: "These seem to be nice."

"Yes," replied Fred, holding up one of the cigarettes and studying it with judicial calm, "they're fine."

"You're not drinking your beer, old man."

"Oh, I'll drink it all right. How is it—strong?"

"Not very. I don't like beer if it's too light."

"Neither do I."

They puckered their lips and took a sip apiece and then sat in silence for awhile, dreamily pulling at the cigarettes.

Then Ollie suddenly asked: "Say, old man, do you like my Tuxedo coat?"

"Yes; I think it's all right."

"Billy Pendleton said he thought it was too long."

"The dickens he did! He needn't talk, dog-gone it! You know those new shirts of his?"

"Yes."

"Uncle Bob got some exactly like them two years ago in New York. Billy thought they were something new."

Both of them smiled wearily at the expense of Billy Pendleton, and settled further down in their chairs.

Ollie resumed the conversation.

"Crossley's got some dandy hatbands," he said.

"Yes. I was looking at them. They're fine."

"I bought—"

But just then the orchestra broke in and the remainder was lost.

WHEN FATHER MEETS FATHER[27]

An "L" train had come to a grinding stop at the second station of the inbound trip. The big man came along the aisle until he saw a seat with only one man in it. His Chicago training asserted itself. He hurriedly pre-empted the place. The man already in the seat moved over toward the window. The big man said "Thanks," secretively, and leaned back to waste seventeen minutes of this precious life.

In the seat opposite, and facing them, were two women and one baby.

The younger woman held the baby, and the young woman's mother superintended. Once she said: "I think you'd better keep your hand on his back, Ida. The car jolts so."

Soon after she advised strongly against allowing "him" to chew the newspaper, advancing a theory that printer's ink is not a wholesome food for infants.

Ida, who was all eyes for "him," followed directions placidly, and three times she addressed him as "precious rascal," which doubtful compliment was utterly ignored.

The baby was a round-faced, pinkish creature with big, blue eyes. As babies go, doubtless he was a very fine specimen. When he opened his mouth to crow, he showed two unimportant teeth. His gown was a scramble of lace, and the bonnet was fastened under his plump chin with an enormous bow.

He pawed the air with two milk-white fists until his mother turned him around squarely. Then he sat very still and studied the two men on the other seat.

The big man with the black moustache wore a blue suit, a broad straw hat, and a striped négligé shirt with a loose cravat falling down the front of it.

His neighbour was a smaller and rather pale man, with a short patch of side-whiskers in front of each ear. His coat was of black silk, the cravat was of white lawn, and the rim of his straw hat was much narrower than that of his neighbour's.

The baby stared at one and then at the other. The pale man stood the scrutiny for a time and then began to smile. The baby smiled in return, and the pale man winked and shook his head in a threatening way, causing the infant to become serious again and turn to the big man.

The latter pointed his finger and, using his thumb as a trigger, discharged a loud cluck, which so delighted the child that it waved its arms and gurgled.

Once more he clucked and this time the demonstration of delight was so earnest that the mother looked out of the window in pleased embarrassment and the grandmother smiled and said: "Oh, you bad boy, you're not afraid of any one."

The big man put his forefinger against the baby's ribs and said; "Kitchey, kitchey, kitchey, kitchey, kitchey."

Leaning with his elbows on his knees the pale man watched this performance with unconcealed delight, especially when the baby laughed so hard that it came very near rolling off its mother's lap.

"Boy or girl?" he asked.

"Boy, and a bad boy, too; now, aren't you?" the mother replied, straightening the bonnet, which had been pulled down over one eye during the frolic. She was blushing proudly.

"No, he ain't a bad boy; no, siree," said the big man. "He's a little corker; that's what he is. Ain't you a little corker?" He advanced his forefinger toward the ribs, and the "corker" went into a kicking fit over the mere prospect of being tickled again.

"What's his name?" asked the pale man.

"Tell the gentleman your name," said the grandmother, shaking him by the arm. But he could see no one except the big man, from whom he was momentarily expecting another attack.

"His name's Walter, but all he can say now is 'Wah'; you see, he's only a little over a year old. How old is he, Ida?"

"Thirteen months and ten days," was the prompt reply.

"You seem to have made a deep impression on him," said the pale man to his neighbour.

"Would he come to me, do you s'pose?" asked the big man of the grandmother.

"Bless you, he isn't afraid of anyone."

"Let's see? Come, Walter, come to me; come on."

While entreating, the big man held out his hands, and the baby, with his round face puckered into a laugh, reached for the big man.

"Just look at that," said the baby's mother, with a little gasp.

The big man received Walter and danced him in the air. He allowed the baby to claw his moustache, and when he said "Ouch," the pale man laughed aloud, and the whole car, which was watching the performance, smiled.

"Oh, you bad boy," said the grandmother, recovering Walter and straightening the bonnet once more. "Ida, the next stop is Thirty-first."

That was where they alighted. The baby looked back over the mother's shoulder and laughed at the two men, who grinned after him like two foolish boys.

Two eager men with newspapers fought their way into the vacant seat, and the friends of the baby found themselves depending upon each other for entertainment.

"Nice baby?" said the pale man.

"A dandy. I like 'em about that age."

"I have one of about that size—a little girl. She'll be fifteen months old on the 17th. She's just beginning to toddle around and we have to watch her all the time."

"That's right."

"The other day my wife left her alone for a little while, and when she came back there was that little tike clear up on the sideboard trying to get the cork out of the vinegar-bottle."

"You don't say so?"

"Yes, sir; she had pushed a chair over to the sideboard and climbed up."

"I've got a boy that's goin' to be a terror," said the big man. "He's only nine months old, but he's big for his age, and I guess he knows more than most children do at a year old. The other morning about six o'clock I was woke up by something poundin' me, and what do you think? That little cuss had squirmed around in bed and had both of his feet in my face kicking away to beat the cars."

"Well, well!"

"I woke up my wife and let her see it. He knew what he was doin', all right, for when he saw me lookin' at him, he commenced to laugh. I'll tell you they begin to learn things early enough."

"They do, for a fact. Now, my second girl isn't five years old, and, of course, we've never sent her to school, but she knows her letters and can read some; just picked it up, you know. My wife and I thought we wouldn't attempt any instruction until she was six, but she simply went ahead and learned anyway."

"I'll bet you! That's the way they do. But say, you ought to see that oldest boy of mine. He's twelve years old and his sister is goin' on nine. They're down in the country now visitin' their grandmother, and I want to tell you, pardner, they think she's the greatest woman in the world. My wife's folks have a fine place, with an orchard and a crick and horses to ride. Why, when they get down there they just own the farm. Turn it upside down."

"I dare say they do," said the pale man, smiling and nodding his head as if he remembered something of the kind himself.

"Yes, you see their grandmother humors them and gives them all they want to eat, and fusses over them. She thinks more of them children than she does of me, but that's all right. My wife was the only child. And their grandfather! He'd bring a team in out of the field any time if the kids wanted to ride."

"I'm sorry I can't let my children get out into the country more than they do. But I send them to the park every pleasant afternoon, and, of course, they enjoy that."

"I'll bet they do, but it's better, of course, if they get clear out into the country, where they can peel their shoes and stockings and raise—Cain. I wish your children could get out there with mine. They'd have great times together."

"They would, indeed; I know *mine* would enjoy it. Is your little boy in good health?"

"Is he? He's a buster. Never cries except when the colic gets in its work. One day about a month ago the nurse set him in a chair and he fell off right on his head. My wife come screamin', thinkin', of course, that he was croaked, sure enough. That boy simply rolled over and started in playin' with his rattle again—never even whimpered."

"This seems to be Congress Street," said the pale man, looking out of the window, and arising.

"Yes, this is where I get off, too."

"Well, I'm very glad to have met you," and he held out his hand.

"The same to you," said the big man, giving a hearty grasp.

"I'll give you my card. Have you one?"

"I think I have, somewheres."

The pale man opened a leather case, and the other searched in his upper vest-pockets.

They exchanged cards while crowding to the platform with the others. Outside, after they had separated, each looked at his card. One read:

> REV. MCLEOD HATLEY,
> Essex Presbyterian Church.
> Residence, 4690 Calumet Avenue.

The other:

> THE SMILAX BUFFET.
> "Billy" Alexander, Proprietor,
> 82 Clark Street.
> Imported and Domestic Wines,
> Liquors and Cigars. Remember the
> Number.
> The Home of the "Looloo" Cocktail.

THE JUDGE'S SON[28]

Two men sat by one of the narrow south windows of the Freedom Hotel. They were tipped back in their straight wooden chairs and their feet rested against the scarred sill of the window.

One of the men was tall, with a tan-colored moustache and a goatee. He wore a black slouch hat, which was pulled forward over one eye so that it gave him a suggestion of rural bravado. The other man was younger, hollow-cheeked, and with hair and beard of dead blackness. His light-coloured stiff hat seemed preposterously out of season, for a slow but steady sift of snow was coming down.

Both men wore clothes of careful cut, but the shape had gone from the garments. The elbows were shiny, the vest buttons were not uniform and the fronts were sadly spotted.

In the room with the two men were some fifty other men, marked by adversity, most of them holding with weakened pride to some chattel of better days.

As many as could find places at the windows sat and looked with fascinated idleness at the rushing money-makers outside. Others put their backs to the dim light and read from scraps of newspapers. There was a smothering odor of pipe-smoke, which floated in vague ribbons above the clustering heads. Sometimes—but not often—the murmur of conversation was broken by laughter.

It is a good thing the Freedom Hotel calls itself a hotel, otherwise it would be a lodging-house. These men in the bare "office" were being sheltered at a weekly rate of $1.50, and each had a cubby-hole for a home—a mere shell of wood open at the top. The upper floors of the Freedom Hotel were subdivided into these tiny pens. Here the tired and discouraged men came crawling every night. From these boxes the frowsy and unrested men emerged every morning.

The wreckage on an ocean beach washes together as if by choice and the wrecks of a city mobilize of their own free will. The man who is down must find some one with whom he can rail at the undeserving prosperous.

The Freedom Hotel sheltered a community of equals, all worsted in the fight, some living on the crumbs of a happier period, some abjectly depending on the charity of friends and relatives, and some struggling along on small and unreliable pay.

There was a 400-page novel in every life there, but the condensed stories of the two men at the window must suffice for the present.

The older, the one with the slouch hat—son of a wealthy merchant in an Indiana town—inherited money—married—learned to gamble—took up with Board of Trade—wife died—more reckless gambling—moved to Chicago—went broke—Freedom Hotel.

The younger, with black hair and beard—son of a judge in a Western city—reared with great care by mother—sent to college—learned to drink—repeatedly forgiven by father through the intercession of the mother—mother died—father cast son from home—son in Chicago, employed in a collection agency—went on a drunk—Freedom Hotel.

The victim of gambling did most of the talking.

"They can't always keep me down, now, you can bet on that," he said, nervously combing his goatee with thumb and finger. "I wish I could have had about ten thousand last week. I'd have shown some of these fellows."

"If I had ten thousand I wouldn't chance a cent of it," said the other, his eyes twitching.

"Well, I'll beat the game yet, you see if I don't. I've got three or four fellows in this town to get even with—fellows that I spent my money on when I had it; fellows that could come to me and get fifty or a hundred just for the askin' of it, and there ain't one of 'em today that'd turn over his finger to help me—not one of 'em. That's what you get when you're down, young man. If you want to find out who your friends are, just wait till you go broke."

"I know all about it," said the other. With a shaky hand he took the last cigarette from a package.

"I was thinkin' when I turned in to my bunk last night, 'Well, this is a devil of a place for a man that had a room at the Palmer House, when it was the talk of the whole country,' That was when I used to drive my own trotter and hire a man to take care of him. When I'd come to Chicago, the hotel clerks used to jump over the counter to shake hands with me. If I wanted a steak, I went to Billy Boyle's for it. If I was over on Clark Street and wanted a game, I could get a private roll. It was 'Phil' here and 'Phil' there, and nothin' too good for me. Do you think I could go to any one o' them today and get a dollar? A dollar! Not a cent—not a red cent. That's what you get when you're in hard luck."

"You can't tell me anything about it," said the other, in a restrained voice, for his lungs were filled with cigarette-smoke, which he was breathing slowly through his nostrils. "Didn't I go to college with fellows that live right here in this town, and don't they pass me on the street every day or two without recognizing me? Why, when I think that I came of a family that—ah, well, it's all right. Money talks here in Chicago, and if you haven't got money you're little better than a tramp."

"Well, I'll have it again and I'll make some of these fellows sorry they ever threw me down. I'll make 'em sweat. If I don't—" and he ran into profanity.

"Here's a telegram for you," said some one at his elbow.

It was the "clerk" of the Freedom—a short man with an indented nose, who went about in his shirt-sleeves.

"For me?" asked the speculator, in surprise.

"That's what it says here—Philip Sanderson. It came over for 136."

"That's right."

"I signed for it."

He tore open the envelope and read the message. It seemed that he gazed at it for a full minute without speaking or moving. Then he arose and hurried away. The judge's son rubbed his eyes and felt vainly for another cigarette.

"Your partner's gone," said the clerk that evening.

"Who—Sanderson?" asked the judge's son.

"Yes, this afternoon. He didn't have much packin' to do. What do you think? An old aunt of his died down in Indiana and he told me he'd come in for about five thousand."

"Well, I'll swear," said the judge's son, "and he didn't leave any word?"

"Nope."

A week later the judge's son was walking in State Street.

The cold north wind was blowing.

His summer derby had to be held in place. The other hand was deep in his trousers' pocket.

His old sack-coat was tightly buttoned and the collar was turned up. The judge's son seemed to be limping in each foot, but it was not a limp. It was the slouch of utter dejection.

He was within thirty feet of the main entrance to the Palmer House when he saw a man come out.

The judge's son had to take a second look, to be sure of his own senses. Instead of the old and crumpled slouch there was a new broad-brimmed felt hat of much shapeliness. The winter overcoat was heavy chinchilla, with a velvet collar. Sanderson was smoking a long cigar. He had been shaved recently. His shoes were brightly polished. As he stood back in the sheltered doorway he worked his left hand into a blood-red glove.

The judge's son stood some fifteen feet away and hesitated. Then he slunk to the shelter of a column and spoke to his partner.

"Well, Sanderson, they seem to be coming pretty easy for you."

Sanderson looked at the speaker, squinting through the smoke.

He said nothing. His hand being well into the glove, he fastened the clasp at the wrist with a springy snap. With a satisfied lick he turned his cigar once over in his mouth. A flake of ash had fallen on the chinchilla coat. He brushed it off. Then he pushed through the swinging doors and went back into the hotel.

NOTES ON THE SHORT STORIES

1. From *Artie* (Chicago: Herbert S. Stone & Company, 1896).
2. Joe Weber (1867–1942) and Lew Fields (1867–1941). The Weber &

Fields vaudeville team was one of the most popular that played the major city "circuits" from the turn of the century to the demise of vaudeville, about 1920. See J. E. Di Meglio, *Vaudeville USA* (1974).

3. From *Pink Marsh* (Chicago: Herbert S. Stone & Company, 1897). Originally in the *Chicago Record*, September 8, 1894.

4. From *Doc' Horne* (Chicago: Herbert S. Stone & Company, 1899).

5. In *Small Town Chicago* (Port Washington, N.Y.: Kennikat Press, 1980) James De Muth argues that "the common intention which links Dunne, Ade, and Lardner—which distinguished their art form from [that of] the Chicago novelists—is their attempt to interpret Chicago in the nostalgic terms of a small American community" (p. 105). See a review of *Small Town Chicago* in the *Indiana Magazine of History* (December, 1980), pp. 369–370.

6. The population of Chicago, in 1980, was 3,005,072.

7. From *In Babel* (New York: McClure, Phillips & Co., 1903). This story was selected as "one of Ade's best" by W. D. Howells for his anthology *Great Modern American Stories* (1920). The story appeared originally in the *Chicago Record*, March 13, 1896.

8. From *Stories of the Streets and of the Town, 4th Series* (1895). Originally in the *Chicago Record*, May 10, 1895. Reprinted in *Chicago Stories* (Chicago: Caxton Club, 1941).

9. From *Stories of the Streets and of the Town, 4th Series* (1895). Originally in the *Chicago Record*, April 30, 1895.

10. From *In Babel* (1903).

11. William Cowper, *The Task* (1784), Book III, l. 41.

12. From James Thomson, "The Seasons" (1728).

13. Song of Sol. 2:12.

14. John Milton's *Paradise Lost* (1667), Book IV, ll. 598ff.

15. Alexander Pope, "Essay on Man" (1734), Epistle I, ll. 95ff.

16. From Nathaniel Parker Willis, "The Month of June," *Poetical Works* (1888).

17. From Eugene Field, "The Little Peach" (1896).

18. *The Iliad*, Book XXII, l. 106 (Alexander Pope's translation, 1720).

19. From *In Babel*.

20. From *Stories of the Streets and of the Town, First Series* (1894). Originally in the *Chicago Record*, February 27, 1894.

21. From *In Babel*.

22. From *In Babel*.

23. From Thomas Moore's "Farewell!" *Irish Melodies* (1834).

24. From *Stories of the Streets and of the Town, First Series* (1894). Originally in the *Chicago Record*, March 24, 1894.

25. From *Verses and Jingles* (1911). Printed by Bobbs-Merrill for the Indiana Society of Chicago. Copyright ©1911 by the Indiana Society of Chicago. Notice that Mr. Tyler names his two main characters Mr. and Mrs. Taylor.

26. From *Stories of the Streets and of the Town, Third Series* (1895).

27. From *In Babel*.

28. From *In Babel*.

III

Plays

AUNT FANNY FROM CHAUTAUQUA[1]

A Comedy in One Act

CHARACTERS

FANNY SHERLOCK *is a well preserved, lively woman anywhere from 30 to 40—well dressed and just a little on the show-girl order, but nothing eccentric. At first appearance she is supposed to have come from the train and is dressed for traveling.*

BEVERLY LATTIMORE *is a well dressed bachelor of about 40—he and* FANNY *should pair off as a good-looking couple. He is a man of leisure, good manners, but not too bright—an amiable, slow-witted, nice sort of fellow.*

FLOSSIE SHERLOCK, FANNY'S *niece, must be a gushing, affected, artificial and shallow-minded young girl of bursting social aspirations—should be about 20—must play a little on the piano.*

NORA *is a well-trained housemaid who goes in and out quietly and attends to her own business.*

Scene: A living room in the Sherlock home. Essentials are: Piano at Right of Center and diagonal so that anyone playing will have back to sofa or divan at Left of Center. Over against wall at Left, a buffet or sideboard with a few decanters and glasses. Several pictures on wall, including one at Center which is a painting of a country girl of 10 or 12.

Probably the entrance from hallway will have to be at Center although it could be at Left and upstage. At Right is a doorway leading off to another apartment. These are the only two doors actually required. There may be a table at Center with a vase of flowers, magazines and books, and of course, several chairs placed effectively. Try to get the effect of a drawing room in the home of a well-to-do-family.

At rise of Curtain, FLOSSIE *is propped up on sofa or in easy chair, in a comfortable but undignified attitude, reading "Town Topics"—she should hold it so that cover can be seen from front. For curtain music play the refrain of the song by Von Tilzer,*[2] *"All Alone"—continue music softly after curtain is up.* FLOSSIE *is deeply interested in paper—*NORA *enters with card on tray and brings it to her, being compelled to almost push it between her and the paper in order to attract her attention.*

FLOSSIE [*startled*]. Oh! [*Sees card and takes it—is impressed.*] Mr. Lattimore! [*Jumping up.*] You told him to wait?
NORA. Yes'm. [*Or may simply nod.*]
FLOSSIE: [*primping—going to mirror if there is one*]. Just think—Mister Lattimore!—I didn't expect him— He's so exclusive! [*Goes to table or mantel and exchanges "Town Topics" for a copy of "Outlook"—Goes back to divan, adjusts herself in a graceful attitude.* NORA *is waiting near Center. After* FLOSSIE *has settled herself, she speaks to* NORA *again.*] Show him in.
        [NORA *exits Center to Left and* FLOSSIE *continues business of posing and fixing herself. She is apparently intent on magazine when* NORA *comes to doorway Center and stands just inside.* LATTIMORE *enters with hat in hand and coat on arm, and stops inside doorway.* NORA *out Center and exits Right.*]
LATTIMORE [*hesitating*]. Ah—Miss Sherlock.
FLOSSIE [*apparently startled*]. Mister Lattimore—this is a surprise. [*Arises and goes toward him with magazine in hand—extremely cordial.*] Delighted to see you. [*Shake hands well up—do not burlesque.*]
LATTIMORE. I just came over—I—that is—you see—
FLOSSIE [*seeing hat and coat*]. That stupid maid—your hat and coat.
LATTIMORE. No, really—[*He allows her to take them.*] I mustn't disturb you. [*She puts hat on chair and throws coat over back of it.*]
FLOSSIE [*meaningly*]. Disturb me—I'm always glad to see you.
LATTIMORE. Thanks. [*Forcing a smile.*] Very kind I'm sure—
FLOSSIE. The trouble is I don't see you often enough. When I tell the

girls that you've been to call on me they'll be simply wild with jealousy. [*She must keep up a gushing and affected manner.*]

LATTIMORE. Well—you see—it isn't really a call.

FLOSSIE [*pretending to be disappointed*]. Why—Mister—Lattimore.

LATTIMORE. I mean—it's like this—I'm sitting in a poker game at the club—your father comes in and takes the place next to me—so I drop out.

FLOSSIE [*motioning him to chair or divan*]. Why?

LATTIMORE. A man who inherits his money should never play poker with a self-made millionaire.

FLOSSIE [*puzzled*]. Why not?

LATTIMORE. Because—that's the way he got the million.

FLOSSIE. You mean—by being lucky?

LATTIMORE. You are his daughter—we'll let it go at that.

FLOSSIE. You were saying—

LATTIMORE. The game proceeded—I was looking on. Boy brought in telegram for your father—your father said he would have to drop out—five other players stood up on their hind legs and said he couldn't drop out.

FLOSSIE. Couldn't?

LATTIMORE. He had all the chips.

FLOSSIE. It seems to me that was the very time to quit.

LATTIMORE. You try it some time.

FLOSSIE. Anyway?

LATTIMORE. He wanted you to have the telegram—so I volunteered to run across the street with it, [*Producing it from pocket.*] and here it is.

FLOSSIE. Thank you ever so much—[*Taking telegram from envelope, already opened.*] I hope it's nothing serious—[*Glances at it—gives a shriek indicating surprise and horror.*]

LATTIMORE. Great Scott! Someone dead?

FLOSSIE. Oh-h-h-h. Worse than that. Someone is coming.

LATTIMORE. Coming?

FLOSSIE [*grabbing him by the arm and swinging him around, calling his attention to picture on wall which must be placed to show plainly*]. Look at that—That is what is coming.

LATTIMORE. You mean that little girl?

FLOSSIE. Little girl! That picture was painted the year of the Centennial at Philadelphia.

LATTIMORE. Who is she?

FLOSSIE. Aunt Fanny.

LATTIMORE. Aunt Fanny?

FLOSSIE. Father's only sister—lives at Chautauqua—

LATTIMORE. Chautauqua!

FLOSSIE. Doesn't that tell the whole story? Think of anyone living at Chautauqua!

LATTIMORE. Why this agitation? What's wrong with her?

FLOSSIE. Listen! When she was eight years old she could recite one thousand verses of Scripture.

LATTIMORE. Great Heavens!

FLOSSIE. At ten she began making her own dresses.

LATTIMORE [*looking at picture*]. I believe it—after looking at the picture.

FLOSSIE. All my life she's been held up to me as a model—Aunt Fanny this—Aunt Fanny that—Oh-h-h! I can just imagine her—a thin old maid of forty—carries a bird cage—drinks catnip tea—looks under the bed every night.

LATTIMORE. You mean—you've never seen her.

FLOSSIE. The first time I was at school—the second time I ran away—this time there's no escape. [*Bell rings off Left.*] Sakes alive! She's arrived!

LATTIMORE. I'll be going.

FLOSSIE [*agitated*]. Don't—please—you can help me.

LATTIMORE. How?

FLOSSIE. Step into the other room—I'll tell her that I have a caller—send her to bed—then you come back and I'll tell you all about her—

LATTIMORE. Very well—I—[*Sees decanters on sideboard. Pointing.*] Look!

FLOSSIE. What is it?

LATTIMORE. Bottles! If she saw those, she'd faint.

[FLOSSIE *hurries over to sideboard—unfolds napkins and covers decanters. As she is doing so* LATTIMORE *looks around room—may see picture that he thinks would shock a pious lady so he hurries to it and turns it to wall. As he and* FLOSSIE *are at this business,* NORA *the maid, comes to Center doorway from Right and stops in doorway. Bell rings again.*]

NORA. Are you at home, Miss?

FLOSSIE. Nora—listen—if it's a funny female who claims to be my aunt, keep her in the hall till I say "When."

NORA. Very well. [*Exits Left.*]

FLOSSIE. Oh-h-h! [*More of a scream than an exclamation—rushes to table in Center and grabs box.*]

LATTIMORE. What is it?

FLOSSIE. Cigarettes! [*Runs and pushes the box under table or into some corner.*]

LATTIMORE. [*picking up book from Center table—starting to read title*]. By Elinor—[*Hurries and puts book under piano cover or some other convenient hiding place.*]

FLOSSIE [*looking about apprehensively*]. Isn't it a terrible thing—to have relatives?

LATTIMORE [*going toward her—taking her hand*]. My dear Miss Sherlock—there's a skeleton in every closet.

FLOSSIE [*shaking her head*]. And the worst kind is the one that won't stay in the closet.

LATTIMORE [*taking out a cigar*]. I'll smoke a quiet cigar in the next room—when your antiquated auntie is safely tucked away for the night, I'll come back and have you sing to me.

FLOSSIE. I'd love to—[*He is going toward Right—she follows a step or two.*] and I'll never forget how you helped me in this terrible situation.

LATTIMORE [*is at doorway Right—turns and speaks again—amused*]. May I peek in?

FLOSSIE. Don't! I wouldn't have you see her for the world.

 LATTIMORE *laughs and exits Right.* FLOSSIE *turns and takes last survey of room to be sure everything is quite respectable. If stage manager thinks we are not over-elaborating, let her discover an ornament which may seem a little bold and change it, say taking a lamp shade from lamp or a throw from back of chair and covering statue—then goes to doorway Center and beckons off Left—may call "All right,* NORA*"—and then retreat somewhat to Right of Center and wait, trembling, nervous and embarrassed. If entrance music is desired, let it begin on cue "All right,* NORA*" and be something misleading, such as "Reuben, Reuben, I've been thinking" or "When Reuben comes to Town" or even a few bars of some hymn.* NORA *comes and stands inside of doorway.* FANNY *enters briskly—sees* FLOSSIE*— pauses.*]

FANNY. It can't be—it is—little Flossie! [*Hurries to her—embracing and kissing her—continues.*] Say, I could pick you out in a crowd—you're the living image of your mother—she was a nice woman but, oh, what a fuzzy housekeeper!

FLOSSIE [*amazed*]. Are you—really my Aunt Fanny?

FANNY. Am I? I have all the strawberry marks to prove it.

FLOSSIE. I—I—expected someone different.

FANNY. Different?

FLOSSIE. That is—older.

FANNY. S-h-h-! I'm old enough, girlie, but I tore up my birth certificate ten years ago and I've been twenty-eight ever since! [*Removes gloves and wraps during above talk.*]

FLOSSIE. I—I suppose you want to go to your room.

FANNY [*startled*]. You suppose—what?

FLOSSIE. You must be tired after your journey—it's nine o'clock.

FANNY. Nine o'clock is the mere fringe of the night. I've got a lot of
sleep in the bank—If there's a bed in my room, you might as well
move it out. [*Giving wraps to* NORA.]

FLOSSIE. Father is at the club.

FANNY [*preparing to make herself at home.* NORA *exits Center Right with
wraps*]. I'll wait till he comes back—then I want him to take me to
some place with a million electric lights, a Hungarian orchestra
and a bunch of blondes.

FLOSSIE [*horrified*]. Blondes!

FANNY. I've got a lot of Chautauqua to get out of my system—I'll tell
you that. [*Begins to sniff and move around.*] Say, I smell a man.

FLOSSIE [*surprised*]. A what?

FANNY. Cigar smoke. Good cigar too. [*Sees hat and coat thrown across
chair—goes over and picks up hat.*] Do these belong to your father?

FLOSSIE. No—you see—I have a caller.

FANNY. Oh! That's why I was stood up in the hallway—like an old
umbrella.

FLOSSIE. You see—Mister Lattimore—

FANNY. Lattimore? That's the name of the man that built the railroad through our town.

FLOSSIE. Yes—this is the son of the railroad.

FANNY. Rich?

FLOSSIE. He must be—all the newspapers say the most terrible things
about him.

FANNY. Young?

FLOSSIE. He's past forty.

FANNY. Good-looking?

FLOSSIE [*hesitating*]. Well—

FANNY. Hold on. I withdraw the question. If he's forty and worth a
barrel of money, his looks don't make any difference.

FLOSSIE. He's very exclusive.

FANNY. IS he? Where did you put him?

FLOSSIE [*she is frightened by her aunt's manner, and answers quite
promptly*]. In the other room.

FANNY. Did you tell him I was coming?

FLOSSIE. Yes—he thought his presence might annoy you—so he stepped into the other room.

FANNY. Bachelor—forty years old—millionaire—he wouldn't annoy me—I have been keeping company all winter with a piano tuner. You ought to see the men we've got up in Chautauqua—most of them have long whiskers and wear overshoes—

FLOSSIE [*nervous and uncomfortable*]. Really, Auntie, why don't you get a good night's rest—then tomorrow—

FANNY. Tomorrow? Mr. Lattimore won't be here tomorrow.

FLOSSIE [*surprised*]. You mean that you want to meet him?

FANNY. Certainly I want to meet him.

FLOSSIE. Perhaps—perhaps you don't understand, he meets very few people.

FANNY. Same here—the iceman, the milkman and the postman.

FLOSSIE. I mean he is exclusive—awfully swell—belongs to one of the old families.

FANNY. Well, Great Grief, that's the kind I want to meet.

FLOSSIE. Well—I'll speak to him. [*Starts Right.*]

FANNY. [*as* FLOSSIE *is near doorway at Right*]. If he balks at meeting me, you tell him I belong to one of the first families of Chautauqua—as you drive into town. If he asks how old I am, tell him that you don't know.

FLOSSIE. If he comes in, I hope you will remember about his family—and social position, and all that.

FANNY. Leave it to me.

[FLOSSIE *exits Right in frightened manner, leaving* FANNY *standing at Right of Center. She watches* FLOSSIE *off and then laughs in amused manner indicating that she understands why her niece wanted to get her out of the way. She looks about room and sees articles covered on the sideboard, goes over and removes napkins, discovering decanters; then in turn moves about room, reversing picture that was turned to wall, taking lamp shade off of statuette, discovering cigarettes, book and whatever other things were put out of the way, indicating by that that she gradually understands what her relatives thought she was going to be. In conclusion she walks over and picks up hat and coat belonging to* LATTIMORE—*reaches in side pocket and finds some folders of steamship companies. She may look at one and read aloud "North German Lloyd." She finds also a letter in a square envelope—it has been opened—she smells of it and then looks at address—says aloud.*] Woman's handwriting—blue ink—chorus lady. [*Pushes papers back in pocket, as she evidently hears someone coming.*]

FLOSSIE [*enters from Right—hurries toward* FANNY]. He's coming.

FANNY. Good.

FLOSSIE. Remember what I told you. He doesn't meet everybody.

FANNY. Well, I should hope not!

FLOSSIE. And you mustn't treat him as if he were just an ordinary person.

FANNY. Watch me.

    [LATTIMORE *enters Right.*]

FLOSSIE. Aunt Fanny—I wish to present Mr. Beverly Lattimore.

LATTIMORE [*advances offering hand*]. Delighted. [*As he looks at her, he is surprised to find her so attractive—he looks at her intently, then turns and looks at picture on wall and then back at her.*] I say—you've changed.

FANNY. Oh, the picture—that was taken nearly fifteen years ago—I was just a little tot at the time.

    [FLOSSIE *re-acts to this.*]

LATTIMORE. You are from the country, I believe.

FANNY. Country! I should say not. We have a Mayor and a policeman—sprinkle the streets—get New York papers the same day—every house in town has a mortgage on top of it and a motor car standing in front—Oh, we belong.

LATTIMORE [*laughing*]. That's very good.

FANNY. Be seated. [*Indicating divan.*]

LATTIMORE. Thanks.

    [*Walks over to divan followed by* FANNY. FLOSSIE *has been watching her aunt, dazed by her boldness and flippancy. She drops on piano stool as they seat themselves.*]

FANNY [*to* LATTIMORE, *as they seat themselves*]. You are visiting here in the city?

LATTIMORE [*surprised*]. Visiting! I live here.

FANNY. Oh!

FLOSSIE [*aghast*]. Why, Auntie, surely you've heard of Mr. Lattimore. He belongs to all the clubs—leads the cotillions—his father—

LATTIMORE [*making gesture toward* FLOSSIE]. Don't—please! Miss Sherlock never heard of me—I'd rather she found out for herself just who and what I am.

FANNY. I'm beginning to find out already. [*With a meaning look at* LATTIMORE.]

FLOSSIE [*shocked*]. Why, Auntie.

LATTIMORE. Really?

FANNY. I'm a student of human nature. I know the good points of a thoroughbred as soon as I see him.

LATTIMORE. You don't say so!

FLOSSIE [*spitefully*]. She's had a lot of experience.

FANNY [*forcing a smile*]. No, dearie, I've been a student. All those long winter evenings up in Chautauqua I've been reading up on physiognomy, phrenology, palmistry—I can feel of your head and look at your palm and tell what is in your heart.

LATTIMORE [*interested*]. By Jove! So you're a palmist?

FANNY. I've been working on it for eight years—ever since I was twenty years old.

[FLOSSIE *re-acts.*]

LATTIMORE [*interested*]. I say—would you mind trying to see what you can do with me?

FANNY. Not at all. That's what I'm here for—to see what I can do—with you.

[*Give this a double meaning.*]

FLOSSIE [*piqued*]. I don't believe in fortune telling.

FANNY. Honey, this is not fortune telling—this is scientific investigation. I've spent years learning to do this kind of work and I love to do it.

LATTIMORE. Go ahead—do.

FANNY. Your hand—please. [*he holds out whichever hand will help to put them into a chummy and confidential position.*]

FANNY [*taking his hand in both of hers and looking at it admiringly*]. You have the hand of an artist. [*She looks across Right and sees* FLOSSIE *staring at her, evidently much annoyed, but she pretends not to notice and addresses* FLOSSIE *sweetly.*] My dear, I need a teeny bit of soft music—something drippy and sentimental—that's a good little girl.

FLOSSIE [*half to herself—furious*]. Little girl! [*Nevertheless she turns on the stool and begins something soft and simple—something on the order of the "Traumerei" or the "Spring Song"—keep it well down.*]

FANNY [*still holding* LATTIMORE'S *hand in both of hers*]. Nothing helps a reading so much as a little music. [*Leaning toward him and looking into his eyes with a rather yearning and sentimental manner.*] It helps to bring the two souls into a closer communion—you understand, don't you?

LATTIMORE [*flustered but pleased*]. I—I think so.

[FANNY *looks across at* FLOSSIE *who is attempting to play and look back over her shoulder at them at the same time.*]

FANNY [*to* FLOSSIE]. By the way, dear, no matter what happens don't stop the music—I always seem to do better with my subjects if I have music.

FLOSSIE. I should think it would help.

FANNY. I really prefer a conservatory and a dim light, but this will do. And, darling, [*In her sweetest manner.*] I'll ask you, please, not to speak—you might interfere with some of my results. [*During the preceding scene she has been nursing and fondling* LATTIMORE'S *hand—does not exaggerate but makes it apparently unconscious on her part.*]

LATTIMORE. Do you know—I'm quite impatient—

FANNY [*interrupting him—glancing at palm*]. Look at that life line! Look at it! [*Traces it across his palm and wrist and up to cuff and then lifts cuff and tries to peek up his sleeve to see the end of the line.*] If you keep away from flying machines, you'll live to be a hundred years old.

LATTIMORE [*interested*]. You're quite sure?

FANNY. Never take out any life insurance—you'll lose money. [*Looking at palm and shaking her head in admiration.*] You have a wonderful palm—wonderful. On this side, Napoleon, [*Indicating one side of palm.*] on the other side, Shakespeare.

LATTIMORE [*interested—serious*]. Really?

FANNY. And oh, what a life history!

LATTIMORE. You mean—you can tell what my life has been—by looking at my palm?

FANNY [*ignoring question—gazing fixedly at palm and holding hand firmly, speaking in low but distinct dramatic monotone*]. I see a young man—handsome—rich—the son of a great builder—a builder of railways—

LATTIMORE [*half to himself*]. Railways—Father built railways—It's wonderful!

FANNY. He is courted by society—he has many friends but they do not know him—they never have fathomed the depths of his generous nature, never have understood the aspirations of his secret soul.

LATTIMORE [*impressed*]. By George, you're right.

FANNY. He meets many women—some mercenary—some frivolous—some young and childish and inexperienced [*Let slight agitation on the part of* FLOSSIE *be indicated in the playing.*] not one of them is worthy—he is a man who never will be happy until he finds a soulmate.

LATTIMORE [*intensely interested*]. Yes—what kind?

FANNY. A woman young enough to preserve the charms of her sex—wise enough to understand a man of noble character and mold herself to his ambitions.

LATTIMORE [*solemnly*]. Do you know, I feel that you are speaking the truth.

FANNY. The man I see has met—I—I—[*Hesitates.*] No—I must be wrong.

LATTIMORE. What is it? Go ahead.

FANNY. I see a woman—a taxicab—bright lights—yes, it is a theater.

LATTIMORE. Sh-h! [*Alarmed.*] Do you mean Lottie?

FANNY. Yes, Lottie.

LATTIMORE. Merely a harmless flirtation—I swear it.

FANNY. Then what does this mean? I see the man [*Gazing at palm.*] going aboard a great ship—a German ship—

LATTIMORE [*emphatically*]. I call that marvelous—you know—I'm going to Europe on a German ship, and yet, five minutes ago, you never heard of me. But how did you know it?

[FLOSSIE, *playing at piano, puts in a hard note or two to indicate her disgust with the proceedings.* FANNY *looks across at her a trifle annoyed, and proceeds.*]

FANNY. I see you going across the gang-plank—

LATTIMORE. Yes?

FANNY. You are not alone.

LATTIMORE. No?

FANNY. I see a woman—yes, a woman—I can go no further— [*Releases his hand.*]

LATTIMORE. I say—what's the matter?

FANNY. The strain—the nervous tension—I feel weak—I— [*falls gracefully over into arms of* LATTIMORE *who is startled and alarmed.*]

LATTIMORE. Goodness Gracious, she's fainted!

FLOSSIE [*stops playing and comes across—angry and out of patience*]. Fainted? You don't mean to say she's working that, too?

LATTIMORE [*with his arms around* FANNY—*looking up at* FLOSSIE *in surprise*]. Working what, too?

FLOSSIE [*out of patience*] What excuse did she have for keeling over in a faint?

FANNY [*with her head on his shoulder—her eyes closed*]. I see the man— brave, distinguished, handsome—yes, he is going to Europe—and the woman is still with him—his wife.

LATTIMORE [*agitated—exclamatory*]. Wife!

FLOSSIE [*losing all patience*]. Will you please tell me what all this means?

LATTIMORE. Sh-h! She's a clairvoyant! She's in a trance!

FLOSSIE [*disgusted*]. Trance!

FANNY [*half opening eyes*]. A little stimulant—there on the sideboard.

LATTIMORE [*repeating*]. Quick, on the sideboard.

FLOSSIE [*hurries over to sideboard*]. What does she want? [*Must indicate by her manner that she has no sympathy with the whole performance.*]

LATTIMORE [*with his face very close to hers—tender and sympathetic tone*]. What is it you want?

FANNY [*faintly*]. A tall glass.

LATTIMORE [*repeating order to* FLOSSIE]. A tall glass.

FLOSSIE [*picking up glass—repeating as she does so*]. Tall glass.

FANNY. Ice.

LATTIMORE [*repeating order*]. Ice.

FLOSSIE [*dropping chunks of ice from bowl into glass*]. Ice.

FANNY. Gin.

LATTIMORE. Gin.

FLOSSIE [*picking up decanter of water and pouring in liberally*]. Gin.

FANNY. French Vermouth.

LATTIMORE. French Vermouth.

FLOSSIE. French Vermouth. [*Pouring it in.*] And she came from Chautauqua!

LATTIMORE [*to* FANNY—*tenderly*]. Anything else, my dear?

FLOSSIE [*startled*]. Dear!

FANNY. Italian Vermouth.

LATTIMORE [*repeating*]. Italian Vermouth.

FLOSSIE [*as she grabs another bottle and pours in generously*]. Italian Vermouth. Anything else?

FANNY [*her eyes still closed*]. Mix it.

LATTIMORE [*repeating*]. Mix it, please.

FLOSSIE [*grabbing spoon and stirring drink savagely*]. First I'm an orchestra and now I'm a mixer. [*Taking glass over to her—it should look like a very big drink.*] Auntie dear, [*With sarcastic emphasis.*] here's your Bronx Cocktail.

    [FANNY *sits up promptly—takes it and drinks all of it. Put in plenty of ice, use water for gin and cold tea for the Vermouth and the drink can be managed easily.* FLOSSIE *and* LATTIMORE *gaze at her, fascinated, as she slowly drains the large cocktail.*]

FANNY [*handing glass back to* FLOSSIE]. I feel better already.

FLOSSIE. I should think you would.

    [LATTIMORE *takes glass and arises to take it over to sideboard—he crosses and joins* FLOSSIE *at Left.*]

LATTIMORE [*to* FLOSSIE]. Your aunt is a remarkable woman.

FLOSSIE [*with emphasis*]. She—certainly—is.

FANNY. [*gradually composing herself*]. Mr. Lattimore. [*He gives glass to* FLOSSIE *who puts it on sideboard as he turns.*]

LATTIMORE. Yes.

FANNY. I wonder if I did wrong in telling you—sometimes it is better that one should not know.

LATTIMORE. I'm glad you told me—I feel that it's going to come out just as you predicted.

FANNY. It must.

FLOSSIE [*standing in background—desperate*]. I'm afraid we're detaining Mr. Lattimore.

LATTIMORE. Not at all—I have a taxi across the street.

FANNY. By the way, could you drop me at the Knickerbocker?

FLOSSIE [*aghast*]. Knickerbocker!

FANNY. I'm starving.

LATTIMORE. Why don't you let me take you to the Knickerbocker?

FANNY [*calmly*]. That's just what I was leading up to. [FLOSSIE *re-acts.*] Dearie, will you get my wraps?

FLOSSIE. Me—I—[*Dazed.*]—your wraps? [*Choking.*]

FANNY. Hurry, please! That's a good little girl. [FLOSSIE *exits Center and Right, stunned by the proceedings.* FANNY *goes over and gets his coat.*] I'll help you with your coat.

LATTIMORE. No—really—I—

FANNY. Nonsense! Every man likes to have a woman help him with his coat.

LATTIMORE [*rather flattered*]. I believe you're right.

　　　[FANNY *is getting him into coat as* FLOSSIE *re-enters with* FANNY'S *wrap and hat, which she takes to her in a dazed and mechanical manner.*]

FANNY [*taking them*]. Thank you, dear. [*Putting on hat.*]

FLOSSIE. What shall I say to Father?

FANNY. Tell him not to wait up. When he hears that I'm with Mr. Lattimore, he'll know that I'm safe.

FLOSSIE [*meaningly*]. Yes, he'll know that you're safe.

FANNY. You must turn in right away—it's long past your bedtime.

FLOSSIE [*crushed—weakly*]. Very well.

LATTIMORE [*coming to bid* FLOSSIE *good-night—taking her hand in his*]. Good-night. Do you know I'm completely upset by what your aunt has told me.

FLOSSIE [*with sarcasm*]. About going to Europe?

LATTIMORE. How did she know? I've already bought my ticket. Now she says I'm not going alone.

FLOSSIE [*shaking her head sadly*]. She probably knows.

[*Begin curtain music "All Alone"—same as at rise.* FANNY *is all ready for street.*]

FANNY. Come, Mr. Lattimore, we'll talk it over at the Knickerbocker. [*Takes his arm.*] Good-night, dearie.

[*They exeunt Center and Left as* FLOSSIE *collapses on piano stool.*]

CURTAIN

MISS TYNDALL'S PICTURE[3]

Scene: The parlor of the Hazelden house, near the north shore. MRS. HAZELDEN *is seated by the window, reading a magazine. The door-bell rings.* MRS. HAZELDEN *lowers the magazine and listens. A mumble of voices outside. The housemaid comes to the door, followed by* MR. CUSTER, *who offers to* MRS. HAZELDEN *a slight and embarrassed bow.* MRS. HAZELDEN *rises.*

THE HOUSEMAID. He wants to see about the house.

MRS. HAZELDEN. Oh!

MR. CUSTER. Yes—ah—they told me at the agency that you wished to rent your house for the summer. I—my name is Custer.

MRS. H. Yes? Won't you be seated?

[*They sit*]

MR. C. My uncle, Judge Custer, of Custer & Bland, you——?

MRS. H. Oh, yes, indeed, quite often.

MR. C. I—ah—my brother and his wife wish to spend the summer here. My brother is a professor in Runyon College. We thought it would be pleasant to take a house for the summer—something pretty well away from town and near the lake. I'm tired of hotel life, and, besides, I belong to the Edgwater Golf Club and could put him up there. I thought it would be——

MRS. H. I'm sure it would be. You would like this neighborhood, too. It's so near the lake—you can see it from the upper windows—and it's entirely away from the traffic and the smoke.

MR. C. Yes'm.

MRS. H. Really, you know, I've never had a house that I liked any better. I'd be very well satisfied to remain here all summer, but Mr. Hazelden has a cottage on Lake Tomowoc, and he is very fond of boating and fishing, so he wants to be there all summer.

MR. C. Yes'm.

MRS. H. I suppose you want to look through the rooms. [*She rises.*] There are no children?

MR. C. [*rising*]. No, only the three of us. [*Looking around.*] This is a pretty room, isn't it? I like the high ceilings. Hello! [*Walks over and looks at a mounted photograph on the mantel.*] That's Miss Tyndall, isn't it?

MRS. H. [*cordially*]. Why, do *you* know Fannie Tyndall?

MR. C. I met her a few times on the south side—with Jim Wescott.

MRS. H. [*less cordially*]. Oh!

MR. C. You know they were——

MRS. H. Yes, I know all about it. I suppose you heard why it was broken off.

MR. C. [*calmly*]. I heard something of the details—yes.

MRS. H. *His* side of the story, I presume.

MR. C. Well—yes. Jim didn't tell me himself, but I think it came from him.

MRS. H. Do you know Mr. Wescott quite well?

MR. C. Yes, I might say that I know him intimately. We went to school together.

MRS. H. Indeed! Well, what's wrong with him, anyway?

MR. C. [*surprised*]. Wrong with Jim? It never occurred to me that there was *anything* wrong with him.

MRS. H. Isn't he—*odd?*

MR. C. I don't think so. Of course, he's a studious fellow, and isn't quite as—effervescent, you might say, as most of the other fellows in his set, but he's all right.

MRS. H. Well, he was out here with Fannie two or three times last summer—they came out to the golf club—and, do you know, the man actually embarrassed me. Whenever you spoke to him he had such a cold, indifferent way of smiling back at you and saying "Oh, indeed!" and then he would wait for you to say something more. He impressed me as being rather—well, I should say—conceited. He always seemed inclined to patronise women and treat them as creatures of minor intelligence, and yet he never said anything bright or clever himself to back up this calm assumption of superiority. I was perfectly delighted when I learned that the engagement had been broken off. Fannie is such a lovely girl.

MR. C. She's a very *pretty* girl, certainly.

MRS. H. Yes, and she's just as nice as she is pretty. You know the Tyndalls used to be neighbors of ours on the south side, and I came to know them ever so well. I always said that Fannie was the *dearest* thing that ever lived.

MR. C. Isn't she inclined to be a little bit—lively?

MRS. H. *Oh—h! No,* indeed! Why, *really!* In what *way?*

MR. C. Well, perhaps I shouldn't have used that word. I'll admit I don't know her very well. She's charming enough, I suppose, but I've understood that Jim broke the engagement because she received too many attentions from other men.

MRS. H. [*with flashing eye*]. *Jim* broke the engagement! Jim, *indeed!* Why, Mr.—ah——

MR. C. Custer.

MRS. H. Did he tell you, Mr. Custer, that *he* broke the engagement?

MR. C. No, he hasn't said much about it to anyone, but that's what I understood.

MRS. H. Well, there isn't a word of it so. I heard the straight of it from one of Fannie's chums. It seems that he started in to lecture Fannie about dancing with two or three men he didn't like, and she simply refused to be lectured, and ended the engagement then and there. I think that's what any plucky girl should have done, under the circumstances.

MR. C. Isn't it possible that Jim knew more about these young men than Miss Tyndall did?

MRS. H. Oh, pshaw!

MR. C. Oh, well, it's all over now, and I honestly think it was better for all concerned. From what I learned of Miss Tyndall, I don't think she would have made the right kind of a wife for him.

MRS. H. [*slightly ruffled*]. Well—the right kind—what do you mean by that? I suppose she wasn't *good* enough for Mr. Wescott.

MR. C. Well, I think she was too frivolous. I don't consider frivolity a crime, but in some cases it ought to be a hindrance to matrimony. She was a charming girl, in many respects, but [*laughing*] it always seemed to me that she had a sort of—matinee education, as you might say. I don't think she aspired to anything higher than chocolate creams.

MRS. H. Great heavens, Mr. Custer, she's a *girl!* She's hardly nineteen. If she had been a studious thing with spectacles, and her hair all plastered down, do you suppose Mr. Wescott would have ever given her a second look? No, indeed! I don't mean any disrespect to your friend, but, really, I think it would have been a positive calamity for Fannie to have married that man. I don't understand why she was attracted to him in the first place. He isn't handsome, is he?

Mr. C. No, he isn't particularly handsome, but he isn't repulsive, either. He has the usual number of features. He's a brainy chap.

Mrs. H. Oh, you'd be sure to take the man's part. [*Bell rings.*] I wonder if that's some one else to see the house. We've been standing here——

Mr. C. Yes, I've been listening to you slander poor Jim.

Mrs. H. Well, really, Mr. Custer, if you knew Fannie as I do, you'd be out of patience, too, with any man who didn't appreciate her. [*Housemaid tiptoes in and hands a large, square envelope to* Mrs. Hazelden.] It was the postman. Thank you, Mary. Mr. Wescott may be popular among the men, but—ooh! he's such an iceberg. [*Drawing an inner envelope from the large one.*] Fannie never would have been happy with such an unsympathetic—Mercy me! [*Staring at the card folder which she has taken from the envelope.*]

Mr. C. What—er—excuse me.

Mrs. H. Oh—h—h! If that—well! What do you think?

Mr. C. I don't know, I'm sure.

Mrs. H. [*shaking the card folder at him*]. Do you know what this is?

Mr. C. I haven't the slightest idea.

Mrs. H. A wedding-invitation.

Mr. C. Theirs?

Mrs. H. Theirs. [*Reading.*] "To the marriage of their daughter Fannie to Mr. James Duncan Wescott"—and she said she'd never— [*compresses her lips*].

Mr. C. Evidently there has been a reconciliation.

Mrs. H. *Evidently.* What could that child have been thinking of? [*Sighs.*] Poor Fannie!

Mr. C. Poor—I beg your pardon.

Mrs. H. Isn't that just like a girl?

Mr. C. I suppose so. I didn't think Jim would, though.

Mrs. H. Oh, pshaw! *Jim!* Jim, indeed! Mr. Custer, women are deceived once in a while, but every man is a perfect greenhorn. Come on. I want to show you the dining-room.

CURTAIN

THE SULTAN
OF SULU[4]

*An Original Satire
in Two Acts*

THE SCENES

ACT I.—*An open place in front of the Sultan's palace, city of Sulu or
Jolo, Philippine Islands,* 1899.

ACT II.—*The hanging garden of the Sultan's palace. One day is supposed to elapse between the two acts.*

ACT I

Scene: An open place in Sulu.[5] *The* SULTAN'S *palace, with Sulu flag
flying in front of it, at stage right. Suggestion of tropical vegetation at stage
left. Beyond, the open sea.*

*Time: Early morning. During the opening chorus, the stage gradually be-
comes lighted with the glow of sunrise. Native men and women on stage,
kneeling.*

OPENING CHORUS

The darkness breaks! The day's begun!
Hail to the Sultan and the sun!
One cannot rank above the other;
The sun is but the Sultan's brother.
Behold the sun! Majestic sun!
He is the Sultan's brother.

Well may he ride in crimson pride,
He is the the Sultan's brother.

With regal sway, the King of day;
And this the reason, we should say,
He is the Sultan's brother!

[*Six of the wives of* KI-RAM *enter, romping. They are:* MAURICIA,
SELINA, NATIVIDAD, PEPITA, NATALIA, RAMONA—*young and attractive
things.*]

THE SIX WIVES

In early morn, at breakfast-time
　It is our wifely duty
To greet the Sultan with a rhyme
　And to cheer him with our beauty.
So we come, a sweet sextette
　Of most unwilling brides,
To tap upon the castanet
　And do our Spanish glides.

[*Dance*]

In early morn, at breakfast-time,
It is our wifely duty
To tap upon the castanet
And do our Spanish glides.

ALL
Behold the sun, etc.

[*At conclusion of the chorus, the natives salaam to wives and retire as* HADJI *comes from the palace, pausing on the upper step to salute the cluster of wives.*]

HADJI. [*Mysterious and sotto voce.*] Oh! oh! Ladies, not so much noise! *Not* so much noise?! Our beloved ruler is now taking his beauty sleep in the inner chamber. Are all of the Sultan's loving and obedient wives present at the morning round-up?

WIVES. [*Ad lib.*] Here! Yes. Present, etc. [HADJI *gesticulates for silence. Wives group about in sitting posture.*]

HADJI. In order to make sure, we shall proceed with the usual roll-call. [*He consults a book containing the official list of wives.*] Mauricia! Mauricia!

MAURICIA. Here!

HADJI. Selina.

SELINA. Here!

HADJI. Daily catechism. Do you love your husband?

SELINA. What is the answer?

HADJI. The answer is, "I adore him."

SELINA. All right; put it down.

HADJI. Such devotion is touching. [*Calling.*] Natividad!

NATIVIDAD. Here!

HADJI. [*Calling.*] Pepita—Pepita—Pete! Where is the Gibson girl of the Philippine Islands?

PEPITA. Here!

HADJI. Pepita—a question from the book. Suppose the Sultan should die—would you remarry?

PEPITA. What is the answer?

HADJI. The answer is, "Never!" Shall I so record it?

PEPITA. *Never!*

HADJI. Oh, how she loves that man! [*From the book again.*] Natalia— naughty little Natty!

NATALIA. Here!

HADJI. Ramona! Ramona! Blithesome creature, where art thou?

RAMONA. Here!

HADJI. Ramona—a question from the book. Do you—

RAMONA. [*Interrupting.*] Yes.

HADJI. I am delighted to hear it. [*Calling.*] Chiquita! Chiquita! Has any one seen the sunny soubrette of the southern seas? [*Cadenza heard outside.*] Aha! Gallivanting as usual. [CHIQUITA *enters and salaams.*]

HADJI. Now that our entire domestic household has assembled, I wish to make an announcement. It has come to the ears of our august ruler that your uncle, the Datto Mandi of Parang, is encamped near the city. [*The wives arise, with various exclamations of surprise. The news appears to please them.* HADJI *invokes silence.*] He has come to recapture you, but never fear. We, editorially speaking, will protect you.

CHIQUITA. But we *wish* to be recaptured. We *want* to go back to dear old Parang.

HADJI. [*Injured tone.*] Oh, Chiquita! Thus do you repay Ki-Ram's single-hearted devotion?

CHIQUITA. [*Confronting* HADJI.] Single-hearted fiddle-sticks! How can a man have a single-hearted devotion for eight different women? We were brought here as captives. When it came to a choice between an ignominious death and Ki-Ram, we hesitated for a while and then chose Ki-Ram.

HADJI. Such impertinence! I shall inform his Majesty. [HADJI *goes into palace.*]

· · ·

[*Boom of cannon heard in the distance, followed by rattle of musketry. Wives retreat to rear of palace in frightened confusion as* HADJI *comes out and stands on the steps.* DINGBAT, *a native guard, with drawn sword of the kris shape, rushes on from left.*]

DINGBAT. What do you think, sir?

HADJI. I'm a private secretary. I'm not permitted to think.

DINGBAT. A large white ship has come into the harbor.

HADJI. A ship—in the harbor?

DINGBAT. It is crowded with soldiers.

HADJI. Soldiers?

DINGBAT. The flag is one of red, white, and blue, spangled with stars.

HADJI. Never heard of such a flag.

DINGBAT. What's more, sir, they're coming ashore.

HADJI. Soldiers on this side. [*Indicating left.*] Mandi on this. [*Indicating right.*] How glad I am that I am merely a private secretary! [*Distant boom of cannon.*] Aha! That seems friendly. They are firing a salute.

[*Shell, with fuse sputtering, rolls on from left and disappears behind palace. Sound of explosion.* HADJI *disappears headlong into the palace, followed by* DINGBAT. *The broken volleys of musketry become louder and louder. In the incidental music there is a suggestion of "A Hot Time in the Old Town." Sharp yells are heard off left, and then a body of United States Volunteers in khaki and marines in white pours on the stage in pell-mell confusion.* LIEUTENANT WILLIAM HARDY, *in a white uniform of the Regulars, comes down through the center of the charging squad. He has his sword drawn.*]

LIEUTENANT HARDY AND CHORUS OF SOLDIERS

"HIKE"

We haven't the appearance, goodness knows,
    Of plain commercial men;
From a hasty glance, you might suppose
    We are fractious now and then.
But though we come in warlike guise
    And battle-front arrayed,
It's all a business enterprise;
    We're seeking foreign trade.

REFRAIN

We're as mild as any turtle-dove
    When we see the foe a-coming,
Our thoughts are set on human love
    When we hear the bullets humming.
We teach the native population

What the golden rule is like,
And we scatter public education
   On ev'ry blasted hike!

We want to assimilate, if we can,
   Our brother who is brown;
We love our dusky fellow-man
   And we hate to hunt him down.
So, when we perforate his frame,
   We want him to be good.
We shoot at him to make him tame,
   If he but understood.

REFRAIN
We're as mild, etc.

[*During the second verse, the wives and native women return timidly, drawn by curiosity. They gather about the soldiers and study them carefully, more or less frightened but not altogether displeased.* LIEUTENANT HARDY *addresses the company of natives.*]

HARDY. I am here to demand an audience with the Sultan.

CHIQUITA. [*Stepping forth.*] *Indeed!* And who are you that presumes to demand an audience with the Bright Morning Light of the Orient?

HARDY. Why, how do you do? I am Lieutenant Hardy—a modest representative of the U.S.A. [HADJI *cautiously emerges from the palace.*]

HADJI. [*Overhearing.*] The U.S.A.? Where is *that* on the map?

HARDY. Just now it is spread all over the map. Perhaps you don't know it, but we are the owners of this island. We paid twenty millions of dollars for you. [*All whistle.*] At first it did seem a large price, but now that I have seen you [*indicating wives*] I am convinced it was a bargain. [CHIQUITA *has lighted a native cigarette and is serenely puffing it.* LIEUTENANT HARDY *addresses her chidingly.*] You don't mean to say you smoke?

CHIQUITA. Don't the ladies of your country smoke?

HARDY. The *ladies* do—the women *don't*. [HADJI *observes the confidential chat between the officer and the principal wife, and he is disturbed in spirit.*]

HADJI. Lieutenant! [*More loudly.*] *Lieutenant!* Did you come ashore to talk business or to break into the harem?

HARDY. Beg pardon. [*Stepping back into a stiff, military attitude.*] Does the Sultan surrender?

HADJI. He says he will *die* first.

HARDY. *That* can be arranged. We are here as emissaries of peace, but we never object to a skirmish—eh, boys? [*The soldiers respond with a warlike shout, which frightens the native women. The lieutenant reassures them.*]

HARDY. Young ladies, don't be alarmed. We may slaughter all the others, but *you* will be spared. Meet us here after the battle.

HADJI. The *battle!* [*He falls against* DINGBAT. *Then he dejectedly moves over to centre and addresses the wives.*] Mesdames Ki-Ram, his Majesty is about to dictate to me his last will and testament. In one hour you will be widows—all of you. You had better begin picking out your black goods.

CHIQUITA. And I never *did* look well in black. [*Sound of gong heard in palace.*]

HADJI. Excuse me. [*Exit into palace after* DINGBAT.]

[LIEUTENANT HARDY *resumes his confidential relations with wives and native women.*]

HARDY. Young ladies, you never saw a real Yankee girl, did you?

CHIQUITA. What is she like?

HARDY. The American girl? The most remarkable combination of innocence and knowledge, of modesty and boldness, of school-girl simplicity and married-woman diplomacy.

[*Native boys, running on from left, call attention to the approach of the American party. All the natives bow with their arms extended in a deferential salaam. Soldiers come to "present arms."*]

WELCOME CHORUS

Welcome, Americanos!
Welcome, in Oriental style!
Welcome, Americanos!
Welcome, in Oriental style!
Sulu bids you welcome!
Sulu bids you welcome!

[COLONEL JEFFERSON BUDD, HENRIETTA BUDD, WAKEFUL M. JONES, PAMELA FRANCES JACKSON, *and the four school-ma'ams enter, with smiling acknowledgments of the vocal greeting.* HENRIETTA *is a very attractive girl, in a stunning summer gown.* COLONEL BUDD *is large and imposing, somewhat overburdened with conscious dignity. He wears a colonel's service uniform.* WAKEFUL M. JONES *is a brisk young man in flannels.* MISS JACKSON *is a sedate and rigid spinster. Her attire indicates that she has made a partial compromise with the dress-reformers, but has a lingering fondness for stylish garments that fit. After the entrance,* HENRIETTA *advances from the group and breaks into the anticipated song.*]

HENRIETTA BUDD AND CHORUS

"PALM BRANCHES WAVING"

Palm branches waving
A welcome to the queen of the day,
While from above the birds seem to join in the lay.
Long have I sought thee,
O charming little tropical isle!
Here let me dwell—let me dwell awhile.
Softly comes the southern breeze—
Land so bright, of pure delight,
Oh, how I have longed for thee!

HENRIETTA AND CHORUS

'Neath the shade of spreading trees—
Ah, Sulu, fair Sulu,
'Tis the land I have longed to see.

HENRIETTA

Long have I sought thee,
O charming little tropical isle!

Here let me dwell—let me dwell awhile.

HARDY. [*Addressing company of natives.*] Ladies and gentlemen, Colonel Budd! [*Pointing out that august personage.*] His daughter, Miss Henrietta Budd! [*Jones calls attention to Miss Jackson.*]

JONES. And this is Miss Pamela Frances Jackson, a lady who knows as much as any man—and then some more.

PAMELA. [*Inquiringly.*] The Sultan?

CHIQUITA. He is within—making his will.

HENRIETTA. His will?

CHIQUITA. He expects to be captured. They are going to do something dreadful to him.

BUDD. [*Impressively.*] We are going to assimilate him.

CHIQUITA. Yes, that's why he's making his will.

JONES. If he really expects to die, now is the time to talk life insurance. [*He starts towards the palace, whereupon the alarmed wives crowd in front of him.*] No! And why not?

CHIQUITA. For entering that majestic presence unheralded, the punishment is death.

ALL. Death!

[*Jones smiles disdainfully and buttons his coat.*]

JONES. Watch me! [*He motions them to right and left and hurriedly enters palace. The natives are amazed at his audacity.*]

CHIQUITA. Poor man!

HARDY. Don't worry about Mr. Jones. He's from Chicago. [*Looking about, sees soldiers warming up to wives.*] I'm afraid my men are in danger. [*MISS JACKSON comes to the rescue.*]

PAMELA. Young ladies! You are rather young to be trifling with soldiers.

CHIQUITA. *Not* so young. We are married—*all* of us.

PAMELA. What, married women flirting! It is an uncivilized country. Gather about me. [*They come to her and she advises them in a patronizing manner.*] When you have become Americanized you won't follow soldiers. You'll compel *them* to follow *you*. [*The expeditious* JONES *comes from the palace, gleefully waving a paper.*]

JONES. I have insured his life for fifty thousand pesos. I convinced him that he would be a dead man in less than fifteen minutes.

BUDD. [*Preparing for an effort.*] Soldiers of the republic!

ALL. Hear! Hear!

BUDD. For the first time you are about to stand in the presence of royalty. Stiffen yourselves for the ordeal, and remember, no deference, for each of you is a sovereign in his own right.

CHORUS TO SULTAN

Sultan! Mighty Sultan!
　　Thrice glorious in defeat.
Sultan! Wretched Sultan!
　　This great affliction meet.

[*There is a slow thrumming of Oriental music, during which* HADJI *appears on the steps of the palace and makes a mournful announcement.*]

HADJI. Ladies and gentlemen, his Majesty is coming prepared to die according to contract. He has only one request to make. It is that you do not ask him to die a cheap and common death.

[*The natives prostrate themselves.* KI-RAM *comes from palace, accompanied by his two Nubian slaves,* DIDYMOS *and* RASTOS. *The Sultan is attired in funereal black and is the picture of woe.*]

KI-RAM

[*Recitative.*] What do you think? I've got to die;
My time has come to say good-bye
To my upholstered Sulu throne
And all that I can call my own.

[*He comes down and dolefully sings what he believes to be his swan-song.*]

KI-RAM AND CHORUS

"THE SMILING ISLE"

We have no daily papers
To tell of Newport capers,
　　No proud four hundred to look down on ordinary folk;
We have no stocks and tickers,
No Scotch imported liquors,
　　To start us on the downward path and some day land us broke;
We've not a single college
Where youth may get a knowledge
　　Of chorus girls and cigarettes, of poker and the like;
No janitors to sass us,
No bell-boys to harass us,
　　And we've never known the pleasure of a labor-union strike.

REFRAIN

And that is why, you'll understand,
I love my own, my native land,

My little isle of Sulu.
  [*Chorus*.] Sulu!
Smiling isle of Sulu!
  [*Chorus*.] Sulu!
I'm not ready to say good-bye,
I'm mighty sorry that I have to die.

We have no prize-fight sluggers,
No vaudevillian muggers,
  No one of us has ever shot the chutes or looped the loop;
No cable-cars or trolleys,
No life-insurance jollies,
  No bank cashiers to take our money 'ere they fly the coop;
No bookies and no races,
No seaside summer places;
  No Bertha Clays and Duchesses to make the females cry;
We have no dairy lunches,
Where they eat their food in bunches,
  And we don't insult our stomachs with the thing they call mince-pie.

REFRAIN

And that is why, etc.

We have no short-haired ladies
Who are always raising Hades
  With their finical and funny old reformatory fads;
No ten-cent publications,
Sold at all the railway stations,
  With a page or two of reading and a hundred stuffed with "ads";
We never chew in Sulu
Any pepsin gum or tofu—
  In fact, we're not such savages as some of you might think;
And during intermission
We always crave permission
  Before we walk on other people just to get a drink.

REFRAIN

And that is why, etc.

We have no politicians,
And under no conditions
  Do we tolerate the fraud who cures by laying on of hands;
We have no elocutionists,
No social revolutionists,
  No amateur dramatics, and no upright baby grands;
We don't play golf and tennis,
And we never know the menace

Of a passing fad or fancy that may turn the nation's head;
I'm proud of my dominion
When I voice the bold opinion
That we'll never know the tortures of a patent folding-bed.

REFRAIN

And that is why, etc.

[*The song being ended,* KI-RAM *stands apart in an attitude supposed to signify heroic resignation.*]

KI-RAM. Now, then, for a farewell speech that will look well in the school histories. I die—I die that Sulu may—

BUDD. Why, your Majesty, you are not expected to die.

KI-RAM. No? [*With an expression of glad surprise.*]

BUDD. We are your friends. We have come to take possession of the island and teach your benighted people the advantages of free government. We hold that all government derives its just powers from the consent of the governed.

ALL. Hear! Hear!

BUDD. Now, the question is, do you consent to this benevolent plan?

[*The soldiers bring their guns to "charge bayonets."* KI-RAM *looks right and left and finds himself walled in by threatening weapons. He hesitates.*]

KI-RAM. Are all the guns loaded?

BUDD. They *are*.

KI-RAM. I consent.

BUDD. Good! The education of your neglected race will begin at once under the direction of these young ladies.

[*He calls attention to the school-ma'ams standing in the background. When* KI-RAM *sees the luscious quartette he is visibly impressed.*]

KI-RAM. Young ladies? Oh-h-h! Who are they?

BUDD. Four of our most interesting products—four highly culti-vated, dignified, demure New England school-ma'ams. [*The school-ma'ams advance, stepping rather high, and introduce themselves.*]

THE FOUR SCHOOL-MA'AMS

"FROM THE LAND OF THE CEREBELLUM"

From the land of the cerebellum,
  Where clubs abound and books are plenty,
Where people know before you tell 'em
  As much as any one knows,
We come to teach this new possession
  All that's known to a girl of twenty;

And such a girl, it's our impression,
  Knows more than you might suppose.

You may judge by our proper bearing
  That we're accomplished, proud, and haughty,
Those simple little gowns we're wearing
  Proclaim our innocent style.
You must not think because we're frisky
  That we're *re*-ally bold or naughty;
We never flirt when it seems risky,
  Except for a little while.

KI-RAM. [*Gazing at them with unconcealed admiration.*] Are they going to open school here?

BUDD. This very day.

KI-RAM. I'll be there early with my face washed and a red apple for my dear teacher.

BUDD. We believe that in three weeks or a month we will have you as cultured as the people of my native State.

KI-RAM. And what State is that?

BUDD. The State of Arkansaw! [*On the word "Arkansaw," the Colonel removes his cap reverently, and the soldiers solemnly lift their hats.*]

KI-RAM. Arkansaw? Never heard of it.

BUDD. What! Never heard of Arkansaw? Then permit me to tell you that in Arkansaw they never heard of Sulu. Hereafter, you understand, you are not a Sultan, but a Governor.

KI-RAM. A Governor! Is that a promotion?

BUDD. Most assuredly! A Governor is the noblest work of the campaign committee. Ladies and gentlemen—

ALL. Hear! Hear!

BUDD. [*In oratorical fashion.*] I take pleasure in introducing to you that valiant leader, that incorruptible statesman, that splendid type of perfect manhood, our fellow-citizen, the Honorable Ki-Ram, next Governor of Sulu. [*Cheers.*] He will be inaugurated here in one hour. I request you to prepare for the festivities.

[*Another cheer and all exeunt except* KI-RAM, BUDD, *and* CHIQUITA. *The principal wife seems disposed to loiter near the Colonel and admire him.*]

KI-RAM. Chiquita, run along; don't annoy the Colonel. [CHIQUITA *goes into the palace, but before doing so she gives the Colonel a lingering glance, which seems to warm him considerably.* KI-RAM *grasps* BUDD *by the hand.*] Colonel, I want to thank you. It was great! [*Attempting to imitate* BUDD'S *oratorical flight.*] That some-kind-of-a-leader, that

umptatallable statesman, that—that—Say, where did you learn that
kind of talk?

BUDD. You mustn't mind that. I'm in politics. I say that about every
one.

[KI-RAM *blows whistle, which he carries suspended on a cord about
his neck.* DIDYMOS *and* RASTOS *bring stools and then exeunt, dancing in
unison. As they go into the palace,* KI-RAM *and* BUDD *seat themselves.
At the same moment* GALULA *comes from behind the palace carrying a
large, long-handled fan of Oriental pattern. She is an elderly female, all
of whose native charms have long since disappeared. Think of the
homeliest woman you ever saw; multiply her unloveliness by two, and the
reader will have* GALULA. *She timorously approaches* KI-RAM *and begins
fanning him from behind.*]

KI-RAM. Colonel, you'll excuse me for mentioning it, but you are one
of the handsomest men I ever saw. I—I— [*He pauses with an expression of alarm growing on his countenance.* GALULA *continues to fan
him.*] Colonel, do you feel a draft? [*Turns and sees* GALULA.]
Oh-h-h! Galula, I know you love me, and I don't blame you, but
you want to remember one thing, "Absence makes the heart grow
fonder." [*She exits, looking back at him yearningly.*] That's one of
them.

BUDD. One of *what?*

KI-RAM. One of my wives. She is the charter member. I've tried to
lose her, but I can't. The other seven were those society buds that
you saw here a moment ago. I captured them about a month ago.

BUDD. You *captured* them? [*Eagerly.*] Then the beautiful creature
with whom I was chatting—she did not marry you voluntarily?

KI-RAM. Galula is the only one that ever married me voluntarily.
The others I— [*Gesture of reaching out, taking hold of something, and
pulling it in.*] Did you ever hear of the Datto Mandi of Parang?

BUDD. What is it—some new kind of breakfast food?

KI-RAM. Certainly *not.* The Datto Mandi is a warlike gentleman who
holds forth on the other side of the island. About a month ago I
needed a new batch of wives. I turned the former assortment out
to pasture, then I went over to Parang and stampeded seven of
Mandi's lovely nieces. This annoyed Mandi.

BUDD. Naturally.

KI-RAM. He is now encamped outside the wall, waiting for a chance
to recapture *them,* and incidentally carve *me* into small, red cubes.
Now, then, if I'm to be Governor here, I shall expect you to protect *me* against *him.* [COLONEL BUDD *arises and bursts into oratory.*]

BUDD. Most assuredly! Wherever our flag floats there human rights shall be protected, though the heavens fall. Oh—

KI-RAM. Shake out the parachute, Colonel! [*Arises.*] Come down! I understand all that. And just to prove that I appreciate what you have done for me, and what I expect you to do for me in the future, do you know what I am going to do?

BUDD. I can't imagine.

KI-RAM. Well, I'm going to set 'em up.

BUDD. Set 'em up?

KI-RAM. I'm going to set 'em up to the wives. [*Makes a profound bow.*] Have a wife on me. Take your pick of the eight. Do me a favor. Choose the one with the fan.

BUDD. What, your Majesty! Take another man's wife? Barbarous! Barbarous!

KI-RAM. Barbarous, perhaps, but it frequently happens.

BUDD. Besides, I—I—[*hesitating*]—may as well tell you that I have proposed marriage to Miss Jackson, the Judge Advocate. The Judge has the matter under advisement.

KI-RAM. That's all right—marry both of them.

BUDD. My *dear* sir, do you realize that under our laws a man is entitled to only one wife?

KI-RAM. How *could* a man struggle along with only one wife! Suffering Allah! I wonder if they'll try to work that rule on me? [KI-RAM *starts to enter the palace, when* JONES, *entering at right from rear of palace, accosts him sharply.*]

JONES. Governor!

KI-RAM. Well?

JONES. Are you ready for the reception?

KI-RAM. What is a reception? Something civilized?

JONES. [*Taking him by the arm.*] A reception, Governor, is a function at which a large number of people assemble in order to be exclusive. The entire population files past. You shake hands with each person, and say, "I am happy to meet you."

KI-RAM. That's what I say, but *am* I happy?

JONES. Probably not.

BUDD. However, you must pretend to enjoy these little tortures.

JONES. At least, until the other people are out of hearing distance.

KI-RAM, BUDD, AND JONES

"OH, WHAT A BUMP!"

JONES

At a musicale, a five-o'clock,

Or social jamboree,
'Tis there the swagger people flock
  For a bite and a sip of tea;
    And this is what you hear:
"It's been a charming afternoon";
    "Delighted, don't you know";
"Sorry I have to leave so soon,
    But really I must go."
        But after she's away
        In her coupé,
      What *does* this self-same woman say?

KI-RAM AND BUDD

Well, what *does* she say?

JONES

"That was the tackiest time I've had
    In twenty years or more.
The crowd was jay and the tea was bad
    And the whole affair a bore."

TRIO

Oh, what a bump! Alackaday!
    'Twould darken her whole career,
Could the hostess know what people say
    When she's not there to hear.

BUDD

The bashful youth who's rather slow
    When he has made a call,
Receives a message, soft and low,
    At parting in the hall.
      And this is what she says:
"Now come as often as you can.
    I love these little larks.
It's seldom that I meet a man
    Who makes such bright remarks."
        But when he tears away
        From this fairy fay,
      What does the artful maiden say?

KI-RAM AND JONES

Well, what *does* she say?

BUDD

"Of all the dummies I ever met
  He's the limit, and no mistake.
As a touch-me-not and mamma's pet,
  That Johnnie takes the cake."

TRIO

Oh, what a bump! Alackaday!
  'Twould darken his whole career,
Could Harold know what Mabel says
  When he's not there to hear.

KI-RAM

Did you ever feel like saying—
  When some precocious brat
Recites a piece called "Mary's Lamb"
  Or "Little Pussy Cat"?
    And this is what you say:
"What marvellous talent she does possess
  For one of her tender age.
I think she'd make a great success
  If you'd put her on the stage."
    But later in the day,
    When you get away,
    What do you then proceed to say?

BUDD AND JONES

Well, what *do* you say?

KI-RAM

"If that awful kid belonged to me,
  I'll tell you what I'd do—
I'd keep *it* under lock and key
  And spank it black and blue."

TRIO

Oh, what a bump! Alackaday!
  'Twould darken the child's career,
Could parents know what callers say
  When they're not there to hear.

JONES

Perhaps the most terrific bump

Is found in politics.
The campaign speaker on the stump
  Is up to all the tricks,
    And this is what he says:
"Oh, fellow-citizens, I see
  Before me here today
The sovereign voters, pure and free,
  Whom I shall e'er obey."
    But when he's won the race,
    Gets a nice, fat place,
    What does the people's servant say?

KI-RAM AND BUDD

Well, what *does* he say?

JONES

"Well, maybe I didn't con those yaps
  With that patriotic bluff.
Now that I've landed one of the snaps,
  I'm going to get the stuff."

TRIO

Oh, what a bump! Alackaday!
  'Twould darken their whole career
Could voters know what bosses say
  When they're not there to hear.

KI-RAM

Some ladies of the smartest set
  Met on the boulevard.
They shook hands most effusively
  And kissed each other *hard*.
    And this is what one said:
"Why, Alice, dear, what a zippy gown!
  The fit is perfectly fine;
And that dream of a hat! How swell you look!
  Good-bye, dear. Drop me a line."
    But when she said good-day,
    And wafted on her way,
    What did this gushing lady say?

BUDD AND JONES

Well, what *did* she say?

Ki-Ram

"Did you ever see such a fright of a dress?
    It was wrinkled all *up* the back,
And those feathers, too—she's had them dyed;
    They were on her last winter's hat.
        [*Spoken.*] The *upstart!*"

Trio

Oh, what a bump! Alackaday!
    'Twould darken her whole career,
Could a woman know what her friends all say
    When she's not there to hear.

[*A dance concludes this number, and the three exeunt into the palace as* Henrietta Budd *enters, followed by* Lieutenant Hardy, *who appears to be expostulating and pleading.*]

Henrietta. Mr. Hardy, it cannot be. My father objects to you in language which I dare not repeat.

Hardy. He objects to *me*? [*Indignant and surprised.*]

Henrietta. He told me only yesterday that I must *never* marry you.

Hardy. But I had not proposed to you yesterday.

Henrietta. True, but I knew what was coming. I have been engaged many times, and I notice that the man who intends to propose acts very strangely for a day or two in advance. So I went to father and said: "Lieutenant Hardy is about to propose to me."

Hardy. Whereupon he said—

Henrietta. "My child, never marry a Regular. There are no heroes except in the Volunteer service. The Volunteer goes home and is elected to Congress. The Regular keeps right ahead, a plain fighting man."

Hardy. Plain fighting man, perhaps, but even a plain fighting man may love, and I love you, Henrietta—I love you as only a West-Pointer *can* love the one girl in sight. [*Kisses her impetuously.*]

Henrietta. [*Retreating the usual number of steps.*] Lieutenant! Is it proper?

Hardy. It is customary among engaged couples. And we *are* engaged, aren't we?

Henrietta. Yes, I suppose we are—in a sort of a way.

HENRIETTA AND HARDY

"ENGAGED IN A SORT OF A WAY"

HARDY

Sweetheart, doubt my love no more;
　　Believe me, I'm sincere.
I love no other on this tropic shore;
　　You're the only girl that's here.

HENRIETTA

Lieutenant, I cannot withstand
　　A man who pleads like you;
So here's the promise of my heart and hand,
　　At least for a month or two.

HARDY

We are engaged in a sort of a way.

HENRIETTA

And we will truly love each other.

HARDY

Though it may chance there will soon come a day
When I can learn to love another.

HENRIETTA

I take this man on probation.

HARDY

And I will take her just the same.

BOTH

For it is simply a slight variation
Of the same little flirting game.

HENRIETTA

Marriage is a doubtful state.
　　I think of it with dread.
Still, an engagement need not indicate
　　That we really mean to wed.

HARDY

Henrietta, you are quite correct.
  I have been engaged before.
Frankly, I'll tell you, also, I expect
  That *I'll* be engaged some more.

HARDY

We are engaged, etc.

[*The waltz refrain continues.* HARDY *and* HENRIETTA *waltz away as* KI-RAM *comes out of the palace, followed by* PAMELA FRANCES JACKSON. KI-RAM *is greatly interested in the waltz. As* HARDY *and* HENRIETTA *disappear he turns and puts his arm around* PAMELA, *and they execute a waltz characterized by activity rather than poetry of motion. At the conclusion,* KI-RAM *is somewhat "blown" but altogether delighted.*]

KI-RAM. Oh, my! Pamela, that is simply hilarious. What do you call that?

PAMELA. It is called a waltz, your Majesty.

KI-RAM. Well, it may not be *proper*, but it *is* enjoyable.

PAMELA. It is quite proper, I assure you.

KI-RAM. Is it? I had no idea that anything as pleasant as that could be proper. [*He wraps his arm about her.*] Pamela, I suspect that we are going to be very jolly playmates.

PAMELA. Your Majesty! [*She is horrified at his presumption.*]

KI-RAM. What is it?

PAMELA. Your arm!

KI-RAM. Yes—what about it?

PAMELA. You have your arm around me.

KI-RAM. I know it. You said it was proper.

PAMELA. It *is* proper, when we are moving about. As a stationary form of amusement, I am afraid it would cause comment.

KI-RAM. *All right!* Let's move about. Anything to be civilized. [*He does a few eccentric dance steps without releasing his hold on* PAMELA.]

PAMELA. Why, your Majesty, how strangely you act! [*Breaking away from him.*]

KI-RAM. Pamela, when I first saw you, do you know, I was not particularly attracted to you. But now—now—[*He approaches her and she retreats. He pauses and reflects.*] I wonder if that cocktail had anything to do with it.

PAMELA. Cocktail? [*Surprised and pained.*]

KI-RAM. When the Colonel took me aside in there he said he was going to make me acquainted with one of the first blessings of civilization. He told me that the constitution and the cocktail followed the flag. Then he gave me an amber-colored beverage with a roguish little cherry nestling at the bottom. And, oh, little friend, when I felt that delicious liquid trickle down the corridors of my inmost being, all the incandescent lights were turned on and the birds began to sing. I felt myself bursting into full bloom, like a timid little flower kissed by the morning sunlight. So I ordered two more.

PAMELA. Three cocktails! Oh!

KI-RAM. I've had three, and I wish I'd made it thirty-three. I believe I'll climb a tree. You pick out any tree around here and I'll climb it. [*Unable to control his joyous emotions, he begins to run around in a circle until stopped short by* PAMELA, *who is determined to be severe with him.*]

PAMELA. Your Majesty, a little bit of advice! Beware of the cocktail. [*She sits on one of the stools.*]

KI-RAM. Beware of nothing! I'm going to drink cocktails all day and waltz all night. I'm going to be so civilized that people will talk about me. Pamela, Pammy [*seats himself beside her*], did you ever think you would like to live in a palace and have Sultana printed on your visiting-cards? [GALULA *comes on and begins to fan from behind.*]

PAMELA. Perhaps I have had my little ambition. Who hasn't?

KI-RAM. Well, I think I can fix it for you. Of course— [*He pauses, full of suspicion. To* PAMELA.] Do you feel a draft? [*Turns and sees* GALULA.] Oh-h! Galula, according to the *Ladies' Home Journal*, it is not considered good form for a wife to hang around when her husband is proposing marriage to another lady. [GALULA *exits, much disheartened.*] Sometimes I am almost sorry I married that one.

PAMELA. [*Aghast.*] Is she your wife?

KI-RAM. You don't think I would be so impolite to a lady who was *not* my wife, do you?

PAMELA. And she *is* your wife?

KI-RAM. She's *one* of them.

PAMELA. *One!*

KI-RAM. I have eight.

PAMELA. *Eight!* [*Rising and shrinking from him.*]

KI-RAM. Eight or nine, I forget which; I have them coming and going all the time.

PAMELA. Eight wives already, and you—[*he arises and retreats*]—you dare to make this scandalous proposition, and to me—to *me!*

KI-RAM. You didn't expect to have me all to yourself, did you?

PAMELA. Colonel! Colonel! [*Calling.*]

KI-RAM. Sh-h! I'll take it back—honestly, I will.

PAMELA. Colonel!

KI-RAM. Say, what's the matter with you? Can't you take a joke? [BUDD *comes from palace.*]

BUDD. My dear Miss Jackson, what *is* the matter?

KI-RAM. Don't believe a word she tells you.

PAMELA. Colonel, this babarian has had the monumental effrontery to ask me to join his harem.

BUDD. Wha-a-a-t!

KI-RAM. It was your fault—you gave it to me with a cherry in it.

PAMELA. [*To* KI-RAM.] Silence! [*To* BUDD.] I know that at one word from me you would run this contemptible foreign person through and through. But I do not ask it. I can execute my own revenge for this hideous insult. Tomorrow I am to be Judge-Advocate. Then shall the law deal with this miscreant. To-morrow—you—you—[PAMELA *enters palace greatly agitated*.]

BUDD. Your Majesty, why—*why* did you propose marriage to Miss Jackson?

KI-RAM. Do you know—I'm beginning to ask myself that question.

BUDD. Didn't I tell you, sir that *I* intended to marry her?

KI-RAM. That's it! I knew she was engaged to you, and therefore I argued that she could not possibly marry me, so I would not be taking any chances in proposing. What do you suppose she is going to do to me?

BUDD. I suspect, sir, that as Judge-Advocate she is going to compel you to give up those eight wives.

KI-RAM. [*Much pleased*.] I'm going to get rid of Galula at last! Colonel, I want to celebrate. Let's go into the palace and drink three more of those things that follow the flag.

BUDD. You will excuse me if I don't refuse. [*They start towards palace.* HENRIETTA *and* HARDY *stroll on, in loving attitude;* BUDD *sees them; stands on steps watching them.* KI-RAM *enters palace*.] Henrietta, once more I must remind you that you are the daughter of a military hero who expects to go to Congress. Come. [HENRIETTA *starts towards him, regretfully. At the palace steps she turns and throws a kiss to* HARDY *and exits after* BUDD.]

HARDY. By George! I thought this being engaged would prove a lark. It's serious business. I wonder if Henrietta really loves me. If I but knew. [HARDY *enters palace. School-ma'ams enter, followed by a flock of wives, natives, and soldiers.*]

ALL

Give three cheers for education—
   Hurrah! Hurrah! Hurrah!
Give three cheers for education—
   Hurrah! Hurrah! Hurrah!
A tiger, too, for education.
   How we love our teachers dear!
An attractive aggregation
   From the Western Hemisphere.
Give three cheers—
   Hurrah! Hurrah! Hurrah!

[PAMELA *comes from the palace and stands on the top step, regarding the educational movement with a smile of gratification.*]

PAMELA. I am glad to see that the school has opened with so much enthusiasm. I will grant a short recess, as I have something of great importance to communicate to the wives of Ki-Ram.

NATIVE WOMEN AND SOLDIERS

[*Singing as they march away*]
Oh, the knowledge we are gaining
  In our little school!
Modern methods they're explaining
  In our little school!
We shall learn, from day to day,
What to do and what to say,
In the truly Newport way,
  In our little school!

[PAMELA *beckons the wives to her.*]

PAMELA. I have good news for you. Ki-Ram is no longer your husband.
WIVES. No-o-o?
PAMELA. The new law allows a man but one wife. You shall be divorced tomorrow. If the governor objects, he can then be imprisoned for bigamy—or, rather, octagamy. If he consents, then he will have to pay alimony to all of you.
MAURICIA. What is alimony?
PAMELA. Pin-money, my child—plenty of it. You are to be free and have plenty of spending-money. *That* is usually a novelty for a married woman. By the way, Didymos! Rastos! [*The two slaves approach.*] You are slaves no longer, but free citizens of Sulu. Serve the Governor, if you choose, but compel him to pay union wages and tip you liberally. You understand? [*She enters palace.*]
CHIQUITA. Tomorrow we shall be American grass-widows. Now for the soldiers.
PEPITA. We must be careful.
CHIQUITA. Nonsense! We have nothing to fear from these gentle strangers after being courted by Sulu sweethearts.

CHIQUITA AND WIVES, DIDYMOS AND RASTOS

"MY SULU LULU LOO"

In Sulu once there lived a belle
Whose winning ways had cast a spell
Upon a chief of great renown—
  He was smitten sore.
He followed her both night and day;

He tried to steal this girl away;
And underneath her window he
Repeated o'er and o'er:

REFRAIN

Lulu, you're my Sulu Lulu Loo!
Lulu, do take pity on me, do!
I want no one else but you!
Lulu, you're my Sulu Lulu Loo!

If she went out to take a stroll,
This palpitating, eager soul
Would wave his snaky knife at her,
  Saying, "Fly with me!"
In jungle deep she thought to hide,
Since she could not become his bride,
When all at once she heard this song
  From out a bamboo-tree:

REFRAIN

Lulu, you're my Sulu Lulu Loo, etc.

[CHIQUITA, DIDYMOS, RASTOS, *and wives exeunt with dance as* KI-RAM *enters with the four school-ma'ams. He has two on each side and is making a sincere effort to embrace all four at the same time.*]

KI-RAM. Why not? I think you might—to oblige a friend. Young ladies, I have only eight. I need some blondes to help out the color scheme. I've fallen into the habit of marrying nearly all of the ladies I meet.

A SCHOOL-MA'AM. We didn't come over here to marry. We are interested in education.

KI-RAM. Married life is an education.

  [*A blare of trumpets.* BUDD, HADJI, DINGBAT, DIDYMOS, *and* RASTOS *come from palace. The natives kneel, and one of the slaves advances towards* KI-RAM *a silken pillow on which is a shaggy silk hat of the kind seen at State conventions.* KI-RAM *is mystified. He looks at the hat.*]

KI-RAM. What's that?

BUDD. The insignia of your new office.

KI-RAM. [*Picking it up to examine it.*] My! My! What is it—animal, vegetable, or mineral?

BUDD. It is called a hat. This is the kind worn by all Governors.

KI-RAM. With the fur rubbed the wrong way?

BUDD. A true statesman invariably has the fur rubbed the wrong way.

HADJI. [*Announcing.*] They are coming for the inauguration.

BUDD. [*To* KI-RAM.] Did you hear that? Get ready.

KI-RAM. Colonel, there is only one thing that will get me ready.

BUDD. And what is that?

KI-RAM. You know—it has a cherry in it.

[*They hurriedly enter palace. Volunteers, marines, fife-and-drum corps, wives, natives, and various members of the American party enter from right and left and mass in front of the palace.*]

CHORUS

CHORUS TO THE GOVERNOR

Ki-Ram, the new-made chief!
　　Our ruler democratic,
From recent state of grief,
　　Transferred to bliss ecstatic.
Forgetful of his scare
　　And its attendant pallor, he
Accepts this job, so fair—
　　Also the salaree!

[BUDD *comes from palace and takes his place in front of the soldiers.* KI-RAM *comes to the palace steps, proudly exhibiting the hat.*]

KI-RAM

No crown for me of ordinary gold;
A Governor I'm to be, and I've been told
That this, which the Colonel calls a hat,
Is the proper gear for a democrat.

BUDD

'Tis emblematic, chaste, and pat,
He's proud to wear a hat like that.

[KI-RAM *comes down and faces the assemblage. He puts on the hat, which falls over his ears.*]

KI-RAM

[*Recitative.*] How do I look?

ALL

Glorious! Wonderful!
What do you think of that?
Could anything excel
The simple beauty of a hat?

[*The boom of a cannon is heard. A sergeant lowers the Sulu flag from the tall pole in front of the palace.*]

HARDY

Let all at strict attention stand,
The blessed moment's nigh.
When o'er this liberated land
The stars and stripes shall fly.

[*Another gun salute. The stars and stripes break from the top of the flag-staff to the music of "The Star-Spangled Banner." A roll of drums, and* HENRIETTA *enters and comes down front.*]

HENRIETTA

If I would be a soldier's bride,
I must not grieve, whate'er betide,
But laugh the tear-drops from my eye,
And cheerily wave the last good-bye.
And every girl who's left behind
    Civilian love will spurn;
For never a one will change her mind
    Till the Volunteers return.

ALL

March, march, hearts are light,
    Step with jaunty pride
To the fight! To the fight!
    Where each may win a bride.
For they know the girls they're leaving behind
    All civilian love will spurn,
And never a one will change her mind
    Till the Volunteers return.

[*During this chorus* KI-RAM, *on the palace steps, consumes many cocktails brought to him by* DIDYMOS *and* RASTOS. *At conclusion of the chorus all turn and salute the flag.*]

CURTAIN

ACT II

Scene: *The hanging garden of the palace. A half-open apartment. The architecture is gorgeous and Oriental. Free entrances up stage at right (the left, as one faces the stage), and also down stage at right, are supposed to lead to outer stairways. Up stage at left is a boxed-in stairway leading down to* KI-RAM'S *sleeping apartment. At left, and down stage (that is, towards the footlights), is a broad stairway leading to the second floor of the palace. Beyond the fanciful turrets and minarets may be seen the tropical vegetation, and beyond that the placid sea. At the rise of the curtain, native men and women are gathered on the stage singing a restful lullaby to* GOVERNOR KI-RAM, *who is over-sleeping himself in the apartment below.*

LULLABY CHORUS

Slumber! Slumber!
Forgetting, while you sleep,
Small and great affairs of state
While we our vigil keep.
Slumber on! No cares encumber
One who's lost in peaceful slumber.
Slumber! Slumber!
Forgetting, while you sleep,
Small and great affairs of state
While we our vigil keep.

[*They withdraw quietly, still singing softly, and* KI-RAM *comes from below. He wears a suit of pajamas of exaggerated pattern. His head is wrapped in a large towel. He carries in one hand a water pitcher and in the other the silk hat presented by the government at Washington. He moves slowly and dejectedly, and the expression on his face is one of extreme misery. He squats and removes the towel from his head, dips it into the ice-water, and holds it against his throbbing brow. Presently he lowers it with a heaving sigh, and discovers several specimens of the insect creation moving about on his person and disporting in his immediate vicinity. He battles with them for several moments, and then breaks into doleful song.*]

KI-RAM

"R—E—M—O—R—S—E"

The cocktail is a pleasant drink;
It's mild and harmless—I don't think.
When you've had one, you call for two,
And then you don't care what you do.
Last night I hoisted twenty-three

Of those arrangements into me.
My wealth increased, I swelled with pride,
I was pickled, primed, and ossified;
But R—E—M—O—R—S—E!
The water wagon is the place for me.
I think that somewhere in the game
I wept and told my real name.
At four I sought my whirling bed;
At eight I woke with such a head!
It is no time for mirth and laughter,
The cold, gray dawn of the morning after.

I wanted to pay for ev'ry round;
I talked on subjects most profound;
When all my woes I analyzed,
The barkeep softly sympathized.
The world was one kaleidoscope
Of purple bliss, transcendent hope.
But now I'm feeling mighty blue—
Three cheers for the W.C.T.U!
R—E—M—O—R—S—E!
Those dry Martinis did the work for me;
Last night at twelve I felt immense,
Today I feel like thirty cents.
My eyes are bleared, my coppers hot,
I'll try to eat, but I cannot.
It is no time for mirth and laughter,
The cold, gray dawn of the morning after.

[JONES *appears on the landing up stage and looks at the suffering executive, then comes towards him.*]

JONES. Governor, this isn't right. Remember, I've insured your life for fifty thousand pesos.

KI-RAM. Jones, civilization may be all right, but I took too large a dose right at the start. And you know that hat? [*He puts it on. It is many sizes too small.*] The constitution, the cocktail, and the katzenjammer follow the flag.

JONES. A bit of advice. If you had too many cocktails last evening, take one or two this morning. [*He gives a signal.* DIDYMOS *and* RASTOS, *smartly attired as waiters, come on and await orders.*]

KI-RAM. The American practice?

JONES. It is—especially among politicians. [DIDYMOS *and* RASTOS *do an impertinent breakdown, and crowd upon* KI-RAM, *who indignantly resents their familiarity.* JONES *restrains him.*]

JONES. Governor, be careful. You are now an office-holder. This is the president and vice-president of the waiters' union. You can't afford to antagonize the colored vote. I'll attend to them. [*Goes over to* DIDYMOS *and* RASTOS *and bows humbly.*] Gentlemen, if you will be good enough to prepare for us a few pick-me-ups we shall esteem it a personal favor and remember you with the usual piece of silver. [*They break and exeunt.*] Governor, I am here to announce the first review of the imperial troops.

KI-RAM. The imperial troops?

JONES. They landed here yesterday as soldiers of a simple republic. Today they are soldiers of the new empire. As such they have assumed an imperial splendor.

KI-RAM. I suppose you provided the uniforms?

JONES. I *did.* By the way [*taking paper from pocket*], a few articles selected by your wives.

KI-RAM. [*Taking the paper.*] What's this?

JONES. The bill.

KI-RAM. [*Reading.*] Eight morning gowns, eight afternoon gowns, eight evening gowns, eight night—eight suits of silk pajamas—Look here, sir. This is a terrible thing to bring around before breakfast. [*With increasing dismay.*]Eight diamond tararums eight automobiles, eight picture-hats, eight straight-fronts, eight habit-backs, eight rats— Rats! What can they do with rats? [HARDY *enters at right.*]

JONES. I'll explain. A rat—

KI-RAM. You needn't explain, I've been seeing them all morning—blue ones with acetylene eyes.

HARDY. [*Saluting.*] Governor! [*They turn.*] Governor, the Imperial Guards are approaching.

KI-RAM. Oh, very well. Jones and I are going into the life-saving station for a few moments.

[KI-RAM *and* JONES *go into the palace as wives and other natives come flocking on, cheering for the Imperial Guards, who march in from the right, under command of* COLONEL JEFFERSON BUDD, *and escorted by the fife-and-drum corps and the school-ma'ams. The Imperial Guards wear elaborate and costly uniforms of white and gold, with top-boots, plumes, and helmets. The* COLONEL'S *uniform is especially magnificent.*]

SONG OF THE IMPERIAL GUARDS

We are troops of the twentieth century kind,
    With our gaudy colors brightly flashing;
The pride and the joy of our native land—

For the records we are smashing.
Our former isolation makes us smile, sir,
    We've learned to sing a different tune,
It may keep us busy for a while, sir,
    But we shall come to like it soon—
        We'll come to like it soon!
        We'll come to like it soon!

BUDD. Imperial Guards! This is a proud day for all of us. I have
wanted to wear this kind of uniform ever since I was a boy in
Arkansaw and felt my pulse leap at the stirring measures of the
grand old "Jay-Bird."

BUDD AND CHORUS

"JAY-BIRD"

BUDD

When I was a boy in Arkansaw,
I worked in a hat and cap emporium.

REFRAIN

Umpalorium! Umpalorium!
Hat and cap emporium!

BUDD

After that I studied law,
    But I longed for a soldier's life,
And my heart would bound
At the martial sound
    Of the drum and the piercing fife.
Hark to the strains, so clear and loud!
Along the street a cheering crowd;
The sweetest music ever heard—
The thump and tootle of the old "Jay-Bird."

REFRAIN

Hark to the strains, etc.

BUDD

I've heard the Nibelungenlied,
And all the gems of Cavalleria.

REFRAIN

Cavalleria! Cavalleria!
Gems of Cavalleria!

BUDD

They're rather tuneful, I'll concede,
　But, to swell a colonel's chest,
They will not compare with the swinging air
　That I always have loved the best.

REFRAIN

Hark to the strains, etc.

[*At conclusion of the song the Imperial Guards break ranks and hurry to the wives and native women, with whom they are becoming well acquainted, this being their second day on the island.*]

BUDD. Make ready to receive his Excellency.
　[*All move into lines, facing the broad stairway at left. A roll of drums.* DIDYMOS *and* RASTOS *come down stairway and salaam to the left.* HADJI, *at the top of the steps, announces the approach of the executive.*]
HADJI. The Governor!
　[KI-RAM, *in a gaudy native costume, comes down the steps very nimbly and acknowledges the deferential salute.*]
KI-RAM. Good morning, troops! [*Sees* BUDD *and is staggered by the glory of his apparel. In the mean time* PAMELA, *wearing a Portia cap and gown, and very much on her official dignity, has entered from the right.* KI-RAM *addresses* BUDD.] My! My! Colonel, you are without doubt the handsomest man I— [PAMELA *interrupts.*]
PAMELA. Governor Ki-Ram!
KI-RAM. Oh-h! Here she is again. I don't believe I'm going to like her very well.
PAMELA. I have granted divorces to seven of your wives.
KI-RAM. Oh, very well!
PAMELA. The court holds that you may keep *one.*
KI-RAM. *One!* Oh, say, Judge, let me keep two; now, don't be stingy. Let me keep two little ones instead of one big one.
PAMELA. You heard the law—*one.*
KI-RAM. Much obliged. I suppose I can keep house with only one. It has been done.
PAMELA. I suggest that you select that unhappy creature who is to remain under your roof. Am I right, Colonel?

BUDD. Quite right, Judge. [BUDD *and* PAMELA *exeunt to the right.*]

KI-RAM. [*Calling after her.*] You have a pleasant way of putting it. [*He turns to the wives, who are hobnobbing with the soldiers.*] Mrs. Ki-Ram, step forward. [*The wives leave the soldiers and stand in a row, looking at him with saucy indifference. He is serious.*] Ladies, you are about to lose a good thing. [*They burst into laughter and return to the soldiers.*] I am glad to see that you bear up under the grief. Now for the sad farewell. Which one shall I keep? [HENRIETTA *appears on the landing up stage. She wears a most fetching summer gown and a sweepy hat. She carries an arm-load of fresh flowers.* KI-RAM *gazes at her in speechless admiration and is struck by a sudden inspiration.*] The American girl! Why not? [*To the wives*] I've made up my mind. I'll not keep *any* of you. Ladies, you are free. [*They rush to the arms of the soldiers, with exclamations of delight.*] Leave your keys at the office as you pass out. [*Then* KI-RAM *approaches* HENRIETTA, *who has sauntered down stage. He leans over her shoulder and addresses her flirtatiously.*] Linger here after the others go; I have something to tell you. [*To the others*] Ladies and gentlemen, I shall not detain you longer. [*All except* KI-RAM *and* HENRIETTA *romp away, the soldiers and native women paired off.* HENRIETTA *seats herself on a low stool and calmly awaits developments.* KI-RAM *approaches her, beaming and struggling with pent-up emotion.*] In the excitement of being inaugurated and granting all those divorces, I fear that I have overlooked you— *darling!*

HENRIETTA. *Darling?* Isn't this rather sudden?

KI-RAM. Not for *me.*

HENRIETTA. Before you go too far, I want to give you warning. As you are a titled foreigner, you have a right to know it. I am an American girl, but *not* an heiress.

KI-RAM. Henrietta, you wrong me. I am Sulu, not English.

HENRIETTA. Very well, go ahead.

KI-RAM. Henrietta, it appears that I am entitled to only one wife. Having been married to sixty-odd already, I feel that I can justly claim to be a connoisseur. It may flatter you to learn that you suit me. You are my first choice, and there is no second. You are *it.* Oh, Henrietta! Oh, Henry—Henny—Hen! I love you with an equatorial passion that no thermometer can register. [*He falls on his knees and attempts to embrace her. She breaks away from him.*]

HENRIETTA. But I am more or less engaged already.

KI-RAM. Which—*more or less?*

HENRIETTA. I mean that I am engaged—in a sort of way.

KI-RAM. What you mean to say is that you're engaged, but you're not
  sure that it's going to take.
HENRIETTA. That's it.
KI-RAM. Oh, Henrietta, I don't know who the other fellow is, but his
  love is a cheap rhinestone imitation compared to mine.

KI-RAM AND OTHERS

"SINCE I FIRST MET YOU"

KI-RAM

[*Singing to* HENRIETTA]

I am a dashing, gay Lothario;
I've a reputation as a gallant beau;
Courting pretty girls is a habit hard to break;
I'm a bold coquette and rather reckless rake.
I've told my love to many a girl,
  But never a word was true,
For my passion intense, it was a mere pretense
  Until I encountered you.

REFRAIN

Since I first met you,
Since I first met you,
The open sky above me seems a deeper blue;
Golden, rippling sunshine warms me through and through,
  Each flower has a new perfume,
  Since I met you!

I've been courting many, many times;
  In the most exclusive circles I'm a pet—
Writing little notes and inditing tender rhymes
  To the maids of every station that I've met.
I've sworn that each was my first love,
  But never a word was true,
For I never knew bliss of a kind like this
  Until I encountered you.

REFRAIN

Since I first met you,
Since I first met you,
The open sky above me seems a deeper blue;
Golden, rippling sunshine warms me through and through,

Each flower has a new perfume,
Since I met you!

[*As he starts to repeat the refrain,* HARDY *is heard singing it outside.* HARDY *saunters on and* HENRIETTA *hurries to him. The two look into each other's eyes and sing the refrain with much feeling, while* KI-RAM *looks on, crushed. As they conclude, the same refrain is heard off at the left, and* JONES *comes down the stairway, singing to* CHIQUITA. *While* KI-RAM *is staring at them and trying to comprehend this new outcropping of the American invasion,* BUDD *and* PAMELA *come on from right and join in the tender refrain. After which, various wives and soldiers appear as loving couples, and "Since I first met you" becomes a general chorus of love-making, the climax of which is reached when* HADJI *brings* GALULA *on. All the others stroll away, still singing the refrain, and* KI-RAM *is left alone, bewildered and dismayed. He can think of but one relief for the painful situation.*]

KI-RAM. To the life-saving station! [*Starts to exit left, when* PAMELA, *entering from right, calls to him.*]

PAMELA. Aha! Viper! There you are!

KI-RAM. Viper? She is referring to me.

PAMELA. You have exceeded your authority. You cannot divorce *all* of your wives. You must keep *one*.

KI-RAM. [*A horrible suspicion dawning upon him.*] Which one?

PAMELA. The one you married first of all—Galula! [KI-RAM *emits a groan of mortal agony.*] She is a good soul. [HADJI *enters, carrying a volume of Arkansaw law.*]

KI-RAM. Judge, I sometimes think she is too good to be true.

PAMELA. Now, then, in regard to the alimony. Private Secretary, read the section.

HADJI. Judge, I hate to read it to him—he has a weak heart.

PAMELA. Go ahead!

HADJI. Well, here it is. [*Reads*] "When a divorce is granted, the wife is entitled to alimony equivalent to one-half of the income of the husband."

KI-RAM. [*Stunned.*] I don't understand.

PAMELA. It means that each of your eight wives is entitled to one-half of your total income.

KI-RAM. Eight wives! Each entitled to one-half—one-hof?

PAMELA. You heard the law.

KI-RAM. I don't believe I can manage it.

PAMELA. I'm sure you can't, and that is why I expect to have the pleasure of committing you to jail.

KI-RAM. What are you talking about? The brother of the sun and cousin to the moon locked up in a common jail? Ho! I laugh—not boisterously, it is true, but still I laugh! Ha! Ha!

PAMELA. Private Secretary, read the second section.

HADJI. [*Reading*] "Take the whites of six eggs, beat to a froth, and add powdered sugar—"

KI-RAM. Hold on! What's that?

HADJI. That's not right. Judge, you have been filing your recipes in here. Here it is. [*Reads.*] "If a husband fails to pay alimony at the time and place designated by the court, he may be committed to the county jail—to the county jail."

KI-RAM. I heard you the first time.

PAMELA. At five o'clock, Ki-Ram, you pay four times your income for this month or to jail you go. This is my revenge for the insult of yesterday.

KI-RAM. Well, there's nothing the matter with it.

PAMELA. At five o'clock! [*She flaunts out, leaving* GOVERNOR KI-RAM *staring blankly into space.*]

KI-RAM. Isn't she the hasty Helen? [*Looking after her.*] You can make it six o'clock if you like. The prison doors stand open invitingly, and over them is an evergreen motto reading as follows: "Welcome, little stranger."

HADJI. It's the law, Governor.

KI-RAM. How can a man pay out four times his income?

HADJI. It *will* be a difficult matter.

KI-RAM. Difficult! Say my income is ten thousand pesos a month. Each wife is entitled to one-half of that, or five thousand pesos. Eight wives—forty thousand pesos. In order to keep out of jail I must raise forty thousand pesos.

HADJI. That's right.

KI-RAM. But look here. The moment I increase my income to forty thousand pesos, each wife is entitled to twenty thousand. Eight wives, one hundred and sixty thousand pesos. If by any miracle of finance I could get hold of that much money, then each of the eight would be entitled to eighty thousand. Eight times eight is eighty-eight—eight times eighty-eight is eight hundred and eighty-eight thousand, and— Oh, what's the use! I'm broke! And the more money I get the worse I'm broke. [*Collapses.*]

HADJI. You'll have to decrease your income.

KI-RAM. Even if I do decrease it, I am still required to pay four times as much as I can possibly get. Oh, Hadji, why did I ever hook up with that Ladies' Glee Club? I wish the Datto Mandi had them back again—the whole seven.

HADJI. Your Excellency, that is the solution of the whole problem.

KI-RAM. What is?

HADJI. The Datto Mandi. He is still encamped outside the city. Why not permit him to come in and recapture them? If *they* disappear, then *you* can't be required to pay alimony to them.

KI-RAM. [*A great light breaking in upon him.*] Hadji, you have been drawing salary for seven years and this is the first minute you earned it. As Governor, I send that dazzling array of Imperial Guards over to the north wall to repulse an imaginary attack. Then the Datto Mandi can come in by the south gate and capture his nieces. Now, then, some one must get through the lines with a message to Mandi. Do you happen to know of a good, trustworthy man who fears no danger?

HADJI. Send Mr. Jones.

KI-RAM. No, we must have a brave man—an intrepid character, a—Hold on! I know the man.

HADJI. You do?

KI-RAM. Yes! He's a short, stout, thick man, with bushy eyebrows, and he wears a yellow raglan.

HADJI. I don't believe I know him.

KI-RAM. It's you.

HADJI. *Me!*

KI-RAM. Don't say "me"—say "I". Be grammatical, even if you are scared. [HADJI *exits at left as* BUDD *and* PAMELA *come on from right, engaged in a business-like conversation.*]

PAMELA. If he fails to pay, Colonel, I shall expect the military to see that he is incarcerated.

KI-RAM. [*Aside.*] Somebody is talking about me. I can feel my left ear burn.

BUDD. The military will do its duty, Judge Jackson.

KI-RAM. [*Addressing them defiantly*] Don't you folks worry about me. I'll come out all right. I'm not the only man in the world that owes four times his income. But, Colonel, I have a feeling—

BUDD. Yes?

KI-RAM. That I loved not wisely, but too often. [*He goes into the palace.* BUDD *gazes at* PAMELA *and evinces all the sentimental longing compatible with his dignity.*]

BUDD. Pamela! Pamela!

PAMELA. Judge, if you please.

BUDD. I was hoping to make this a love scene.

PAMELA. If you wish to make love to me, come around after business hours. [*She exits to right, haughtily, leaving* BUDD *rather ruffled.*]

BUDD. Very well, madam, if I find, after business hours, that I am still in love with you, you may expect me. [*He starts away and encounters* CHICQUITA, *who has tripped in, carrying a large coconut, with the original husk still intact. She holds it toward* BUDD, *who looks at it and is puzzled.*] For me?

CHIQUITA. For you, mighty warrior.

BUDD. What is it?

CHIQUITA. A coconut—the first of the season. I want you to wear it next your heart.

BUDD. Next my heart? How romantic! Arise, Chiquita; now that you have been adopted by the administration at Washington, you must kneel to no one—not even to *me*. [*He puts his arm around* CHIQUITA *in a fatherly demonstration of affection.* HARDY *and* HENRIETTA *come on from right and catch the picture.*]

HARDY AND HENRIETTA. Oh! Oh!

BUDD. [*Intensely annoyed.*] Why do you interrupt us just as she was becoming assimilated?

HENRIETTA. Father, your blessing.

BUDD. Why a blessing?

HARDY. We are engaged.

BUDD. What! Again?

HENRIETTA. Father, don't be unreasonable. You know I'm not happy unless I'm engaged to some one.

BUDD. [*Striking an oratorical pose.*] Fifteen years ago, when your sainted mother was alive, I promised her that I would watch over you—[HENRIETTA *puts her hand on his arm.*]

HENRIETTA. Father, wake up!

BUDD. Well, what is it?

HENRIETTA. If you object, say so, but please don't make a speech.

BUDD. I do object. [*To* HARDY] Young man, why do you aspire to become the son-in-law of one who, when the call of duty sounded—

HARDY. Good day, Colonel. [*Exits, right.*]

BUDD. Humph! Au revoir, Chiquita. Come, Henrietta. [*He departs with his daughter, leaving* CHIQUITA *disconsolate.* KI-RAM *comes from left and sees her.*]

KI-RAM. Ah, Chiquita, wife that was! [*Embraces her.*] Let's pretend we were never married. [*She moves away from him, and he sings with feeling:*]

> Since I first met you,
> Since I first met you,
> My whole existence seems to be a deeper blue;

This assimilation process pains me through and through,
>   For I've been up against it hard—
>   Since I met you.

Chiquita, you and your innocent sisters are not safe here. There are too many things following the flag.

CHIQUITA. "They never proceed to follow the flag, but always follow me."

KI-RAM. From "Tannhäuser," I believe. Exactly what I mean. Why not go back to Parang?

CHIQUITA. And leave the dear Colonel?

KI-RAM. Take the dear Colonel with you—and Galula.

CHIQUITA. Even with Galula on your hands, you advise other people to marry?

KI-RAM. I'll tell you—after a man has been initiated, his only fun in life is to see somebody else get it. As for me, I am an expert on matrimony. I've made a study of women. I like you individually and collectively, but all of you have one fault.

CHIQUITA. What's that?

KI-RAM. You're always a trifle late.

KI-RAM AND CHIQUITA

"ALWAYS LATE"

KI-RAM

See the lady at the station,
>   Starting on a trip!
> In a state of perturbation,
>   Slightly off her dip.

CHIQUITA

"All aboard!" she hears them calling,
>   Then they ring the bell;
> While she starts in to count up all her parcels
>   And to kiss her friends farewell.

KI-RAM

She tells each one good-bye,
>   And then she starts to cry;
> The man who's at the gate
> Says, "Hurry, you'll be late!"

CHIQUITA. [*To be spoken. The bell is ringing outside, and* KI-RAM, *as gateman, is busily collecting tickets and crowding the passengers through the turnstile*.] Well, good-bye, good-bye, good-bye! Write, won't you? And don't forget to feed the bird. Where's my— Oh, here it is! And, say, there was something else— Oh yes, be sure and give the goldfish fresh water every day. I'll *bet* I've lost that parasol. I lose *more* parasols— It just seems to me that I lose something every time I start to go anywhere. Oh, *you've* got it, have you? What was that other—I remember now. Tell Laura that I left that dress pattern in the upper left-hand drawer of my bureau—*Yes*, where I keep the frizzes. And if any of the children get sick, tel-egraph me the first thing—[*whistle*]—and—*Oh, mercy!* there goes my train.

Ki-Ram and Chiquita

Late! Late! Always late!
Railway trains should learn to wait.
They should take their time in starting,
When a woman is departing,
For she's always a trifle late—late—late—
She's always a trifle late.

Ki-Ram

Guests assembled for the wedding
  Of a happy pair;
Female friends their tears are shedding
  On the bride so fair.

Chiquita

'Tis the moment for the entrance
  To the drawing-room,
But when the preacher's ready to begin the service,
  No one's there except the groom.

Ki-Ram

Mamma must hug the bride;
Some fourteen friends beside
Must smack her once again,
And straighten out the train.

Chiquita. [*To be spoken while the orchestra softly plays wedding-march, to give effect of being in an adjoining room.*] Oh, ma-mah, isn't it dreadful! But *please* don't carry on so. I'm not going far away. We'll come and see you every day. Where's my bouquet? Yes, yes, *I'm* coming— Ethel, how does that veil hang? It feels all squidgy in the back. *Gracious goodness!* There goes the music. Where's my bouquet? Why, I've *got* it, haven't I? Lordy, do you know, I never was so scared in all my life! This is my first time. I dare say that makes a difference. What's *that*? The others have gone *in*? Jiminy crickets! Where's my— Ah, yes— Louise, I'll *bet* I look as if I'd been crying—*don't* I, really? Well, here goes. Gee! look at all the people. This is the last time *I* ever get married.

KI-RAM AND CHIQUITA

Late! Late! Always late!
Even Cupid learns to wait.
There's no need to fuss and worry,
Woman's never in a hurry,
And she's always a trifle late—late—late—
She's always a trifle late.

CHIQUITA

When you're settled snug and quiet,
   To enjoy a play,
Some one starts a small-sized riot
   In the main parquet.

KI-RAM

Seats are raised and seats are lowered,
   Ushers come and go,
And what is taking place behind the footlights
   No one really seems to know.

CHIQUITA

To reach an inside seat,
She walks on people's feet,
And never seems to care,
Though they may turn and stare.

[KI-RAM, *on upper landing, impersonates the actor engaged in a serious and sentimental scene, while* CHIQUITA *plays the bustling lady who comes in at 9:05 and demoralizes the performance.*]

CHIQUITA. Oh, my! The curtain's gone up, hasn't it? I wonder if we missed anythng. I don't s'pose we have, because the first part of a show never amounts to anything, anyway. Oh, fiddle! See where our seats are! Why didn't you get aisle seats, Fred? I always want to sit in the aisle. Shall I go first? I wonder if these people are going to let us in. Oh, my! did you see the look that woman gave me? Come *on!* We'll *have* to crowd in some way. Did you get any programmes? I wonder who that is on the stage now. I do hope Faversham hasn't been out yet. [*A subdued "Sh-h-h!"*] Well, what do you think of *that?*

CHIQUITA AND KI-RAM

Late! Late! Always late!
Doesn't start till half-past eight.
There's no need to fuss and worry,
Woman's never in a hurry,
And she's always a trifle late—late—late—
She's always a trifle late.

[*Dance.*]

[*At conclusion of dance,* CHIQUITA *exits and* HADJI *comes from the palace.* KI-RAM *gives him the message to* MANDI.]

KI-RAM. Now all you have to do is to get through the lines and deliver that message to Mandi—
HADJI. They may shoot at me.
KI-RAM. If any one shoots at you, you dodge. [HADJI *exits.* KI-RAM
calls after him.] And tell Colonel Budd I want to see him.
[*Soliloquy.*] If he doesn't get through with that message, I have a
panel photograph of little Bright Eyes doing a solitaire specialty
in a cold-storage warehouse. [*Enter* BUDD.] Colonel, bring out
your standing army, feathers and all. [BUDD *gives signal and
soldiers enter.*] What do you think? We're going to be attacked—
ALL. Attacked?
KI-RAM. —By the Datta Mandi—this very afternoon. Colonel, my
advice— My! Colonel, you are one of the handsomest men—
BUDD. [*Impatiently.*] I know it! I know it! Proceed!
KI-RAM. My advice is to take all of these peace commissioners over to
the north wall. Let them shoot at everything in sight, while I,
being merely an office-holder, will take the women into the
palace grounds, near the south gate, so as to keep them out of
danger.
BUDD. An excellent plan.
KI-RAM. [*Solemnly.*] And may Allah give you victory. [*He summons the
natives, who come in, followed by the Americans.*]

CHORUS OF NATIVES

Drive the foe into the sea!
Allah! Allah! Strike for thee!
Winds and furies, wild and free!
Allah! Allah! Strike for thee!
Allah—il—Allah!

[BUDD *and the other Americans listen to the chorus, and appear to be in* *pain. Evidently the Oriental music does not appeal to them.*]

BUDD. Stop it! Stop it! That is the worst I ever heard. What do you call it?

KI-RAM. It is our Sulu battle-hymn. We always sing that just before we fight.

BUDD. That's enough to make any one fight.

KI-RAM. I'm sorry you don't like it. It's very popular over here.

JONES. *Popular! Popular!* Would you like to hear some of the *popular* songs of a truly progressive and refined people?

KI-RAM. If it isn't too much trouble.

JONES. Very well, your musical education begins right here. We'll give you some of our characteristic numbers with the usual trimmings. [JONES *gives a sheet to* KI-RAM *and then comes down centre with the school-ma'ams.*]

JONES

Oh, sing no more of the crescent moon
    Above the mango-tree,
Or of the bold and free monsoon
    That fans your local sea.
I've something here of a classic turn
    Which you should learn to sing,
As true musicians you must learn
    To do this sort of thing.

[*He breaks into the familiar American song and dance with walk around.*]

Rosabella, Rosabella Clancy,
She has caught my idle fancy;
Simply a stenographic girl,
But a priceless princess and a pearl.
Rosabella, Rosabella Clancy,
She is ever bright and glancy,

Cute, coquettish, song-and-dancey—
Rosabella, Bella Clancy.

[All repeat, with dance.]

KI-RAM

And now I'll ask a chord in G
For this sad roundelay,
About the girl of Manistee
Who up and went away.

[He looks at the song, trembles with emotion, and is unable to proceed.]

KI-RAM. Colonel, I can't sing this. It's too sad.
BUDD. Go on; try it. All true Americans love sad songs.
KI-RAM. Where *is* Manistee?
BUDD. In Michigan.
KI-RAM. That makes it sadder still. *[Sings.]*

Oh, darling sister, come back to Manistee;
Come back to Manistee; come right away!
For mother is waiting for you back in Manistee;
Come back to Manistee; don't go astray!

[At the conclusion he breaks down and sobs convulsively, while the entire chorus repeats the pathetic appeal with much feeling. After which KI-RAM, BUDD, JONES, and DINGBAT sing it as a "close harmony" quartette–the kind heard at amateur entertainments for the benefit of something. As they conclude, a rifle-shot is heard near at hand. The company is thrown into confusion, and KI-RAM retreats to the palace.]

BUDD. What's that? Are we attacked ahead of schedule time? *[HARDY comes on from right.]*
HARDY. They have captured a man trying to get through the lines. *[Two marines enter with HADJI between them. His garments are torn and he is badly mussed up.]*
A NATIVE. Why, it's Hadji!
HARDY. We found this. *[He gives the intercepted message to BUDD.]*
BUDD. This looks suspicious, but I can't make it out. Will you translate it? *[He hands it over to JONES, who, during the twenty-four hours he has spent on the island, has mastered the Sulu language.]*
JONES. It is to the Datto Mandi of Parang. *[Reads.]* "The south gate of the city will be unguarded at four o'clock. Your eight nieces may be found in the palace garden."

BUDD. Why, this is treason! Where is the Governor? [KI-RAM *comes from palace, practicing the "Rosabella" dance.* BUDD *calls to him.*] Governor!

KI-RAM. What's the matter, Colonel?

BUDD. We have captured a traitor.

KI-RAM. A traitor?

BUDD. Yes—look. [KI-RAM *sees* HADJI *and shows consternation.*]

JONES. Read that. [KI-RAM *takes the message and reads as he goes towards* HADJI.]

KI-RAM. North wall—south gate—isn't that terrible? [*To* HADJI.] Oh, Hadji, you whom I have trusted—you whom I have known since boyhood—you in a conspiracy! How could you! [*Chokes him.*] Not a word! [*Aside.*] If he speaks, I'm lost.

PAMELA. The question is, who sent him with that message?

KI-RAM. That is the question, undoubtedly, "*Who* sent him?" [*To* HADJI.] Why didn't you swallow it?

HADJI. I couldn't. My heart was in my mouth.

PAMELA. Do you happen to know of any one who would like very much to see those young ladies disappear and never return?

KI-RAM. Why, Judge, what *do* you mean? [*To* BUDD.] At least, Colonel, you don't suspect *me?*

PAMELA. Let the prisoner speak!

KI-RAM. No, I protest. He's a private secretary. I wouldn't believe him under oath. [*The palace clock strikes, one–two–three–four–five.* KI-RAM *listens apprehensively, flinching at each stroke.*]

PAMELA. Five o'clock! The alimony!

KI-RAM. [*Helplessly.*] Judge—

PAMELA. As I suspected—you can't pay. Very well, to jail with both of them.

KI-RAM. I think you are the meanest judge— [*Marines seize* KI-RAM *and* HADJI.]

PAMELA. To jail! [*They are marched away.* BUDD *summons* LIEUTENANT HARDY.]

BUDD. Lieutenant Hardy, take a detachment. Bring in this Datto Mandi. If you capture him, my election to Congress will be assured. [HARDY *salutes.*] Fellow-citizens, the military will assume command. Until there can be an election by the people, I will be Governor of Sulu.

CHORUS TO BUDD

Loudly we shout,
    With unaffected din,

Ki-Ram goes out
    And Budd comes in!
Ki-Ram goes out
    And Budd, and Budd comes in!

[*Soldiers and all the others exeunt to the marching chorus, the wives and native women waving their good-byes.*]

MARCHING CHORUS

For they know the girls they're leaving behind
    All civilian love will spurn,
And never a one will change her mind
    Till the Volunteers return.

[*As the chorus dies away,* HENRIETTA *comes from palace and crosses to the upper landing, mournfully watching the departure.*]

HENRIETTA. Gone! The only man I have loved this week! The only lieutenant in the command! With what joy shall I await his return! [*Sings.*]

"WHEN MAIDENS WAIT"

When maidens wait for lovers far away—
    How long each moment then!
They sigh impatient through the lonesome day—
    Sigh for the absent men!
    Sigh for the absent men!
Yet this reflection cheers my woeful plight
    And brings relief from pain—
The longer he's away, the more delight
    To see him back again!
    To see him back again!
Since he departed I have drooped and sighed—
    I wear a downcast air.
My deep anxiety I do not hide—
    It's noticed ev'rywhere!
    It's noticed ev'rywhere!
A girl whose sweetheart to the war has gone—
    A touching picture she!
And yet the longer I am left alone
    The more concern for me!
    The more concern for me!

[*She enters the palace.* KI-RAM *and* HADJI, *in modified prison stripes, humanely cut on the evening-dress pattern, enter from right. Each has a heavy iron band padlocked about his waist, and they are chained together. A very tall and formidable native guard accompanies them. They are exceedingly dejected.*]

KI-RAM. [*To guard.*] You tell the warden that we'll be back about nine o'clock, and tell him not to lock us out. [*Guard exits.* KI-RAM *looks at* HADJI.] You appear to be sad about something.

HADJI. I *am* sad.

KI-RAM. You appear to be *very* sad.

HADJI. The future seems quite dark to me.

KI-RAM. As for me, I'm a little discouraged about my future, more or less ashamed of my past, and not exactly delighted with my present.

HADJI. Only to think, branded as a criminal!

KI-RAM. Hadji, after having been a private secretary for years, I shouldn't think you'd mind a little thing like this. Besides, it's no disgrace to be a convict. Science has but lately discovered that crime is a disease. We are not really wicked; we are full of microbes.

HADJI. It's a consoling reflection, isn't it?

KI-RAM. What's more, I have a plan. I find in that volume of Arkansaw law that when a divorced woman becomes desperate and remarries, then the first victim doesn't have to pay any more alimony.

HADJI. Well?

KI-RAM. Shall I move in a portable black-board and diagram this for you? Don't you see that if I can induce those dreamy gazelles to commit matrimony, then I shall be free and can take my place as Governor once more?

HADJI. What good will that do *me*?

KI-RAM. After I am Governor once more, you apply for a pardon.

HADJI. And then?

KI-RAM. Then your application will be placed on file.

HADJI. After which?

KI-RAM. Nothing ever happens after an application is placed on file.

HADJI. I can't see that the situation is clearing up as far as I am concerned.

KI-RAM. You don't seem to understand. This plan of mine is intended to get *me* out of trouble. It's not any widespread, benevolent undertaking of a Carnegie character. It's simply a very foxy

plan by which your uncle Ki-Ram is going to give the loud, metallic ha-ha to Hasty Helen.

HADJI. And what, oh Towering Intellect, is your plan? [KI-RAM *gives him a card, which he reads*.] "Ki-Ram and Hadji, matrimonial agents." Then I am a partner in the enterprise?

KI-RAM. In order to get my parole, I had to bring you along, so I thought I might as well make you a partner. No one but a blacksmith can dissolve this partnership. [NATIVIDAD, *one of the wives, comes from the palace and down the broad stairway. She is overwhelmingly attired in a Parisian gown, and has adopted a languid, society manner*.]

KI-RAM. [*Gazing at her*.] Merciful Manila! See what she has been doing with my money! [*He approaches her in the humble manner of a tradesman soliciting patronage*.] Good evening! Would you do me a slight favor? I want you to marry a—

NATIVIDAD. [*Haughtily*.] Oh, really! [RAMONA, *another wife, follows* NATIVIDAD. *She and the others, who come later, wear superb evening costumes*.]

KI-RAM. [*To* RAMONA, *offering card*.] Would you require anything in our line?

RAMONA. I beg pardon, but have we met?

KI-RAM. We were married for a while, but, of course, *that* is a mere detail. [*She passes on as* MAURICIA *comes down the steps.*]

HADJI. Oh, look at *this* one!

KI-RAM. [*To* HADJI.] Did you ever see so much alimony in one evening? [*To* MAURICIA.] We have in stock a choice assortment of husbands—short ones, tall ones—

MAURICIA. Indeed! [*Passing on.* SELINA *approaches and* KI-RAM *bows to her.*]

KI-RAM. Madam, matrimony follows the flag. Our husbands are guaranteed—

SELINA. What strange-looking creatures!

KI-RAM. And my money paid for it. [*Looking at the gown.* PEPITA *follows, and he addresses her.*] An American husband is a very convenient thing to have around the house. He is a permanent meal-ticket and can be taught to eat from the hand.

PEPITA. I should rather like to have one. [*Passing on.*]

HADJI. *That* is the first ray of hope. [NATALIA *enters.*]

KI-RAM. [*To* NATALIA.] Laura, why not?

NATALIA. My name is *not* Laura.

KI-RAM. Isn't it? Well, it's a wise husband that can remember all of his wives. [*She passes on and he continues to importune her.*] Madam, a husband can be thrown in with the lease and moved out with the furniture. Now—[*Sees* CHIQUITA, *who comes with a flourish of her finery.*] Oh-h-h-h!

CHIQUITA. [*Sweeping up and down to display gown.*] We are *Americanized*.

KI-RAM. *I* am paralyzed.

HADJI. And I [*looking at wives, who are disdainful*] seem to be *ostracized*.

KI-RAM. You are simply *under*sized. That lets you out.

CHIQUITA. As I live, it's that fellow Ki-Ram.

KI-RAM. Yes, ma'am, I *am*, I *am* Ki-Ram, and I'd like to say something to complete the rhyme.

CHIQUITA. [*To the wives.*] We must not be seen talking to any one below us in social station.

KI-RAM. This is one of the heaviest frosts ever known in the tropics. [BUDD *and* HENRIETTA *enter together as* KI-RAM *continues to address the wives on the business proposition.*] Ladies, matrimony is an institution that no family should be without. True happiness— [HADJI *sees* BUDD *and* HENRIETTA, *and attempts to call* KI-RAM'S *attention to them. He tugs at the chain*]—true happiness—[HADJI *pulls the chain once more.* KI-RAM *to wives.*] Excuse me, I'm getting a cable message.

HADJI. The Colonel. [*All wives except* CHIQUITA *exeunt as* BUDD *and* HENRIETTA *come down stage.*]

CHIQUITA. [*Hurrying to* BUDD.] Oh, Colonel!

HENRIETTA. [*Seeing* KI-RAM *in prison suit.*] Governor!

KI-RAM. Henrietta, don't call me Governor! I am plain convict number forty-seven. The globule of merriment fastened to the other end of this daisy chain is number forty-eight. Even my private secretary outranks me one point. Henrietta, help us. Every man likes to see his wife happily married. I want these fairy fays to marry the soldiers.

HENRIETTA. I think that *every* girl should marry a soldier.

KI-RAM. Good! [*Offering card to Colonel.*] Colonel!

HADJI. Colonel, we hope—

KI-RAM. You keep still. You are the silent partner. [*To* BUDD] Have a card.

BUDD. [*Reading the card.*] "Ki-Ram and Hadji, matrimonial agents. Husbands and wives supplied while you wait. Satisfaction guaranteed or goods will be exchanged." [*To* CHIQUITA.] That seems reasonable.

KI-RAM. Exactly. Our object in life is to make people happy, it being a well known fact that all married people *are* happy. [*Aside.*] Heaven help me! [*To* BUDD *once more.*] Take *your* case. There is Chiquita—she loves you dearly.

BUDD. Really—

HADJI. I should say so. Everybody in jail has been talking about it.

KI-RAM. Take a good look, Colonel. She's amiable, young, fascinating. I don't see how you can get along without her.

BUDD. Really—I see no objection. [*Enter* HARDY.]

CHIQUITA. Oh, Colonel! [BUDD *and* CHIQUITA *embrace.*]

HENRIETTA. [*Scandalized.*] Father!

KI-RAM. [*Delighted.*] Too late!

HARDY. Colonel, congratulations on your wonderful victory.

BUDD. *My* wonderful victory.

HARDY. We have brought in the Datto Mandi.

KI-RAM. Mandi here? *I'm* going back to jail.

HADJI. But the matrimonial bureau?

KI-RAM. That's so.

HENRIETTA. [*To* BUDD.] If you and Chiquita are to be married, why not Mr. Hardy and I?

BUDD. On various occasions I have—

KI-RAM. Look out everybody, he's going to make a speech.

BUDD. I *will* permit you and the Lieutenant to stand up with me and

Chiquita. [BUDD *and* CHIQUITA *stroll up stage together, leaving* HENRIETTA *disconsolate.* KI-RAM *beckons to her.*]

KI-RAM. Henny! Henny, come here! If you and this reckless youth wish to marry, cultivate Chiquita. Hereafter *she* will be the general manager of the Budd family.

HENRIETTA. I'll do it. [*Goes over to* CHIQUITA.] Chiquita! Or perhaps I had better learn to call you "mamma."

KI-RAM AND HADJI. [*Aside.*] Mamma! [*They dance with glee.*]

CHIQUITA. What is it, my *daughter?*

KI-RAM AND HADJI. [*Aside.*] Daughter! [*They embrace each other in rapture.*]

HENRIETTA. [*To* CHIQUITA.] Come! Help me to select a nice soldier for each of your sisters.

CHIQUITA. *Indeed* I will. [*To* BUDD.] Star of my soul! [*Looks at him tenderly and goes over to join* HARDY *and* HENRIETTA.]

KI-RAM. [*To* HADJI.] Star of her soul! That's what she used to call *me*.

BUDD. [*Cordially.*] Gentlemen, we seem to be threatened with an epidemic of marriages.

HADJI. It hasn't affected *me* yet.

KI-RAM. Don't you worry—I'm going to give you Galula. [*To* BUDD.] Colonel, do you know what I've been thinking about ever since I went to jail?

BUDD. [*Interested.*] Tell me.

KI-RAM. I forget the name, but it had a cherry in it.

BUDD. A cocktail! Come! [*They start towards the palace.* KI-RAM *finds himself held back by the chain attached to* HADJI. *He is embarrassed.*]

KI-RAM. Colonel!

BUDD. Well?

KI-RAM. I don't like to ring any one in on you, but there are certain reasons why we shall have to take number forty-eight along with us. [BUDD *shrugs his shoulders and exits.*] About face! Forward, march! To the life-saving station! [KI-RAM *and* HADJI *off left, keeping step.*]

HARDY. [*Looking at* CHIQUITA.] Chiquita, simply marvelous! In two days you have become quite assimilated. Permit me. [*Kisses* CHIQUITA. *Exclamation of surprise from* HENRIETTA.] What's the matter? Haven't I a right to kiss my mother-in-law?

HENRIETTA. You have the right, but it is so *unusual.*

HARDY. And a charming mother-in-law, too. Only to think— yesterday morning an untamed creature of the jungle, and now, thanks to our new policy, a genuine American girl.

CHIQUITA. Yes, a genuine American girl, for I'm going to get married right away.

HENRIETTA AND CHORUS

"FOOLISH WEDDING-BELLS"

When you are feeling out of gear
   And blue as indigo,
The world devoid of any cheer,
   Your spirits rather low,
Now this is what you ought to do, and that without delay:
Go seek the matrimonial mart—get married right away.

REFRAIN

For men they come, and men they go,
   Don't wait until tomorrow;
For those who wait too long may know
   A spinster's lot is sorrow.
Shut your eyes; grab a prize;
Choose a male at the bargain sale;
To single joys your last farewells,
And ring those foolish wedding-bells.

[*As she is singing the refrain, the wives and Imperial Guards come in, attended by pages who carry cushions.* BUDD *comes back from left and joins* CHIQUITA. *A stately dance follows the repeat of the refrain, at the close of which the men are kneeling on the cushions, each in front of the maiden of his choice.* KI-RAM *and* HADJI *come from palace.*]

HENRIETTA. [*To* KI-RAM.] I have arranged everything.

KI-RAM. Talk about your matrimonial jack-pots! Now, then, who's going to perform the ceremony?

HENRIETTA. I have sent for the Judge-Advocate. [PAMELA *enters and comes down center.*]

KI-RAM. Oh, fie, fury, fiddle, and fudge! [*Falls in* HADJI's *arms*]

PAMELA. Well, what is required?

CHIQUITA. [*Mischievously and triumphantly.*] We want to get married— *all* of us.

PAMELA. *Married!* You, *too*, Colonel?

BUDD. [*Embarrassed.*] I'm afraid so.

PAMELA. Oh, Colonel, how *could* you! [*Signs of breaking down.*]

KI-RAM. He couldn't, so we arranged it for him.

PAMELA. *You* arranged it? Aha! I *see*. [*To the women.*] You have been deceived. [*Men arise.*]

WOMEN. *Deceived?* [*Pages remove cushions.*]

PAMELA. Don't you remember what I told you? If you remarry, you lose all interest in the royal estates. Marry, and that moment you are *paupers*.

CHIQUITA. You forget. We are now *American girls*, and *they* never marry for money. [KI-RAM *and* HADJI *applaud loudly.*] Begin the service.

PAMELA. *No!* If you will not save yourselves, then *I* will save you. *Listen* to this order of the court. The divorced wives of Ki-Ram shall not marry within the year. [*A general exclamation of disappointment. Soldiers embrace the wives sympathetically.*]

PAMELA. [*To* KI-RAM.] Now, what do you say?

KI-RAM. I don't dare to say it, there are ladies present. Have mercy, Judge. [*She spurns him.*] Have a card.

    [*She looks at him contemptuously and stalks away, followed by the sorrowful couples, leaving* KI-RAM *and* HADJI *alone with their misery. They squat at center, utterly discouraged.*]

KI-RAM. Hadji, pull down the blinds. The matrimonial agency is busted. [GALULA *slips on from left and stands behind him, gently fanning. He sits up, alarmed. Looks at* HADJI.] Do you feel a draft? [*Turns and sees* GALULA.] Oh, Galula, don't you think I'm having trouble enough? [*She exits to left, crestfallen, as the* DATTO MANDI *of Parang, a fierce and bearded warrior, brandishing a long sword, comes stealthily from right and approaches* KI-RAM.]

HADJI. I wonder what's going to happen next. [KI-RAM *sees* MANDI *and falls over in mortal terror.* HADJI *scrambles to the end of the chain.* MANDI *has his sword up and is about to despatch* KI-RAM, *when* JONES *comes on from right and stops him.*]

JONES. You mustn't kill this man. I've insured his life for fifty thousand pesos.

    [*Loud cheering heard outside.* KI-RAM, HADJI, *and* MANDI *listen, surprised.*]

HADJI. What's that? [JONES *runs up steps and looks out.*]

JONES. Aha! The campaign clubs are coming, and the two candidates for Governor.

KI-RAM. Candidates for Governor?

JONES. Certainly. Politics follows the flag.

    [*More cheering. A crash of brass-band music, and a political parade comes into view. First, "The Sulu Democratic Marching Club," with a large banner. Soldiers, natives, wives, etc., march four abreast. Then the "Sulu Republican Marching Club," with banner, tin horns, badges, etc. The Democrats mass at the left, and Republicans at right.* BUDD, PAMELA, HARDY, HENRIETTA, CHIQUITA, *and* JONES *in the center.* DIDYMOS *and* RASTOS, *in frock-coat costumes and tall hats, come down and do a lively dance.*]

KI-RAM. Colonel, what in the name of Aguinaldo[6] does this mean?

BUDD. I will explain. When you went to prison, *I*, as military commander, became Governor *pro tem.*, until the people could elect a new governor. The first political campaign is now in full swing. Permit me to introduce the Honorable Mr. Rastos, the people's choice, Republican candidate for Governor of Sulu. [*Cheers and horn-blowing on the Republican side.* RASTOS *bows to the ovation, and then looks at* KI-RAM *scornfully.*] And the Honorable Mr. Didymos, the workingman's friend, Democratic candidate for Governor of Sulu. [*Cheers and horn-blowing on the Democratic side.*]

HADJI. [*To* KI-RAM.] What are we—Populists?

KI-RAM. No. We are Prohibitionists. Colonel!

BUDD. Well?

KI-RAM. Colonel, this is the final blow. Take me back to prison. Lock me in the deepest, darkest, dampest dungeon, and keep me there forever. [*Boom of cannon heard.*]

BUDD. What's that? [*Enter* Soldier.]

SOLDIER. The despatch-boat has arrived with orders. [*Gives official-looking paper to* BUDD *and one to* HARDY.]

HARDY. [*Looking.*] What's this? [*Reading.*] "For bravery displayed in the capture of the desperate and bloodthirsty Mandi, you are made a brigadier-general."

HENRIETTA. A brigadier-general!

HARDY. Yes! Of Volunteers, too! A hero at last! [*He embraces* HENRIETTA.]

KI-RAM. A hero! Now he'll have to be investigated.

BUDD. [*Looking at paper.*] Aha! This is important. [*Reads.*] "The Supreme Court decides that the constitution follows the flag on Mondays, Wednesdays, and Fridays only. This being the case, you are instructed to preserve order in Sulu, but not to interfere with any of the local laws or customs. [*To soldiers.*] Release him! He is no longer convict number forty-seven. He is—the Sultan!

[*The soldiers hastily remove the chains. One hands* KI-RAM *his royal Sulu head-gear. As he puts it on there is a blare of trumpets. All the natives salaam humbly.* DIDYMOS *and* RASTOS *kneel in trepidation.* KI-RAM *swaggers back and forth in front of the assemblage.*]

KI-RAM. [*To* DIDYMOS *and* RASTOS.] You two *statesmen* hurry and get me a throne.

CHIQUITA. [*Sadly.*] And are we still your wives?

KI-RAM. Not if I can help it. You go to Parang with Mandi.

CHIQUITA. We don't want to go.

KI-RAM. I don't care where you go, but the alimony ceases. [*He mounts an improvised throne at center.*] Judge Jackson!

PAMELA. [*Coldly.*] Well, sir?

KI-RAM. Back to Boston! As for the brother of the sun, he will resume operations as the Sultan of Sulu.

FINALE

KI-RAM

And this is why, you'll understand,
I love my own, my native land,
 My little isle of Sulu!
 Smiling isle of Sulu!
I wasn't ready to say good-bye,
And I'm glad that I didn't have to die.

[*All repeat*]

CHORUS TO AUDIENCE

Since we first met you,
Since we first met you,
The open sky above us seems a deeper blue;
Golden, rippling sunshine warms us through and through
 Each flower has a new perfume,
 Since we met you!

CURTAIN

NOTES ON THE PLAYS

1. *Aunt Fanny from Chautauqua*, although published in 1949, was written about 1906, the year Ade wrote several one-act plays, including *Marse Covington, Nettie,* and *Speaking to Father*. According to biographer Lee Coyle (*George Ade*, Twayne Publishers, 1964), p. 141, Ade was "a life-long agnostic." Ade's supercilious attitude toward Chautauqua, New York, as "the home of piety, prayers, and psalm-singing" (see Letter to Louise Dresser) is reflected in Flossie's remark that "when Aunt Fanny was eight years old she could recite one thousand verses of Scripture." In 1873 John Heyl Vincent (1832–1920), a Methodist bishop, along with his associates, designed an eight weeks' summer Sunday school and institute that included not only religious but also secular courses in science, the arts, and the humanities. The next year hundreds of participants attended; and in the following

years, thousands each summer. In 1912 the enterprise was organized com-
mercially, with branches in many areas beyond the state of New York. Although Chautauqua remains a family place, it has broadened its facilities,
activities, and entertainment far beyond its original, narrower ambience.
The lodging accommodations now range from modest cottages to elaborate
hotels. The range of summer sports and recreation is augmented by legiti-
mate theatre productions and cinema, by opera and rock concerts. See J. H.
Vincent, *The Chautauqua Movement* (1886; 1971), and Gay MacLaren, *Morally
We Roll Along* (1938).

2. Albert Von Tilzer (1878–1956) of Indianapolis was a publisher and
composer. He remains best remembered for the song "Take Me Out to the
Ball Game," written in collaboration with Jack Norworth.

3. From *In Babel* (New York: McClure, Phillips & Company, 1903).

4. *The Sultan of Sulu*, with music by Alfred Wathall, was produced by the
Castle Square Opera Company, under the direction of Henry Savage, at the
Studebaker Theatre, Chicago, March 11, 1902. Ade's best friend, John T.
McCutcheon, had designed the sets and the costumes. The play was first
published in 1903 by R. H. Russel, New York; the music in the same year by
M. Whitmark & Sons, New York and Chicago.

There had been no pre-Chicago tryouts. However, certain revisions
prompted an out-of-town tryout the next month—on Thursday, April
24—at the Lafayette, Indiana, Opera House. A special train was chartered,
and the company stayed briefly at the Lahr Hotel. In the *Lafayette Courier*
writeup of April 25, George Barr McCutcheon declared "Ade's book a masterpiece of satire," praised Mr. Wathall's music, along with "the women, who
were pretty and could sing"; observed that the Purdue boys, who packed the
gallery, "cheered at all the right moments"; reported that Ade and John T.
gave command speeches after the final curtain, Ade saying he was glad to be
home, and John T. saying that in his costume designs he had not followed
the Sulu styles too closely, "preferring not to shock the ladies." See A. L.
Lazarus and Victor H. Jones, *Beyond Graustark* (Port Washington, N.Y.:
Kennikat Press, 1981), p.70.

The first Boston performance was at the Tremont Theatre on December
1, 1902. The first New York performance was at Wallack's Theatre on December 20, 1902, whence the play ran for over 100 consecutive performances.

Ade's inspiration for this play was no doubt his friend John T. McCutcheon's real-life encounter with some Sulus in 1899 shortly after his
swashbuckling exploits in the Battle of the Philippines. For McCutcheon's
account, see his "Sultan of Sulu," Chapter 20, in *Drawn from Memory* (Indianapolis: Bobbs-Merrill, 1950), pp. 142–148.

5. George Ade's Program Note about Sulu:

Sulu, or Jolo, is the largest of the southerly islands in the Philippine
group. The chief ruler of the island [in 1899 was] Hadji Mohammed
Jamalul Ki-Ram, Sultan of Sulu and Brother of the Sun. His rule
[had] been disputed by certain dattos or chiefs, with whom he kept
up a running warfare. One of the characteristic features of that warfare: the abduction of women. The natives of Sulu [were] Moham-
medans, polygamists, and slaveholders. The American troops landed

in Sulu in 1899 and after some parleying came to a peaceable agreement with the Malay ruler. He renounced his title of Sultan and became Governor at a fixed salary. "The Sultan of Sulu" is not an attempt to show what subsequently happened, but merely what might have happened.

The Sultan of Sulu is in the public domain and may be performed without fee. Although the musical score is also in the public domain and hence requires neither permission fee nor royalty, photocopies of archival copies may be *purchased* from the New York Public Library, the Chicago Public Library, or the Los Angeles Public Library. Copies of the score may also be *rented* from theatrical music research companies. One such is The Monterey Orchestration Rental Service, P.O. Box 462, Monterey, California 93942.

6. Emilio Aguinaldo (1869–1964), Phillippine leader in the 1896 insurrection against Spain.

IV

Essays

HOME COOKING[1]

Each spring, as we say good-bye to the final buckwheat cake of reluctant spring and go forth, wearing garlands, to greet fried chicken, we are again reminded that what every woman knows can never be learned by a chef.

Regard the two items listed in the preamble.

When the first killing frost whitens the fields, Aunt Libbie compounds a large crock of batter which is bubbled on top and has a yeasty aroma. She keeps it in a warm spot and, by judicious replacing, dips from the earthen vessel, during the cold months, say 2800 to 3000 buckwheat cakes which are as much superior to the factory-made flapjacks of hotels and restaurants as roses are more fragrant than rutabagas.

Here is a question never yet answered: Why cannot hotels and clubs and cafes master the simple technique which seems to be nature's gift to every housewife?

Why is it that when you put a white cap on a man and pay him $18,000 a year he can think of nothing except sauces?

Is he too proud to go to Aunt Libbie and find out how to rush from the griddle a product that is thin and hot and snappy and crispy and altogether enticing?

He has a million recipes with French labels, but when he serves an order of strawberry shortcake, he simply advertises his shame.

Certain dishes may be regarded as the culinary corner-stones of domestic tranquility.

She who makes good oyster soup deserves every honor accorded Joan of Arc.

Oyster soup? Why should it be a hidden and unattainable secret to any one?

And yet, when you get among the onyx columns and the Alsatian noblemen and the symphony orchestras, the glorious blending of savory ingredients becomes a tepid pool in which oysters at high-fever temperature are struggling feebly.

Any man who has lived in a civilized home knows the ritual in connection with poultry of the adolescent kind.

He knows that the carcass should be dismembered into the largest possible number of units and that these priceless tidbits need to be soaked in cold water before they are rolled in flour and committed

181

to the hot skillet. Then there is a precautionary steaming just before they are hand-forked to the platter.

Year after year the patrons lined up at public eating racks have been ordering "Fried chicken, country style," hoping in vain that some day or other they will get what they want.

It is now a crime to shake up a cocktail and yet thousands of caterers who try to fry one half of a spring chicken in one individual segment are permitted to stay out of jail.

Shall we take up the matter of waffles? How about rice pudding?

Did you ever find in a four-million-dollar hotel the kind of layer cake served by the ladies of the M. E. Church?

Fillet of sole as done at the Marguery—yes! Cottage cheese, mince pie, new asparagus in cream, light biscuit cookies, noodles—no!

THE MONEY PRESENT[2]

Bless the little ones! We must remember them at Christmas, and what could be more appropriate to the glad season than a small money deposit in some reliable bank.

We are a business people. We admit it. Why not give our children a long, running start toward a business education?

The Noah's Ark animals become scattered and splintered. The drums are punctured and the cast-iron fire engine goes into the scrap-heap before May 1st, but the money in the bank endures as a permanent asset.

Candy sometimes causes stomach-ache and the nuts of commerce contain such a large percentage of oil that a small child having partaken too freely becomes oleaginous, and complains of twinges in the digestive regions. Even books lose their value after a first reading and are pushed away and neglected.

But the money in the bank never plays out. It is right there, ready to be borrowed by papa if he chances to run short and overdraw his own account. And there is no hurry about returning it, because the money is always deposited on condition that it cannot be withdrawn until the child is twenty-one.

Picture: It is the cold grey of Christmas morning. The youngster has slept uneasily and has seen Santa Claus, with smoky breath and frosty coat, peeking into his room. In his fitful naps he has reviewed a procession of red sleds and stood under a festoon of steel skates, tempered to a handsome blue.

At last his eyelids part reluctantly and the first light of morning is squared out at the window. His heart gives a few thumps and he squirms among the warm covers, shaking off his drowsiness and hoping hard that there will be something in the stocking.

This is Christmas morning at last! He has been counting the mornings, "Seven more until Christmas," and then "Six more until Christmas" and so on until it is not even one more morning until Christmas, for the day and the morning have come. He wonders if the skates are there. He is impatient to find out, and yet almost afraid to slip out in the cool ghostly silence and investigate. Not that he is afraid of the shadows and the stillness, but he is faltering at this last moment and wondering if his very politic remarks in regard to skates, a steam engine and plenty of candy were taken seriously.

He cannot lie there and struggle with uncertainty. His two bare feet strike the rug simultaneously and he patters swiftly to the front room.

There hangs the stocking—limp and empty. The hot tears blind his eyes and he has a smothery feeling at the throat. With a despairing sniffle he seizes the stocking and—what is this? There is something inside, after all.

Hope rises faintly within him. He draws out a little hand-book and sees on the first page, in a firm business hand, the entry, "Cash, $5."

Oh, what a sweep of joy engulfs the young soul at that moment! He has not been forgotten by good old Santy! No indeed! He has five dollars locked up in the bank.

Although he will be unable to get at the money, the knowledge that it is in the custody of a responsible corporation and can be withdrawn in fifteen years, should be sufficient to warm the imagination of any child and set the carols to singing in his heart.

With what ecstasy he scampers away to tell papa and mamma of his great fortune. He waves the bank-book above his head and his gleeful shouts break the dull silence of dawn. What cares he now for skates, picture-books, nuts or candy?

"Oh, look, papa!" he exclaims. "See! I have five dollars deposited to my credit with the savings department of the Herculanaeum Bank and Fundamental Reserve Trust Company! Am I not to be congratulated?"

Witness, also, the glad scene after breakfast.

Papa has taken little Robbie on his lap and together they are figuring out the compound interest on $5 for a period of fifteen yearts, at 4 per cent per annum.

How the little one's eyes sparkle with understanding as he studies the long row of figures and realizes that within the next twelve months his deposit will earn twenty cents interest.

While he is at school, striving to improve his mind, and while he is playing with his youthful companions, perhaps forgetting his deposit in the excitment of the moment, his money will be increasing at the rate of one and two-thirds cents a month.

What a child needs is a bank account. When a boy is six years old it is time that he be made to grapple with the sombre responsibilities of commercialism. If he weeps and does not seem to feel the advantage of having five dollars secreted in a bank, explain to him the beauties of business economy and load him down with maxims.

What a Christmas we could have if parents would refrain from giving their children boxes of candy, sacks of nuts, fairy tales, winking dolls, sets of dishes, games, building blocks, mechanical toys, jumping jacks and such fripperies, and, instead, gave each child a hand-written certificate of deposit! Santa Claus should wear side-whiskers and a tall hat and carry a burglar-proof safe in the back of his sleigh. . . .

AFTER THE
SKYSCRAPERS, WHAT?[3]

Every time the down-town confusion of roofs, chimneys and towers is viewed from some eminence there must come to the mind a query: "When will Chicago reach the era of stability?"

Over there to the northwest a cluster of men no larger than flies are hacking away at a roof from which arises dry clouds of dust. The first blow is struck at the cornice, and the destruction is not to cease until the last foundation stone has been rooted out of the clay.

To the northeast is a right-angled web of steel towering above black roofs and showing like the skeleton of a great monument.

There has not been a time in years when the destruction and

construction were not to be seen from this same window, and even the old residents who have watched the ceaseless and marvelous changes of the business district say it is apparently as much unfinished as it was fifty years ago. They may come back in spirit a few centuries hence to view the same old tearing down and building up.

* * *

Chicago need not complain because the critics are not satisfied with this town. The town is never satisfied with itself. A man builds a six-story brick building with a stone front, across the top of which is a tablet bearing his name. It fills with tenants, the foundation settles into place and is ready for permanency. The man snaps his fingers and says: "Pshaw, this will never do! I must have been an idiot—building for a village!" Out go the tenants, bag and baggage; in goes the wrecking crew, and behold! there remain only a hole in the ground and a barricade of rubbish, and the pedestrians have to walk in the street to avoid the horrors of improvement.

This business region is like a household which never settles down—where the "cleaning" goes ahead the year round.

To-day the drawing-room is full of ladders and buckets.

To-morrow the dining-room is having doors hacked through its walls and a new floor is being put down.

The down-town thoroughfare no sooner adopts a tidy front and an unbroken row of bright windows before a vandal army wrenches a building to pieces, puts a rough wooden shed over the sidewalk and begins the clamorous work of driving the earth full of enormous piles, on which is to rest the towering structure of bolted steel. Then the way is strewn with bricks, sand and riveted slabs of metal.

"It's an ugly locality while the work is in progress, but wait until the skyscraper is completed and the litter taken away." That's the consolation. When the day comes the vandals rush upon a building next door, and once more—Babel.

After the skyscraper, what?

The corner building lot on the busy corner held in the '30s a two-story frame with a peaked roof. It was a likely building, but the '40s wouldn't have it.

Then there came a three-story frame with a square front to the street and a double storeroom down-stairs. And the '50s sneered at it.

Nothing would do but brick. The new building was longer and had stone steps in front, with fancy work along the cornice and the inside doors were "grained." They called it a "block." But long before the fire wiped it away it stood abashed in a neighborhood of larger buildings and the tenants were third-class.

There came an opportunity after the fire to build a magnificent business structure which should anticipate the growth of the city rising from its ashes. What if the people did call the builder reckless when he made the entire front of heavy stone, which overhung in carved folds? Why not heed the lesson of the fire and build something to stand forever? It was a pride indeed—five stories high, finished inside with hardwood and a multiplicity of gas-jets. There was a passenger elevator and the windows had plate glass. At last it deserved the name of "block" and its offices were greedily taken.

•   •   •

In a matter of a very few weeks the gaunt triumph of new methods was completed. It had the architectural proportions of a hitching-post and it had been reduced in rank from a "block" to a "building." But it was a great success. Men passengers clung to the bars and women shrieked in hysteria when one of the lightning elevators made a rocket leap for the roof. There was a restaurant in the basement, a cigar-stand in the main lobby and a barber-shop on the eleventh floor, to say nothing of mail-chutes, a telegraph office and a bureau of clean towels.

The owner was satisfied. He had reached the climax once more and was just as certain of it as his predecessors had been back in the '30s, '40s, '50s and '70s. But after the skyscraper, what?

A BREATHING-PLACE AND PLAY-GROUND[4]

Comparisons between the three divisions of the city [of Chicago] are always odious.

One cannot rhapsodize too much over the advantages of the

Lincoln Park

south side without rousing the wrath of the numerous west-siders, while the statement that either the south side or the west side affords a pleasanter location for a residence than the north side simply moves every north-sider to a broad smile of contempt.

Each division has something to be proud of, and after hurrying the visitor through a fringe of slums can show him certain "views" intended to excite his admiration. On the west side it will be a view south on Ashland Avenue, a majestic thoroughfare which always seems ready to be put in a picturebook, or a glance at Union Park and the delightful panorama of Washington Boulevard.

On the south side Michigan Avenue and the branching boulevards to the south, the flowery gateway to Washington Park and the imposing pile of buildings overshadowing the lake front will be submitted as about the best things that the town can show a stranger.

The north side has Lincoln Park,[5] the Lake Shore Drive and those exclusive residence thoroughfares, the "places" and "courts" running east to meet the lake. It also has Washington Square, and to many people this is the most picturesque bit in all the great division, because it is a green spot standing in a framework of noble architecture and bearing a certain dignity which comes only with age.

Washington Square is bounded by Clark Street, Walton Place, Dearborn Avenue and Washington Place. At the west the bright-colored cable cars chase back and forth all day. On the east is the smooth, white boulevard, alive at every hour with flying wheelmen and handsome carriages. Between these thoroughfares lies a patch of nature almost undisturbed. The two diagonal pathways meet in the center where a fountain splashes into a rocky basin. The trees are high and gnarled, throwing great irregular areas of shade on the ground.

The landscape gardener has done but little for the square. It stands as nature decreed it and as the great fire mercifully spared it.

• • •

The fire of 1871 scorched to death nearly all the large trees on the north side. It happened, luckily, that there were few houses immediately west or southwest from the square. The Unity Church, of which the Rev. Robert Collyer was pastor, stood, as it now stands, at the corner of Dearborn Avenue and Walton Place. North from the square stood the Ogden house, one of the two houses in the burned district that escaped destruction. It was sheltered by the trees. As soon as the fire crossed the river many people hurried north to Washington Square with such goods as they could convey and put them in the square, thinking they would be safe there. Later, when the fire rushed northward with such rapidity, these people were compelled to fly for their lives, leaving their property behind. It was soon ignited by flying sparks and burned up. In a few hours the scorched trees of the square and the Ogden house, which they had sheltered, stood alone in a desert of strewn ashes.

• • •

Just across Walton Place from the square is the Newberry Library, its massive stone front of Spanish renaissance rising even above the highest trees. Unity Church and the New England Congregational Church face the square on the east. Each has a broad

"In pleasant weather the square is crowded"

Gothic front, which is beginning to show respectable signs of age. Facing the square from the south and standing at the corner of Dearborn Avenue is the Union club house, with its dark and heavy stone front. West of it is a row of tall, prim and freshly painted apartment houses.

With the venerable trees and the prospect of fortress walls and ponderous stone doorways to north, south and east, Washington Square has a charm peculiarly its own.

It is what one might expect to find in a city of a few centuries' growth, but in Chicago it is always supposed that the trees are to be set out in straight rows and the houses are to smell of fresh plaster and have the litter of the builders scattered around the front door.

· · ·

This particular portion of the north side, especially from Dearborn Avenue to the lake, is said to have had a more stable population during the last twenty-five years than any other region in Chicago. The men whose homes were burned in the great fire rebuilt on the same sites and assisted in rebuilding the churches. The congregations remained almost intact, while those in other parts of the city had to be reorganized. The neighborhood, not being subject to violent changes, settled down to eminent respectability and fixed habits of life, and these seem to find expression in the shady old-fashioned square.

In pleasant weather the square is crowded. The children come from a mile around to roll in the shade and dip their bare feet in the basin where the water falls. The nurse-maids wheel baby-carriages by day and the housemaids come with their young men at night. Men in working clothes sleep under the trees. Other men squat against the trees reading newspapers. The employe who picks up scraps of paper with a long sharp stick has to go around every hour or so.

It is a meeting place of all classes. The boys hauling their brother in a soap-box mounted on two wheels march ahead of a lavender-canopied baby-carriage. The dressed-up children from Dearborn Avenue, who dare not take off their shoes, are the only unhappy youngsters ever seen in the square. They suffer for awhile and then disobey the parental orders, just as they might be expected to do.

IN CHICAGO
BUT NOT OF IT[6]

Even the entrance to the Art Institute is not at all like Chicago. It has too many broad landings and too little regard for space. The great terraced front is spread over enough ground to make the site of a skyscraper. Then when the door is opened, instead of stepping into a corridor behind whose grated walls the elevator cages rise and fall, the visitor finds himself tip-toeing over the polished tiles, afraid to make any noise.

Any place as quiet as the Art Institute is a relief. The walls are dark-hued and restful, and there can be no more deadly silence than that made by a roomful of heroic casts and bronzes. The people who move along, usually two and two, fingering their catalogues and reading the unpoetic sticker labels, converse in whispers or a mumble. An occasional bell or whistle on the Illinois Central tracks interrupts for a moment, but the rattle of wheels on Michigan Avenue seems a long distance away.

The Art Institute is beginning to realize all hopes. During the summer of 1893 there was no room in it for the muses. It was in the possession of the busy delegate. Numberless typewriters were rattling away in the side rooms, the halls echoed with addresses of welcome which could not be easily located. There were many rooms and some kind of a "congress" in each that was large enough for a stage and a row of chairs. Morning, noon and night came the crushing at the doorways. Men and women with badges, catalogues and manuscripts elbowed one another. Policemen stood guard at every corner and told people to "take it easy." The place became littered with tracts and appeals and stray lace mitts and plain parasols.

Those were busy days—the days of the congresses when everything had to be discussed by some one—everything from esoteric Buddhism down to chop-feed. The delegates were for putting in as many hours as possible, so they ate at a café in a basement. Imagine the smell of cooking in a temple of art! The place certainly did not satisfy any artistic cravings. At the east were two huge temporary sheds made of wood and leaning in pitiful contrast against the classic pile. But even the stonework had a disturbing appearance. Some of it was white from the chisel and some blackened by the vandal influence of the smoke nuisance.

. . .

And now the change! The sheds have disappeared. The last blackboard chart and orator's glass pitcher were carted away many weeks ago. The kindly soot has made the whole exterior one unvaried shade of dinginess, suggesting an age equal to that of the pyramids. The committee-rooms and lecture halls have been given over to sculpture and architecture. Every bust, print or painting has found its niche. The whole interior glistens with cleanliness. In place of the congress orator you find the girl with the apron.

She is certainly more interesting, as a study, than a learned man with a passion for alpaca coats and white neckties. She is a student of art. As she would doubtless put it, she "is going in for art, and it's perfectly lovely." She has an easel and a boxful of rattling implements and a large square of paper marked with some strange beginnings, and a pair of coldly poised eye-glasses and the big gingham apron. Thus equipped she rambles, searching for that which she may make her own.

When you see her, you will say she is a refreshing sight. She spreads her easel in front of some plaster god, studies it in rapt ad-

At the Art Institute

miration for a few moments and then begins making marks. She holds the pencil out at arm's length and, sliding her finger back and forth, gauges the distances and proportions. Such industry and such painstaking are surprising in one who would be expected to waste her time on chocolates and matinées. Almost any day there are a score of the aproned young women at the Art Institute. When they become weary of sketching they huddle together on the big soft divans and take turn-about in raving over the Bonheurs, Geromes and Chases on the lower row of paintings.

•   •   •

Chicago isn't old enough to have very many artists who dare to affect long hair and it has no quarter where the art students flock, but the Institute seems destined to become the home of the enthusiasts. They avoid the Sunday crowds and come around on quiet afternoons to look and gloat. The average visitor passes along a row of pictures, giving about thirty seconds to each. If any one picture is unusually bold as to size, color or execution he pauses to nod his head and say: "Pretty good."

This is the visitor who does the place simply as one of the sights of the town. He may be following a guide-book program such as: "In the morning go to the Art Institute on the lake front; in the afternoon visit the stockyards; at night attend a meeting at the Pacific Garden Mission." The enthusiast does not walk up and down the room. He plants himself before the "work" to be admired and begins a critical analysis of color, shade, technique, feeling and all the other things which critics find in a painting. He looks at it as though he were trying to count the buttons on the coat of the man in the far background.

Take one of Rembrandt's, for instance. The ordinary visitor would call it a man wearing his hat. The enthusiast would not call it anything. He would only lift his eyes in unspeakable thankfulness that he had lived to stand before it.

MUSICAL COMEDY[7]

When the first piano was built the owner needed something to put on top of the piano, so the popular song and the light opera were invented. As the musical taste of succeeding buyers developed and improved, light opera became lighter and lighter until at last they had to weight it down to keep it on the piano. There came a time when the manufacturers were prohibited under the Pure Food Law from using the opera label. They had to call the output something or other, so they compromised on "musical comedy."

Musical comedy has done a great deal for our fair land. It has depopulated the laundries, reduced the swollen fortunes of Pittsburgh, and bridged the social chasm between the honest working girl and the pallid offspring of the captain of industry.

It has taught William Shakespeare how to take a joke. It has developed a colony of angels and incidentally it has given the foot-power piano an excuse for being.

A good musical comedy consists largely of disorderly conduct occasionally interrupted by talk. The man who provides the interruptions is called the librettist. I would advise any man who hasn't the nerve to be a foot-pad or is too large to get through a transom, to become a librettist.

> I'd rather be a burglar than the man who writes the book,
> For the burglar is anonymous—a self-concealing crook;
> When they catch *him* with the goods he merely does a term in jail,
> While the author has to stand and take a roast from Alan Dale.

I wrote this years ago, but it is still true.

The so-called music of musical comedy must be the kind that any messenger boy can learn to whistle after hearing it twice. At the same time it must satisfy the tall-browed critic who was brought up on Tschaikowski and Bach. As for the dialogue, it must be guaranteed to wring boisterous laughter from the three-dollar patron who has a facial angle of thirty degrees, and a cerebellum about the size of an olive; also it must have sufficient literary quality and subtle humor to please the dead-head who is sitting in the fourth row with a hammer in one hand and a javelin in the other.

Every young man who goes into the libretto business thinks he is going to revolutionize the American stage. He is going to begin where W. S. Gilbert left off. He gets a fountain pen, a pad of paper, and a few pounds of opiate, and then he dreams it all out. He is going to write a musical play with a consistent and closely connected plot, an abundance of sprightly humor and nothing said or done that would bring the blush of shame to the cheek of the most sensitive manager.

His getaway is usually very promising. By way of novelty he has an opening chorus. A lot of people are standing around in aimless groups there in the green sunshine. Occasionally the green sunshine changes to amber. They tell all about themselves and explain their emotions. Then the principals begin coming on and tell why *they* are present, and the wedding is announced and the people in front begin to get a faint outline of plot. This goes on for about ten minutes until a beautiful blonde, who was educated for grand opera and then changed her mind, suddenly says, apropos of nothing in particular, "Oh, I am so happy today I could sing my favorite song, 'Won't you be my little gum-drop?'"

That is what is known as a "music cue." That is where the author goes into the side pocket and the producer becomes the whole proposition.

First the beautiful blonde sings it all by herself. Then the beautiful tenor with talcum powder all over his face comes out and helps her. Then the refined comedian, recently graduated from vaudeville, breaks in and they do the gum-drop number as a trio. The soubrette arrives, merely by accident, and the song regarding the gum-drop now becomes a quartette. Then eight young ladies in Spanish costumes come out and sing it, introducing a dance. Then eight young ladies in white are lowered from the flies and they sing it while hanging in the air. Then the lights are turned out and the entire company sings it in the moonlight. Then the sunshine is turned on again and all sing it by daylight.

The man who leads the orchestra is a mind-reader. He knows that the public wants more verses of the gum-drop song whether it applauds or not. This is what is known as the "noiseless encore." The reason he is so willing to respond to encores is that he wrote the song.

At last, after the entire company has sung and danced itself into a state of staggering exhaustion, and even the iron-handed ushers have become satiated, the whole covey disappears and that grand old annoyance who shows up in every musical play, the bride's father, wanders on the stage and tries to collect the shattered fragments of plot. Of course nobody pays any attention to him. All the people in front are lying back limp and groggy, trying to recover from the excitement of that gum-drop affair. They have forgotten all about the fragment of "story" that showed up a half hour before. Father, however, starts in to remind the audience of the wedding day and the bride and the birthmark and the picture in the locket and the other essentials, and just about the time he is getting a foothold the Egyptian dancers glide on and everything is once more floating upside down in the air. The morning newspapers say that the plot did not seem to be well sustained.

I do not wish to be understood as attacking musical comedy. It has helped a great many people who belong in trolley cars to ride in motor cars. It provides mental relaxation for the tired business man who doesn't want to think. Probably if he ever stopped to think, he would get up and go out.

Musical comedy has educated the public. When it was first introduced the American people were devoted to such simple and old-fashioned melodies as "Roll On, Silvery Moon," "Then You'll Remember Me," "When the Corn Is Waving, Annie, Dear," and "The Gypsy's Warning." The campaign of education has been going on for years and now we have worked up to a midnight show on a roof, with songs which would be suppressed by the police if the police could fathom the significance of the *double entendre.*

It is said that every man in the world thinks he can edit a newspaper, manage a hotel and write a comic opera. I have been in the newspaper business and I have gone against operas that were trying to be comic. I am still sure that I can manage a hotel.

THE JOYS OF
SINGLE BLESSEDNESS[8]

The bachelor is held up to contempt because he has evaded the draft. He is a slacker. He has side-stepped a plain duty. If he lives in the small town he is fifty per cent joke and fifty per cent object of pity. If he lives in a city, he can hide away with others of his kind, and find courage in numbers; but even in the crowded metropolis he has the hunted look of one who knows that the world knows something about him. He is led to believe that babies mistrust him. Young wives begin to warn their husbands when his name is mentioned. He is a chicken hawk in a world that was intended for turtle doves. It is always taken for granted that the bachelor *could* have married. Of course, he might not have netted the one he wanted first off. It is possible that, later on, circumstances denied him the privilege of selection. *But* it is always assumed by critics of the selfish tribe, that any bachelor who has enough money in the bank to furnish a home, can, if he is persistent, hound some woman into taking a chance.

Undoubtedly the critics are right. When we review the vast army of variegated males who have achieved matrimony, it seems useless to deny that the trick can be turned by any man who is physically capable of standing up in front of a preacher or whose mental equipment enables him to decide that he should go into the house when it rains.

If Brigham Young, wearing throat whiskers, could assemble between thirty-five and forty at one time, how pitiful becomes the alibi of the modern maverick that he never has managed to arrive at any sort of arrangement with a solitary one!

We know that women will accept men who wear arctic overshoes. Statistics prove that ninety-eight per cent of all those you see on station platforms, wearing "elastics" on their shirt-sleeves, have wives at home.

The whole defense of bachelorhood falls to the ground when confronted by the evidence which any one may accumulate while walking through a residence district. He will see dozens of porch-broken husbands who never would have progressed to the married state if all the necessary processes had not been elementary to begin with, and further simplified by custom.

Even after he is convinced, he will stubbornly contend as follows: "Possibly I am a coward, but I refuse to admit that all these other birds are heroes."

At least, he will be ready to confess that any one can get married at any time, provided the party of the second part is no more fastidious and choosey than he is. . . .

At this point we get very near to the weakest point in the general indictment against bachelors: Is it generally known that bachelors privately receive encouragement and approbation from married men?

Not from all married men, it is true. Not, for instance, from the husband of any woman who happens to read these lines. But they *do* receive assurances from married men, of the more undeserving varieties, that matrimony is not always a long promenade through a rose bower drenched with sunshine. The word "lucky" is frequently applied to single men by the associate poker players who are happily married.

The difficulty in rescuing the hardened cases of bachelorhood is that the unregenerate are all the time receiving private signals from those supposed to be saved, to lay off and beat it, and escape while the escaping is good. Many of them would have fallen long ago except for these warnings.

There are times when the most confirmed, cynical, and self-centered celibate, influenced by untoward circumstances and unfavorable atmospheric conditions, believes that he could be rapturously content as a married man, and that he is cheating some good woman out of her destiny. Conversely, the Darby who wants the world to know that his Joan is a jewel and his children are intellectual prodigies and perfect physical specimens—even this paragon, who would shudder at mention of a divorce court, tells his most masonic friends that it must be great to have your freedom and to do as you darn please.

No matter which fork of the road you take, you will wonder, later on, if the scenery on the other route isn't more attractive.

The bachelor, being merely a representative unit of weak man-kind, isn't essentially different from the Benedict. Probably at some time or other he wanted to get married and couldn't. Whereas, the married one didn't want to get married and was mesmerized into it by a combination of full moon, guitar music, and roly-boly eyes. . . .

Bachelors are willing to be segregated or even separately taxed, but they don't wish to be branded with too hot an iron. They come to regard themselves as potential married men who never received notice of their inheritances. Married men are merely bachelors who weakened under the strain. Every time a bachelor sees a man with an alpaca coat pushing a perambulator, he says, "There, but for the grace of God, goes me!"

Whatever excuses the bachelor may secrete in his own mind, the following definite counts have been drawn against him:

1st. It is the duty of every good man to become the founder of a home, because the home (and not the stag boarding-house) is the cornerstone of an orderly civilization.

2d. It is the duty of every high-minded citizen to approve pub-licly the sacrament of marriage, because legalized matrimony is the harbor of safety. When the bachelor ignores the sacrament, his example becomes an endorsement of the advantages offered to travelers by that famous old highway known as "The Primrose Path."

3d. It is the duty of every student of history and economics to help perpetuate the species and protect the birth rate. . . .

The bachelor, as an individual, may sell very low in his im-mediate precinct; but the bachelor, as a type, has become fictionized into a fascinating combination of Romeo and Mephistopheles.

You never saw a bachelor apartment on the stage that was not luxurious and inviting. Always there is a man servant: It is midnight in Gerald Heathcote's princely lodgings. Gerald returns from the club. Evening clothes? Absolutely!

He sends Wilkins away and lights a cigarette. There is a brief silence, with Gerald sitting so that the fireplace has a chance to spot-light him. It is a bachelor's apartment and midnight. Which means that the dirty work is about to begin.

If, at any time, you are sitting so far back in a theatre that you cannot get the words, and you see a distinguished figure of a man come on R.U.E., self-possessed, debonair, patronizing—no need to look at the bill. He is a bachelor, and the most beautiful lady in the cast is all snarled up in an "affair" with him. . . .

That's the kind of a reputation to have! Never too old to be wicked! Lock up the debutantes—here come the bachelors!

ONE AFTERNOON
WITH MARK TWAIN[9]

It was in the late summer or early autumn of 1902, as nearly as I can fix the date, when Dr. Clarence C. Rice, a long-time friend and traveling-companion of Mark Twain's, came to me at my hotel in New York City and invited me to accompany him on a pilgrimage to the One and Only.

Of course I accepted the invitation. Probably no person, then alive and gifted with a pair of movable legs, would have done otherwise. And especially so myself. For a good many years I had been waiting and hoping to meet Mark Twain. I think I had read everything he ever wrote. With great admiration and respect I had witnessed his "come-back" in the early nineties, during which he re-paid a mountainous debt as a matter of honor, not of personal legal responsibility.

How unappreciative we often are, at the time, of the red-letter days in our lives! I cannot say that I was not impressed with the importance of the invitation to visit Mark Twain. I certainly was. But what was in my mind at the time was the belief that he would live for many more years; and that, having met him on this occasion with Dr. Rice, I would later visit him alone and at greater length.

My recollection is that I planned to have the next visit take the form of a newspaperman's interview. I knew that such an article would be in ready demand at a good price. But it was not the money I wanted; it was the honor of having written an article about Mark Twain, all-time Dean of American Literature, commanding figure in this country and throughout the world. Kipling had done a fine job of his interview with Twain at Elmira in 1889, as published in "From Sea to Sea" in 1899. Probably I was just enough conceited in those days to make a try at outdoing Kipling. I can't remember as to this. Time mercifully blots from our memories many of the follies of early life.

Although, at that time, I was regarded in some quarters as being a bit of a humorist myself, I do definitely recall that I had no thought of conferring with Mark Twain as a fellow fun-maker. Beside his towering fame, my own stature was something like that of a child's mud-pie man, placed alongside the statue of Rodin's "Thinker."

And thus it happened that I made no notes recording the details of the most momentous meeting of my life. I went; I saw and heard;

I came away. The tragic events of the few remaining years of Mark Twain's life made it impossible for me ever to talk with him again. I never wrote that masterpiece of an interview I was going to write. I have never before set down on paper the few impressions of our one meeting that still remain fixed in my mind.

Yes, if I had known that I was never again to meet Mark Twain, I would have come provided with a handful of pencils and my pockets bulging with copy paper. I would have carefully recorded the date, the state of the weather—every word he spoke, every trifling detail of that pilgrimage to the shrine of this immortal American.

Vaguely, I can recall that Dr. Rice and I journeyed up the Hudson by rail and alighted at a station which should have been named Riverdale. I was being escorted by Dr. Rice and paid little attention to the route. I don't even remember what kind of a vehicle it was that met us at the station and carried us up to a delightful, rambling, homey-looking old house on a hillside, surrounded by huge, wide-branching trees.

He stood alone on the porch, waiting to greet us. I can recall that he wore a white or tan-colored suit, loose and comfortable-looking, but not ill-fitting. From the moment that he took my hand in his firm clasp, he was the soul of kindliness, cordiality and affability. I can recall only his eyes. I lack words to describe them. Probably the word "imperious" comes close to describing the calm, penetrating, unwavering gaze he enveloped me with during the first few moments of our meeting. I was several inches taller than he, so that he must have looked upward into my eyes: yet I did not sense the difference in height. It seemed, indeed, as if he were looking downward on me.

We seated ourselves in roomy rocking-chairs on the porch. Courteously, Mark Twain asked about my trip to New York. He remarked that he and I would have been born in adjacent states if the damned geographers had not maliciously thrust Illinois between Indiana and Missouri. From then on, Dr. Rice and I did little talking. Our host was happy, expansive. He began his discourse by warning me that I was soon to be made the victim of a fantastic plan, evolved by a woman of family acquaintance, to translate some of my "Fables in Slang" into French.

"She cannot possibly find any French equivalents for your specimens of American vernacular," said Mr. Clemens, "but she is determined to make the effort and I am waiting until it is done so that I can watch some Frenchman go crazy while trying to read it."

I mentioned to him the fact that the "Jumping Frog" had been done into French, with disastrous results, and I said that I would not be a party to turning the "Fables" into that language. . . .

MARK TWAIN—EMISSARY[10]

Men and women in all parts of our spread-out domain, the men especially, cherished a private affection for Mark Twain. They called him by his first name, which is the surest proof of abiding fondness. Some men settle down to kinship with the shirt-sleeve contingent, even when they seem indifferent to the favor of the plain multitude.

Mark Twain never practiced any of the wiles of the politician in order to be cheered at railway stations and have lecture associations send for him. He did not seem over-anxious to meet the reporters, and he had a fine contempt for most of the orthodox traditions cherished by the people who loved him. Probably no other American could have lived abroad for so many years without being editorially branded as an expatriate.

When Mr. Clemens chose to take up his residence in Vienna nobody hurled any William Waldorf Astor[11] talk at him. Everyone hoped he would have a good time and learn the German language. Then when the word came back that he made his loafing headquarters in a place up an alley known as a *stube* or *rathskeller*, or something like that, all the women of the literary clubs, who kept his picture on the high pedestal with the candles burning in front of it, decided that *stube* meant "shrine." You may be sure that if they can find the place they will sink a bronze memorial tablet immediately above the principal faucet.

Of course, the early books, such as "Innocents Abroad," "Roughing It," and "The Gilded Age," gave him an enormous vogue in every remote community visited by book-agents. The fact that people enjoyed reading these cheering volumes and preserved them in the bookcase and moved out some of the classics by E. P. Roe[12] and Mrs. Southworth[13] in order to make room for "Tom Sawyer" and "Huckleberry Finn," does not fully account for the evident and accepted popularity of Mark Twain. Other men wrote books that went into the bookcase, but what one of them ever earned the special privilege of being hailed by his first name?

Is it not true that when a man has done his work for many years more or less under the supervising eye of the public, the public learns a good many facts about him that are in no way associated with his set and regular duties as a servant of the public? Out of the thousand-and-one newspaper mentions and private bits of gossip and whispered words of inside information, even the busy man in the street comes to put an estimate on the real human qualities of each notable, and sometimes these estimates are surprisingly accurate, just as they are often sadly out of focus.

Joseph Jefferson[14] had a place in the public esteem quite apart from that demanded by his skill as an actor. Players and readers of newspapers came to know in time that he was a kind and cheery old gentleman of blameless life, charitable in his estimates of professional associates, a modest devotee of the fine arts, an outdoor sportsman with the enthusiasm of a boy, and the chosen associate of a good many eminent citizens. When they spoke of "Joe" Jefferson in warmth and kindness, it was not because he played "Rip Van Winkle" so beautifully but because the light of his private goodness had filtered through the mystery surrounding every popular actor. William H. Crane[15] is another veteran of the stage who holds the regard of the public. It knows him as a comedian and also it knows him as the kind of man we would like to invite up to our house to meet the folks. The sororities throb with a feeling of sisterhood for Maude Adams[16] because the girls feel sure that she is gracious and charming and altogether "nice."

Mark Twain would have stood very well with the assorted grades making up what is generally known as the "great public" even if he had done his work in a box and passed it out through a knot-hole. Any one who knew our homely neighbors as he knew them and could tell about them in loving candor, so that we laughed at them and warmed up to them at the same time, simply had to be all right. Being prejudiced in his favor, we knew that if he wanted to wear his hair in a mop and adopt white clothing and talk with a drawl, no one would dare to suggest that he was affecting the picturesque. He was big enough to be different. Any special privilege was his without the asking. Having earned one hundred per cent of our homage he didn't have to strain for new effects.

His devotion to the members of his family and the heroic performance in connection with the debts of the publishing house[17] undoubtedly helped to strengthen the general regard for him. Also, the older generation, having heard him lecture, could say that they had "met" him. Everyone who sat within the soothing presence of the drawl, waiting to be chirked up on every second sentence with a half-concealed stroke of drollery, was for all time a witness to the inimitable charm of the man and the story-teller.

Furthermore, is it not possible that much of the tremendous liking for Mark Twain grew out of his success in establishing our credit abroad? Any American who can invade Europe and command respectful attention is entitled to triumphal arches when he arrives home. Our dread and fear of foreign criticism are still most acute. Mrs. Trollope[18] and Captain Marryat[19] lacerated our feelings long ago. Dickens came over to have our choicest flowers strewn in his pathway and then went home to scourge us until we shrieked with pain. Kipling simply put us on the griddle. Even to this day, when a frowning gentleman surrounded by shawls and Gladstone bags is discovered on the Cunard pier, we proceed to search him for vitriol. George Bernard Shaw peppers away at long range and the London *Spectator* grows peevish every time it looks out of the window and sees a drove of Cook tourists madly spending their money.

It is a terrible shock to the simple inlander who has fed upon Congressional oratory and provincial editorials, when he discovers that in certain European capitals the name "American" is almost a term of reproach. The first-time-over citizen from Spudville or Alfalfa Center indicates his protest by wearing a flag on his coat and inviting those who sit in darkness to come over and see what kind of trains are run on the Burlington. The lady whose voice carries from a point directly between the eyes, seeks to correct all erroneous impressions by going to the table d'hôte with fewer clothes and more jewels than any one had reason to expect. These two are not so much in evidence as they were twenty years ago but they are still gleefully held up by our critics as being "typical."

Probably they are outnumbered nowadays by the apologetic kind—those who approach the English accent with trembling determination and who, after ordering in French, put a finger on the printed line so that the waiter may be in on the secret.

There are Americans who live abroad and speak of their native land in shameful whispers. Another kind is an explainer. He becomes fretful and involved in the attempt to make it clear to some Englishman with a cold and fish-like eye that, as a matter of fact, the lynchings are scattered over a large territory and Tammany[20] has nothing whatever to do with the United States Senate and the millionaire does not crawl into the presence of his wife and daughters and the head of the House of Morgan[21] never can be King and citizens of St. Louis are not in danger of being hooked by moose. After he gets through the Englishman says "Really?" and the painful incident is closed.

Once in a while an American, finding himself beset by unfamiliar conditions, follows the simple policy of not trying to assimilate new rules or oppose them, but merely going ahead in his own way, conducting himself as a human being possessed of the standard human attributes. This unusual performance may be counted upon to excite wonder and admiration. Benjamin Franklin tried it out long ago and became the sensation of Europe. General Grant and Colonel Roosevelt got along comfortably in all sorts of foreign complications merely by refusing to put on disguises. But Mark Twain was probably the best of our emissaries. He never waved the starry banner and at the same time he never went around begging forgiveness. He knew the faults of his home people and he understood intimately and with a family knowledge all of their good qualities and groping intentions and half-formed plans for big things in the future, but apparently he did not think it necessary to justify all of his private beliefs to men who lived five thousand miles away from Hannibal, Missouri. He had been in all parts of the world and had made a calm and unbiased estimate of the relative values of men and institutions. Probably he came to know that all had been cut from one piece and then trimmed variously. He carried with him the same placid habits of life that sufficed him in Connecticut and because he was what he pretended to be, the hypercritical foreigners doted upon him and the Americans at home, glad to flatter themselves, said, "Why, certainly; he's *one* of us!"

INDIANA[22]

Indiana has a savor not to be detected in Ohio. It is decidedly un-Michigan-like. Although it tinges off toward Illinois on the west and Kentucky on the south, the community is neither nebulous nor indefinite. It is individual.

Indiana is not Out West or Way Down East or Up North or south in Dixie.

It is true that, west of the Platte River, Indiana is supposed to be under the wither and blight of Eastern decay. Conversely, as one leaves Columbus, Ohio, and moves toward the region of perpetual sea-food, he encounters people to whom Terre Haute and Cripple Creek are synonymous.

The Hoosier refuses to be classified by those who lack information. He knows that his state is an oasis, surrounded by sections. Our people are clotted around the exact centre of population. Boston is not the hub. It is a repaired section of the pneumatic rim.

When a state is one hundred years old (Indiana is beyond the century mark) it escapes the personal recollections of the pioneer, and is still so young that newspapers do not burn incense before the grandchildren of eminent grandparents.

We have grown some ivy, but we have not yet taken on moss.

Indiana has made history, but it figures that the present and the future are more worthy of attention than a dim and receding past.

Indiana has cemeteries and family trees, but does not subsist on them.

If the Hoosier is proud of his state, it is because the state has lived down and fought down certain misconceptions. Even in Cambridge, Massachusetts, the fact that Indiana produces more gray matter than hoop-poles is slowly beginning to percolate.

For a long time the Hoosier was on the defensive. Now he is on a pedestal.

Forty or fifty years ago the native son who went traveling owned up to an indefinite residence somewhere between Chicago and Louisville. Today the Hoosier abroad claims Indiana fervently, hoping to be mistaken for an author.

The Indiana man respects his state because it has grown to importance and wealth without acquiring a double chin or wearing a wrist watch.

The sniffy millionaire and the aloof patrician do not cause any trembles in the state of Indiana.

Even our larger cities have no thoroughfares shaded by the gloomy strongholds of caste. Some of the more enterprising comrades are unduly prosperous, but they continue to reside in homes.

The state is short on slums and aristocratic reservations. In other words, we are still building according to specifications.

The number of liveried servants residing within the boundaries is incredibly small and does not include one person born on the banks of the Wabash.

We have a full quota of smart alecks, but not one serf.

Because Indiana is not overbalanced by city population and is not cowed by arrogant wealth and has a lingering regard for the cadences of the spellbinder, an old-fashioned admiration for the dignified professions, and local pride in all styles of literary output, the Hoosier has achieved his peculiar distinction as a mixed type—a puzzling combination of shy provincial, unfettered democrat and Fourth of July orator. He is a student by choice, a poet by sneaking inclination, and a story-teller by reason of his nativity.

Indiana has been helped to state consciousness because a great man arose to reveal the Hoosiers to themselves. The quintessence of all that is admirable in the make-up of the native was exemplified in James Whitcomb Riley.

No wonder he was beloved and has become the central figure of our Walhalla. Why shouldn't we be proud of our own kin?

The state is full of undiscovered Rileys, inglorious but not necessarily mute.

Your passer-by looks out of the car window and sees the Hoosier on the depot platform, necktieless and slightly bunched at the knees. According to all the late cabaret standards, the Hoosier is a simpleton, the same as you observe in the moving pictures.

Alight from the train and get close to our brother before you turn in your verdict.

Forget that he shaves his neck and remember that many a true heart beats under galluses.

Pick out a low, roomy box on the sunny side of the general store and listen with open mind, while he discourses on the crops, and bass fishing, and preparedness for war, and General Lew Wallace, and Christian Science, and how to find a bee-tree. Do you want a line on Booth Tarkington or Albert Beveridge[23] or Tom Taggart?[24] He will give you the most inside information and garnish it with anecdotes.

The Hoosier may wear the wrong kind of hat, but he is alert on men and affairs and living doctrines. For sixty years the state has been a crucible of politics. It was a buffer between crowding factions all during the Civil War.

Just as the Hoosier emerges from the cradle he is handed a set of convictions and learns that he must defend them, verbally and otherwise. So he goes into training. He may turn out to be a congressman or a contributor to the magazines, but even if he escapes notoriety he will always be a belligerent, with a slant toward the intellectual.

What happened away back yonder to make Indiana different? Listen! There were two migrations early in the nineteenth century. From the seaboard there was a movement to the west. From the Carolinas and the mountain regions there was a drift northward across the Ohio River. Indiana was settled by pioneers who had the enterprise to seek new fields and the gumption to unpack and settle down when they found themselves in the promised land.

Indiana is a composite of steel mills and country clubs, factories and colleges, promoters and professors, stock-breeders and Chautauqua attractions, cornfields and campuses. It grows all the crops and propaganda known to the temperate zone.

If a high wall could be erected to inclose Indiana, the state would continue to operate in all departments, but the outsiders would have to scale the wall in order to get their dialect poetry.

Here's to Indiana, a state as yet unspoiled! Here's to the Hoosier home folks, a good deal more sophisticated than they let on to be!

HOOSIER HAND BOOK[25]
And True Guide for the Returning Exile

The train departs from Dearborn Station which is in Polk Street. The first few miles of the journey are devoid of special interest but a genuine thrill is guaranteed when the train emerges from the smoke-banks of Chicago, hurdles the state barrier and begins to amble through the sun-kissed plains of INDIANA...

After passing the ball park, please notice the Stock Yards on the right. You can't see them but you will notice them, if the wind favors.

ENGLEWOOD. 6.6 MILES. Discovered by a vaudeville comedian in 1880 and immortalized by the following joke, now rated as a classic:

JOKE

"Have you any children?"
"Yes—two living and one in Englewood."

Further along, BURNSIDE, where the whiskers come from.

The train passes near the works of the Ryan Car Company, making cars to ship Indiana novels, and moves swiftly through the suburbs of HEGEWISCH, the town advertised by the accomplished prize-fighter, Mr. Bat Nelson, who recently served a term as mayor.

Near the STATE LINE observe the intricate system of interlocking switches. This is said to be the most amazing display of switches to be found anywhere in the world, outside of Barnham's Hair Store.

The train crosses the STATE LINE and eagerly enters Indiana.

Note the smiling faces, the added tinge of green in the luxuriant vegetation, the simple majesty of the buildings that decorate the broad sweeps of the Hoosier Campana, and the peculiar turquoise blue of the sky—something like Italy, only more so.

Northeast from the point at which we enter our native state, lies the important town of WHITING, a distributing point for the late Standard Oil Company. Crude oil is piped to Whiting from many far-distant points in other states, and it is a significant fact that no matter how crude the oil may be when it arrives, after remaining in Indiana for a short time, it becomes refined.

HAMMOND. 20.7 MILES. For a long time the largest and busiest town in Lake County, Indiana, and not at all disposed to yield the supremacy over to Gary, which lies 8 miles directly east. The present population of Hammond is about 27,000.[26]

When the town was regarded as an unimportant suburb of Chicago, half lost in the marshes and sand-hills, it was said to have two seasons every year, viz.: the season in which huckleberries were ripe and the season in which huckleberries were not ripe. Far be it from any native Hoosier to jeer at the huckleberry, the ne plus ultra pie-filler of the civilized world, but it is a pleasure to record the fact that the huckleberry is no longer the principal export of Hammond.

After we have crossed the Grand Calumet river and as we approach the arch of triumph marking the entrance to Hammond, we will observe a great building set in an attractive park. This is the publishing plant of W. B. Conkey, a valued member of the Indiana Society. He gives employment to 1,000 persons, mostly literary experts, and is responsible for the fact that today the chief article of export is or are books.

The large plant of the Hammond Distilling Company, to be seen from the train, is owned by John E. Fitzgerald, also a member of this Society. Every day he converts 4,000 bushels of corn into an article of commerce intended to encourage political activity and foster the literary impulse.

Formerly the region about Hammond was the rendezvous of depraved characters from Chicago who came across the line to pull off prize-fights, dog-fights and chicken-fights. Not being satisfied with the sanitary arrangements and the table board in the Lake County jail, they have abandoned these forms of Sunday amusement. In fact, it is said that the tide of criminal emigration is now moving in the opposite direction.

The Grand Calumet river, which we see as we approach Hammond, is to be an important arm in the Lakes-to-Gulf[27] deep waterway project. Even now the Government is estimating the cost of dredging the river to a width of 200 feet and a depth sufficient to carry the great lake boats. This work is expected to be ordered by the war department at any moment.

Entering the city, the Monon parallels the Erie and the Nickle Plate roads, over which all the main line trains of these two systems pass. In the heart of the city is the crossing of the Monon and the Michigan Central. This crossing is one of the most dangerous in the world and is controlled by an electric interlocking tower. The Michigan Central line is a four track system which, with the other lines, makes a network of nine different tracks in the heart of the business district of the city.

The Monon depot is a relic of the golden days of railroading in Indiana and is about the oldest Hoosier in the state. The old building is soon to be torn down to make room for a handsome modern station.

The train rolls away from the factory suburbs and enters the farming country.

DYER. 29 MILES. Very near the Illinois state line; train crosses Michigan Central tracks. The town has a population of 400,[28] with a creamery and a flour mill.

The old Sac Indian trail, also known as the old Michigan City-Joliet trail, runs east and west through the center of the town. It will be seen after passing the station and is now a macadam road.

Dyer is on the direct motor route from Chicago to Indianapolis.

The farming country on either side becomes more attractive as the train draws away from the state line. Notice the excellent roads. Every highway is a boulevard, even in the most lonesome and sparsely populated corner of Lake County.

ST. JOHN. 33.5 MILES. 300 inhabitants;[29] settled by the Germans away back in 1837. The town is surrounded by a fertile and favored region and the Germans still own it, speaking and writing their own language in preference to English.

CEDAR LAKE. 39.5 MILES. The lake is at the left, 3 1/2 miles long and 1 to 1 1/2 miles wide, surrounded by low, wooded hills. It has about nine miles of shore line; is well known as a picnic and fishing resort. The large ice houses at the left, just as the train approaches the lake, were built by Armour & Company, but now belong to the Knickerbocker Ice Company. The large white building across the lake is Lassen's Pavilion, a dance hall and refectory. . . .

The train skirts the shores of the lake, past the little station of Creston, and we find ourselves once more in a beautiful farming country, with clean white houses and big red barns, good crop prospects and first-class roads everywhere.

Soon after leaving the lake, there will be seen on the left a pike road, parallel with the railroad. This road is a part of the Cobe Course over which the Automobile Road Race of 1909 was run.

LOWELL. 44.8 MILES. A prosperous agricultural town with a population of 1250.[30] The Crown Point–Lowell race course runs through the center of the town, and the speed maniacs from the city help to make life more interesting and uncertain in the sylvan retreat. . . .

Soon after leaving Lowell, the train passes from the rolling country devoted to farming and grazing, and we see on either side the flat, green expanse of the Kankakee marshes, with a level line of timber in the back-ground. . . .

SHELBY. 52.6 MILES. Has a population of 200,[31] and the Kankakee river is just ahead. . . .

The Kankakee is in great favor with fishermen, and there are club-houses at Water Valley, east of where the train crosses the river.

ROSE LAWN. 56.5 MILES. This town with the beautiful name has a population of 300.[32] Members are invited to look for the rose and the lawn from which the town derives its name.

After bidding good-bye to Rose Lawn, the train passes through a region formerly more or less submerged. The sand hills, with their growth of scrub and jack oak, mark what were once islands.

FAIR OAKS. 63.2 MILES. The north and south road which we cross at Fair Oaks is a branch of the Chicago & Eastern Illinois, running north to La Crosse, Indiana. Fair Oaks has a population of 250,[33] and ships every year 20,000 nursery trees, 1,200 tons of hay, 10,000 bushels of pickles and 3,000 bushels of onions.

Near the station is a 40 acre watermelon patch; also 14 acres devoted to the raising of ginseng and other medicinal herbs.

RENSSELAER. 72.8 MILES. The town lies some distance west of the tracks. Rensselaer is the county seat of Jasper County and is about as old as Chicago and is said to be better preserved as regards morals. The census of last year gave a population of 2,373,[34] since which time two old citizens have dropped dead on hearing that the Monon was about to build a new depot.

St. Joseph College, a Catholic School for boys, is just south of the city. It has an enrollment of 400 and is growing rapidly.

To assist the pilgrims in getting their bearings, it may be explained further that Rensselaer is 13 miles northeast of Hazelden Farm,[35] where the Indiana Society got together just one year ago.

Our own beloved James Whitcomb Riley once put this town into a characteristic bit of child's verse. He called it "Little Cousin

Jasper," probably referring to Jasper County. It is the plaint of a
small-town boy who is awed and humbled by a visit from a cousin
who lives at the wonderful county seat.

Here is a portion of "Little Cousin Jasper":

> Little Cousin Jasper, he
> Don't live in this town like me,—
> He lives 'way to Rensselaer,
> An 'ist comes to visit here.
> He says 'at our courthouse-square
> Ain't nigh big as theirn is there!—
> He says their town's big as four
> Er five towns like this, an' more!
> He says ef his folks moved here
> He'd cry to leave Rensselaer—

For 16 miles after leaving Rensselaer, the train will bowl across a
level region composed principally of green fields, fences and strolling live stock. This portion of Indiana is not mountainous. On the
contrary. We pass several little flag stations, and then pull into

MONON. 88.4 MILES. Monon is a collection of pleasant homes,
paved streets and shade-trees; population about 1,500.[36] The school
building cost $40,000. Division point on the Monon railroad and the
junction with the division running south through all of the colleges
of Indiana[37] to Louisville, and north to another penal institution at
Michigan City.

At the south edge of the town flows a rapid little stream called
the Monon . . . derived from the Indian word "Monong," meaning
"swift running water," and since the recent local option law went into
effect, nothing else is allowed to run in Monon.[38]

The train will stop [next] at

MONTICELLO. 98.6 MILES. The population of Monticello
2,500[39] except the year the census was taken when it happened to be
2,168. It stands on a high bluff, overlooking the beautiful Tippecanoe; has been a town ever since 1834. . . .

It is asserted that Noah unloaded the original pair of black bass
into the Tippecanoe river at this point.

Two high bridges span the Tippecanoe and the views up and
down the river, to say nothing of the boating and fishing, would well
repay any Hoosier for a special visit to this interesting town.

Beginning at about Monticello, we traverse an older region and
one with a greater diversity of scenery. We will find occasionally the
old time log house, the rail fences and the venerable orchard. . . .

One mile after leaving Monticello, we cross the Tippecanoe; beautiful view on either side. Two miles further on is the village of PATTON, with a population of 75 people, guaranteed by the postmaster to be "among the best on earth."

DELPHI. 111 MILES. The name of the town is a friendly little compliment to another town, well-known in Greece and the head-quarters of the Oracle.

One mile before arriving at Delphi, we cross the dear old Wabash river. Logansport is about 20 miles up stream and Lafayette about 20 miles down stream.

Delphi stands on an eminence, half buried in stately trees, and is a most pleasing town from any angle. The Wabash Railway runs through the town and between the Wabash river and the town, we see the old bed of the Wabash & Erie Canal, famous in its day. Along this section of the canal, President Garfield, when a bare-footed boy, worked as a mule-driver.

Delphi is wealthy. It has three banks and two loan and trust companies, with combined deposits of over $2,000,000 which is going some for a town of 2,200.[40] It has a splendid system of water works supplied by natural springs.

Delphi is on the banks of Deer Creek, which we see from a high bridge after leaving the city. . . .

Anyone who has been along Deer Creek will agree with the Hoosier Poet when he says:

On the banks o' Deer Crick! there's the place fer me!—
Worter slidin' past ye jes' as clair as it kin be:—
See yer shadder in it, and the shadder o' the sky,
And the shadder o' the buzzard as he goes a-lazin' by;
Shadder o' the pizen-vines, and shadder o' the trees—
And I purt' nigh said the shadder o' the sunshine and the breeze!
Well—I never seen the ocean ner I never seen the sea:—
On the banks o' Deer Crick's grand enough fer me!

Capt. Johnnie Lathrop is still leading the Delphi Silver Cornet Band. If you happen to be in town any Thursday evening, go up to the court house yard and listen to the concert.

A jealous journalist of Frankfort once wrote: "Delphi is a lonely old woodpecker, sitting on a dead snag in the Wabash valley. Its inhabitants thrive on reminiscences and journey once a week to the cemetery to repeat the Psalm of Life."

This is officially denied in Delphi.

Two miles farther on, a long trestle over the north fork of Wild

Cat creek; then the little town of OWASCO with about 100 inhabitants, 2 churches and a school building. We are now 122 miles from Chicago.

ROSSVILLE. 125.6 MILES. Population 800.[41] It is in Clinton county, one mile south of the Carroll county line, 16 miles due east of Lafayette, on the banks of Campbell's Run and has five miles of cement walks. Don't overlook Rossville.

More pleasing scenery of a varied agricultural description and then

FRANKFORT. 136 MILES. County seat of Clinton County and one of the important smaller cities of Indiana; population about 9,000. A town of handsome residences, well kept lawns and shady streets. It has one of the largest parks now maintained by a city of less than 10,000.[42] . . .

Further on, CYCLONE, 142.3 MILES, a very boisterous name for such a well-behaved little place.

More farm-houses and fields and fences. The tall wavy grain nearly ready to cut is wheat. The shorter and greener growth is oats. The corn is planted in single hills and about three feet apart.

KIRKLIN. 146.9 MILES. Population, about 1,000.[43] One of the oldest towns on the Monon between Indianapolis and Chicago. It was founded in 1832 on the Michigan road, a highway 100 feet wide. . . .

Observe the new $40,000 school building on the right as you approach the town. Quite a change from the little red shack of your boyhood days!

Look out of the car window anywhere between Frankfort and Sheridan and you will find a most satisfactory rural landscape, not only good to look at but wearing all the outward evidences of being populated by enterprising and progressive people. The word "progressive" is not used in a political sense.

Just after passing TERHUNE, 151.5 MILES, notice the stately grove of forest trees at the right.

Nearly every town in this favored region has a tile factory. The ovens for baking the tile look like coke ovens. The drainage tile made at these yards is used by the farmers for carrying water away from the low spots on their land. With the drainage and good roads the farmer no longer fears the wet weather.

Four miles after passing Terhune and just before entering the town of Sheridan, notice excavation on the left. Why the large hole in the ground? Well, 900 carloads of soil were dug up and shipped to Chicago and spread on the race course out at the Hawthorne

Track. It was decided, after much investigation, that Indiana soil helped to encourage a high rate of speed. . . .

George Boxley, the first white settler, came here in 1829 from Virginia, bringing with him a number of negro slaves, all of whom he liberated. . . .

Mr. Boxley was the first Socialist in this region. He insisted on sharing all his worldly goods with his neighbors and refused to pay any taxes.

HORTON. 159.9 MILES. Population about 300; in the heart of a fine farming region. The land hereabout will grow anything from a turnip to No. 2 wheat, but it makes a specialty of yellow dent corn.

Horton was a station on the "underground railway" before the war. . . .

Among the attractive features of Horton are 14 widows and a Methodist preacher who is also a first-class paperhanger.

SHERIDAN. 155.4 MILES. Population 2,000.[44] We are now in Hamilton County and only 28 miles from Indianapolis.

WESTFIELD. 163.4 MILES. Population about 800.[45] The town lies northeast from the station and is almost hidden by a grove of old maples. Important terminus of "underground railway." One of the very few towns of its size that never had a saloon. . . .

This is the smallest town in the state to secure and maintain a Carnegie Library. . . .

The factory just north of the station, with 13,500 panes of glass in the windows, is headquarters for the Hoyt Light for motor cars. East of the station is a cannery, handling tomatoes, corn, beans, and pumpkins.

Westfield is overwhelmingly Republican and for several years about the close of the Civil War, there was not one Democratic voter in the precinct. The Democrats explain that this was before the building of the new school house. . . .

We cross the Central Indiana tracks at Westfield.

CARMEL. 167.8 MILES. Population 700.[46] Only 16 miles from the Claypool. Grand farming country. One of the few Indiana towns still using natural gas.

Many miles before we really come to Indianapolis, we begin to see the suburbs, which indicates that the real estate men of all large cities smoke the same brand.

After passing Carmel the train will continue through a most inviting region. The home places seem to have the flavor of age and the log houses are actually venerable.

The train crosses the White River at

BROAD RIPPLE. 175.3 MILES. This spot will be remembered for ages because it was here that a railway train was wrecked, thereby instigating the poem by the Bard of Alamo[47] and contributing to English Literature the immortal couplet:

> Then I heard a poor man say,
> Cut, Oh, cut my leg away!

After passing Broad Ripple, Kingan's Ice House on the left.

Next the State Institute for the Blind, at the left.

Next the Mecca for every farm-hand, the State Fair Grounds, at the left.

We cross Fall Creek, the stream along which Gen. John Lipton floated when he was looking for a site for the capital of Indiana.

We pass Howland Station and the Belt Railway at 22nd Street and begin to move right into the city.

We cross Washington Street, which is part of the old National Road leading straightway from Washington to St. Louis.

After a glimpse of the famous Pogue's Run, we find ourselves at Union Station.

INDIANAPOLIS. 183.5 MILES. Population last year, 233,650. Population today and tomorrow, 500,000.[48]

Growing at the rate of 7,000 a year.

The city was laid out in 1821 and began on a capital of nothing. It now has, in the entire United States:

The Largest Saw Works

The Largest Hominy Mills

The Largest Buggy Factory

The Largest Manufacturers of High Grade Automobiles [e.g., Duesenbergs]

The Largest Motor Speedway

Home of James Whitcomb Riley, Benjamin Harrison, Albert J. Beveridge, Booth Tarkington, Meredith Nicholson.

And—The Largest Hearted People in the World. . . .

NOTES ON THE ESSAYS

1. From *Single Blessedness and Other Observations* (Garden City, N.Y.: Doubleday Page & Company, 1922).

2. From *In Babel* (New York: McClure, Phillips & Company, 1903).

3. From *Knocking the Neighbors* (Garden City, N.Y.: Doubleday Page & Company, 1912).

4. From *Knocking the Neighbors*.

5. Lincoln Park had been created under the leadership of Alderman Lawrence Proudfoot, the father of George Barr McCutcheon's wife, Marie.

6. From *Knocking the Neighbors*.

7. From *Single Blessedness*.

8. From *Single Blessedness*.

9. From *One Afternoon with Mark Twain* (Chicago: Mark Twain Society, 1939). The Mark Twain Society of Chicago was founded in 1939. In 1941 it became the Mark Twain Society of America. Its first president was George Ade.

10. From *Single Blessedness*.

11. William Waldorf Astor (1848–1919), American-British financier; son of John Jacob Astor (1822–1890).

12. E[dward] P[ayson] Roe (1838–1888), American clergyman and novelist. He wrote over 60 novels. His first, *Barriers Burned Away*, was based on Chicago's great fire of 1871. See Mary Roe, *EPR, Reminiscences of His Life* (1899).

13. Mrs. Southworth—Emma Dorothy Eliza Nevitti (1819–1899)—American author of over 60 novels, including *The Hidden Hand* (1859), which sold millions of copies. See R. L. Boyle, *Mrs. E.D.E.N. Southworth* (1939).

14. Joseph Jefferson (1829–1905), American actor, famous for his role in *Rip Van Winkle*. See his *Autobiography* (1890).

15. William H. Crane (1845–1928), American stage idol who ended his career in the movies.

16. Maude Adams, stage name of Maude Kiskadden (1872–1953), American actress best known for her role in James M. Barrie's *Peter Pan* (1905). She was a protégée of New York theatre manager Charles Frohman until 1915. In 1937 she became a teacher at Stephens College. See Phyllis Robbins, *Maude Adams: An Intimate Portrait* (1956).

17. In 1883 Mark Twain established his own publishing company, which lost a considerable amount of money, especially on a biography of Ulysses Grant. On the advice of Twain's friend Henry Rogers (of the Standard Oil Company), the publisher declared bankruptcy. But he still made good, eventually, on all of his debts—thanks to the subsequent financial success of his books published by Harper & Brothers. See Charles Neider, ed., *Mark Twain's Autobiography* (1958).

18. Frances Trollope (1780–1863) was the mother of the well-known English novelist Anthony Trollope (1815–1882). Also a novelist she is now remembered chiefly as the author of the travelogue *Domestic Manners of the Americans* (1832), recounting her visit to America and offensively criticizing her hosts.

19. Frederick Marryat (1792–1848), an English naval officer and novelist, whose best-known novel remains *Mr. Midshipman Easy* (1836). Marryat sojourned in the United States and Canada from 1837 to 1839; his *Diary in America* (1840) contains some unflattering observations.

20. The Society of Tammany, founded in New York City in 1786 (reor-

ganized 1789), at first championed Federalist causes but ultimately the modern Democrats. "Tammany Hall" came to be associated, in the public consciousness, as the center of boss-type politics, and its best known boss was William Tweed (1823–1878). In the late 1860s and early 1870s, during the reformers' campaign against Tweed, some devastating cartoons and caricatures, mostly by Thomas Nast (1848–1902), appeared in *Harper's Weekly*. See D. T. Lynch, *Boss Tweed* (1927).

21. John Pierpont Morgan (1837–1913), banker and philanthropist, leading contributor to and supporter of the New York Public Library and the Metropolitan Museum of Art.

22. From *Single Blessedness*.

23. Albert Beveridge (1862–1927), Hoosier statesman; author of *Life of John Marshall*.

24. Tom Taggart, mayor of Indianapolis from 1895 to 1901.

25. From *Hoosier Hand Book and True Guide for the Returning Exile* (Chicago: Indiana Society of Chicago, 1911), a humorous and nostalgic Baedeker that Ade wrote for his fellow Hoosier "exiles," members of the Indiana Society of Chicago, on the occasion of their Monon train excursion "back home to Indiana" on June 23, 1911. The *Hand Book* depicts summer scenes from the train on its progress from north (Chicago) to south (Indianapolis). For scenes in the reverse direction (from Lafayette to Chicago) during a snowy winter, see the poem "Boneless on the Monon," in *The Indiana Experience*, ed. A. L. Lazarus (Indiana University Press, 1977), pages 399–400.

26. Hammond, in 1980, had a population of 93,714.

27. The Lakes to Gulf Waterway project was completed in 1933. It connects Chicago and other Lake Michigan cities (including Burns Harbor, Indiana) with New Orleans and the Gulf of Mexico via the Illinois and Mississippi Rivers. Ade did not, of course, live to see the completion in 1959 of the St. Lawrence Seaway, which connects Chicago with the Atlantic Ocean.

28. Dyer, in 1980, had a population of 9,555.

29. St. John, in 1980, had a population of 3,974.

30. Lowell, in 1980, had a population of 5,827.

31. Shelby, in 1980, had a population of 14,989.

32. Rose Lawn (now spelled Roselawn) was not incorporated in the census year 1980.

33. Fair Oaks was not incorporated in the census year 1980.

34. Rensselaer, in 1980, had a population of 4,944.

35. Hazelden Farm was George Ade's estate in Brook (near Kentland), Indiana.

36. Monon, in 1980, had a population of 1,540.

37. The colleges of Indiana at that time were Purdue (Lafayette), Wabash (Crawfordsville), DePauw (Greencastle), Indiana University (Bloomington), and Indiana State University (Terre Haute).

38. Monon voters had just opted to go dry.

39. Monticello, in 1980, had a population of 5,162.

40. Delphi, in 1980, had a population of 3,042.

41. Rossville, in 1980, had a population of 1,148.

42. Frankfort, in 1980, had a population of 15,168.

43. Kirklin, in 1980, had a population of 662.

44. Sheridan, in 1980, had a population of 2,200.

45. Westfield, in 1980, had a population of 2,783.

46. Carmel, in 1980, had a population of 18,272.

47. Ade here misquotes one of the more obscure "Bards of Alamo": James Buchanan Elmore (1857–1942) of Alamo, Indiana, whose poem "The Monon Wreck" is reprinted in full in the anthology *Hoosier Caravan: A Treasury of Indiana Life and Lore* (Bloomington: Indiana University Press, 1951, 1975). A less obscure Alamo Bard was Joaquin Miller (1841?–1913), a native of Liberty, Indiana, whose 1836 poem "Defense of the [Texas] Alamo," although equally undistinguished, was widely anthologized during the late 1800s.

48. Indianapolis, in 1980, had a population of 700,807.

V

Verses and Songs

THE COLLEGE SERENADE[1]

When the chapel bell struck the midnight hour
And the campus lay asleep,
We'd count the strokes from the ivy tower,
Then out from our dens we'd creep;
And the guiding star in the lonely night
For all of that rollicking crew,
As it gleamed afar—'twas the signal light
Where she waited for me and you.

Oh, sweet co-ed! Oh, college maid!
The one we went to serenade.
Oh, star-lit night!
Oh, glimpse of white,
At the window overhead!
Back, through the years
Of smiles and tears,
I'll dream of that rare co-ed.

WHAT MAN DARE SAY?[2]

What man dare say that he is quite immune
  From charms and spells that ev'ry girl possesses?
A budding love is like the warmth of June,
  That lulls and dulls his senses ere he guesses;
Yet who should seek to fly from such attack?
  Though stricken sore, I hold my charmer blameless;
My truant heart I would not summon back,
  I leave it in the care of one who's nameless.

He jests at scars who never felt the blow
  That comes when love first smites and sends him reeling;
The stinging arrow speeds and brings him low,
  While pain and pleasure blend in that new feeling.

221

I care not if the wound will never heal;
  My weakness I proclaim in manner shameless;
I'll never see her more and yet I feel.
  I'll love thro' all the years the one who's nameless.

THE WOMAN WITH AN ORDINARY PAST[3]

I

The folks in Section A
Who watch a problem play
Of the kind C. F.[4] imports for Ethel Barrymore
  Will pity quite a lot
  Poor Sadie in the plot
Who has such a load of grief she couldn't carry more.
  At present she is more discreet
  She's pale and wan and sad and sweet;
  But once she went a trifle fast—
    This woman with a past.
This woman with a past is quite engaging
In plays by Mister Henry Arthur Jones[5]
  We look at her with streaming eyes;
  We very deeply sympathize
When she relates her sins in melting tones.
Now I've a past of quite another color;
In humble walks of life my lot was cast;
  I've nothing sinful to confess
  I've been too well-behaved, I guess,
  The woman with an ordinary past.

II

There's no poetic charm
In living on a farm,
If you can't be lured away by some Lothario.
  The girl who sticks at home,
  With villains does not roam,
She can never break into a real scenario.
  I've not endured the tragic woes
  Dealt out by men in evening clothes;

What chance have I to head the cast?
    I have no spotted past.
The woman with a past is fascinating
She enters and the others fade away.
    But one who's led the simple life
    Till she becomes a lawful wife
Cuts mighty little figure in a play.
I ran a boarding house till I was thirty
Connected with a bank account at last;
    No need of taking up your time;
    I've not committed any crime—
I'm sorry, but I haven't got a past.

III

    I've never learned as yet
    To smoke a cigarette
Or to wear a gown that's very much de*col*le-tay.
    I don't know how to drape
    My simple western shape
In a clinging gown of most expensive quality.
    I've got a man I call my own;
    I leave all other men alone;
    My reputation you can't blast;
    I haven't any past.
The woman with a past gets in the papers
With pictures of the men that she has known,
    But one without her first divorce
    Has not a claim on fame, of course;
The scandal sheets all leave her quite alone.
Her life is quite devoid of all excitement;
She never sets the social world aghast;
    Oh, pity the unhappy lot
    Of one whose life's without a blot—
    The woman with an ordinary past.

THE MICROBE'S SERENADE[6]

A love-lorn microbe met by chance
At a swagger bacteroidal dance,
A proud bacillian belle, and she

Was first of the animalculae.
Of organisms saccharine,
She was the protoplasmic queen;
The microscopical pride and pet
Of the biological smartest set;
And so this infinitesimal swain
Evolved a pleading, low refrain:
"Oh, lovely metamorphic germ!
What futile scientific term
Can well describe thy many charms?
Come to these embryonic arms!
Then hie away to my cellular home
And be my little diatome."

His epithelium burned with love;
He swore by molecules above
She'd be his own gregarious mate
Or else he would disintegrate.
This amorous mite of a parasite
Pursued the germ both day and night,
And 'neath her window often played
This Darwin-Huxley serenade—
He'd warble to her ev'ry day,
This rhizopodical roundelay:
"O, most primordial type of spore!
I never saw your like before,
And though a microbe has no heart
From you, sweet germ, I'll never part;
We'll sit beneath some fungus growth
Till dissolution claims us both."

LEAVE IT TO THE BOYS IN THE NAVY[7]

I

From the rousing times of old Paul Jones[8]
Down to the present day,
There's one good toast we all can boast

If we live in the U. S. A.
When the lights are up and the music swells
And the waxen floor it gleams,
Each maiden fair says, "Where, oh where
Is the hero of my dreams?"
Up steps the neat little middy,
Up steps the gay cadet,
Broad of shoulder, he can hold her
In a way she won't forget.
The Annapolis style of dancing
Is the one the girls all like
With partners in demand
Civilians cannot land—
Leave it to the boys in the navy.

II

Decatur[9] kept the flag on high
And Farragut[10] never quit;
Old Fighting Bob[11] while on the job
Was full of nerve and grit.
At the present day we've heroes still,
They're never known to stop,
When cold champagne comes down like rain
They never miss a drop.
Up come the men from the squadron,
Up to the banquet hall;
Meet all comers—they are hummers;
Never a one will fall.
Off in the foreign countries,
Where they are wined and dined,
They answer each request
And finish with the rest—
Leave it to the boys in the navy.

III

When Teddy[12] told the navy boys
To sail around the world,
Till every land would understand
Our flag was still unfurled;
The weaklings were beset by fear,
But not the boys in blue.
Through stormy straits they braved the fates

And brought each vessel through.
Here's to the men who are sailing
Far in the distant seas;
They're not boasting—simply coasting,
Learning their A, B, C's.
A cheer for the men on the flag-ship,
For the little gun-boat, too.
When work is to be done,
Or when there's any fun,
Leave it to the boys in the navy.

IV

We don't go looking for a scrap;
We're friendly as can be,
But we sleep each night with hearts more light
When we count our ships at sea.
There have been wars, there may be wars,
When the crowding nations meet:
We'll sit back tight—be sure we're right,
And then turn loose the fleet.
Trust to the men in the navy,
Commodore to cadet;
Strong and steady, always ready,
Never have failed us yet.
They shoot very straight in the navy
And they don't know how to run
From any sort of fellow, whether white
    or whether yellow—
Leave it to the boys in the navy.

"THE LA GRIPPE"[13]

I am not hypercritical on points of punctuation;
  A misplaced comma now and then is surely not a sin;
I overlook the sundry breaks of common conversation
    And do my wincing inwardly when some "I seen" creeps in.

To wretched double negatives some friends are quite addicted;
  They knife the good King's English and then revel in its gore;
These crude idiosyncrasies are never contradicted,
  For I would not seem pedantic or appear a learned bore.

Yet the whiskered proverbs tell us, and I know they tell us truly,
  That forbearance as a virtue cannot always be construed,
And the camel's dorsal vertebrae, if weighted down unduly,
  Will sustain a compound fracture with a fatal promptitude;
And when a college maiden, intellectual and charming,
  Sends me a little perfumed note, regretful in its tone,
"To learn that all your symptoms are especially alarming,
  And the doctor fears that the 'la grippe' has claimed you for its
    own";
Then I howl and curse a little, and I stamp upon the letter,
  And I boil with indignation to think that any one,
Who long has studied French, should not, apparently, know better
  Than to write it "the la grippe," when but one "the" would have
    done.
A break like this affects me in a manner almost fatal,
  'Tis even worse than the "la grippe"—
Heavens! I have gone and done it myself!

THE GAMES
WE USED TO PLAY[14]

  Back in the golden days of youth,
    On a farm in I-o-way;
  Happiest days of all were they,—
    If you don't care what you say.
  Nothing to do but milk the cows,
    And feed the gentle stock,
  And work like a Turk from early morn
    Till nearly eight o'clock.
  The only joy of the country boy,
    To fill his soul with glee,

On a frosty night, when the moon shone bright,
    Away to the husking bee.

Go to the East, go to the West,
    Go to the one that you love best;
If she's not here to take your part,
    Choose another with all your heart.
Down on this carpet you must kneel
    As sure's the grass grows in the field,
Salute your bride and kiss her sweet,
    And then you rise upon your feet.

Oft' I recall the girl I loved,
    In the days of long ago;
Muscular maid of six feet two,
    With a cheek of rosy glow.
I would escort my Genevieve
    To many a husking bee,
And she at the call of "ladies choice"
    Would always grab for me.
With a sudden swoop and a merry whoop,
    She'd mop me 'round the floor,
And though I'd resist, I was always kissed,
    Sing hey, for the days of yore!

I think I hear the rain-crow say,
    I think I hear the rain-crow say,
I think I hear the rain-crow say,
    "It ain't a-goin' to rain no more."
Swing your true love, swing her back again,
    Swing your true love, swing her back again,
Swing your true love, swing her back again,
    It ain't a-goin' to rain no more.

Best of the pleasure that we knew,
    In the days that now have fled,
Snuggled so warm and holding hands,
    In the big old-time bob-sled.
Calico damsels just as proud
    As any queen in silk,
And we didn't take them out to dine,
    They lived on mush and milk.
But the noisy fun when the work was done,
    And the cider flowing free,

With a "balance all," at the fiddler's call,
  We'd swing in the jamboree.

I long and sigh for the days gone by,
  I pine for the rustic charm
Of the dear old games, the queer old games
  We played down on the farm.

FLUTTER, LITTLE BIRD[15]

Observe the loving mother bird,
  Up in the spreading tree,
Correct with stern but loving word,
  Her tender chickadee.
The feathered youngster tries to flap
  His embryonic wings,
While mother cheers the little chap,
  As to the bough he clings.
He makes a most heroic jump,
  Alas, it is in vain,
She says: "Don't mind a little bump,
  Just try it once again."

Flutter, little bird and keep on trying,
  By and by you will be flying;
You can do it, take my word,
  Keep on fluttering, little bird.

NOTES ON VERSES AND SONGS

Other verses or songs, made popular by *The Sultan of Sulu*, in which they occur (See Part III), include "Hike," "The Smiling Isle," "My Sulu Lulu Loo," "When Maidens Wait," and "R-E-M-O-R-S-E."

1. From *The Fair Co-ed* (1909).

2. From *The Old Town* (1910).

3. Written for, but cut from, *The Old Town*.

4. C. F. were the initials of Charles Frohman (1860–1915), a New York theatre syndicate manager. For a profile see A. J. Lazarus and Victor H. Jones, *Beyond Graustark* (Port Washington, N.Y.: Kennikat Press, 1981), pages 117–118.

5. Henry Arthur Jones (1851–1929), English playwright; author of over 60 plays including *The Case of Rebellious Susan* (1894) and *The Triumph of the Philistines* (1895). See Richard Cordell, *Henry Arthur Jones and the Modern Drama* (1932; 1968).

6. "The Microbe's Serenade" was written for, but cut from, *The Sho-Gun* (1904). Ade liked this piece so much he recited it at banquets, even handed out copies.

7. From *The Fair Co-ed*.

8. John Paul Jones (1747–1792), American naval hero who in 1779 from his ship *Bonhomme Richard* (named in honor of Ben Franklin's "Poor Richard") shouted to the captain of the British frigate *Serapis* "Sir, I have not yet begun to fight!" See Samuel Elliot Morrison, *John Paul Jones* (1959; 1964).

9. Stephen Decatur (1779–1820), American naval hero who during the War of 1812 captured the British frigate *Macedonian*. One of his slogans was "Our country . . . may she always be in the right, but our country right or wrong!" See the biography by Helen Nicolay (1942).

10. David Farragut (1801–1870), American admiral celebrated for his exploits during the War between the States. One of his slogans: "Damn the torpedoes . . . full speed ahead!" See the biography by Christopher Hartin (1970).

11. Old Fighting Bob alludes to Robley Evans (1846–1912), commander of the U.S. battleship *Iowa*, which in 1898 helped defeat the Spanish Admiral Cervera's fleet near Santiago Bay, Cuba.

12. Teddy alludes to Theodore Roosevelt (1858–1919), who was all for "speaking softly but carrying a big stick." See the biography by G. W. Chessman (1969).

13. Written for *Souvenir*, a Purdue University variety show of 1890.

14. From *The Sho-Gun*.

15. From *The Sho-Gun*.

VI

Selected Letters

The Opera Bus

TO JESSIE MC CUTCHEON[1]

Chicago [Illinois]
Nov. 16-1899.

My Dear Jessie:

Your letter came to me while I was in the sunny south. When I came home and walked into my transformed apartment I understood your reference to decorating. Certainly the room has been greatly improved. I walk softly across the floor now for fear that I will "joggle" down one of the canes and not be able to hang it up again—Ben [McCutcheon] and Mr. Casey of the Record will be in La Fayette on Saturday to see the football game and I should like very much to accompany them but I am due to attend a dinner at the Athletic Club. You may be aware that Grand Opera is now raging in Chicago. The engagement will continue for two weeks after this and if you find it possible to come up during the season I will promise you a couple nights of it. That is about as much as I can stand at one time. John [McCutcheon] wrote a long letter from Yokohama, which came last week. He was about to start for Manila. Trumbull White of the Record, who has just returned from a trip around the world, saw John in Japan and spent an afternoon with him. He said John was well and quite contented to remain in the Philippines until the close of the war. On Monday I forwarded a Christmas present of an ascot tie and a scarf pin. The tie was the best to be had in Chicago and the pin was of solid gold, a sort of unicorn design with pearls in it. I know that John has a weakness for swell cravats and old scarf-pins—You may be interested to know that the "Fables in Slang" has proved a success beyond all reasonable expectations. It promises to outsell "Artie" three to one. [Herbert S.] Stone [and Co.] cannot get them out rapidly enough to fill the orders. All of which is very satisfying. Remember me to your mother and to George [Barr McCutcheon] and let me thank you for your valuable services as a house decorator.

Very sincerely,
George Ade

TO JOHN M. STUDEBAKER[2]

May 10, 1907

UNDERSTAND YOU ARE NEGOTIATING WITH CHARLES DILLINGHAM REGARDING LEASE OF STUDEBAKER THEATRE. SINCERELY TRUST YOU MAY COME TO AGREEMENT WITH HIM AS I BELIEVE HE IS MOST ENTERPRISING AND RELIABLE OF THE MANAGERS. AM WRITING MY NEW PLAY FOR HIM AND HOPE IT CAN BE PUT ON AT STUDEBAKER THIS FALL. BELIEVE WE CAN DUPLICATE SUCCESS OF THE COUNTY CHAIRMAN AND THE COLLEGE WIDOW.

GEORGE ADE

TO WINTHROP ELLSWORTH STONE[3]

Chicago, Illinois
4th January, 1915.

My dear Dr. Stone:

I have your letter, and before it came I had learned something about the scrapping between the coaches and the Athletic Director.

I hesitate to make any definite suggestion at this time. I believe that the final and proper solution of the problem of directing athletic contests will be to have the general control vested in a Board in which the faculty, the alumni and the undergraduates will be equally represented. I do not believe that the alumni representatives should be members of the faculty. They should be men of sufficient age and experience to permit them to stand as a kind of buffer between the intemperate zeal of the under-graduates and the restraining conservatism of the faculty. I believe you will find out that in colleges which have adopted this plan of control the faculty and alumni usually work together to correct and modify the too-ambitious projects of the students. I believe this Board should select a good coach for each department of sport and that it should have a capable business manager who has no connection with the work of coaching. The plan of having one Athletic Director and giving him supreme control might work out all right if you could accomplish the miracle of getting a man who would command the loyal affection of the students and win a large majority of his games. Chicago has [Alonzo] Stagg[4] and for a long time Huff[5] came very near being the boss of Illinois, but even Illinois has changed her plan and George Huff is very much in favor of giving the students a voice in the management.

I can well understand that faculty members often become discouraged when compelled to abide by student legislation, but we must remember that the men in college average more than 21 years of age and are supposed to be ready to go out and manage important business affairs, and I believe the modern policy will continue to be to give the under-graduates certain legislative powers, even if they do muss things up once in a while.

A Board, such as I have suggested, would control the general athletic policy of the University and select the coaches, but it would not undertake to deprive the faculty of the right to pass upon the eligibility of any athlete, supervise the financial management or reserve a final veto power if some action of the Board went squarely against the best traditions of the school. I think that even in Yale and other eastern schools, where student control is very strong, the faculty would always have the power of a kind of supreme court, if it cared to assert it.

I am, with best wishes,

Sincerely,
George Ade

TO WILLIAM ALLEN WHITE[6]

Hazelden[7]
Brook, Indiana
April 17, 1916.

My dear White:

I find awaiting me the book[8] you were good enough to send and I sure thank you for remembering me, and for the pleasure I have found in the reading. No doubt you are enjoying the political spectacle just at present. Our old friends of the old party are in a bad way. One year ago, it seemed certain that all they had to do was name some dignified old party wearing a frock coat, and having a church connection, and land him right in the White House. It is now evident that the voters have no hankering for any old fluff who refuses to admit that there is a war in Europe. I don't know what is going to happen, but it looks as if the Colonel [Theodore Roosevelt] might be in evidence.

I am with best wishes,

Sincerely,
George Ade

TO THEODORE ROOSEVELT

Hazelden
Brook, Indiana
June 12—1917

My Dear Colonel Roosevelt—

I thank you for your friendly letter. The other day a harelipped man working for me stopped me and said he wished to ask a question. I told him to shoot, so he said: "I want to find out who got us into this war. I know [Woodrow] Wilson kept us out, but I can't find out who the dickens got us in."

You are quite right. We cocained ourselves into believing that the war was no quarrel of ours and now, when asked to arouse ourselves, we are still a bit dopey and incredulous. A medley of mellifluous sounds is not always a battle hymn. Probably we will have to be kicked a couple of times in some vital spot before we get fighting mad.

I am on our State Council of Defense and trying to be of some help. We find it hard work to induce the farmers and other small investors to take the Liberty Loan bonds. They have been talked at so much from so many different angles that some of them seem to be in doubt as to the wisdom of taking advice from any one. The enlisting in this northern half of Indiana was active and continues so, I am happy to report.

We have a hefty job ahead of us but I suppose the only thing to do is go ahead and use the tools at hand. We must not even think out loud, but ever and anon give three silent cheers for some of the lawyer-politicians down at Washington.

I am, with best wishes,

Sincerely,
George Ade

TO JESSE L. LASKY[9]

[Florida]
8 March, 1922

My dear Mr. Lasky:

Thank you for your telegram and for your very kind offer to assist the Indiana Society. The date for the dinner has not been set and it probably will depend upon the time when the picture can be secured. The whole idea is being worked up by the officers of the club in Chicago. I would much prefer to find out what we have in the way of a picture before we try to make a splurge with it. If you have any inside information as to how the darned thing is working out, I wish you would let me know and, if you can now make a guess as to when the picture might be secured for a private showing before the Indiana Society, I will be very much obliged.

Now, in regard to "Back Home and Broke": The treatment accorded me by you and all of your associates has been such that I am extremely prejudiced in your favor. I would rather do a picture for you than anybody else. As I wired you, I have been disposed to wait and see what we had accomplished with "Our Leading Citizen" before I tackled another continuity. I have been connected with the show business long enough to find out that nothing must be taken for granted and that no play is a success until the returns are in. Also, I have always hoped that sometime or other authors writing for the screen might be paid on a royalty basis. I never have made important money selling stuff outright. Each successful play which I did for the stage brought me in a great deal more than the sum you are now offering. The two failures which I had out of a total of fourteen plays on which I drew royalties brought me practically nothing, as I never in my life asked or accepted an advance payment until I signed the contract with you for "Our Leading Citizen." Two or three pieces that were moderately successful brought as much, or more than I am able to get for a screen play, and the real winners such as "The College Widow," "The County Chairman" and "Father and the Boys" ran as high as a hundred thousand dollars for a single play before the piece was finally sent to the stock companies. Always in writing for the stage I had a chance to get some real money provided the producer got his. Of course I am not pretending that I know anything about the details of your business. Under present conditions and when you are compelled to take a gamble on an untried story, I can understand that you would not feel disposed to offer large money, but on the other hand the author who has only a few stories ready to market can see no prospect of juicy returns so long as he sells his stuff outright. I am convinced that sooner or later the plays for the screen will be produced on a percentage basis. The percentage would not have to be high. At present undoubtedly a good many writers would possibly be skeptical as to the bookkeeping methods of some of the companies, but I would not be afraid to trust your organization. . . .

I shall be at this hotel until March 18th, and then for a couple of weeks I will be at the Hotel Alcazar, St. Augustine, Florida. I will notify the studio as to my movements after that time.

I am, with best wishes,

Sincerely,
George Ade

TO WILL HAYS[10]

Hazelden
Brook, Indiana
29th June, 1922.

My dear Will Hays:

Just for your information and so that you may keep track of some of the absurdities of the present methods of censorship. I want to tell you what happened to *Our Leading Citizen* in Pennsylvania. I would have sworn that this picture was fumigated, deodorized and scrubbed up until even the most finicky censor in all the world could not find a scene or a word of text which might not properly have been shown in any church on a Sabbath evening. It remained for one of the wise birds in Pennsylvania to detect in a sub-title a phrase which he must have regarded as unpatriotic to the point of treason, for he had the words cut out.

You will remember in the picture that after Dan Bentley meets the girl in France, she comes home and talks to the women's club as to her experiences at the front. This scene is preceded by the following text:

After the Great Disturbance had ended, and people were trying to find out what it had all been about, Katherine Fendle was telling them—back in Wing-field—that Foch and Pershing and Major Dan Bentley really won the war.

The Board of Censors in Pennsylvania cut out:

and people were trying to find out what it had all been about.

Why? Of course the phrase was put in as a mere pleasantry, but also it was meant to suggest the fact that everywhere, since the war, people have been discussing the issues involved and trying to discover the hidden causes of the great conflict. I don't think the censors meant to dispute the suggestion that people have been talking about the real causes of the war. It is pretty hard to fathom the mental operations of the feeble-minded, but I suppose these censors figured that I was trying to put over an implication that there was really some doubt as to the righteousness of America's participation in the war. Of course we meant nothing of the sort and I can't imagine any one detecting dangerous propaganda in such a harmless little paragraph.

All of which is submitted merely for your information. I don't know that we can do anything in the premises.

I am, with best wishes,

Sincerely,
George Ade

TO THE EDITOR, *HERALD-TRIBUNE*

Hazelden
Brook, Indiana
Sept. 8, 1926

My dear Sir:
You have asked me if Theodore Dreiser in his novel of Sister Carrie[11] incorporated in one of his early chapters part of a story which I had written for The Chicago Record. . . .
Along about 1898 I wrote for The Record a story in fable form

called THE TWO MANDOLIN PLAYERS AND THE WILLING PERFORMER. In that story I had a character known as Cousin Gus from St. Paul. He was of the type then known as "a swift worker." Probably we would call him a "sheik" today, seeing that we have made such tremendous advances in recent years. In my little story I detailed the tactics which would be employed by Gus if he spotted a good looker on the train between St. Paul and Chicago.

When the very large and important novel called SISTER CARRIE came out I read it and I was much amused to discover that Theodore Dreiser had incorporated, in a description of one of his important characters, the word picture of Cousin Gus which I had outlined in my newspaper story and which later appeared in a volume called FABLES IN SLANG. It is true that for a few paragraphs Mr. Dreiser's copy for the book tallied very closely with my copy for the little story. When I discovered the resemblance I was not horrified or indignant, I was simply flattered. It warmed me to discover that Mr. Dreiser had found my description suitable for the clothing of one of his characters. . . .

Most certainly I do not accuse Mr. Dreiser of plagiarism, even by implication or in the spirit of pleasantry. I have a genuine admiration for him. To me he is a very large and commanding figure in American letters. While some of us have been building chicken coops or, possibly, bungalows, Mr. Dreiser has been creating skyscrapers. He makes the old three-decker novel look like a pamphlet. He is the only writer in our list who has the courage and the patience and the painstaking powers of observation to get all of one human career into one story.

Theodor Dreiser was born in Indiana and we other Hoosiers are very proud of him. I knew rather intimately his brother, Paul Dreiser,[12] who wrote so many popular songs and the one song so highly esteemed here at home, THE BANKS OF THE WABASH. . . .

I am rather sorry that some one has reminded The Herald Tribune, of which I am a constant reader and regular subscriber, that Mr. Dreiser got into his novel something which read like something written by me before his novel came out. It all happened so many years ago! It seems to raise the absolutely preposterous suggestion that Mr. Dreiser needs help. Anybody who writes novels containing approximately one million words each doesn't need any help from any one. . . .

Sincerely,
George Ade

TO LOUISE DRESSER[13]

Hazelden
Brook, Indiana
Sept. 9, 1927

My dear Louise Dresser:

I am interested to have a letter from you. Of course, nothing would make me happier than to deliver to you a story which could be worked up into a good picture but I am not sure that I have the knack of outlining the kind of stories that the directors like. . . . I had a story outlined once but never did anything with it. It was called AUNT FANNY FROM CHAUTAUQUA.[14] A very rich man with a modern family gets word that his sister, whom he has not seen for many years, is coming to visit him. He has a large country place and the young people are getting ready for an important house party. They know nothing about Aunt Fanny and the fact that she is about to land in on them is bad news. Father has only one picture of her and that was taken at the World's Fair in Chicago and shows her as a funny-looking little country girl. It appears that she is forty or forty-five years old. To a flapper of 18 that is just the same as ninety. Besides she comes from Chautauqua, the home of piety, prayers and psalm singing.

The idea of the comedy would be to demonstrate that a good many women of 40 who do not live in the cities are still snappy and up-to-date. The aunt lands in and sizes up the situation. The guest of honor is a rich and distinguished bachelor, one of these handsome dogs of the Louis Stone variety, a little gray around the temples, but very good looking and what the young girls would call "distang-gay." The bachelor is just what Aunt Fanny is looking for. He is a little older than she is and has a fine social position and money and looks so there begins a battle between the flappers and the old maid. They plot to expose her real age and her country breeding and she evens up by cooking all sorts of things for the bachelor and making him talk about himself. The young ones are trying to impress him with their importance, the old one is trying to impress him with his importance. Of course, for the purposes of the drama the older one must win out. I will confess that this outline, as far as we have got with it, doesn't contain very much drama but possibly a few exciting episodes could be worked in. As I said, I probably could not do a real serious play and I don't know that this story which I have vaguely in mind would work into anything, although the character of Aunt Fanny would be a good one.

I am, with best wishes

Sincerely,
George Ade

TO SAMUEL FRENCH, INC.

Hazelden
Brook, Indiana
June 27, 1928.

Gentlemen:

I suppose there is no sadder moment in the life of an author than when he is compelled to return a check sent to him by a publisher. The enclosed letter and remittance from you to me will explain itself after you have carefully gone over it again. I was delighted and surprised to receive a check of this size but when my assistant and I began to check over the items we found on page 6 some addition which filled us with grief, because there was an error of $1,000 and it was not in our favor! I hope I have not brought trouble upon one of your valued employees by calling attention to this error. Perhaps the sportsmanlike thing for me to do, in order to protect your bookkeeper, would have been to pocket the check and say no more about it, but, it seems, there is one New England conscience out here in Indiana and so I am sadly returning the whole thing and will ask you to go over it again and send me the amount really due, which I fear is exactly $1000 less than the amount you sent.

I am, with best wishes

Sincerely,
George Ade

TO FRANKLIN P. ADAMS[15]

Miami Beach, Florida
Dec. 8, 1929.

Dear Frank:

I am interested to hear from you and I am compelled to reply that various press agents at different times had me engaged to all of the young ladies mentioned in your letter and several others including some I never met. Because I didn't run around much with the gals back of the foot lights the publicity boys seemed to think it was a great joke to float these wild-eyed stories about my pursuing Dorothy Tennant or Helen Hale or Irene Frizelle or Elsie Janis. The story about Tennant was the one most widely circulated although I knew her very slightly and had spoken to her timidly a couple of times at rehearsals.

I trust you are well and happy.

Sincerely,
George Ade

TO JAMES KIRBY RISK[16]

Hazelden
Brook, Indiana
Sept. 17, 1930.

Dear Kirby:

I have your letter of the 15th and I can hardly find time to tell you all of the things I have done around Purdue. When the Memorial Gym was planned and Purdue had to raise a certain sum to meet an appropriation by the state, the University fund was still short $2500 on the last day and I chipped in with the amount required. I helped out on the Harlequin shows for a number of years and bought the boys about $2000 worth of scenery, including the plush drop curtain still in use. I directed the building of the Sigma Chi

The Purdue campus in 1889. The sign reads,
"I am being initiated"

house and spent about $25,000. Also I handled the alumni magazine for a number of years. Dave Ross discovered the site for the Stadium and showed me the layout. We bought sixty-five acres of land for $40,000 and later matched up contributions made by alumni so that our total contribution to the project was somewhere between $60,000 and $70,000. I have no accurate record of the amount we spent. It is not my desire to blow about the things I have done for Purdue because I derived a real pleasure from getting in on such large and worthy enterprises. You must remember that Dave Ross and I are old bachelors. Every person who begins to grow old must adopt something. Old maids adopt cats and canaries. Dave Ross and I adopted Purdue. It is only fair to add that Dave has done much more for the University than I have done. The amount of work he has given to the school and the amount of money he has given, without many people knowing about it, entitle him to first place among the alumni and I want it distinctly understood that I am not presuming to put myself in his class as a Purdue benefactor.

As I wrote before, I have no suggestions to offer as to placing the story. The young lady could find no better medium than The Saturday Evening Post.

I am, with best wishes

Sincerely,
George Ade

TO JULIAN STREET[17]

Hazelden
Brook, Indiana
May 29, 1932.

Dear Julian:

I have postponed replying to your last letter of inquiry because I wanted time to look up some dope, including some from John McCutcheon, but he is quite ill and on his way west, so I will take a little time off this Sunday morning and attempt to help you out.

You are right about our accepting conditions as we found them

without endeavoring to investigate causes or psychoanalyze ourselves. For instance, I lived in Chicago all during the nineties when it
was the wildest and most wide open town in the world and to me all
the conditions seemed perfectly proper and natural and the picturesque trimmings of city life. . . .

The Ross-Ade Stadium was promoted by Dave Ross and myself.
He is now President of the Board of Trustees. It is exactly the size of
the original stadium near Athens and will seat about 23,000. It has a
beautiful sight on a hill top overlooking the Wabash Valley and the
playing field, because of the soil and drainage conditions, is said to
be one of the best in the country.

Now regarding George Barr McCutcheon. He continued as City
Editor of the LaFayette Evening Courier long after John [McCutch-
eon] and I went to Chicago. He wrote many plays and novels and
submitted them to managers and publishers but they were turned
down year after year. One day he came into our office in Chicago
and said that Herbert Stone had offered him five hundred dollars
cash for the script of a novel. I advised him to accept it but not to
promise any future deliveries at any rate. My argument was that if
Stone got the book cheap he would boom it and spend on advertis-
ing the money which might otherwise be paid in royalties. I told
George that if he made good on this first book he could name his
own terms on later books but he simply had to get a start somehow
and so he signed the contract and took the five hundred dollars. The
book was GRAUSTARK, which brought him fame and fortune.

When George was about 18 he became stage struck and joined a
traveling company. . . . The show busted over in Illinois and he
walked all the way home. The family living out at Elston, a suburb of
LaFayette, were at Thanksgiving dinner when they saw George looking in the window. They brought him in and thawed him out and
asked him to sit down and have some dinner but he said he had just
eaten a hearty meal over at the junction. As a matter of fact, he had
not eaten for two days. Finally he was persuaded to sit down and
have a bite and they did not get him away from the table until late in
the evening.

While he was at Purdue his father was sheriff. John was only
sixteen. His family lived in the residence of the jail and he helped
supervise the prisoners. One day a tough criminal knocked him
aside and jumped through the doorway and ran into the open street.
John got a revolver and chased him five blocks and into a lumber
yard and popped at him five times before the prisoner threw up his
hands and surrendered. He got a great write-up in the local papers.

I am going to call it a day but I will help you later on if you have any special queries.

I am, with best wishes

George Ade

TO RUSSELL DOUBLEDAY[18]

Hazelden
Brook, Indiana
July 26, 1933.

Dear Mr. Doubleday:

I am interested to have your letter. The story about Lilly Mars was one of the most captivating things that [Booth] Tark[ington] has ever done. Perhaps I can tell of one yarn which you may edit up to suit yourselves.

Some of us were walking with him along Meridian Street in Indianapolis. He was on his way to make a call on some lady who had been hospitable and he carried a large bouquet to be presented to his recent hostess. Across the street he saw a portly negro wench, waddling along with a bundle of "wash." Tark saw her and suddenly left us and walked across the street, confronted the portly negress, removed his hat and made a sweeping gesture with his hat and a low bow. Then he poured upon the dark lady the most lavish compliments ever bestowed any member of her sex, removed the covering of the bouquet and presented it to her. We had to walk all the way back with him while he bought another bouquet but Tark was smiling and happy. He had defeated the conventions, brought a burst of sunshine into the life of a lowly worker and given a certain dark female something to talk about for days to come.

I am, with best wishes

Sincerely,
George Ade

TO DAN RESNECK

Hazelden
Brook, Indiana
Aug. 27, 1933.

Dear Mr. Resneck:

I have your inquiry from Kentland and will answer briefly and according to my best ability. In nearly all of my writing I have tried to be a realist and to tell about people and things as I saw them, endeavoring to find the element of "human interest" and possibly some phrases which might be amusing or entertaining. I have not had in my mind's eye a very definite or very critical audience but I have attempted to interest all people of fair intelligence who might have an abiding interest in plain people and every day happenings. I cannot give the names of the "literary masters" who might have influenced my preferences or affected my style but I suppose I was very much under the influence of [Charles] Dickens when I was young and later I no doubt got some inspiration from Mark Twain and Robert Louis Stevenson. In regard to my short stories written in the vernacular, I have merely entertained the hope that because they told the truth about people and events of contemporary interest they might be of interest to coming generations as a partial record of our times.

I am, with best wishes

Sincerely,
George Ade

TO DAMON RUNYON[19]

Miami Beach, Florida
March 8, 1934.

My dear Damon Runyon:

Up to date you have batted one thousand with those stories in Collier's. I cannot begin to tell you how much I liked them because you not only get a story but you spice it with the correct vernacular of the non-virtuous night-hawk and what's more, you bring out his singular point of view, which combines the innocence of childhood with all of the less gentle traits of the Bengal tiger. I'm not a raver by habit. Some of my other preferences are P. G. Wodehouse, Harry Leon Wilson, Westbrook Pegler and, with reservation, Irvin Cobb, when they are hitting on all cylinders.

Sorry I was not in the other evening when you called. I think it was the day of the party for Eddie Cantor. As a matter of fact, I received no invitation or notification and neither did John Golden and so we must not be accused of running out on our little pop-eyed friend. Please drop in again and maybe I will be at home.

Convey my best wishes to Mrs. Runyon,

Sincerely,
G. A.

TO JOHN EDGAR HOOVER[20]

Hazelden
Brook, Indiana
August 8, 1939

Dear Mr. Hoover,

I am more than glad to have the annual report of your Bureau. It is a model of compactness and tells a lot in a very few pages. You and your associates have certainly made a record of which you may well be proud.

I suppose you operate what might be called a glorified detective agency. You are different from other detective agencies with which I have been familiar because you play no favorites. All criminals look alike to you. It happens that I knew William A. Pinkerton. He managed a very successful detective agency; however, he made no effort to apprehend criminals except those who committed offenses against his clients. He represented the organized bankers. A good many safe blowers made it a rule not to rob any safe or vault which bore the protective label of the organized bankers. Bill Pinkerton got most of his information regarding bank robberies from the safe blowers with whom he was on friendly terms. They were always ready to snitch on the other boys in order to get immunity for themselves. It was a strange situation, this secret partnership between the Pinkerton Agency and a certain group of law breakers who were playing safe. In the old days in Chicago, I came into close contact with the partnership existing between crooks, police, and police court magistrates. Such a partnership still exists in some cities. I am glad to learn that you and your boys are doing your best to break it up. Your personal crusade against crime is sure to bring good results. You are doing a whale of a job and earning the respect and the confidence of all intelligent citizens.

I am, with best wishes.

Sincerely,
George Ade

TO CYRIL CLEMENS[21]

Hazelden
Brook, Indiana
September 13, 1940

Dear Mr. Clemens,

I have your postcard of inquiry. I am very strong for Mr. [Wendell] Willkie but I most certainly am not going to take the stump for him or anyone else. I appeared at Convocation in the vast Music Hall at Purdue night before last and I am quite sure that my act was a flop. I wouldn't get very far as a stump speaker. For one thing, I am a semi-invalid and I must take things easy. That is why I probably will not find it possible to accept your invitation to lunch or supper.

I am not sure regarding the first book I ever read. It may have been by Oliver Optic or it may have been ROUGHING IT by Mark Twain. The latter was certainly one of the first books that I read after I was old enough. I trust you are well and happy.

Sincerely,
George Ade

TO MEREDITH NICHOLSON[22]

Miami Beach, Florida
December 1, 1940

My dear Nicholson:

I am delighted to have your letter and to learn that you approved of my Purdue speech on Mr. [James Whitcomb] Riley. I tried to tell the truth about him but, of course, I had to enthuse a little. I couldn't help it. He was the most interesting human being I ever knew. You knew him much better than I did but I saw a great deal of him in his latter years. I am especially interested to know what you say about his drinking habits. I heard him refer, once in a while, to the fact that he had fought various battles with the Demon Rum but, believe it or not, I never saw him take a drink and I never saw him after he had taken a drink. So as far as my personal observation is concerned, his conduct would have been approved by any member of the W.C.T.U. I am convinced with you that most of the fellows who told about getting drunk with Riley were just plain liars. I am glad you approved of what I said regarding his non-bohemianism. You are right in saying that he had a great sense of personal dignity. I always called him "Mr. Riley" and I never heard anyone call him "Jim." There was only one Riley and I doubt if we shall ever see another.

You will note by the heading that I am in Florida and I plan to remain here until April. The weather just now is lovely. There is every indication that we will have a very busy season here. I am taking the liberty of enclosing to you a little piece concerning Mark Twain in one of his more eruptive moods. Thank you again for your very friendly letter. You have my best wishes at all times.

Sincerely,
George Ade

NOTES ON SELECTED LETTERS

The letters to William Allen White (April 17, 1916) and Theodore Roosevelt (June 12, 1917) are used by permission of the Library of Congress. The letter to James Kirby Risk (September 17, 1930) is used by permission of the George

Ade Memorial Society of Kentland, Indiana. The letter to Cyril Clemens (Sept. 13, 1940) is used by permission of the Lilly Library, Indiana University. These letters, along with all the others in this section, appear in Terence Tobin, ed., *Letters of George Ade* (Lafayette, Indiana: Purdue University Studies, 1973, © 1973 by the Purdue Research Foundation, and are used with permission.

1. Jessie McCutcheon was the sister of Ben, George, and John T. McCutcheon. For her role as volunteer decorator of the Lafayette McCutcheons' (and Ade's) Chicago rooms, see A. L. Lazarus and Victor H. Jones, *Beyond Graustark* (Port Washington, N.Y.: Kennikat Press, 1981), page 72.

2. John Studebaker, along with his brothers, was owner of the Studebaker Car Company (originally Wagon Company) of South Bend, Indiana, at the turn of the century the largest vehicle works in the world. John Studebaker built and contributed to Chicago the Studebaker Theatre, where at this time Ade was adapting *Artie* (1896) for stage production (1907). See Kathleen Smallzried's profile of the Studebaker brothers in *The Indiana Experience* (Indiana Univ. Press, 1977), pp. 108ff.

3. Stone was President of Purdue from 1900 to 1921. Although Ade's advice in this letter may not seem presumptuous or gratuitous given the fact that Ade (along with his friend David Ross) was Purdue's most generous benefactor, it does foreshadow Ade's subsequent campaign to have Stone fired.

4. Alonzo Stagg (1862–1965), after a career in coaching football, became director of athletics at the University of Chicago.

5. George Huff was director of athletics at the University of Illinois.

6. William Allen White (1868–1944), Editor of the *Emporia, Kansas, Gazette,* was the author of the novel *A Certain Rich Man* (1909) and of several widely anthologized essays, including "Mary White," about his daughter who died in a horseback-riding accident when she was seventeen. On May 25, 1916, Ade wired White, requesting that he endorse Theodore Roosevelt for President. White did so.

7. Hazelden was the name of Ade's country estate, near Kentland, Indiana. Notice that McCutcheon's sketch, "George Ade's Home in Brook," (see Introduction) although faithfully photographic, is also satirical in its perspective.

8. The book was White's *God's Puppets* (New York, 1916).

9. Jesse Lasky (1881–1958) was at this time chief executive officer of Famous Players, Inc. Ade had declined Lasky's $5,000 advance.

10. Will Hays (1879–1954), a native of Sullivan, Indiana, served as Chairman of the Republican National Committee from 1918 to 1921. He then became, upon the election of President Harding, Postmaster General (1921–1922). But Hays is best remembered as President of the Motion Pictures and Distributors of America (1922–1945) and as the "czar" of that industry's self-censoring morals (the Hays Code of 1934). For details of the incident alluded to in this letter, see Ade's article "Censorship in America," *Indianapolis Star* (January 14, 1923).

11. That the charge of plagiarism was preposterous can easily be seen by comparing Chapter I of Dreiser's *Sister Carrie* (1900), in which Charles Drouet meets Carrie, with the "Fable of the Two Mandolin Players . . ." in Part I.

12. Theodore Dreiser's brother Paul published songs under the name of Dresser.

13. Louise Dresser (née Dreiser), although a native of Terre Haute, was not related to the brothers Theodore Dreiser and Paul Dresser. But she was a good friend of Paul's, and it was he who suggested that she change her name to Dresser.

14. The play *Aunt Fanny from Chautauqua* is found in Part III.

15. Franklin Pierce Adams (1881–1960), a native of Chicago, was best known for his *New York Herald-Tribune* column "The Conning Tower," which he signed "F.P.A." Contributors to this column, besides Ade, included Ring Lardner and Dorothy Parker.

16. James Kirby Risk, a Purdue benefactor, was owner of the Lafayette, Indiana, electrical supply company that still bears his name.

17. Julian Street (1879–1947), a native of Chicago, was best known, along with Harry Leon Wilson, as one of Booth Tarkington's collaborators in playwriting, which they did on the Isle of Capri. Street was also a friend of Ade's and of George Barr McCutcheon's. (Street and Tarkington were fellow members, with G B Mc, of the Dutch Treat Club in New York City; and during the summers were his neighbors near Kennebunkport, Maine.) A party which Ade gave in Rome, Italy, for his friend "Buffalo" Bill Cody was described by Street in his article "When We Were Very Young," *Saturday Evening Post* (August 20 and November 19, 1932). In that article there appears Street's quatrain "Somehow I always like to think / of GEORGEADE as a Summer Drink, / sparkling and cool, with just a Tang / of Pleasant Effervescent Slang."

18. Russell Doubleday was one of the owners of Doubleday, Doran & Company, which had just published Tarkington's *Presenting Lily Mars* (1933).

19. Damon Runyon (1884–1946), a native of Manhattan, Kansas, was best known for his stories about New York City underworld characters. His works include *Guys and Dolls* (1931), basis for the 1950 musical comedy.

20. J. Edgar Hoover (1895–1972), a native of Washington, D.C., was best known as Director of the Federal Bureau of Investigation. He reached the height of his popularity when his bureau cracked down on criminals and terrorists, for example on John Dillinger (of Indianapolis) when he was "Public Enemy No. 1" (1934). Ade's praise in this letter is understandable. However, since Ade's death Hoover's reputation has become somewhat tarnished. (See the biographies by J. R. Nash and H. Messick, both published in 1972.)

21. Cyril Clemens (b. 1902), a native of St. Louis, Missouri, and a relative of Mark Twain's, was founder of the Mark Twain Society (1936) and editor of *The Mark Twain Quarterly*.

22. Meredith Nicholson (1866–1947), a native of Crawfordsville, Indiana, served as the U.S. Minister to Paraguay (1933–34) and to Nicaragua (1938–1941). He was also the author of several histories, many essays, some mystery novels, including *The House of a Thousand Candles* (1905), and the romantic novel *A Hoosier Chronicle* (1912).